HIGHLAND LOVE COMES CALLING

HOUSE OF CLAN SUTHERLAND

CELESTE BARCLAY

0 9 8 7 6 5 4 3 2 1

Published by Oliver Heber Books

❦ Created with Vellum

To all my imaginary friends who feel like family.

Happy reading, y'all,
Celeste

SUBSCRIBE TO CELESTE'S NEWSLETTER

Subscribe to Celeste's bimonthly newsletter to receive exclusive insider perks.

Have you read *The Highland Ladies Guide*? Learn all the behind the scenes details to *The Highland Ladies* series! This FREE book is available to all new subscribers to Celeste's monthly newsletter. Subscribe on her website.
Subscribe Now

PREFACE

Welcome to *House of Clan Sutherland*, the newest installment in the medieval Highlander world I've been lovingly creating since 2018. This series a spinoff from my *The Clan Sinclair, The Clan Sinclair Legacy, The Highland Ladies,* and *The Highland Ladies Always* series. The next few pages will explain how these series are connected, so you have a sense of the different parts that make up my version of medieval Highlands. They will also give you insights into the historical facts I'm passionate about incorporating into my stories. It's the former history teacher in me. I also divulge where I took creative license.

This book, *Highland Love Comes Calling,* is a prequel for this series. This particular one is set fifty years before the other stories that will join it. *House of Clan Sutherland* series takes place roughly twenty years after *The Clan Sinclair* and about ten years after the final installment of *The Highland Ladies Always.* It flows parallel to *The Clan Sinclair Legacy.*

In my first series, *The Clan Sinclair,* I never explicitly stated who ruled Scotland at the time; however, I alluded to King Robert the Bruce and Queen Elizabeth de Burgh, who appear throughout *The Highland Ladies* and *The Highland Ladies Always.*

By the time this new series takes place, the Bruce is dead, and his son, David II, is on the throne. You will discover more about King David's complicated reign in later books in this new series.

When I decided to create second generation stories, I knew I wanted to branch out from the Sinclair Clan and include their cousins, who I introduced readers to during *The Highland Ladies* (*A Wallflower at the Highland Court, A Saint at the Highland Court,* and *A Beauty at the Highland Court*). This decision gave me the opportunity to allow my imagination to explore Hamish and Amelia's love story, which many readers have clamored for me to write. When I created Hamish in *Their Highland Beginning*, then had Hamish and Amelia make cameos in several subsequent stories, I never envision they'd one day have their own story. One of my greatest regrets was deciding to have Kyla Sutherland Sinclair die before the beginning of *The Clan Sinclair*. I couldn't have fathomed what these make-believe people would come to mean to me. It fills me with happiness that I was about to bring Kyla into this story just as I described her in so many others.

As you join the Sutherlands' second generation, you may recognize heroes and heroines from previous series. For some of you, it may be a chance to become reacquainted with old friends. For those who haven't read my previous series, take heart: all of my books can be read as standalones, so you don't have to read the earlier series to enjoy this one. Many readers of the original books wondered what would become of the couples from my *The Highland Ladies* and *The Highland Ladies Always* series. Fear not. The children of several of those couples will have their chance to find love with the younger Sutherlands and their Sinclair relatives over the course of twenty books.

As I mentioned earlier, this book takes place roughly fifty years before the rest of the series. The other five books in *House of Clan Sutherland* tell love stories against the tumultuous reign of King David II, the son of Robert the Bruce. *Highland Love Comes Calling* is set against the backdrop of the early days of the First

War of Scottish Independence. I take you back to late August and early September of 1297, just before the pivotal Battle of Stirling Bridge on September 11, 1297. If you've read any of my previous books, you know my passion for incorporating accurate history into my stories, but some creative license is inevitable.

The raid on Carlisle, the Sack (or Siege) of Berwick, and the Battle of Dunbar were three of the earliest events of what would become more than a decade of war between the Scots and the English. They set the scene for *Highland Love Comes Calling*, which begins roughly eighteen months after those initial battles. While the contentiousness between the Rosses and Sutherlands is based on truth, I took creative license, moving the time period to suit my stories. The discord, in fact, stemmed from the Sutherlands lending support to the Mackays. In *Their Highland Beginning*, I ended the Sutherland and Sinclair feud, which was also a true event in history, but not during the time I wrote. The alliance between the Sutherlands and Sinclairs became a key characteristic of many of my subsequent stories, and if you've read any of my other Highlander books, you've likely encountered it.

Since I wished to set this book during the early days of the war, I decided Stirling would be a convenient place for our couple to meet. In reality, King John Balliol had already abdicated on July 6, 1296. By the time the English arrived in September of the following year, they found Stirling Castle virtually abandoned. That didn't work for my storytelling purposes, so I created a slightly alternative timeline.

The Earl of Ross, the antagonist of this story, was one of the seven earls who led the attack on Carlisle. However, Roy Ross, our heroine's father in this story, is entirely the product of my imagination, as are all the characters besides the known members of history. The first piece of dialogue from William Wallace, toward the end of the book, is a quote from him. However, the second piece is from my imagination. However, what he did to his fallen enemy is true. I don't know what Andrew Moray shouted, if anything, as he entered the battle, but I thought I created something fitting. The wound he suffered was significant, and many historians believe it led to his death a couple months later.

The landscape and events during the Battle of Stirling Bridge scene are true to history, with the exception of the clans I name who followed Andrew Moray. Despite how I searched, I couldn't find an accurate list. I found which clans arrived alongside Wallace, but not Moray. Consequently, I researched which clans were present at Stirling Bridge, but who I couldn't attest to being with Wallace, and made them part of Moray's forces. I foreshadowed some of what was to come as the Bruce fought for his claim to the throne, and I mentioned other heroes of the day, like Duncan "the Black" Campbell, who I alluded to was Brodie and Dominic Campbell's father (*A Hellion at the Highland Court* and *A Harlot at the Highland Court* respectively).

King Edward I, "Longshanks" and "Hammer of the Scots," based his claim to intervening in the Scottish heredity crisis because of his tangled family lineage. Queen Isabella de Warenne's familial ties I name are true. Beyond being related to Queen Margaret of Scotland (the last queen before Isabella), she was not only John Balliol's wife and King Edward's cousin, but the daughter of John de Warenne, 6th Earl of Surrey. De Warenne was the man who led the English forces against the Scots at the Battle of Stirling Bridge. As I wrote in one of my previous books, "Oh, what a tangled web we weave, when at first we practice to conceive."

The true historical family lineages were complex. Similarly, as my world continues to grow, the family trees have many intertwining branches now. Be sure to check the family trees I provide in my books to help keep the ever-expanding families straight.

The wedding vows are ones I discovered while researching *An*

Enemy at the Highland Court, so they may sound familiar to modern day ones, but there are some significant differences in wording. I often incorporate traditional handfast vows, so I wanted to include the historic Catholic vows when I've incorporated the spoken parts of a wedding into my books.

Thank you for taking this trip back in time with me. It's a period that fascinates me, and I enjoy weaving it into my tales of strong men and fierce women.

Happy reading,

Celeste

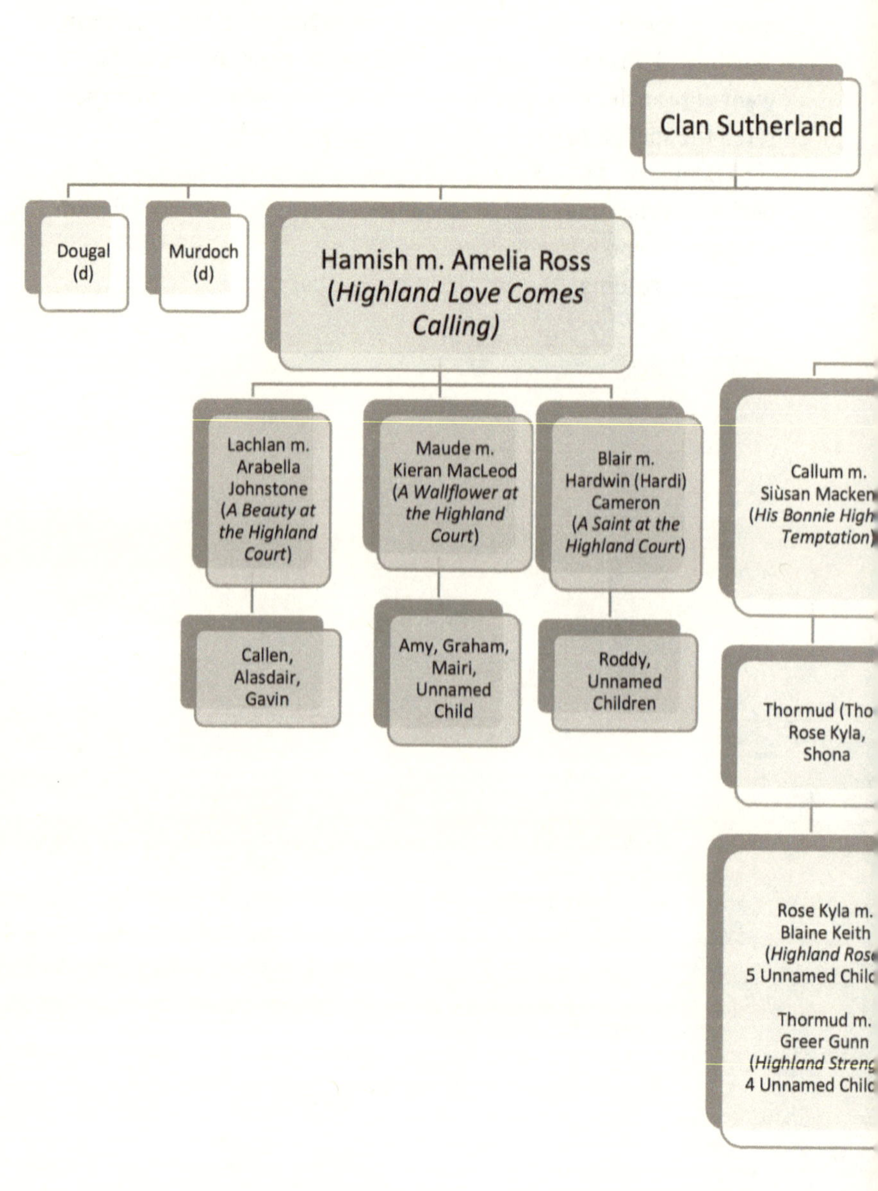

Clan Sutherland

Dougal (d)

Murdoch (d)

Hamish m. Amelia Ross (*Highland Love Comes Calling*)

Lachlan m. Arabella Johnstone (*A Beauty at the Highland Court*)

Maude m. Kieran MacLeod (*A Wallflower at the Highland Court*)

Blair m. Hardwin (Hardi) Cameron (*A Saint at the Highland Court*)

Callum m. Siùsan Macken (*His Bonnie High Temptation*)

Callen, Alasdair, Gavin

Amy, Graham, Mairi, Unnamed Child

Roddy, Unnamed Children

Thormud (Tho Rose Kyla, Shona

Rose Kyla m. Blaine Keith (*Highland Rose* 5 Unnamed Child

Thormud m. Greer Gunn (*Highland Streng* 4 Unnamed Child

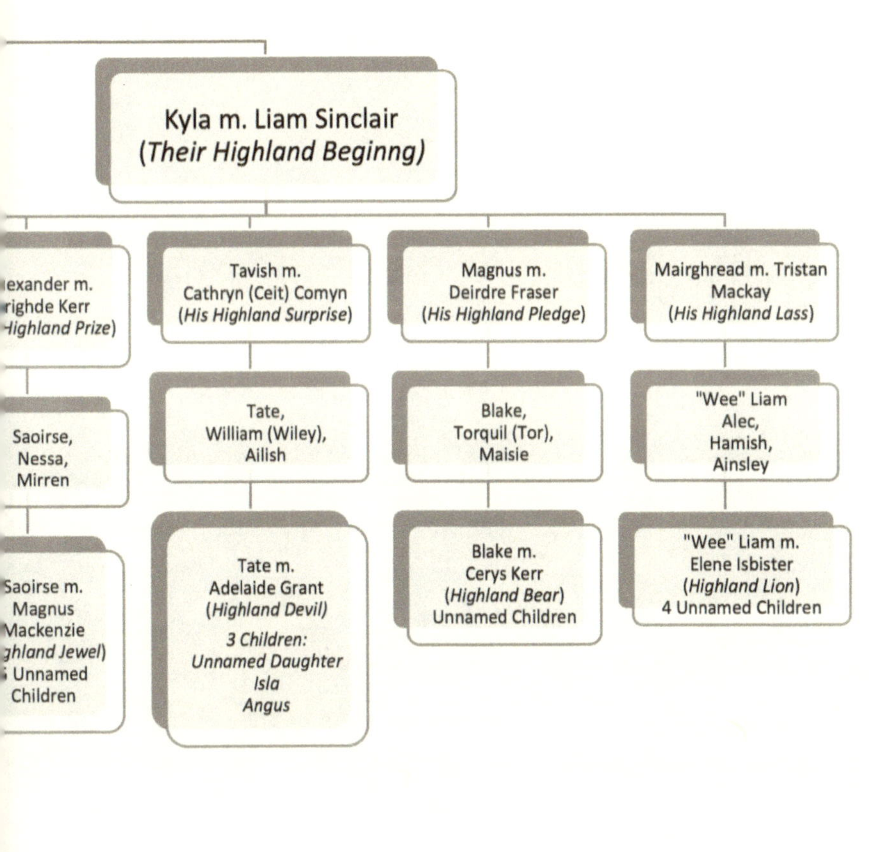

Kyla m. Liam Sinclair
(Their Highland Beginng)

exander m.
righde Kerr
Highland Prize)

Tavish m.
Cathryn (Ceit) Comyn
(His Highland Surprise)

Magnus m.
Deirdre Fraser
(His Highland Pledge)

Mairghread m. Tristan
Mackay
(His Highland Lass)

Saoirse,
Nessa,
Mirren

Tate,
William (Wiley),
Ailish

Blake,
Torquil (Tor),
Maisie

"Wee" Liam
Alec,
Hamish,
Ainsley

Saoirse m.
Magnus
Mackenzie
ghland Jewel)
Unnamed
Children

Tate m.
Adelaide Grant
(Highland Devil)

3 Children:
Unnamed Daughter
Isla
Angus

Blake m.
Cerys Kerr
(Highland Bear)
Unnamed Children

"Wee" Liam m.
Elene Isbister
(Highland Lion)
4 Unnamed Children

CHAPTER 1

*H*amish Sutherland would rather be back in battle against the English. The sacking of Berwick and Battle of Dunbar a year-and-a-half earlier seemed preferable to another evening in the Great Hall at Stirling Castle. He felt utterly out of place during this first visit to the royal court as an adult. While there wasn't the blood and slashed limbs strewn across the Great Hall's floor like one finds in battle, the stench was almost as overpowering. Far too many overheated bodies in too confined a space. He didn't belong here. He belonged back in his beloved Highlands at his home, Dunrobin Castle. The wild and open space along with the fresh air beckoned him. If another courtier called out to him tonight, he might run from the chamber, the keep, and the town.

That is, if he even recognized his name when they did. When people addressed him as Laird Sutherland, or worse, the Earl of Sutherland, he still instinctively looked for his father. But his father was recently dead, may he rest in hell. At least, that's where Hamish was certain his father's soul, along with his two brothers', went to spend the afterlife. Their deaths were the reason he was forced to remain at court. He was in the midst of feuding civilly with the Rosses while beneath the king's roof. It had been uncivil back home when his family slew dozens of Rosses in a needless battle, only to have their nemeses chase after his father and brothers, killing them just beyond Dunrobin's barmkin.

He pushed away from the wall he propped up when he saw the enchanting woman who'd caught his attention the past two nights finally step away from the other dancers to go in search of a mug of ale. He didn't dare ask about her since he didn't want to draw unnecessary attention to himself, nor did he want to risk the young lady-in-waiting's reputation. But he no longer wished to observe. He wanted to meet the woman with the alder wood hair. He doubted she would find that a compliment. He recalled the tree was frequently found in swampy areas upon which lichen often grew. He was a woodworker and loved to carve, so he'd made furniture from the tree many times. At least the tree had curative properties, so perhaps she wouldn't loathe the comparison.

He wove around the crowd, noticing another man making his way toward the woman with whom he wished to dance. He bumped into a courtier, his larger frame pushing the man into his rival's path. Now that he'd found his nerve, he wasn't to be deterred. He reached the nameless beauty first and smiled at her. She stared at him in return before her gaze darted to the other man who she clearly recognized. But her attention shifted back to Hamish, and his competition seemed soon forgotten.

"Good evening, ma lady."

The woman's dark eyebrows rose at his brogue. There were few Highlanders at court and even fewer who allowed their accents to flavor their speech. However, Hamish didn't believe in being anything besides who he was— a Highland warrior. That was all he thought life ever meant him to be. Now he was a Highland warrior laird. He reminded himself: a Highland warrior earl. He wondered how many more moons it would take to accustom himself to that title. The woman stared at him, and he realized she'd returned his greeting and awaited his response.

"Would ye care to dance?"

"Aye. Thank you."

The couple moved into position for a set that would keep them together. Hamish wished to breathe a sigh of relief. He didn't want the woman in his arms to float away to another partner.

"Ma lady, I'm Hamish."

She waited for him to offer his clan name, but he said nothing more. After word spread through court that he and Laird Roy Ross, Earl of Ross, nearly came to blows in the king's Privy Council chamber, he figured everyone at court knew his now notorious name.

"I'm Lady Amelia." Amelia Ross waited to see a spark of recognition in her partner's eyes, but there was nothing. After the afternoon brouhaha she heard her father caused, she assumed everyone knew her now infamous relation to the enraged, redheaded laird. When Hamish merely smiled, she took his lack of familiarity with her family as a blessing. She wouldn't offer her clan name if he was disinclined to offer his.

"Are ye one of the queen's ladies?" Hamish hoped he hadn't just asked another man's wife to dance. But he'd seen no ring on her finger, nor had she paid particularly more attention to one man than the others.

"I am. I've served Her Grace for three years." *Three vera long years.*

"Ye must have traveled much of Scotland in that time. Do ye have a favorite place?" Hamish prayed he'd chosen a neutral topic that could allow them to talk for a while.

"I have traveled some, but the queen rarely goes on procession with King John. She has Prince Henry, so she prefers to remain with him." Amelia knew that was the excuse the woman gave because she cared little for her ten-year-old son. She'd already raised Edward and Agnes and believed she was finished with bairns and weans until Henry came along. Truly, Queen Isabella de Warenne didn't enjoy her husband's company, so she avoided time trapped with him on the road and in tents. "I'm from the Highlands, so I've been to our gatherings."

"If ye havenae realized, I'm a Highlander. I dinna recall ye at the gatherings."

"Do ye ken everyone in the Highlands?" Amelia chuckled. "I ken I dinna. There are hundreds who come to the gatherings each year."

"Nay. I dinna ken everyone, but I would have remembered ye."

Amelia's cheeks flushed, uncertain what she should say, especially when she wanted to say she would have remembered him too. She wished to steer the conversation back to where they'd started. "When I've traveled with Her Grace, it was often to the Lowlands. But I've enjoyed our journeys to the Highlands far more. I miss the wide expanses of hills, forests, and mountains. I miss the way our air smells."

Hamish nearly missed a step when Amelia described the same things to which he longed to return. He supposed it was in their blood. The good Lord hadn't made Highlanders to be cooped up in towns that stunk of refuse or in castles where morality was selectively applied to most situations. "Do ye ken when she might release ye from her service, and ye can return home?"

Amelia's brow furrowed. "Most ladies-in-waiting aren't released until they wed."

Hamish glanced between them, staring at his feet. He'd been to court twice before, but they'd been when he was much younger. He'd mostly spent his time in his family's suite, where children could neither be seen nor heard. It hadn't mattered to him back then. Now he felt woefully unprepared yet again. "Ma father presented ma sister at court a few years ago, but she is married now. Our father didna arrange for her to remain here as a lady-in-waiting but to announce she was eligible to wed. We needed her since our mother died while ma brothers, sister, and I were weans."

He wouldn't admit his father hadn't been bothered to arrange anything for Kyla except for her marriage to end a feud. His sister left Dunrobin to meet her bridegroom terrified and virtually alone, with only their uncle accompanying her with a handful of guards. Hamish had feared for her life from the moment his father mumbled the name Sinclair until the day he rode through the gates of Kyla's new husband's keep two moons ago to announce their father's and brothers' demise. He'd found Kyla happier than he'd ever imagined a new bride could be. She was deeply in love with her husband, Liam, and the man clearly returned her affection.

Amelia slid her gaze around the chamber, noting anyone who might pay them too much attention. When it satisfied her that no one took an interest in them, she lowered her voice. "Your sister missed naught by not serving Her Grace. I wish I'd never come here. They say Stirling straddles the Highlands and Lowlands, but this isn't our home. Look around. Even the other High- landers wear hose and doublets. No one speaks Gaelic in fear of King John finding out. He tolerates us."

Amelia knew what she risked admitting such things to a stranger. Perhaps she was testing him to determine his trustwor- thiness. Or perhaps she already trusted him, and that's why she confessed those thoughts. She wasn't certain. It hadn't escaped Hamish's attention that he and his men stood out because of their size, and his men wore their Sutherland plaids. There were Mackays and MacLeods of Lewis in attendance, and they wore their plaids, too. But other clans, like the Rosses, conformed to courtly attire. He only trapped his bollocks in such a vise because he knew his appearance had to befit his new station as an earl. He preferred the roominess of his *breacan feile*, or great plaid.

"I would speak to ye in Gaelic if ye miss it. I speak Scots as well as anyone else, but I dinna care for it. I definitely dinna care for English, and French is only for dealing with the king."

Amelia's lips twitched at Hamish's last comment. "Dealing with the king" was exactly how she felt about the man and his insufferable wife. "Mayhap another eve. If you could travel anywhere in Scotland, where would you go?"

"Home, of course!" Hamish grinned. "I already live in the Highlands, so why would I leave God's most glorious creation? I dinna care what the Islanders say. It rains God's tears on the Hebrides."

Amelia laughed before covering her mouth, hoping she didn't draw attention from the couples swirling around them. "I wouldn't let the MacLeods hear that."

"Bah. Even the Lord crying over the islands is a far sight better than wading through the Lord's— erm —what the Lord left behind that makes the Lowland marches." Hamish caught himself before he said something profane.

"I don't know if it's safe to dance with you." At Amelia's comments, Hamish's heart lurched. He didn't want her to leave before the song ended. But she laughed again, and the tightness eased. "After all, I don't want to be too near when God smites you for taking His name in vain."

"I did nay such thing, lass. It isnae a sin to speak the truth." When Hamish grinned at her again, it was Amelia's turn to nearly miss a step. He was the single most handsome man she'd ever seen. Tall, braw, funny, and with kind eyes. He seemed perfect from what she could tell. She wondered why he'd come to court, but he'd offered nothing that made her think he wished to tell her. He'd spent more time telling her why he'd rather be anywhere else. She decided to push a little and see what came of it.

"You haven't been here long, and I don't recall you visiting before. Have you come to join King John's forces?" Amelia gazed up at Hamish since she was easily eight inches shorter than him, and many considered her taller than average. Because she did, she could see the underside of his chin and notice his jaw clench for a heartbeat.

"Nay. I have other clan business to handle." When he saw his abrupt answer made Amelia pull back in his arms, he softened his tone. "I've had troubles with ma neighbors as Highlanders do. I'm here to present ma case before the king. We will see what comes of it."

Amelia darted her gaze to the dais where the king and queen sat before meeting Hamish's. "He has been very preoccupied since Berwick. He may keep you waiting. Since that didn't go well for him, he's been in a bit of a— mood." It didn't matter that Berwick and Dunbar were nearly eighteen months ago. The monarch remained perpetually on edge.

"I noticed. He summoned me. I arrived on the date he insisted. But he's kept me waiting for two days. I dinna have forever. I have a clan to return to. Duties." Hamish scowled, but when he saw concern in the lovely woman's eyes, he softened his tone. "I ken what happened in Berwick. King Edward stole one of our most populated cities and massacred the men. Then he marched on the Dunbars and swept through there. He keeps his men garrisoned on *our* land. He's even living on *our* land. *I* ken King John's frustration. But life goes on, and he must continue ruling all of this country." Hamish knew he'd found a crack in the ice, speaking about the king with such discontent, and it was like he was pressing the toe of his boot into it to see if it would crack. Amelia sighed. She didn't disagree. Instead, she appeared resigned.

"I had family at Carlisle. A brutal and futile move that invited Longshanks to march on us. We were fortunate they returned, but not all of my clan did. I suppose not all of yours came home from the borders either." Her father had been one of seven invading earls who marched into England. He was lucky to come away with his head on his shoulders. The result was the sacking of the border town of Berwick, followed a month later by an attack on Clan Dunbar.

"Berwick was just the start," Hamish mused. "There was little to defend once they finished. Neither people nor places. The English had already destroyed much of the royal burgh. The Lowland clans may have rallied to fight several skirmishes with the men Longshanks left behind after the Battle of Dunbar, but there werenae enough of them to carry out our king's orders successfully. They kenned it before they began."

Hamish knew they'd already danced at least two songs. He didn't want to end their conversation, but people would talk if they continued as they were. When the tune ended as he finished speaking, he steered Amelia toward doors that opened onto a terrace. Other people milled around, enjoying a reprieve from the stifling air within the Great Hall. He ensured they remained where people could see them for propriety's sake. Amelia allowed Hamish to guide her outside because the dancing had only made her more overheated. Her hair was thicker than most women's by at least double. She wore it tied back with a ribbon at her nape, but it still stuck to her neck. Its weight always made her perspire sooner than her fellow ladies. It frequently embarrassed her to resemble a wilted rhubarb stalk when the other women appeared like freshly bloomed buttercups.

Amelia lowered her voice now neither she nor Hamish had to speak over the cacophony in the Great Hall. They tread a precariously fine line discussing the conflict with England. "That must have been frustrating for those men and even more terrifying than most battles. At least, I would imagine so. If warriors enter most battles believing they will win, I would think that gives men courage. But to enter a fight they know they'll likely lose must make warriors feel defeated— even dead —before they start." Amelia realized what she said and wished to bite her tongue. "I didn't mean winning is the only thing that gives men courage. Or that they'd go into any battle without courage. I—"

"Lady Amelia, I kenned what ye meant. I didna take offense. Ye arenae wrong like ye fear. It is demoralizing to ken ye enter a battle ye will probably lose. And all battles are terrifying, but kenning how outnumbered ye are only makes it worse. We shouldnae have antagonized King Edward. Things are already bad enough with the way he treats us like vassals." *If Ross and his bluidy friends hadnae ignited the fire that burned up Longshanks' arse, we wouldnae have had battles to lose.*

"Aye. Just because Edward's sister wed King Alexander doesn't entitle him to our throne. He has no blood to his claim. We don't need him hovering like a father waiting to punish his naughty wean." Amelia glanced in the direction she knew King John Balliol sat beyond the wall. Everyone knew the Scottish king had a loose claim to the throne upon which he sat. He wasn't the only man to vie for the position, but he was the one King Edward believed most malleable to his wishes. She knew Scotland would rue the day they invited the English king to assist in the succession decision. They'd invited the wolf not only to the door but inside for a dram of whisky.

"We are where we are, but I dinna think we will remain here long." Hamish didn't know the young lady with whom he spoke. He wouldn't go so far as to say he didn't believe Balliol would remain their monarch for much longer. He foresaw the man abdicating, being forced from the throne by the Scottish nobles, or killed in battle.

Amelia understood the thinly veiled prediction, and she agreed. "But where we go next may be where we've already been." If Balliol had no clear successor, it would draw them back into conflict among the claimants. It would invariably give Edward more reason to assert himself across the border.

"Ye are right, ma lady. Hopefully, one mon has a keen sense of direction."

"They say those with red hair have the temper needed to win the most heated arguments." There was one man who stood among many, and it wasn't his height. Amelia darted her gaze around to ensure no one took an interest in their conversation or could overhear her treasonous statement.

"Aye. The Bruce." Hamish named the man who many argued had just as strong a claim to the throne as Balliol. Those who supported him argued he was more experienced in battle and a more decisive leader. No one believed Edward could bend Robert Bruce to his will. He'd spent time at Edward's court, and he knew how the man thought. He could predict Edward's actions better than their current Scottish king.

"Aye. His only fault is that he's a Lowlander." Amelia grinned.

"Nae everyone can be perfect." Longing to kiss her overtook Hamish, testing his good sense. She had a keen understanding of politics he suspected came from an observant nature. This wasn't a topic likely discussed among the women at court. Amelia must have learned from listening to the men. Hamish appreciated that she trusted him enough to share her thoughts, and he found her sharp mind made her even more alluring than her beauty.

Amelia chuckled. "Such a Highlander."

"Aye, lass. Born and bred." His smile was irrepressible and unrepentant. She might have grown up in the Highlands, but he was unlike any man she knew. None in her family welcomed her opinions, and she'd never dared share them at court. Something about the colossus before her put her at ease. He could easily force her to his will, kill her before she could make a sound. But he had a gentleness that belied the experience as a warrior she knew he must have.

A lull in the music made them both look toward the Great Hall. The crowd thinned significantly while they chatted. Neither noticed that it was well into the middle of the night. Both knew they should retire, but neither wished to walk away. The decision was taken from her when a woman stepped outside but remained too close to the doors to see Amelia or Hamish.

"Amelia?"

"Aye, Henrietta. Coming." Amelia hadn't looked away from Hamish. She whispered, "My cousin."

She'd disliked Henrietta Gunn since they were children. The woman had a selfish streak that often made her cruel. As adults, she wielded her tongue as her weapon. As weans, she bit. Amelia couldn't tarry, or Henrietta would investigate. She didn't want her cousin to spy Hamish. She was a gossip of the worst sort, and family bonds meant nothing to her. She couldn't be less like her mother, Amelia's father's sister. She turned away from Hamish but paused. She twisted to look at him. The candles in the Great Hall were being extinguished, so little light shone on them now. She could no longer make out his features.

"I enjoyed our conversation, Hamish. Thank you."

"It is I who should thank ye. Ye are the most interesting person I've spoken to since I arrived, and the only who hasnae treated me like a heathen." The Lowlanders possessed such a low opinion of the Highlanders that they saw them as little more than tamed wildcats. "I hope we can speak again."

"I'd like that very much. Hamish, my cousin isn't kind. It's better she doesn't see me walk back with a mon. I'm sorry."

"Ye dinna need to apologize for someone else's poor behavior. I'll watch to be sure ye make it into the Great Hall, then I'll follow. I'll make sure ye make it safely to yer passageway."

"You can't. She'll know."

"Lass, nay one is seeing me unless I want them to."

CHAPTER 2

*H*amish made good on his promise the night before. He'd followed Amelia and Henrietta through the passageways on silent feet. He watched from a distance, ready to step forward three times when men stepped in front of the women. Henrietta's squawking quickly drove the men away, leaving the cousins untouched. He observed Amelia glance back down the passageway just before she entered her chamber. She was subtle, but Hamish saw the slight tilt of her head. He knew she hadn't seen him and couldn't. He wondered if she doubted he'd kept his word.

This morning, he intended to make his presence known to the king. He was fed up and refused to squander any more time waiting for the king to deign to notice him. He didn't want to remain in the same keep as Roy Ross since every time they encountered one another, which was often thanks to only one place to dine, they were ready to draw their dirks and stab one another. Hamish had many reasons compelling him to return to Dunrobin since he'd only inherited the lairdship two months earlier. His father had been a tyrant, and his brothers learned from his example. It meant Hamish had to work doubly hard to convince his clan he would rule with firmness, but he wasn't unreasonable. Those who lived in and near Dunrobin already knew him, and most recognized the difference in his leadership from the start. But he needed to tour his outlying villages, and that took days.

His Earldom of Sutherland stretched across much of the most northern part of Scotland. His brother-by-marriage, Liam Sinclair, was tánaiste to the Earldom of Sinclair. Caithness covered nearly as much territory as Sutherland. Liam and Hamish's sister, Kyla, returned with him after he shared the news of his inheritance. His two brothers' wives had been woefully neglectful of their duties, neither wanting to be chatelaine. He'd avoided taking a wife since he couldn't imagine subjecting any woman to his family. The alliances they already had through his older and younger brother satisfied his father until his death. Though, toward the end, the man put unbearable pressure on Hamish to marry. When Kyla left to wed Liam, the keep nearly fell down around their ears. She and Liam made it clear her return was as a visit, and Liam made it doubly clear that if anyone mistreated Kyla as her father and two out of her three brothers had, not only would they depart, but the alliance would be over as would their lives.

Hamish had been the second brother and second child out of four. He'd never imagined he would inherit the lairdship. He'd served as his older brother's second-in-command. He was a warrior and leader their men respected. They were glad to follow Hamish when they'd followed his brother purely out of clan loyalty. Hamish's younger brother would have been better suited to become tánaiste one day when their oldest brother became laird. Instead, the titles of laird and earl now rested upon his head. He'd feared Kyla wouldn't come back with him to help him get the keep in order and to adjudicate disagreements that brewed among the women. While they'd been close as children, their father's taunting and physical abuse toward Kyla drove them apart.

Hamish admitted to Kyla he'd found it easier to turn a blind eye than feel helpless to do anything or to have their father turn his abusive temper toward him. Hamish had been the only family member Kyla trusted, even if they'd grown apart before her marriage. By the end of the moon Kyla and Liam spent with the Sutherlands, he and his sister fully reconciled, and he counted Liam as his closest friend. He pulled himself out of his ruminations as he crossed the bailey to join the king on a morning promenade. The monarch joined the queen, so Hamish hoped the ladies-in-waiting would accompany her, too. A particular lady-in-waiting. There were courtiers surrounding the king, but he saw no other petitioners present. Blessedly, that meant the Ross was nowhere in sight. He scanned the crowd of women, but the woman with the alder tree-hued hair wasn't among them. He promised himself he would find a better color to which he could liken the rich mane he wished to run his fingers through.

"Hamish?"

He knew that voice. "Good morning, Lady Amelia. It's a brighter morning for seeing ye." *Where the devil did that come from? I am nae a charming mon, but I seem to be trying.*

"Thank you. It's a beautiful morning for a walk, isn't it?" Hamish's compliment surprised her, making her belly flutter. She feared her question was too forward. Polite society allowed men far more freedom with their words than women.

"It is. I hope to catch the king's attention, but I find I'm less inclined to press for an audience than I was a minute ago." He offered her his arm without consideration for who might watch them. It felt natural, and Amelia didn't hesitate to take it.

"Allow him the ten minutes he feels obligated to spend with his wife. Your best chance is to catch him while he walks from the gardens to the lists. Be prepared though. You'll want to be at the front of the pack since he escapes his wife like a fire were up his arse." Amelia's eyes widened when she realized what she let slip. It wasn't the insult about the royal couple. They'd already established the night before that neither thought highly of the man. It was the crudeness of her comment. But Hamish laughed — loudly. Too loudly.

A roar from behind was the only warning before a weight propelled him forward. He barely released Amelia with a light shove to get her away from his falling body. He landed on the ground with a man straddling him, a fist poised to land on his cheek. He grabbed the fist and bucked, but his attacker was of equal weight and height to him. He threw his own fist at Laird Roy Ross, the Earl of Ross, and he met his mark. From there, it was a clash of titans. Fists flying every which way, the men rolling on the ground, taking turns gaining superiority. It was when Roy grabbed a handful of Hamish's hair and Hamish wrapped his hands around his fellow earl's throat that men finally intervened. It took six of the king's guardsmen to pry them apart. They kept launching themselves at each other. Even the king's orders fell on deaf ears as the two mighty lions roared and fought.

Hamish didn't understand why Roy chose that moment to attack him. Not when the king was only a few yards away, but he had his honor to defend. He'd never fought Roy directly, and he wasn't there during the raid his father led that spurred the Rosses to retaliate. He'd watched the beginning of the near massacre as his family was almost within shouting distance of their keep. The Sutherlands and Rosses raided one another, and Hamish's family had led a successful hot trot to gather the livestock the Rosses had most recently stolen. They'd triumphed initially and regained cattle the Rosses stole. But merely retrieving their animals left his father dissatisfied. He'd wished for revenge. He underestimated Roy Ross, and he died for it. The Rosses chased the Sutherlands back to their land, and before Hamish could ride out from beneath the portcullis, the Rosses slew the Sutherlands and were attempting to snatch the herd. Hamish prevented the theft, but he could do nothing to bring his brothers or father back to life.

But as furious as the need to defend his honor made him, it enraged him that the Ross should attack him with Amelia standing so close. The fighting men could have caught her between them and grievously injured her. Neither man pulled a dirk, but they both had them at the ready. A recklessly slashing blade could have maimed or even killed her. That he couldn't forgive, so he'd been ready to fight his enemy to the death.

"Enough!" King John bellowed. It did nothing to settle either man, who continued to writhe against the men holding them back. Hamish spotted Amelia in tears, and that only reignited his fury. Only when she stepped in front of him did he relent.

"Hamish, ye must stop. Ye canna kill ma father in front of the entire court. Ye will wind up in the dungeon then dead right alongside him." Amelia was so distraught she didn't notice she'd lapsed into her burr.

"Get the bluidy hell away from my daughter, you piece of shite. Amelia, come away from him."

Hamish shifted his focus from Amelia to Roy and back to the woman whose tears he wished to wipe away. They bore absolutely no resemblance to one another. He never would have guessed. He knew Roy had a daughter named Amelia, but it was a common name.

"I'm so sorry, Hamish."

"For what, lass? Ye didna do aught."

"That I'm why ma father attacked ye."

"Lia," the tender diminutive fell all too naturally from his lips, "ye didna cause that. Yer father is a mon with his own barmy mind. He chose to do that. He chose to risk yer safety, and I canna accept that. He could have had it out with me in the lists. He could have drawn me aside. He launched himself at me and could have caught ye in the middle. I dinna wish to kill yer father, but if ye'd been hurt, I might have."

They spoke in lowered voices, but he was sure at least a few people other than the three guards around them heard him. He felt his reaction was entirely justified. Roy did not.

"Get away from my daughter, you bluidy bastard. You'd shame her and defile her before the entire court."

Hamish looked over Amelia's shoulder to where Roy seethed and tugged against the men surrounding him. He stepped forward as far as he could. He tugged one arm free and pressed Amelia behind him. "Move. I willna strike first."

The guard blocking his forward progress looked at his counterparts before taking a step aside. Roy tried to free himself, but his captors weren't as trusting. Hamish walked close enough to keep his voice low but not so close Roy could lunge and tackle him again.

"Ye and I dinna get along. Ye and I would gladly bury each other beneath our boots. Ye and I will have a reckoning one way or another. But if ye ever risk yer daughter's life again by putting her between two men trained to kill, I will kill ye. Neither she nor I have done aught but talk. Neither of us kenned who the other was last eve. We—"

"Last eve? What the devil are you talking aboot? I saw you walking with her here. You were with her last night?"

Hamish wished to bite his tongue. He assumed Roy was angry because he'd learned they danced and talked. That he'd seen them together that morning spurred him to action. Their altercation was entirely because they walked arm-in-arm with plenty of witnesses. This was going to go from bad to worse.

"Aye. I danced with yer daughter. After all that's happened with ye caterwauling to anyone who'll listen, I assumed I didna need to state ma clan name. She didna offer hers. We did naught wrong."

"Liar."

The single word made everyone tense. Roy already called into question Hamish's integrity; now he insulted his honor. Between Highlanders, this was grounds for a personal feud, never mind the enmity between their clans. Hamish's voice was dangerously low when he spoke.

"Say that again, Ross. Say it with nay one holding ye up." Hamish cocked an eyebrow, taunting Roy for still having guards restraining him.

"They don't fear what you can do, so they let you go. They know what I'll do to any Sutherland. I—"

"Enough, Father." Amelia stepped beside Hamish, turned to him, put her small hand on his expansive chest, and gave it a good shove. Her expression told him he'd be wise to remain quiet. She turned to her father; her hands clasped demurely before her. Her gaze locked with his. Hamish still stood close enough that he could hear what she whispered. "You are making a fool of yourself and our clan. You came here to have King John settle this matter. Brawling in the bailey makes it look like you don't trust the king to adjudicate. You're insulting him. We will have more problems than just a few score sheep missing and our bruised egos if you don't relent. Hamish did naught dishonorable last night. He spoke the truth. Neither of us kenned who the other was. I didna ken this morning when *I* approached *him*. He did naught dishonorable this morning by walking with me where there are plenty of people to see neither of us acted improperly. Father, I love you. But you're being a fool."

Amelia leaned back, praying she hadn't just earned herself exile to Inchailloch Priory, a remote nunnery known as the Island of Auld Women. Before her father could say anything more, she turned to Hamish.

"Now that I know who you are, I *know* who you are. You are much too new to your lairdship and earldom to get in fights with an earl twice your age whose held his title for longer than you've been alive. If you want anyone to sympathize with you, then you cannot antagonize the mon. And I don't mean by dancing with me or walking with me. Telling him you'll kill him when half the court can hear will not endear you to the king, who you very much need on your side. Don't be shortsighted, Hamish. You have a clan you must protect now, and that responsibility falls solely on your shoulders. They're broad enough while you're standing up. But if you're lying flat in the ground, who will lead them? You have no heir."

Hamish leaned so he could whisper to Amelia and was certain no one heard him. "What ye say is all true, but I will kill any mon who endangers ye. I dinna care which title he bears or what his connection to ye may be. I will put ye and yer safety first. He'd be wise nae to test me again because I willna change ma mind. I will take yer counsel on everything else, but I willna budge on that, Lia. Dinna bother trying to change ma mind. It's the eleventh commandment."

He straightened and stepped back. He filled his glare toward Roy with such disgust the older man flinched. Hamish was every bit the laird and earl in that moment. His word was law, and he would allow no one to gainsay him. It wasn't his feats on a battlefield. It wasn't his patience awaiting the king. No. That wasn't what just proved him a formidable force few could bend. It was his defense of the woman he planned to marry.

That thought struck him like a poleax to the belly. He didn't intend to marry for some time. While he knew he needed alliances to deal with troubles like the very ones that brought him to court, he wasn't prepared for that. There was too much to remedy within his clan before he could envision bringing a wife into his home or sealing his clan's future in a pact with someone else. His alliance with the Sinclairs suited him well, but even that wasn't without complications. The hostility between the Sutherlands and Rosses didn't stem from heads of sheep. That was merely how they displayed it. The root was the Sutherlands' alliance with the Mackays, who'd battled the Rosses more than once. The Sinclairs and Mackays were on rocky terms, and he already foresaw he'd have to broker peace between them lest they tear him in half.

But Amelia drew him like no woman ever had. He'd been impressed by the way she'd assessed the fight between him and her father with unflinching accuracy, pointing out the even more precarious position it placed them in. It was common sense, but her warning was something that needed saying. He also admired her bravery in being so forthright with her father. He'd feared Roy would lash out at her for insulting him, but she knew her father. She turned away from him before he could, allowing him time to stew over her evaluation of their clan's situation. She'd also shown no timidity in addressing Hamish. He liked that she felt safe enough and trusted him enough to be so plain-spoken. She didn't fear he might rebuke her, and she believed he might take her advice. Nothing about Amelia made Hamish think she spoke just to hear her own voice. The practical side of him knew she would make an outstanding lady of the clan; someone he could rely upon in times of peace and in times of strife. He knew it in his marrow. But he'd also never desired a woman physically as much as the petite— compared to him —brunette. If he had his druthers, he would whisk her away, strip her bare, and revel in every inch of her.

"As for not bothering to try to change your mind, I don't think I could change aught aboot you even if I tried. I don't want to. I like you just as you are." Amelia whispered so quietly Hamish strained to hear her, but he could hear well enough to be certain he understood her. Her seal of approval would bolster him in times to come when his duties made him question himself. It also made him intent upon courting the woman, even if she was his enemy's daughter.

"Ross, Sutherland."

King John stepped forward and interrupted their semi-private conversation. Hamish was uncertain whether the man had remained quiet, hoping the irate lairds would tire of their public battle or if the king felt ill-equipped to deal with them. While John Balliol was a larger man, it wasn't muscle that gave him girth. He could spar in the lists and hold his own on the battle-field. After all, he'd lived long enough to be crowned, but he was no match for the Ross or the Sutherland. Hamish suspected he'd avoided dealing with either of them because he feared them. The thought of facing them both together likely made the royal wish to pish himself. That idea nearly made Hamish's lips twitch.

"Aye, Your Majesty."

"Aye, Yer Majesty."

Both lairds answered together, casting a glower in each other's direction. Amelia softly cleared her throat. It didn't go unnoticed that she remained closer to Hamish than her father. It suited Hamish nicely, but he had enough awareness of what would happen beyond that morning to know Amelia would likely suffer for it. That rekindled the need to protect her.

"We shall adjourn to the Privy Council chamber where we shall address your clash today and what brought you both to my doorstep. Come along."

This time, when Roy and Hamish exchanged a look of disgust, it wasn't toward one another. Neither appreciated being spoken to like children, even if they'd tussled like them. And neither appreciated being told to come like dogs running after their master. While they despised one another, neither was a fan of Balliol, but both had fought on his behalf against the English. The only respect they had for one another was for their prowess on the battlefield. However, they might have found one more thing in common. At least, it seemed a possibility until Henrietta called out to Amelia. Both men whipped their gazes to the woman who remained physically and metaphorically between them.

Amelia could have slapped her cousin. The woman made her presence known because she couldn't go more than fifteen minutes without being the center of attention. The men's confrontation meant everyone else ignored her for at least thirty. Henrietta had drawn attention to the fact Amelia continued to stand between the men and would have to walk away to reach her. The perfect way for Henrietta to make herself a focal point. Amelia smiled up at Hamish before shifting to look at her father.

"I'll see you at the evening meal, Father."

"You can be certain of that tonight." Roy's piercing stare would have made a lesser person shrivel, but Amelia took no notice. At least, she appeared like she didn't. She wished to cringe since her father may as well have screamed he would be her shadow to ensure Hamish came nowhere near her. It wasn't even time for terce, and she already wished she could retire for the night. Her gaze darted to Hamish, who barely dipped his chin, opting to remain silent for now. Her worry for him spiked, knowing there was nothing she could do to mediate once the men walked away. She was certain the king would instigate more trouble before he solved it. He needed to appear as though he could control his subjects.

Amelia stepped away from the men, while each of the two angry lairds had three royal guards escort them into the keep. She wished to drag her feet rather than join her cousin and other ladies-in-waiting. But she noticed Queen Isabella scowling at her. The woman had a face like curdled milk: chunky and sour. She curtsied to the queen before the woman turned away without acknowledging her and began her delayed morning constitutional. When Henrietta wrapped her arm around Amelia's, the latter wished to yank it away. Alas, that wasn't an option.

"Such a braw mon in a barbaric sort of way." Henrietta's stage whisper attempted to give their conversation a conspiratorial tone, but Amelia wasn't interested. She didn't respond. She knew that wouldn't dissuade her cousin from nattering on, but she wasn't about to allow the woman to draw her in and put her in a position to defend herself. "Did you see his muscles when he fought your father? I feared if he'd worn his plaid, he'd have presented us all with a most inappropriate view beneath his plaid." She tittered, and the surrounding women joined in.

Amelia was certain they would have loved nothing more than to see what Hamish's *breacan feile* covered. As her mind conjured lascivious thoughts, she realized she was no better than the others. She merely kept such musings to herself. She considered how he'd felt when she danced in his arms the night before. She recalled how the muscles bunched beneath his leine as her palm rested on his forearm before her father ruined their walk. She thought about how he'd given her a firm but not rough push as he fell to the ground, in an attempt not to take her down with him. She remembered how he'd pressed her behind him before confronting her father about endangering her. She could practically feel his adamance pulsate from him when he pledged his protection was as irrefutable as the Ten Commandments. That it was another commandment all would follow. He made her feel special in a way no one ever had. Her brothers had been protective of her when they were younger, and they worried about her at court. But they'd never been so assertive against those who'd taunted her at Balnagown, the only home she'd known before arriving at court.

"Lady Amelia, how could neither you nor Laird Sutherland know who the other was?" Lady Beitiris Chisholm wondered. "Didn't you notice people staring at you while you danced?"

"We didn't exchange clan names, and neither of us wore our plaids. As he said, he assumed everyone knew who he was. I didn't. I assumed everyone knew who I was because of my father. He didn't."

"But you didn't notice people talking aboot you?" Beitiris pressed.

Amelia's cheeks heated. "I assumed people took interest in him because he's a Highlander and doesn't hide it by sounding like a Scot." *And because he was the vera brawest mon in the Great Hall.*

Henrietta rolled her eyes. "We all wondered why he danced with you. And not just because your father wishes to murder him."

Amelia steeled herself not to respond to her cousin's barb. She was all too familiar with them. She knew if she defended herself, Henrietta would spin their conversation to make herself the victim of Amelia's sharp tongue. It was better to let the topic fade. But her tactics didn't work today. Henrietta persisted.

"Why did he dance with you if he didn't know who you were? He knew, and he did it to antagonize your father. He could only want your company as an excuse."

When Amelia's gaze met Henrietta's, she knew her cousin intended each malicious word she uttered. She would lay the foundation for gossip and hand each brick to the ladies-in-waiting, pointing to where they should place them but never doing the work herself. She was slippery, making it difficult to catch her and pin the blame for vicious rumors upon her.

"Perhaps he wished for a partner who doesn't prattle." Amelia kept her tone light and shrugged her shoulder dismissively. "Lady Anne, how fairs your mother? I heard she's recuperating from the ague." Amelia separated herself from Henrietta and attached herself to the most talkative woman in their group. While she had no interest in her fellow lady-in-waiting or the woman's mother, she knew once Anne launched into her tale, she would barely come up for a breath. It would make it impossible for Henrietta to speak over her. At least, not without looking as desperate as she was for attention.

"Well, our clan's healer told my aunt to tell my mother's cousin to tell my mother that all she needed was to sleep with an onion beneath her pillow for a sennight and bathe with nettles. Now, I've had nettle tea when poorly, so I believe it can cure one's ailments. But have you heard aught so ridiculous as bathing with it? My mother refused, saying the ague was preferable to a rash all over her body. The healer said if Mother was going to refuse to heed the woman's advice, then she wouldn't spend her time treating her and would find patients who truly needed her. That made Mother think twice. She was so poorly that she needed…"

Amelia no longer listened as Anne carried on their one-sided conversation. She looked toward the keep, wondering how Hamish was surviving the royal inquisition. His temper had cooled faster than her father's, and he'd fought to defend her and his honor. She wished one of the king's councilmen would call her father into a meeting again, so he wouldn't be present for the evening meal. Though, even if he weren't, she knew she couldn't dance with Hamish again. That tore her heart in two.

CHAPTER 3

"You cannot brawl in the bailey like a pair of street urchins," King John declared.

The men walked in silence to the Privy Council chamber, but the moment the king sat upon his throne, his disdain for the two Highlanders oozed from him. While he relied on the Highlanders in battle, he could barely tolerate the uncouth creatures he likened to wild animals. His gaze trailed over Hamish from head to toe. His disgust could have only been greater if Hamish had worn his *breacan feile*, leine, and sporran. Roy stared at Hamish with aloof amusement. In turn, Hamish ignored Roy like he would the village idiot. No. He corrected his thoughts. He held empathy for anyone born with challenges. He held no empathy for the arse who prided himself upon being an arse. Aware his mind had wandered, Hamish forced his attention back to the king. He realized he didn't know what the sovereign just said. He schooled his thoughts away from wishing his enemy would wind up a pile of ash in the blazing fires of hell.

"Both of you have slain men needlessly. Men I need to defend our country from those who would steal our freedom."

Both Roy and Hamish fought not to roll their eyes. Balliol had turned into little more than Longshanks' puppet. He was likely to invite the man in for a dram or ten of whisky, then lick shite from his boots. Little did he know that his pomposity might be the one thing that could broker a truce between the men since he fed their mutual disdain for him. The king had already reined for twelve years, and it was his silent condoning of Roy's raid on Carlisle, alongside the other earls, that led to the sacking of Berwick. That said, King Edward never would have made it across the border so casually if Balliol didn't act as though the English monarch was a benevolent patron to all of Scotland.

Hamish squared his shoulders. "I apologize, Yer Majesty." *For aught that risks ma clan. Nae for pummeling the bastard. One more punch, and I might have broken his jaw. Then he wouldnae be able to smirk like the king will choose him as his Christmas goose. He's fit to be tied and roasted.* Hamish kept his expression neutral as he silently volleyed his thoughts toward his neighbor. He could see Roy was veritably ready to snarl at him for apologizing first. Hamish had stolen his thunder. Balliol nodded before looking at Roy with a mien of smug anticipation.

"I apologize, Your Majesty. As a father to a daughter, you understand we must protect their virtue." Roy wouldn't turn down the opportunity to belittle Hamish while forcing the king to take his side.

"Aye. But I would have the sense to not do so in a manner that would crush Princess Agnes." Balliol turned his attention to Hamish. "Your behavior was unacceptable. I don't know how you conduct yourself in the Highlands, but you do not approach one of the queen's ladies-in-waiting and solicit her attention. She is now sullied."

Hamish's subtly shifted to the balls of his feet like he was ready to pounce. There was nothing he could do. Perhaps Amelia's reputation was a little tarnished, but she herself was not. He resented the implication. The courtiers present were worse gossips than a passel of fishwives. He was certain the king's words would circulate before the nooning. King John accomplished his goal. Hamish had no choice but to stay away from Amelia. His rational mind told him it was just as well. But far deeper in his mind, and deep within his bollocks, he knew he would do no such thing. He would find a way.

"You are both dismissed. I must consider your circumstances even more seriously now that you've both behaved so abominably."

Hamish knew the king still avoided adjudicating the feud. He fully believed the king intended to torment them, but he also believed it terrified the king to anger either Highlander further. Neither Hamish nor Roy moved, since neither wished to be the first to walk away. Both hoped the last to leave might gain the king's attention. Or perhaps the king would keep the one who remained and have an extra word with them.

"Be gone." John flapped his hand. Hamish and Roy turned toward one another before turning toward the door. When they arrived at the portal, each gestured to usher the other one out, as though trying to prove they were the bigger man. When that didn't work, they tried to muscle their way through the doorway at the same time. A guard had to open the second door to let them pass.

"Let us be clear, Ross," Hamish snarled. "Lady Amelia did naught wrong. Dinna ever shame her like that in public again. I willna tolerate it."

"And who the bluidy hell do you think you are, giving me orders aboot my daughter?"

Hamish didn't hesitate. "I'm the mon who's going to marry yer daughter."

Tormud and Lionel Ross wove through the crowd gathering to enter the Great Hall for the evening meal. They'd both spotted their father, looked at one another, and elbowed their way forward. When they found their sister, they each grabbed an arm and unceremoniously steered her through the doors opposite from where their father would enter.

"Amy, what have you done?" Tormud whispered.

Amelia understood her younger brother's question, but she didn't wish to answer it. She'd been responding to some variation or another of it all day. She hadn't thought twice about greeting Hamish that morning. She'd had no choice but to walk past him to join the queen. She'd reasoned it would have been abominable manners to walk past without acknowledging him. But she shouldn't have hinted she wished to walk with him. She shouldn't have even considered asking him. She knew she was to blame for everything that had transpired that day. But the impulse overwhelmed her when she saw him standing, awaiting the king. He'd been too handsome to ignore. He'd been so kind the night before. He'd listened to her thoughts after his altercation with her father that morning, and it proved he was the man she suspected. He respected her despite what her father claimed. She'd risked much speaking to her father as she had, but someone had to do it. If they'd been in private, he would have likely lashed out with more accusations and insults. But she'd known he wouldn't attack her in front of so many people for the sake of his own reputation as much as hers. He'd already erred by attacking Hamish in public and with her so nearby.

"I didn't do aught," she replied.

People were already whispering about the incident. The way Hamish came to her defense made her want to twirl on her tiptoes. After he'd been so adamant about her safety, she realized the fight had morphed from Hamish defending his honor against any attack to anger over her wellbeing. If the guards hadn't pulled the two men apart, she didn't doubt the younger and stronger Hamish could have killed her father. She didn't think he would, even though he'd warned her he would kill anyone who endangered her, but she knew he might.

"Henrietta's already told half the court you invited him to walk with you. Is that true?" Lionel demanded.

"Aye. Neither of us knew who each other was."

"I don't believe that for a moment," Lionel scoffed. "Everyone knows who you are."

"Those who come to court or live here do. But Hamish hasn't been to court since before I arrived. I assumed he kenned who I was because of Father's ill fame over the feud. Hamish assumed I kenned who he was for the same reason. Neither of us gave our clan name because we both thought we'd recognize each other. We didn't. Besides, he was already in the garden and was aboot to walk in the same direction."

"Mayhap so, but you didn't need to accept his arm like some common—"

"Finish that thought, Tormud, and I will tell Lady Marion what I walked in on when you called out her name." Amelia crossed her arms as she glowered at the man taller than her but three years her junior at nine-and-ten. She knew he lusted for the widow who thought him still a child and who would gladly boast of his preference. It did him no good since their father already betrothed him to someone else. Lady Una Gillanders was barely more than a lass who appeared sweet to everyone but had already showed her temper to Amelia and Tormud. The latter knew his soon-to-be bride would castrate him the night before the wedding and arrive at the ceremony as the blushing bride.

"I might not finish the thought, but that won't change what other people are saying," Tormud insisted.

"Mayhap not, but you're my brother. You don't have to speak like that to me." Amelia knew her brother thought he was help-ing, but she didn't wish to hear him utter what she'd already heard four other people whisper none too subtly that day. She doubted anyone would have considered her brief moments with Hamish nearly so interesting if their clans weren't feuding. And people would have soon forgotten them altogether if the two behemoths hadn't tried to beat each other senseless.

"I'm sorry, Amy. But you know this doesn't look good for our clan."

Amelia inhaled and held it for a moment before she stepped close enough to her brother that their shoes nearly touched. "You don't need to tell me how to represent this clan at court. You weren't the one dumped here three years ago and left to fend for herself. You weren't the one who gave up a happy life with genuine friends and the respect of a clan to come to this den of iniquity. All I do is think aboot how my actions reflect upon our clan, Father, and you."

As the Ross heir and tánaiste, Tormud was next in line to become laird and earl. Lionel was a consideration, but he didn't weigh as heavily on her mind with each decision she made. Approaching Hamish was the first impulsive thing she'd done since arriving at court, and she knew this was why she always thought about every permutation or consequence before acting. But only a sliver of her regretted it. That sliver was the part worried about unintended consequences for her clan. Lionel was less than a year younger than Tormud. Her father and brothers were adults and could fend for themselves.

"Then why did you do something so reckless?" Lionel queried.

"I told you already. I didn't know who he was."

"That aside, you still approached a mon, Amy," Lionel pressed.

She blew out an aggravated breath. "I needn't be reminded. I must return to the Great Hall. My absence will draw more attention. If Hamish isn't in there, Father will assume I sneaked off somewhere with him or that he's absconded with me. That's all we need."

While they were at court, Amelia could sit with her family.

When they returned to Ross-shire, she would return to the ladies-in-waiting. As much as she usually enjoyed her brothers' company, she enjoyed sitting with the guardsmen who traveled with her relatives more. She heard stories about her friends at Balnagown. She wanted to know about a foal that was her mare's grandchild. Her mare produced the stallion that sired the newborn. She wondered if the animal had its father and grandmother's temperament or a milder one.

She followed Tormud back into the Great Hall, and Lionel brought up the rear. The moment she entered, she saw her father pointing a finger at the Sutherland men. Hamish wasn't there.

Bluidy hell. Just what I feared.

"Tormud, hurry. We need to get to Father before a melee erupts in here." Amelia pushed her brother's back, urging him on. When she was close enough to step around her brother and not bump into someone else, she increased her pace to short of a sprint. "Father."

The man whipped around; his snarl now directed at her. But he schooled his features when he recognized Amelia and his sons. He glanced back at the Sutherlands before staring at Tormud. "Where were you three?"

"Talking in the passageway." Tormud kept his voice low as he stood near Amelia. He could step in front of her if needed. He didn't fear their father striking her, but he was prepared for anything.

"Come along." Roy turned away from his offspring and the Sutherlands, prepared to seek his family's table.

"Ross."

Amelia wished to cringe. She was slower to turn than the men in her family when Hamish called out to her father. Hamish appeared as rugged and unmovable as the Cairngorms. He'd changed into his *breacan feile,* and Amelia marveled at the way the muscles at his knees moved with each step. The hint she could see made her wonder what the rest of his leg must look like. His broad chest surely necessitated at least an extra yard to reach from his waist to over his shoulder. He stopped beside his men's table, leaving a table's length between the Rosses and him.

"Ma mon said ye have been harassing them."

"Did he run and whinge to you like a wee lassie who lost her poppet?"

"Nay. He warned that if I didna arrive soon, all ma men would be in the dungeon for murdering a noblemon."

Amelia gasped. She knew Hamish exaggerated from his tone, but when her gaze darted to the men, she knew each of them could have attacked her father and put up a fair fight. None convinced her that any of them would succeed individually since she knew her father's reputation in battle. She didn't want to witness a test to her theory. But collectively?

"It would take all of them to try. Too bad they'd fail just like yer da." Roy crossed his arms with an arrogant tilt of his head. Amelia steeled herself for the fallout, but Hamish simply stared at her father. It was incredibly unnerving. It terrified her even more than their brawl that morning. She didn't dare speak up like she had in the bailey. But she wanted nothing more than to grab her father's sleeve and drag him away. She shifted her gaze to look at Tormud, who only spared her a glance. She noticed his hand was on the hilt of his dagger.

Hamish hooked his thumbs into his belt and pushed his shoulders back. Amelia knew it was the worst time to daydream about how braw the warrior was, but she couldn't help her body's reaction. She wanted to be in his arms again like she'd been the night before. But for that to happen, he'd have to live.

"Ross, have ye never noticed that the only battles ye've won against ma family are the ones I wasna in?"

Amelia had no idea if that was true, but nothing about Hamish made her think he was a liar. Her eyes darted to her father, waiting for his reaction. His expression didn't change, but his cheeks grew flushed. It was Roy's turn to stand as though his feet had grown roots. She nudged Tormud. Someone had to concede because people were staring. As though he could read her thoughts, Hamish turned away from them, giving her father and brothers— and thus her —his back as though he had no fear anyone would dare stab him. It dismissed them all. He took a seat at the table and accepted a mug from one of his men. The Rosses no longer held his interest.

Tormud stepped beside their father, bringing the older man out of his stupor. Amelia followed them with Lionel once again completing the family procession. She glanced over to Hamish as she rounded a table to take a seat. His attention appeared focused on a Sutherland guard, but she noticed he watched her. Their gazes met, and his chin dipped. But he took a sip a moment later, so she wasn't certain it was an acknowledgement. But his gaze didn't shift until after he placed the mug on the table. Then he had to pay attention to the servant who placed a trencher before him. The woman almost dropped it down the front of him in her attempt to press her breasts to his cheek. Amelia's hands fisted beneath the table while she kept her thoughts to herself.

Ye have nay claim to the mon. He's probably bedding at least one maid or going to a tavern every night for a whore.

That notion made her belly ache, but she observed the moment he was certain he wouldn't wear his dinner. He was watching her again. He watched her from beneath his dark brow, and she wondered if anyone else could tell where he looked. She swept her gaze over the surrounding tables, but no one paid him attention. Plenty watched her father, surely wondering how he would counter the perceived slight. They might not have heard Hamish's question, but they saw him walk away.

When her gaze arrived upon her fellow ladies-in-waiting, several stared at him unabashedly. She wished to be the one to throw a punch. She didn't recognize this side of herself. She'd never been territorial, but she'd enjoyed her conversation with Hamish. She'd entered her chamber the night before with a lightness she hadn't felt since leaving home. She'd realized as she readied for bed that she'd felt appreciated. She longed for that again, and specifically from Hamish. She didn't want to contemplate him with another woman. Lady or whore. She forced her attention to her food and the ensuing courses throughout the meal. When servants pushed the trestle tables and benches aside, and the dancing began, she made her excuses and asked the Mistress of the Bedchamber if she could retire. The woman looked over her shoulder toward her family before assessing Amelia. It wasn't sympathy, but pity. Haughty pity. Once she received permission, she asked Lionel to walk her back to her chamber. She'd noticed Hamish left as soon as he'd finished his last course. She saw no reason to remain once that happened.

"Amy, be careful. Tormud's and my concern is genuine. We don't want you to anger Father. The last thing we want is for him to arrange a betrothal out of anger to keep you away from the Sutherland. He's not rash by nature, but this feud is worse than you know."

"What do you mean?"

Lionel stood beside her door and whispered to her. "Father knows how weak the Sutherlands are right now. Hamish is without anyone to support him since the few men he could rely upon died in the last battle. His uncle is a strong warrior but a useless leader while Hamish is away. With Liam and Kyla gone, no one is there to govern with any force. Father sent raiding parties to three villages to raze them and slaughter the livestock. Hens, sheep, cows. Whatever they can find."

Amelia's heart pounded. "Can he really be so shortsighted? Hamish is already at court. What does he think will happen when word reaches Hamish here? When the king finds out?"

"His people won't know it was us."

"A midnight raid?"

"Aye, and not in our plaids."

Amelia fisted her hands. She knew he didn't mean trews or hose. "Whose plaid?"

"The Gunns."

"Bluidy hell, Lio. This won't distract Hamish. He's more apt to negotiate with the Gunns to rally alongside the Sutherlands, Sinclairs, and Mackays to massacre our people. It's likely what will make peace between the Mackays and Sinclairs." Amelia wanted nothing more than to family suites, find Hamish, and share everything she just learned. But she couldn't. She would never betray her clan. That was an absolute. But there was no way for her to speak to him without others finding out. She felt trapped.

"Are you going to tell him?"

Amelia stared at her brother before her mien hardened. "I ought to, but you know I never would. I'm a Ross. You know that's more than a name or a plaid to me. How dare you?"

"I dare because you were making cow eyes at him all night."

"He's a braw mon, and I'm attracted to him. That doesn't mean I would ever act upon it. And it doesn't mean I would put any mon ahead of my clan. God gave women only one head for a reason. We aren't the ones who need to think twice. I'm not the one trying to measure myself against him, Lio. I know where my loyalty lies. Goodnight." She opened her chamber door and stepped inside. She didn't slam it, but she closed it in her brother's face.

What the bluidy bleeding hell am I supposed to do with this now? I canna tell him. But I canna ken ma clan is going to murder his people and sleep like a bairn. Damn it, Lio. Why did ye have to tell me that? Why did ye decide to test me? Do Father and Tormud think I'd be so treacherous? Mayhap Lio told me by his own choice, or mayhap Father or Tormud told him to tell me. Either way, they're punishing me. How have they nae learned I'm the last person ye want to back into a corner?

CHAPTER 4

*H*amish steeled himself not to tap his toes as he stood before the king once more in the busy Privy Council chamber. He refused to look at Roy, who stood beside him yet again. He suspected they'd been summoned here once more, not because the king had a resolution, but so that he could berate them about the exchange at the previous night's meal. King John shuffled through sheets of parchment, scanning the documents as though they were dire. Perhaps the monarch assumed neither Roy nor Hamish could read, but Hamish deciphered the writing upside down. It was a report about Berwick that was months old and had clearly already been passed from hand to hand many times. Finally, the king leaned back and steepled his fingers, his elbows on the armrests of his throne.

"The pair of you caused yet another scene last eve. You draw more attention than a jester at a fair."

Then resolve the business between us, so I may court Amelia, then take her home to Dunrobin.

"Ross, I expect more from you. You were born to your position."

Hamish's expression didn't change. He understood the slight

was intended, but it was true. He couldn't contest the statement, and he didn't disagree. When it elicited no reaction, the king continued to speak to Roy.

"You are also the elder and should lead by example. You making an arse of yourself does naught to make other clans see the wrongs done to you."

Once more, Hamish ignored the comment. It would only matter to him if the king sided with Roy and not him. Otherwise, he couldn't give a shite if the king taunted him. The monarch watched Roy as though he expected a response, but he'd asked no question. Balliol wouldn't fool the older laird into speaking out of turn. So, both lairds stood with their hands behind their backs, waiting for the king to decide their fate. It made Hamish feel like he was a naughty wean standing before his father, waiting to learn how many lashes with a belt his backside would take. Since his comment garnered no response, Balliol shifted his attention to Hamish.

"You will not win over friends and allies if you pick fights with men more respected than you. What will you do when you face more than one foe?"

"The only foe I have now is standing beside me. One who has his men disguise themselves as though they're from another clan because they dinna have the bollocks to wear their own plaids while they raze ma fields and massacre ma livestock because I am nae on ma land to defend it." Hamish didn't raise his voice to make his proclamation. He didn't need to. The rich timber carried with ease. The courtiers unabashedly turned their attention to the trio rather than pretend they were busy with their work. Hamish's gaze locked with the monarch's, challenging him.

"What are you talking aboot, Sutherland? Who is wearing what plaid?"

"One of ma clansmen arrived this morning. He and his horse were both in a lather. Seems Laird Ross sent men in Gunn plaids to raze ma fields and massacre any animal they could find. A wean's pet rabbit from what I heard. As I pointed out last night, the only battles the Rosses have won are the ones I wasna there for. He waited until I was away to prey on ma people. People who have never raised a weapon against the Rosses. Rather than face *me*, he tried to deceive *us* by drawing in the Gunns." Since Roy was at court to atone for his part in the feud, Hamish felt the other laird's actions while residing in the king's home constituted a slight to them both. At least, that's what he would insinuate. He could make veiled comments, too.

"Is this true?" The king's gaze swung to Roy, and his eyebrows shot toward his hairline. His left hand fisted while his right hand covered it, his elbows still on the armrests.

"Sutherland may allege that—"

"Mayhap Ross would like to speak to his clansmon who traveled with mine."

Both men swung toward him. Roy's face nearly matched his strawberry-blond hair. Hamish could tell it took all of the man's restraint not to lunge at Hamish again. The bailey was bad enough. The Privy Council chamber would seal his fate. The monarch leaned forward, his hands now on the armrests.

"What do you mean, Sutherland?"

"Ma mon had a traveling companion. One of Ross's men didna hie his arse off ma land fast enough. They should be in the passageway now in case ye should like to speak to them, Yer Majesty." He made the last part sound like a generous offer.

King John signaled a guard at the door, and the chamberlain stepped out. They could all hear the man call out the two clan names. Hamish didn't turn like Roy did when the warriors entered. He already knew what he would see. He'd met with his warrior hours before dawn just after the flagging horses practically stumbled through the castle gates. He'd been summoned from his sleep because they kept the gates locked at that hour. Once he knew his clansman had brought a captive, he roused his men from their bunks in the barracks. He ordered them to find an empty storage room and guard the Ross prisoner until summoned. When the king requested Hamish's presence, Hamish had sent for his prisoner.

"Alfred?" Roy demanded.

"Aye, Uncle."

Hamish forced himself not to grin. He heard the man limp to the assembled noblemen. God had offered him a boon. It was his great fortune his clansmen captured Roy's sister's only son who was the same age as Hamish. He knew this because they'd faced each other during the first battle either of them fought. They'd traded barbs until Hamish sliced Alfred's ribs and stabbed him in the side. It was the first and only lesson he needed to learn never to walk away unless he was certain his opponent was dead.

Hamish watched John Balliol to see if the man even knew enough to recognize the plaid pattern the new arrival wore. The Sutherland warrior wore one that was nearly identical to Hamish's, which differed with the slight distinction that he was the laird. King John's near blank expression told Hamish that he didn't know. But he couldn't point out the king's ignorance directly.

"Maxwell, bring the ledger of plaids." Hamish knew there was a record much like the Ragman Rolls that enabled John Balliol to become king. The Rolls were a list of signatures from various clans with their crests imbedded in wax beside their names. The ledger of plaids had a sample from mostly Highland clans, but they forced plenty of Lowlanders to contribute theirs as well.

The Lowland courtier shuffled several leatherbound books until he came to the one he sought. He brought it to the table but was unsure if he should hand it to Hamish or the king. Hamish opted to make it easier for the man.

"Open it to the Gunns, if ye please." Hamish doubted it pleased the man to be drawn into this or to act as his servant of sorts. But the courtier from Clan Maxwell obliged. He placed it on the table once he'd found what he needed. King John stared at the sample for several seconds before turning to the man who now sagged to one side. It was indisputable. Roy Ross acknowledged the man in the Gunn plaid and didn't correct the familial title. Hamish wished to skip with glee, but he made no sign of the smugness he felt. He kept his gaze trained on the king, waiting for the man to side with him. But he wasn't so arrogant as to believe it would be that easy.

"Ross, what say you? Why is a mon who calls you uncle wearing another clan's plaid?"

"My sister is a widow, but she was married to a Gunn. Alfred must have ridden with them." Roy had the temerity to shrug, then turn to face Hamish and wink with the eye farther from the king.

"Aye. And he rode with them six moons ago when he returned to live at yer keep. He thought to remain with the Gunns after his fostering, but they didna want him. Inept is what I believe Tomas called him." Hamish watched Roy's face turn a deeper shade of red, close to crimson, and he was certain the man wished to bare his teeth and growl. "Ye sent him to lead yer raid on ma lands to the north of Dunrobin, thinking that riding around ma border then turning back south would confuse us into believing the Gunns wore those plaids. Tomas Gunn isnae sticking his wee toe onto ma land, and we both ken it."

The man was too busy harrying the Sinclairs to bother the Sutherlands, but even then, Tomas was careful just how far he pushed Hamish's new family-by-marriage, lest Hamish join the Sinclairs and turn on the Gunns. Now that the Sutherlands and Sinclairs were allies, there were few brazen enough to confront them both. Besides trying to pull the wool over Hamish's eyes with the wrong plaids, it was foolhardy to pit the Sutherlands against the Gunns, when the Sinclairs already took issue with the latter. All it would mean was a united Sinclair-Sutherland force against the Rosses for instigating trouble where there was none.

Balliol once more sat back in his chair, his fingers steepled before him. He stared at the Sutherland warrior who was filthy but hale and the Ross warrior who could barely remain upright. He narrowed his eyes a fraction, then assessed Hamish before finally turning his attention back to Roy.

"I shall have to give this some serious consideration. Ross, you are sorely testing my patience and resolve to hold any affinity for you. It's clear Sutherland speaks the truth as it is right before our eyes. You'd do well to cease your covert attacks since they fail. At the rate you're going, I'll cede all your land to Sutherland, and you can call him laird. What say you to that, Sutherland?"

"I have nay desire to have his crumbling pile of stones he calls a keep. Nor do I want to house and feed his people. He can keep them. I want something else." Hamish wasn't about to act on a whim, but he knew he risked everything if the king asked him to what he referred. He might very well die in the next minute since only his exhausted warrior stood close enough to defend him.

"And what is it you want?"

"Permission to court Lady Amelia."

"The hell you will!" Roy roared as he tried to launch himself at Hamish once more. The Sutherland warrior and Alfred roused themselves enough to attempt to restrain the irate earl. But he shook off both of them. Hamish didn't move. He remained rooted to his spot like a monolithic standing stone. He allowed Roy to land one punch to his jaw, which he turned away in time for it to be a glancing blow. Then he reared back and slammed his fist in Roy's chest, sending him sailing onto his backside. He turned back to the monarch.

"I am nae asking for the sake of a truce or an alliance. It is to be entirely Lady Amelia's choice whether I court her. I'm nae asking for anyone's permission but hers. I'm simply letting her father ken." Hamish's gaze locked with the king's, and it was clear his statement applied to his sovereign as well. His hands settled at his waist; his thumbs hooked into his belt. It broadened his chest to its full expanse, making his leine strain across his back, shoulders, and biceps.

"Is Lady Amelia aware of your interest?"

"Nay. Nae yet. I will speak to her when I'm done here." Hamish's stare remained unwavering as he trod a dangerous line between being assertive and winding up with his head severed from his neck.

"And if she declines?"

"Then I ken she isnae interested in me."

"And if she accepts?"

"If she accepts, then mayhap we have a future together. We willna ken if we dinna court."

"And if ye two suit? Would ye put her in the middle?"

"There willna be a middle. She will have made her choice."

"The bluidy hell she will." Roy clambered to his feet, shoving his nephew's hands off him. "Ma daughter isnae going anywhere with this beast. He isnae good enough for ma lass." Roy didn't notice how his brogue came back into his words; his courtly speech abandoned.

King John shook his head. "The lady will decide. My wife shall speak to her."

"Yer Majesty, I will speak to her. Lady Amelia will hear ma request from ma own lips. If she doesnae wish for me to court her, then I will hear her say it maself."

The king stood so fast his throne screeched on the stone floor. "You dare give me orders? You dare disobey me?"

"If ye dinna trust me nae to pressure her, then have the queen and all the ladies watch. But I willna have anyone else pressure her, either."

"Are you questioning my wife's integrity?"

"Nay." Hamish's single word hung in the air. Everyone waited for him to justify his comment, but he saw no reason to explain himself since the king hadn't asked why he made the comment.

"Where do you think to have this conversation?"

"Here, the queen's solar, the Great Hall's antechamber, the

garden. The place isnae as important as Lady Amelia being free from her father harassing a refusal from her."

"Very well. You may speak to her in the antechamber before the evening meal. Two of my guards and both of her brothers will be present," King John decreed. Hamish would accept that as a victory. He nodded as the king turned back to the other earl. "Ross, you will cease and desist all matters with the Sutherland until your daughter decides."

"Your Majesty—" Roy's courtly accent was back in place, even if the monarch only allowed him two words.

"No. Take your nephew and deal with him. Sutherland, take your mon away from here. They both reek like they rolled in a bog." King John turned away, summoning one of his clerks to his side. He spoke to the young man in a low voice that clearly signified he'd finished with Hamish and Roy. Much like the last time they tried to leave the Privy Council chamber, they reached the door at the same time. And just like the last time, guards had to open both for the rival earls to pass.

"I'm serious, Sutherland. Stay away from my daughter."

"Is she already betrothed?"

"No."

"Then she will decide whether she wishes for ma attention." Hamish tilted his head and observed his nemesis. "If ye werenae a Ross, and I wasna a Sutherland, would ye object to me? Or would ye see me as a mon who would care for yer daughter? One who would be faithful to her until ma last breath? One who would respect and seek her counsel? Is it me or ma name?"

"They are, and will always be, one and the same."

"Name a mon who would treat her better. Ye ken me to be naught like ma father or brothers. Ye ken me to be honest, loyal, fair, and kind. I may nae be the last on the battlefield, but I am all of those things off it."

"None of that matters. I will not sell my daughter to you."

"That's fine. I dinna want her dowry and willna accept it. Ma clan isnae without means. We may have much to rebuild, but I dinna need yer money to do it. I wish for Amelia nae yer coin."

"My daughter will not help you rebuild a clan that continues its attempt to slaughter her people."

"Ye think me so dishonorable that I would continue this feud once Amelia becomes ma wife? I dinna wish for her hand to end this, and I wouldnae mistreat ma wife. Trying to kill her father and brothers wouldnae make for a happy life. I—"

The sound of a woman's shoes rushing toward them made them both turn and peer down the passageway. Amelia stumbled as she rounded the corner and found her father talking to the man she sought. She dropped her skirts, having hiked them to her ankles to keep from tripping. She didn't know what to do. They'd seen her, so she couldn't turn around. But neither could she approach Hamish, and she didn't want to speak to her father in front of him.

Hamish decided for her. His long strides carried him to her, and he reached for her hand without thought. Her tiny one sat like a flower in a bear's paw. "Lia, what's wrong?"

"I— Hamish, what happened to your jaw? Dear merciful heavens. Did my father do that?" Amelia lifted her free hand to turn his head, so she could see the bruise forming on his chin. "You fought again?"

"Nay. He punched me in the jaw, and I punched him in the chest. I stayed standing, and he wound up on his arse. Neither of us got hurt." *Well, his pride got hurt.*

"What set you both off this time?

"Amelia! Come away from him now. You will cease throwing yourself at him." Roy's voice carried, and the petitioners still waiting for the king's attention turned toward the trio.

"Stop squawking like a magpie, Ross. Nae everyone needs to ken our business." Hamish looked over the man's shoulder with a pointed stare at those now watching them. Roy didn't need to turn back to know his enemy was right. But the sight of his daughter with a man he loathed made him forget his common sense. He hated Hamish for being a Sutherland, for looking so much like the late Earl of Sutherland, and for being right about everything he'd said only moments ago. He would make the perfect husband for his daughter if he could trust him, which he didn't.

"Father." Amelia didn't know what to say. She'd learned from one of Hamish's men that he was with the king. She'd rehearsed what she would say to warn Hamish without giving away what she knew. She'd barely slept the night before as her mind turned over every conceivable way to tell Hamish about her father's planned attacks without admitting a secret she swore to keep. Now she could say nothing with her father watching them.

"Come, Amelia. Let us find your brothers." Roy offered his arm to Amelia. When she didn't immediately take it, he moved to grab her forearm. Hamish's hand shot out and wrapped around Roy's wrist like a manacle. He squeezed. Hard.

"Dinna manhandle yer daughter, mon. People are watching. Ye have already made a scene. Ye will only make it worse if ye drag her down the passageway. Nay one can see past me, but they will if ye storm off with her in tow."

"Don't you dare tell me—"

"I dare, and ye ken why." Hamish was only a few inches taller than Ross, and they both stood well over six feet. But he raised his chin and looked down his nose at the older man.

Amelia didn't know what to do with yet another round of male posturing. It was like reading about the lions the Romans once set upon one another for sport. Except there was nothing entertaining about the spectacle in front of her. She turned toward Hamish. "What are you talking aboot? What does my father know?"

"I will explain all of it to ye, but I willna do it here where all the walls have ears and mouths." Hamish offered her his arm, and she accepted. She glared at her father, who she was certain caused more harm than good while he and Hamish met with the king again. Hamish looked at Roy and shook his head. "Yer daughter and I will go to the queen's garden and speak there. Lady Amelia will tell ye her decision. Ye will accept whatever it is, Ross."

"You will do the same, Sutherland." Roy spoke with a sneer, certain his daughter would remain ever loyal to the clan of her birth. He would follow at a distance, but he would watch them from a hidden spot in the garden. He would relish the moment his daughter rejected the upstart.

"Ross, try nae to be too obvious when ye listen to us."

CHAPTER 5

Amelia stared up at Hamish, completely at a loss to understand what he and her father discussed with her standing there. She didn't appreciate it, and she grew anxious at the situation she couldn't control. She'd seen their fight in the bailey, and it had terrified her. She hadn't known who to root for, and she'd feared they'd kill each other at her feet. Now she knew they'd struck each other before the king in the man's official solar. She could only imagine what it took for them to not do more damage to one another.

"Hamish?"

"I'll explain everything, Lia. Just nae here. Please trust me."

As she continued to gaze up at him, she realized she not only trusted him, but it was implicit. She hadn't felt that way about anyone she met at court. She was always inherently wary, knowing there was always some secret agenda. But Hamish seemed entirely frank. What he said was what he meant, and he would say nothing he didn't mean. She walked beside him, her hand resting on top of his arm. She longed to wrap her fingers around his, but she worried her father would draw a dirk and hack Hamish's limb off.

The trio walked in silence until they reached the queen's garden. Hamish pointed to a second path that would wind around the outside of the space while he steered Amelia to the path that led to the center. Roy glowered, but he did nothing to stop them when they walked away.

"Hamish?" She repeated the single word she'd said inside the keep.

"What do ye ken aboot the feud?"

"Yer clan aided the Mackays, who are our enemy." Amelia didn't notice her burr was back, but she was so relaxed around Hamish that she didn't feel like she had to maintain any pretense. "That started the reiving between yer clan and mine. Yer father led a raid with yer brothers that gained them back sheep ma father and brothers took from ye. But yer father stole twice as many of our sheep as we had yers. Our clans fought, but yer father had already sent the flock ahead. Ma father followed yer father back to yer land and avenged our people. It wasna far outside the Dunrobin gates that yer family perished. King John ordered ye both to appear."

"Ye are right aboot it all. That is how it happened."

"And I ken ye werenae a part of it. Ye were at yer keep as yer brother's second to protect it while he fought alongside yer father and other brother. Ye rode out to join the fight, but it was already over. I assume yer uncle, who survived the battle, is overseeing yer clan and keep right now."

"He is, and ye're right that I remained behind. Do ye ken what has happened in the past when I've fought yer clan?"

Amelia turned away, no longer able to look at Hamish as she nodded. "I ken ye injured Alfred badly enough that he nearly died. I ken ye've killed two of ma other cousins. They died at the end of yer sword."

"Yet now that ye ken who I am, ye came out here with me. Ye defended me to yer father."

Amelia blew out a sigh and brushed a wisp of hair from her

forehead, something that tempted Hamish to do. But he'd restrained himself. Barely. "Ye are a warrior just as they were. It is what ye were all raised to become. Death is inevitable for all of us. For a warrior, it usually comes sooner and bloodier."

"Do ye think I enjoy what I do?" Hamish feared her answer.

Amelia shook her head. When Hamish said nothing, she assumed he wished to hear her answer. "I dinna think that. Ye strike me as a mon who would prefer peace, but ye are prepared to defend yer people and yer land until yer last breath. That's simply the way of it."

"Ye sound resigned to that. Would ye rather yer future was one without warring clans?"

"Dinna ye?" Amelia thought the question should go without saying, but she asked it anyway.

"I do, but I dinna wish to leave the Highlands or Dunrobin. Ye have already left the Highlands and Balnagown. Do ye wish to return to that or remain here in the Lowlands?"

"What Highlander would ever wish to remain here?" She flinched when she heard the disgust in her voice. But it made Hamish chuckle, a deep rumble. She knew it made his chest vibrate. She'd felt it when they danced. A woman bumped her side, and it had pressed her against him. Her scowl at the clumsy couple had made him laugh.

"So, ye wish to return to yer home." It was statement they both knew every Highlander felt.

"Aye." Amelia enjoyed talking to him, but she grew impatient to understand why they were speaking. Why he was suddenly evasive. "Why are ye asking me this?"

"Because I wish to ken if ye'd consider another part of the Highlands yer home." Hamish observed her, wondering if she'd guess at his real reason. He knew her to be astute, but this was likely the least expected conversation she could have.

"I will marry one day. I willna have a choice."

"And if ye had a choice?"

Amelia turned to stand before Hamish rather than continue to stroll beside him. "If I had a choice, I ken where I would go."

They stood staring at one another before Hamish took both her hands in his. She didn't pull away, which gave him hope she wasn't thinking about marrying a different man. He knew keenly that her father could see and hear everything. He longed to pull her into his arms and kiss her senseless. He wanted her to kiss him senseless.

"Lia—"

"Why do ye call me that? People call me Amy. I never thought that could be ma name."

"Because I am the only one who does, and I'd like to continue to be the only mon who does." Hamish tightened his grip around her hands, but he didn't squeeze. He never wanted her to feel trapped. But she was the one to squeeze his.

"Ye are the only mon who does. The only person who does. Do ye wish it to be a name that only ye have for me?"

"I wish it to be the only name I call ma wife." Hamish feared he'd jumped too far ahead of himself. He waited for the rejection. He watched her gaze dart to her left while she remained facing him. She lowered her voice to ensure it didn't carry on the wind, so Hamish had to strain to hear her.

"It's the only name ma husband will call me."

"Would ye agree to me courting ye?"

"Hamish, are ye serious? I am nae lying aboot wishing to hear ma husband— ye —call me that, but I dinna ken how that's aught more than a dream."

"Yer father and the king ken ma intentions. I'd planned to speak to ye this evening before the meal. We were to meet in the antechamber with yer brothers and a couple of the king's men. But now is even better."

"That's why ma father was livid again and why he follows us."

"Lia, I told yer father I dinna want yer dowry, and I dinna. I'll pay whatever bride price he demands, but I willna accept aught from him but ye. I'm nae doing this for a truce. I hope that comes aboot because I dinna want to take ye from yer family, and I dinna want ye to choose. But I have met nay woman I would consider offering for. I was so reticent that ma father threatened to find the most unsuitable woman he could to punish me for being so unwilling. He likely would have. He would have punished our entire clan to prove his point. I would have submitted for the sake of ma people and found someone before it reached that point. But I nay longer have anyone compelling me to marry. I could wait years if I wished. I'd planned to. Then I met ye."

Amelia knew what she wanted to answer, but she felt unable. She squeezed his hands harder and didn't lighten the pressure. She felt her eyes water as they once again darted in her father's direction before her gaze met Hamish's. "Ye already ken what ma answer has to be. Ye ken what I want it to be. Ye ken they arenae the same. I canna betray ma clan."

"And if I were to sever ma alliance with the Mackays to make peace with yer father? If I were to return all the livestock and pay a bride price?"

"Then ye would be a selfish mon I ken ye are nae. Ye wouldnae sacrifice yer clan for yer wants."

"Wouldnae peace be good for both our clans? I dinna wish to marry ye to end this feud, but ending this feud would mean we could marry."

"Marrying me would ensure ma father never ends this."

"And if the king sanctioned it? Would yer father disobey him further?"

"I truly dinna ken." Amelia stretched to whisper, so Hamish leaned forward. "Ma father led that raid into England alongside the other earls because the king ordered him to. He didna do it because he supports John Balliol. He did it because he will do aught to protect his people from the king's machinations. Ye ken who ye'd both support if ye could."

"Lia, war is coming to Scotland. The English wish to destroy us, and the king is weak. The Bruce is our best choice, and he will rally the clans like nay king ever has before. Ma clan is at peace with the Sinclairs after fighting one another for generations. We are at peace with the Mackays. Yer father attempted to create strife with the Gunns by raiding ma lands and sending his men in the Gunns' plaids. If yer father truly wishes to protect his people, he wouldnae make war with me, and he wouldnae do aught to draw the king's ire. Yer clan, ma clan, and ma allies are the northern Highlands. The lesser clans will do as we do. I came here to broker a truce, but yer father did nae. I will tell ye again that I dinna wish to marry ye to gain the truce. But I will accept the truce to marry ye."

Amelia only half heard the second half of what Hamish said. Her father had done the very thing about which she'd struggled to warn Hamish. "Ma father already ordered those raids?"

Hamish jerked back at her question, but her absent stare made him realize she spoke aloud what she intended to be a silent thought. And misery had filled her tone. "Lia, ye kenned?"

A tear slipped from her glassy eyes, and Hamish brushed it away before cupping her cheek. Her eyelids slid shut as she leaned into his palm. "I found out last night. I didna sleep for trying to conceive of a way to tell ye without betraying ma clan. I promised ma brother I would say naught, and I ken it was ma father's test. He likely believes I'm telling ye right now. That was probably half his objection to us speaking. Hamish, I'm so sorry."

"Ye didna do aught to make this happen. Ye have naught to be sorry for. Yer father planned it before he and I arrived. He did this to take advantage of me being away. He kens he never wins battles where I fight."

"I can be sorry for the lives likely lost, and the harvests likely destroyed. Our considering marriage will only make this worse. I canna court ye, Hamish. It's breaking ma heart, but I canna do it if it risks ye and yer people. It's nae even aboot ma clan anymore. It's aboot protecting yers."

"Do ye truly wish to consider someone else? Or do ye wish to ken if we suit?"

"Ye ken the answer to both questions."

"Then let me court ye for a moon. If we suit, then we find some way to resolve this with yer father. If we dinna, then we part ways."

"Ye canna remain here for a moon. Look at what's happened in the sennights since ye left."

"Even if ye werenae a consideration, I am trapped here. Ye father did this on purpose. He kens I should return to ma people, but he kens if I leave here, he will gain the upper hand with the king. That's why he did it. He's trying to chase me from court. I canna leave because it will hurt ma clan in the long run if I do. I will send a missive to Donnell Sinclair, ma sister's father-by-marriage. I will ask him to send men to reinforce ma border with yers."

"That will only enrage ma father."

"And it will remind him I dinna stand alone. I have more allies than just the Mackays. Lia, he'd do this regardless of whether I'm here. That's why he wants me gone. Ma staying complicates things for him."

"Ye would remain to spite him? Ye wouldnae go home to see how yer people fair?"

"Nay. I told ye. He wishes to gain the upper hand by having the king's ear. If I leave, that's what he gains. I'll lose land, livestock, and coin. I'll lose ye."

"Hamish, I believe ye arenae using me to barter. But mayhap ma father would be more agreeable if ye did. Me in exchange for peace."

"He kens I dinna see it that way."

"And if I tell him I see it as a sacrifice I'm willing to make?"

"Is that how ye see it?"

"Of course nae. I will be the envy of every woman. Ye're nae only the brawest mon at court, ye're wise beyond yer years. Ye're kind and gracious. Ye're thoughtful and gentle when ye could be the opposite of all those things."

"Ye think me braw, do ye?" Hamish waggled his eyebrows and made his chest muscles jump. Amelia giggled, and it lightened her heart.

"And ye make me laugh. Hamish, could this really work?"

"I want to try. That's all I can promise for now. I will do ma best to make this work. But if we dinna suit, or ye canna accept becoming a Sutherland, then I will leave ye in peace."

"I doubt I will find much peace if ye walk away." Amelia reasoned that if they were to spend a life together, then there was no point in being coy. She wanted to know if they suited. With all that stood between them, there was little reason to pretend bashfulness as though she would try to seduce him. He'd already stated his intentions, so she didn't need to capture his attention.

Hamish continued to cup her cheek when he leaned forward to kiss her opposite one. His warm breath against her ear made her shiver. "Ye are the bonniest woman I have ever seen. Ye are the wise one, *leannan*. Ye are the kind and gracious one. Ye're thoughtful and strong when ye could be the opposite of all those things."

Amelia's eyes widened when he repeated nearly verbatim what she'd told him. He'd truly listened. She reveled in him calling her sweetheart. As she gazed up at him, she wondered for the umpteenth time what it would be like to kiss Hamish. If she didn't know her father lurked, she might be brazen enough to lift her chin and part her lips. She wanted more than a peck on the cheek.

"When we are truly alone, Lia, then I will kiss ye properly. I long to taste ye." *All of ye.* Hamish resolved to keep that latter part to himself. He didn't want to send her running into the hills. When her free hand came to rest on his waist, the heat from it nearly scorched him. It was his turn to shiver. She fisted his leine and went on her toes to kiss his cheek. She remained that way to whisper to him.

"I think ye and I long to taste more than our mouths."

Her statement surprised Hamish so much that when he turned his head to see her, their lips brushed. The current of electricity that flowed between them had them both forgetting Roy or anyone else who might watch them. Hamish encircled his arms around her waist and lifted her off her feet as she wrapped her arms around his neck. This was not a peck. This was not a chaste agreement to court. This was a passionate surrender to the desire that had grown between them since Hamish approached her to dance. She opened to him, understanding the mechanics of kissing, even if she'd never done it before.

Hamish was in purgatory. He wasn't quite in heaven despite the euphoria from Amelia's kisses. Just the opposite. It was near hell to hold her pressed against him and know he could do nothing more than kiss her when what he wanted was the strip her bare and lay her down on the grass to ravish her.

"We should stop," he whispered.

"I ken," she murmured.

Neither pulled away, instead molding their lips to each other's again. Hamish could tell Amelia was inexperienced but eager. He had enough experience to know what he was doing, but neither of his brothers had been faithful to their wives. Sharing the women in the village tavern with his whoring brothers had disgusted him. And he would never approach a woman working in his home. He didn't wish to make any fear their employment was based upon their willingness to couple with him. His brothers and father had done that. And he didn't want any to believe they had a right to approach him because of the convenience. He'd sought company the second night he was in Stirling because it had been ages since he'd tupped a woman. But then he'd met Amelia, and the thought of another woman was wholly unappealing. Besides, now that Amelia was in his arms, he would never seek another. He had no need to, nor would he betray her.

When they were breathless, Hamish lowered Amelia to the ground. His arms remained around her, and her hands rested on his shoulders. Neither took a step back to place a more appropriate distance between them. As their gazes held, Amelia cupped his cheek. It was his turn to lean his cheek into her palm.

"Hamish, I'd like us to court."

"Lass, naught makes me happier than hearing ye say aye. Yer father is likely having an apoplexy right now since I'm certain he assumed ye would refuse me. Ye did for a while."

"Ye ken ye didna wear me down. I've always wanted to say aye. I thought I couldnae— and I likely shouldnae —because of ma clan. But I trust ye, and I dinna think it's misplaced. We will figure this out."

"Together, *leannan*."

Amelia's toes curled within her slippers. Between him calling her Lia and now sweetheart, she was ready to melt. "Always together, *m'eudail*." Darling. It felt fitting. It was masculine and not too presumptuous.

"Call me that again, Lia. Please." Hamish thought he sounded desperate. But Amelia's smile was sweet, not snide.

"*M'eudail*."

"I hope to hear ye call me that for the next three score years."

"I'd like naught more."

They stared at one another until they heard voices approaching. Neither knew how long they'd spent talking or how they'd managed to have such privacy. They stepped back, but Hamish offered his arm to her again. She didn't hesitate to wrap hers around it. His other hand rested on top of hers when he drew their arms to his side. It was a possessive move he prayed protected her rather than risked her reputation. Only a moment before the group of ladies met them in the center of the garden, Roy stepped out. His rage etched his face in deep lines.

"You think to stake your claim to my daughter? I will not let you ruin her reputation by being seen alone here. But you are no closer to marrying her than you were the day you were born."

"Father, you may not have heard everything, but I'm certain you saw it. I've agreed to court Hamish. I suggest you get along, or you will make a fool of yourself. I know why Hamish wishes to consider marrying me. To everyone else, it will appear he's the one of sound mind to offer an alliance rather than a war. You'd do well to appear to be just as big a mon." Amelia's speech returned to the one she used at court only because she feared someone might overhear snippets. She'd rather sound like the Highlander she was, and she knew her father hated altering his speech as much as she did. He wouldn't begrudge her proper accent. When she glanced up at Hamish, who refused to pretend to be anything he wasn't, a new resolve passed over her. If she would consider being the next Lady Sutherland, then she would act the part.

CHAPTER 6

Hamish and Amelia remained with their arms linked, and Roy continued to glower at them as the ladies-in-waiting approached with the queen. Hamish drew his arm tighter against his ribs and rubbed his thumb over Amelia's before uncovering that hand. He wouldn't let her go, but he would be circumspect about their displays of affection in front of the worst gossips in the realm. Amelia appreciated Hamish's tact even if she longed for his hand to continue to rest on top of hers. She spied her cousin at the front of the group and wished to cringe. Henrietta would surely have plenty to say, and she wouldn't do it privately.

Hamish and Roy bowed while Amelia curtsied when the queen and her attendants reached them. Queen Isabella appeared unsurprised by the couple, but she looked down her nose at both of them. Isabella de Warenne's lineage connected her to King Henry III of England through her mother, who had been the late king's half-sister. It made her King Edward's cousin. That did little to endear her to the Scottish people any more than King John's subservient manner to his cousin-by-marriage Edward "Longshanks."

"Lady Amelia, I didn't realize the king gave you leave to wander the gardens with Laird Sutherland. I understood his permission stated you were to have proper chaperones in the antechamber before the evening meal."

"Your Grace, my father has been here."

"Mayhap, but he was out of sight for that kiss you exchanged." Queen Isabella's voice seemed to gain volume with each word. If Hamish weren't holding her arm and bolstering her courage, she would have cringed. Instead, she raised her chin and met the queen's gaze before sweeping it over her counterparts. The queen intended to humiliate her, and it wouldn't be the first time since her father led the raid into England with the other earls. Amelia waited for her father to defend her, or at least stand up for himself, but he remained quiet. The queen had asked no questions, so he offered no answers. However, it stung since he'd claimed to waylay them to save her reputation. His silence did the opposite.

"Yer Grace, I hope ye can offer yer felicitations now rather than wait until the evening meal. Lady Amelia consented to allow me to court her." Hamish didn't appreciate the implications of the queen's comment about their kiss since he knew some of the young women by their own dubious reputation. Competitiveness ran deep within the entourage, and they all vied to be the queen's favorite. Though, as the thought came to him, he suspected Amelia was one of the few who didn't beg for Queen Isabella's attention.

"And you sealed that agreement with a kiss. Not a betrothal, but an agreement to find out you may never wish to marry."

Several ladies tittered behind their hands, forcing Amelia to take several calming breaths lest her ire rise and her cheeks flush. She refused to be cowed by the queen or allow any of her fellow ladies-in-waiting believe she was ashamed of what she and Hamish had done. She wasn't. She was proud Hamish chose her. He could have considered any of the women before them, or he could remain a bachelor like he originally planned. Instead, he pursued her.

"Cousin, such wonderful news." Henrietta stepped forward and linked her arm with Amelia's free one. "I must hear all aboot it."

Amelia couldn't extricate her arm from Henrietta's grasp, but she didn't step forward when her cousin tried to yank her back to the group. She stood in her position beside Hamish. Her cousin already attempted to make the situation about her, but she'd seen the flash of anger when Henrietta spotted her with Hamish. She would rather fuel the other ladies' gossip than allow her mealy-mouthed cousin to trap her. At least then the rumors would be about what they saw rather than the corruption of her statements Henrietta would use to fuel the speculation.

"Lady Amelia, join us since your conversation with Hamish is over." Henrietta smiled demurely at Hamish, but he scowled at her.

"Ye and I are nae kin yet. I am Laird Sutherland, Lady Henrietta." Hamish knew what the woman was doing, and he would have none of it. He would allow no hint of familiarity between them. He'd met her upon his arrival, and she'd cornered him into dancing the first night. He ensured he never made that mistake again. Henrietta's eyes grew wide at his abruptness, then her left eye narrowed as she shifted her gaze to Amelia. The latter knew she would pay for Hamish's bluntness later. She also knew he thought he was defending her. While the women had laughed earlier, they stood stunned at Hamish's comment. Everyone was unaccustomed to such brusqueness at court. Amelia found it refreshing, and it tempted her to grin. But that would serve no one well.

"Ma laird, thank ye for speaking to me. I look forward to getting to ken ye." Amelia's arm was still in Henrietta's clutches, but she twisted as best she could to look up at Hamish as she spoke. She registered the surprise, then happiness in his eyes when she allowed the brogue back into her speech.

"Amelia," Henrietta hissed. She would rather have her toenails ripped off than admit she was Highlander. She hid the burr she'd grown up with, and she resented Amelia allowing it to come through her speech since Henrietta had once more acknowledged their family ties just moments earlier. It reflected poorly on her, and her image was everything to Henrietta. She knew it was all she had. She didn't have a large dowry, nor did she have the education Amelia did. The one thing she was certain about was she was far more attractive than her cousin, who she believed was as broad across the hips as a stable. She thought Amelia's bust was entirely too large for a noblewoman. That made her lips twitch. Now she knew why Hamish favored Amelia. He wished to plow her like a barmaid.

"Aye, lass. I look forward to it too," Hamish said. "Will ye allow me to escort ye on yer morning constitutional tomorrow?" Hamish shifted his gaze to the queen, knowing it was the older woman's decision not Amelia's. The queen's nostril curled, but she nodded. Hamish lifted Amelia's hand from his arm and brought it to his lips. He should have kept it a respectable distance from his mouth and merely pantomimed a kiss. But he pressed his lips to the smooth skin, and he felt the electricity once more. It made the tips of his toes tingle. When her fingers curled around his for only a moment, he knew she felt it, too.

When the women retired from the garden, the queen suddenly deciding against a stroll, Hamish and Roy were left together. Hamish braced himself.

"You won't court my daughter when you're dead."

"And if I die, Ross, it willna be difficult to guess at whose hand I did. Ye canna murder a fellow earl and believe nay one will come asking questions ye willna wish to answer." Hamish knew it irritated Roy immensely that they shared the same title. It infuriated him that their earldoms were of a similar size. Roy's was not the only territory that stretched the breadth of the country. Both of theirs stretched from the Moray to the Hebrides. Allied now with the Earldom of Sinclair, Hamish counted the entire northern part of the Highlands as being a force with which to be reckoned. A force that sided with him.

"I haven't lived to my age without knowing up from down, lad."

"Ye've lived to yer age because ye havenae ridden out to meet me." Hamish adopted his usual stance. Hands at his waist, his thumbs hooked into his belt, and his feet hip-width apart. He was twenty years Roy's junior, and his physique showed youth was on his side. Roy was still a warrior to fear and in fine shape, but he couldn't compete with a man nearly half his age who was in his prime. It was why he'd launched the covert attacks when he did.

"You may think you've swayed the king to your side by receiving his permission to court my daughter. But he knows a marriage between our clans will only strengthen mine and weaken yours."

"Why do ye think that?"

"I've already destroyed your family. Your clan may have land and they may have you, but you don't have the men you did even three moons ago. You don't have the crops or animals you did three moons ago. So, you won't have the coin you did three moons ago. You're ripe for the taking, and once Amelia is Lady Sutherland, you will have little choice but to ally with me. You won't kill her father, so you can't stop me."

"Now ye're in agreement with Amelia marrying me. It didna take ye long to sell yer daughter."

"If I'm selling her, then you're buying. Don't pretend to be better than me, lad."

"Ross, ye and I both ken ma father beat the lad out of me. I havenae been one in a score. I wish to marry Amelia because there isnae a better woman alive than her. If our marriage brings a truce, then all the better. But I will marry her, regardless of whether ye and I get along. I willna wage war against ma wife's family. I will strike once, and ye willna recover until yer grandson is laird. A grandson who isnae even alive yet. Dinna doubt that, auld mon."

"Go tup a whore instead of eying my daughter like she's a side of beef." Ross's smugness made Hamish want to bash his teeth in. He took a menacing step forward.

"Compare yer daughter to aught but perfection, and I will make sure ye swallow every word. Unlike ma feelings for ye, I respect yer daughter. I dinna care who ye are. Ye dinna speak that way aboot her. I already knocked the shite out of ye once for endangering her. Dinna think I willna do the same for insulting her."

"You only want my daughter as revenge."

"I wanted to marry yer daughter the night I met her. That was before I kenned who she was. Do ye truly nae see the value of yer daughter beyond her title and dowry?" Hamish waited, but Roy wasn't forthcoming. "Ye are a fool. Yer daughter is a kind soul, but she has a backbone of Damascus steel. She stood up to ye twice and gave ye sound advice. Nae for yer sake, but for yer clan's. She puts them first, unlike ye. She doesnae fear telling me her thoughts either, and I ken her to offer sound counsel. Counsel I respect more than anyone else's. She's beautiful too."

"We both know you exaggerate that last bit. You want her to torment me."

Hamish wrapped his fingers around his belt to keep from being the one to instigate the next fight. But he took another menacing step forward. "I dinna need to exaggerate a damn thing aboot yer daughter. She's beautiful, and well ye ken it. She's bonnier than the bluest Highland sky and the fullest field of heather and thistles. If ye dinna see that, then ye are an ungrateful wretch who doesnae deserve her as his daughter. Ross, I willna keep Amelia from yer family. She can visit

Balnagown whenever she wishes. I will welcome yer wife into ma home to visit whenever she wishes."

"But you won't welcome me."

"I will only compromise so far. What farmer invites pestilence into his barn?" Hamish cocked an eyebrow. If he wasn't careful, Ross would be the harbinger of death for his clan. He prayed his insistence on courting and hopefully marrying Amelia wasn't the most shortsighted and selfish thing he'd ever done. The Rosses weren't the only clan with which the Sutherlands had strife. They were merely the most current. Amelia's insights impressed him, and he knew she would be invaluable to him with her sage advice. He admired that most about her. He wanted to make love to her until his last breath, and his bollocks ached at the mere thought of her. He wanted to know if they could fall in love with one another. He prayed a moon would be long enough to know. He could admit his infatuation, but he thought it was something deeper for both of them.

"And do you think to join my family for Eastertide or Hogmanay? Do you think you'll sip ale around our Beltane fires?" Ross scoffed at Hamish.

"If that is what Amelia wishes, then I can make peace with yer family, at least for those days."

"If she wishes. Do you think she wishes for me to kill the mon so set on marrying her? I will."

"Ye say ye canna separate me from ma name. If I werenae a Sutherland, what could ye complain aboot? I'm a mon who wishes for his clan to prosper but nae at the expense of other clans. I'm a mon who sees the benefit of a truce, even an alliance, with other clans before an imminent war with England. I'm a mon who admires yer daughter and has nay reputation for whoring or abuse. Who do ye believe would make Amelia a finer husband? Who has the capacity to appreciate her more than I do? Who wishes to love her?"

"Ye'd love her dowry."

"I will sign away any claim to it right now. I'd sign it in blood."

"Meet me on the battlefield then."

"Ye wish for me to slay the father of the woman I wish to call wife. *If* ye were successful and killed me, what would that do to Amelia? How would she see ye then?"

"I don't care aboot my daughter's opinion of me. It's inconsequential."

"And when ye force her to marry, and she tells that mon ye canna be trusted?"

"She wouldn't dare."

Hamish cocked an eyebrow again. They both knew Amelia was assertive and didn't prevaricate. Hamish couldn't guarantee she would reveal that, but neither could Roy guarantee she wouldn't.

"Ross, let me have the moon. Let me show ye I care aboot Amelia for who she is. Let us see if she can come to care for me. If at the end of the thirty days, she doesnae wish to marry me, then I will be on ma way. If she does, then ye and I will find a way to get along for her sake."

"You plan to abandon your clan for another moon, so you can swan around after my daughter."

"Ye ken I willna leave before ye, so if it takes a moon or more to get home, then ye are stuck with ma company, regardless. Ye could return to Balnagown."

"And leave ye here alone with ma daughter? Nae bluidy likely." Roy finally lost his temper. He'd fought to keep it reined in, but Hamish pushed him too far by suggesting he would leave Amelia alone at court with Hamish. He stepped forward until their boots nearly touched. "Touch ma daughter again like I saw ye do here, and I will geld ye."

Then I willna let ye see us. "Vera well. But ye dinna interfere. Ye dinna sabotage ma courtship, Ross. Ultimately, this is Amelia's choice. I willna have it any other way." Hamish stepped around Roy and didn't turn back as he walked to the keep. His head ached from the going back and forth. They'd accomplished nothing. They were no further along than they had been in the king's Privy Council chamber. They'd each said their piece. Over and over and over and over. But he'd held his position, so Roy knew he couldn't deter Hamish. That he counted as a success. Hamish could be stubborn, and once he dug his heels in, he was difficult to dissuade. It's why he wasn't yet married. However, wanting to marry Amelia wasn't about stubbornness born from Roy's refusal. Wanting to marry her was like the air he needed to breathe. He didn't know how he'd lived before her, but he'd discovered the woman he needed.

He wouldn't allow infatuation to turn to obsession. He wouldn't set her on a pedestal just for her to fall from it. He wouldn't offer her sainthood when she was a sinner just like everyone else. But he could value her intelligence and her beauty. And he would defend her against anyone who saw her as anything less than he did. He didn't look back as he crossed the bailey. He knew he'd left Roy staring after him, but he cared not what the man did next. Hamish cared about planning his courtship. He wondered if Amelia was thinking the same thing. He would find out that evening.

"HENRIETTA," Roy called out. He watched the young woman halt at the entrance to the passageway leading to the queen's solar. She was Alfred's younger sister, and for at least the millionth time, he wished she'd been born a lad instead of her useless brother.

"Aye, Uncle." Henrietta waited for him to approach. For at least the millionth time, she wished consanguinity wasn't an impediment. That and a living aunt. She admired the older man's attractiveness, but it was his mind that drew her. She appreciated his strategic thinking. His ability to make most bend to his will. The way he need only stare at a man to make him back down. He didn't need his title. Just his bearing. That he still possessed an excellent physique only made the longing greater.

"I saw the way you regarded Laird Sutherland. You tested him with your informality." Roy watched his niece, who he knew wished for more than he would ever offer. He didn't love his wife, but he respected her. He didn't respect his niece because of the way she flaunted herself, and she was a weak substitute for her far more attractive aunt. Ross would never complain about his marital bed. He had no need to. But he would leverage his niece's willingness to do his bidding, hoping to please him.

"Aye. Rude heathen." Henrietta was as much a Highlander as Roy, Amelia, and Hamish. But she aspired to so much more. She sneered at those with a brogue. She refused to wear her plaid even when she returned to Balnagown. She'd walk away from anyone who addressed her in Gaelic, which was the only language most of their clan spoke. She'd arrived at court and immediately found a place next the queen, emulating the woman with the same hero worship she offered Roy.

"Rude heathen that he may be, you want him." Roy had known the woman since the day of her birth. She resembled him more than Amelia did. They shared the same strawberry-blond hair. He knew he would get what he wanted by being blunt. She might be coy with other men and conniving with other women, but she preferred his straightforward manner.

"He's a braw mon looking for a wife. Why wouldn't I want him?"

"Because he's a Highlander. Because he's set his sights on your cousin."

"Which of those is supposed to matter when he's an earl?" Henrietta lifted her chin imperiously. Roy refrained from laughing. It neither made her look superior nor haughty. It made her look like a petulant child. But she was an attractive petulant child. Far prettier than his own daughter. While he was fond of his children, he could see their shortcomings. He knew Amelia was no great beauty having inherited the least memorable features from him and his wife.

"I haven't arranged a betrothal for you, and your mother hasn't pressed for one. You've been very useful here. But you would be far more useful in Hamish's bed at Dunrobin. I suspect you'd like to be in his bed here."

"Uncle!" Henrietta's skirts twirled around her ankles as she spun side to side to ensure no one was near enough to hear him.

"You can act scandalized, but you don't deny it. I ken you won't need chicken's blood to prove your maidenhead. You will give it to him here and be a spy for us when you arrive at your new home. He's a beast who likes to rut. He should at least satisfy you there."

Henrietta's eyes narrowed. She was still an innocent, and she'd allowed no man any improprieties. How did her uncle know her lustfulness? Had he guessed what she wanted with him? "How do you suppose I do that? Should I slip into his chamber and into his bed, then scream the roof down?"

"That would certainly be one way. But that would make you a whore. That is not the reputation we need. You will turn his head from Amelia, and you will ensure everyone sees you. You will *quietly* find your way into his bed, where one of his men will find you."

"Do you believe he would take me to his bed by choice?"

"You think yourself a seductress to at least one mon. See if you are to him. If not, drug him. But we will find you with blood on the sheets and no maidenhead between your legs." Roy's gaze bore into the younger woman, and she felt fully exposed in a way other than he meant for her to be in Hamish's bed. She felt like he saw into her mind, and it made her body ache for him. She took three steps closer, forcing her to look up.

"And why should I do this?"

"Because you loathe Amelia and all that she has because she's the laird's daughter, and you are not. If you were, mayhap then your incestuous mind would be laid to rest. Do as I say, Henrietta, or you will regret disobeying me. I've known your thoughts for years. I haven't acted upon them and never will. But I will tell your mother, and I will see you shut away in a nunnery for them. Test me, lass. I've been at this game since long before you were seed in your father's cock. You will not win. Do as I say, and I will keep your secret."

Henrietta stood aghast, staring at the man who now angered her far more than he attracted her. She took another step forward until she was nearly under his chin. "Don't threaten me, Uncle. Or I will scream the roof down and call foul against you. What do I get in exchange for this? Because if I do this, and he's forced to marry me, it will destroy my reputation. He will not do this willingly. I want something in return."

"You get a roof over your head here, and you become a countess there. You'd do well to appreciate what you have and what I'm giving you. You'd do even better to make the mon fall in love with you. Then there would be no need for deceit." *Nae bluidy likely, but I can hope.*

"And what of Amelia?" Henrietta cared not for her cousin's feelings. She cared about the logistics. She needed the woman out of her way.

"I will take care of that. I will make sure she's too occupied to be available for Hamish to court her."

Henrietta's mind jumped from one possibility to another. She knew her cousin's stubbornness better than Roy did. In public, Amelia was amiable and amenable. In private, she could be as unbending as Henrietta. It wasn't often the latter pushed her cousin to that point, but she'd seen it. If Amelia wanted Hamish, she wouldn't step aside graciously. Henrietta would have to give her a hard shove. And that shove might come at an expense to her own good name. But now that the idea of being a countess took root, she planned to water it and make it grow into a mighty oak.

"You shall owe me a boon that I will choose, and I will demand what *I* want. Agree to that, and I'll start this evening." *And I will be in his bed before the sennight is through.*

melia stifled her groan when she spotted Lionel and Tormud approaching. She was not in the mood for their whingeing about the scene in the garden or about her agreeing to allow Hamish to court her. She'd just changed her gown for the evening meal and was making her way to the Great Hall with two other ladies-in-waiting. She wished there were an alcove in which she could hide or a tunnel to make her escape. The two women with her beamed at her brothers, and it made her want to roll her eyes. Both men were handsome, and both would grow into powerful positions. But for now, they were still her younger brothers, and they were about to annoy her.

"Amy, a word, please," Lionel held out his hand for her. She slipped past her friends, whispering she would join them for the evening meal. She suspected she wouldn't have that chance. She expected her family would insist she dine with them, then they could deny anyone who approached to dance with her. They could deny Hamish.

Her brothers herded her down the passageway to the music chamber. She'd spent hours in there playing the harp for the queen. It was an instrument her mother insisted she learn for exactly this purpose. To entertain the royals while serving as a lady-in-waiting. Her mother had been one to the English-by-birth Queen Margaret. The late queen and current queen were cousins. Queen Margaret had been King Henry's daughter, and Queen Isabella's mother had been the king's half-sister. Amelia's mother insisted the tradition of service continue with Amelia, but Amelia dreaded sending any of her daughters here.

"Father said you ran to Hamish's side unbeknownst Father was already there." Tormud didn't prevaricate.

"I ran to find Father, and Hamish was there." She'd found her father there by accident, but she wouldn't argue semantics.

"If you'd found Hamish alone, you would have told him Father's plan."

"I wouldnae have needed to since Father already sent the raiding parties." Amelia watched her brothers closely. She could read them better than anyone. She would know if they lied. She was the one who'd taught them to school their emotions and let nothing show. She believed it was one of the most important skills any laird or tánaiste could have. It was a skill at which their father excelled, but she knew he would never think to teach them. She'd learned after years of unkind comments about her weight and appearance. She'd developed sooner than most girls her age, and she had an ample bust. It was something she wished her courtly gowns hid better. It made her self-conscious, especially when many men did nothing to hide their interest in that feature. She knew Hamish noticed them, but he never ogled. His interest in her body made her wish to strip naked, so he could taste more than her mouth, just as she'd said. Other men made her wish to wrap herself in her plaid like the Egyptian mummies she'd once read about.

"How do you ken that?" Tormud demanded.

"Because Hamish told me." Amelia crossed her arms, her mulishness emerging.

"But you would have told him," Lionel insisted.

"I gave ma word that I wouldnae. Do ye nae believe ma word is worth what it was?"

"Why do you sound like a Highlander?" Lionel blurted.

"Because I am one. And as one, ye should ken ma honor and ma loyalty were etched into me before I came out of Mother's womb. I would nae have betrayed our clan, but ye are all fools to think that because Hamish is here, he willna retaliate. He may be here, but so are ye and Father. Who is home to lead our clan the way Father can? Uncle Alastair. The mon is half deaf from listening to Aunt Eleanor ranting and raving at him. She may be Father's and Uncle Alastair's sister, but she isnae a woman easy to love. He drinks when Father is gone, and ye ken that. Mother willna get involved. And Marcus may be the captain of the guard while ye are away, but ye ken he doesnae have a head for strategy. Ye willna find a braver or stronger warrior than him, but he isnae a leader. It's why Father elevated ye to the position, Tor, while ye were still so young. Ye two and Father are so blind. Hamish's uncle may nae be a good mon, but he's a competent one. And Hamish has surely dispatched a messenger to Dunrobin with orders aboot how to avenge his people."

Tormud and Lionel glanced at one another. Amelia knew she might have overplayed her hand by pointing that out. Would her family send a messenger now? Balnagown was closer by a day-and-a-half ride than Dunrobin. She'd only found out about the raids that morning. A messenger sent now would reach her home before one could reach Hamish's. But she assumed Henry Sutherland would act with or without Hamish's permission. He'd acted on his own without consulting his now dead brother. He was the first to raid the Rosses.

"You running through a keep was enough to gain people's attention. You—" Tormud didn't get to complete his thought.

"I didna run through the keep. I only hurried once I was nearly to the passageway to the Privy Council chamber. I heard a Sutherland warrior had arrived."

"You embarrassed yourself, speaking to the Sutherland when Father told you to leave," Tormud insisted.

"He never told me to leave. He said he didna want Hamish speaking to me, and he didna want me to walk with Hamish. But he didna tell me I had to leave. Ye are making things up, assuming ye already ken what happened. Ye dinna. Tor, ye willna change ma mind any more than Father can. Hamish Sutherland is courting me, and I intend to say aye." Amelia uncrossed her arms and pushed between her stunned brothers. She was slippery as an eel when Lionel reached for her, twisting to reach the doorway. "Dinna do aught ye canna take back, brothers. Father willna live forever. Ye will need whoever I marry as an ally nae an enemy."

Amelia slipped into the Great Hall as the last diners found seats. She glanced in her father's direction, but she wasn't interested in joining him. It meant facing the gossips and Henrietta, but she would rather that and have Hamish approach her to dance than be invisibly chained to the table beside Roy.

"Lady Amelia, you've caught the Earl of Sutherland's eye. He is lucky to still have both of them from the way your father glares at him," Lady Caroline Johnstone mused. When Amelia said nothing, her opponent accepted the challenge. "What will you do when they fight yet again? Everyone knows you'll be to blame."

"Does either mon look like I can cause them to do aught they dinna want to do?" Amelia's gaze didn't waver from Caroline's. It shocked the other ladies to hear she no longer sounded like a Lowlander. That was cause for a stir. That her focus remained solely on Caroline and hadn't drifted to Roy or Hamish disconcerted many of them. Even Henrietta's squawking voice didn't shift Amelia's attention.

"Why on God's good Earth do you sound like such a blasted heathen? Our mothers ensured we were educated, so we wouldn't sound like barbarians."

"I speak four languages and read six. I'm plenty educated, Henny. Dinna prattle at me." Amelia let slip the childhood name her cousin now detested. But she didn't regret it when she realized what she'd done. However, Henrietta saw it as a slight she couldn't ignore.

"Do you know where Hamish was the second night he was here?" Henrietta paused for effect. "The Merry Widow. Men don't go there for the whisky or the food."

Amelia felt like she'd taken a kick to the gut. But they hadn't met each other then. It was before either of them knew the other existed. She wanted to know if he'd been back, but she wouldn't ask in case he had. "And how would ye ken that, Cousin? Were ye traipsing aboot when ye should have been in yer chamber? Or are ye asking around aboot a mon who hasnae looked in yer direction longer than it took him to tell ye his title?"

Henrietta's face nearly matched her hair as she slanted her eyes at Amelia. The latter knew she shouldn't have antagonized the vindictive woman. She could imagine where her impetuous insults would land her. She knew she'd laid down the gauntlet for Henrietta. The woman had never been her friend, but she was all too prepared to be Amelia's enemy. She'd felt a need to compete against Amelia that was never reciprocated.

"I wasn't the one seen flagrantly kissing him in the queen's garden."

"Aye. Because ye arenae the one he wants." Amelia smirked. In for a penny, in for a pound. She wouldn't back down now.

"If you wish to make yourself known as a slut, then—"

"Ye still havenae told us how ye ken where Laird Sutherland went that night. Were ye there to see him arrive? Were ye sneaking in or out of the keep? Were ye following, hoping he'd let ye call him Hamish like he lets me?" Amelia's hands rested on the edge of the table, so she was prepared to snatch the full chalice from Henrietta before her nemesis could pour it down the front of her. "I wouldnae," Amelia warned. "How will Father react when he sees ye pour wine down his daughter's gown?"

Henrietta placed the goblet on the table a little too hard,

making some wine slosh over the side. Amelia caught herself before she said something she truly couldn't take back. She knew of her cousin's pining for Roy. She thought it disgusting since she could never imagine herself longing for Henrietta's father before he died. She couldn't see herself pining for their mutual uncle, either. She recognized her father was a handsome man, but she and Henrietta were the same age. She had no interest in a man old enough to be her father, but she knew Henrietta did. She knew Henrietta admired Roy and had since she was a lass. She also knew her cousin was scheming and wished to become a countess. If anything befell her mother, Amelia would point the finger at Henrietta.

"You dare to accuse me of—"

"I accused ye of naught. Mayhap it is a guilty conscience that sees it as accusations. I merely asked a few questions. Ones ye still havenae answered. Are ye paying a servant to watch Laird Sutherland?"

"I am not."

"Aye, ye are." Hamish stopped behind Amelia and looked at the table of women whose mouths were open so wide they could catch all the flies in the kingdom. "Lady Henrietta, yer maid is nay more subtle than a wean with a toothache. What are ye clish-maclavering aboot, ma lady?"

Amelia had yet to turn around. She didn't want to take her eyes off Henrietta, and it would put her at an awkward angle to see Hamish. But she couldn't ignore him, either. Just as she shifted on the bench, Henrietta had her own question.

"And where were you the second night you were here? Who were you with?"

Hamish forced himself not to curl his fists. He couldn't strike her despite the temptation. He knew the game she played, and she intended to humiliate Amelia. He wouldn't soon forgive that. "I was at the Merry Widow, and ye can guess who I was with. But how many times have I been back since I met Lady Amelia?"

Henrietta remained silent. Hamish placed a hand on Amelia's shoulder as he leaned forward. His gaze locked with Henrietta's. He kept his voice low, so only the women closest to them could hear when he glared at Henrietta and whispered.

"Ye'd do well to keep yer tongue in yer mouth and nay whipping aboot the breeze. Humiliate me if ye like. Call me a barbarian or a heathen from now until our eternal kingdom. Humiliate yer cousin again, and I willna overlook it a second time." Hamish moved his hand from Amelia's shoulder to offer her his hand. His whisper was even quieter, ensuring only Amelia heard. "Come, ma lady. Lady Gwendolyn has agreed to be our chaperone. Ye may sit with ma clan."

She didn't hesitate to accept the offer even though she knew she threw oil on the fire. She stepped over the bench and accepted Hamish's arm for a third time that day. He escorted her to the table where the matron sat with an open spot beside her. Across from the open spot was another vacant one. Hamish released her arm before she sat, then wound his way around the table to take his seat. Lady Gwendolyn was the oldest woman at court. She was eighty-four, but she had the sight and hearing of a wolfhound. She was the most respected person at court, so Hamish had sought her before the evening meal. It didn't hurt that she was his great-aunt on his mother's side. She'd always had an affinity for him.

"Good evening, Lady Gwendolyn. It is a pleasure to see ye." Amelia smiled at the woman with the crepey skin that held laugh lines from a lifetime of smiling. The old woman's hands showed the cruelty of age as she reached for the chalice they would share.

"It's aboot time a lass at this pile of stones sounded like she has her head on properly. You all sound alike, and it's enough to drive me barmy. Highlanders should sound like Highlanders. Lowlanders already overrun this place." The woman was Welsh and the daughter of the late Lord of Glamorgan, an earldom in the principality of Morgannwg. She'd married a Highlander sixty-five years ago and had made her home there. While her accent was distinctly from her homeland, everyone at court considered her a Highlander. She had the mettle to be one. She'd survived three husbands and four children. Her living children, all daughters, moved slower than she did on the best of days. She'd taken up residence at court when she became the king's ward— a fact she took grave offense to at her age. She was a sprite who still went to the Stirling market once a week and often led the queen's constitutional, insisting the brisk air kept her alive. She had no patience for those— including the queen —who loitered.

Amelia grinned at the dowager countess whose first husband had been the Earl of Crawford. Once widowed, she'd remained in the Highlands. It was how she'd developed a brogue before abandoning it at court. She didn't know Hamish's family tree, but she knew the woman married a Sutherland. She knew not if that was the matron's second or third husband. She enjoyed Lady Gwendolyn's sense of humor, and she'd often wished Lady Gwendolyn was her great-grandmother.

Amelia listened as the dowager chatted with the Sutherland warriors, often teasing Hamish mercilessly. But it was endearing to see that it was always done without malice. Amelia suspected Gwendolyn was one of the few kind people in Hamish's life. She knew his mother died when he was an adolescent, and she knew his father had been a cruel man. But she knew no more about his family than that.

"Lad, how is your sister?" Lady Gwendolyn tilted her head as she spoke to Hamish. Amelia's brow furrowed. It seemed she would get a lesson on his family tree during the meal.

"She is blissfully happy with Liam. I couldnae wish for a better mon than him. He dotes on her, and she on him. It wouldnae surprise me if I have a nephew in the next nine moons." Hamish beamed as he spoke about his younger sister, Kyla. They'd had many strained years between them because of their father and brothers, but it delighted him to see her so happy after so many years of misery.

"A strapping lad, that one." Gwendolyn nodded her head in agreement with her own proclamation. It made Hamish and Amelia smile. She'd called Hamish a lad and now referred to Liam Sinclair, a man known to be among the tallest and strongest in Scotland, as a lad, too. Neither had been one in at least a decade, but to a woman well into her eighth, Amelia and Hamish reasoned everyone was a lad or lass to her. Gwendolyn turned her attention back to the men at the table and began sharing off-color jokes no lady should know. That made them all the more amusing to the warriors. She shot Hamish a momentary wink, and he knew she would distract his men, so he could speak to Amelia.

He darted his gaze to the ladies-in-waiting before locking his gaze with Amelia's. "What happened?"

"I allowed her to goad me."

"Lia, if ye'd asked, I would have told ye where I went. If the topic had come up, I would have been honest. I'm sorry ye heard that from her."

"Is it a place ye frequent?"

"Nay. It was ma first and only time there." Hamish lowered his eating knife, his long legs shifting to bracket hers beneath the table. "I am nae a mon governed by urges. At least, nae until I met ye. I dinna go whoring, Lia. I have a past, but that is where it shall stay. It is nae one I'm embarrassed of, nor one that should shame ye. I dinna want ye to fear meeting a line of women from ma past if ye come to Dunrobin."

"If?" Amelia heard the rest of what he said, but that was the word she latched onto.

"We have a moon to decide whether we suit. I willna assume aught until ye tell me what ye wish." Hamish wished he could reach across and hold her hand, entwining their fingers together. "It had been many moons since the last time I'd sought a woman's company. More important things exist in this world than tupping wenches. I had a clan to rebuild and a keep to set straight. Fortunately, Kyla came to help with the latter, and Liam helped me learn to be a laird. I met ye the third night I was here, but I saw ye the two nights before."

Amelia wondered what he left unsaid. He'd seen her the night before he approached her, and that was the night he'd gone to bed a whore. She wasn't sure how to she felt about that. Why hadn't he approached her sooner? Why the night after bedding another woman?

"Lia, I can hear yer thoughts as though ye were screaming them. This is ma first trip to court as an adult. I didna approach ye because I was unsure of maself. I didna dare ask aboot ye for fear it would make people gossip. That seems rather moot now, but I worried. I went out that second night because I felt restless after seeing ye and nae being able to speak to ye. I went out because I was lonely, and that seemed like a good way to pass the time." He wouldn't share that he'd been picturing her while he tupped the woman from behind. He'd insisted that way her face wouldn't distract him from the one he envisioned. "Ye can ask aught ye wish to ken aboot ma past. I willna hide aught, for better or for worse."

"Why me? I didna see ye dance with many women the night ye came to me. I hadnae seen more than a glance of ye before that."

"I didna enjoy seeing ye dancing with other men."

Amelia waited for him to say more, but nothing was forthcoming. It seemed Hamish expected her to understand his meaning from that single sentence. But she didn't understand.

"We didna ken each other. Why would that bother ye?"

"Because ma patience couldnae last seeing ye in other men's arms. Ye are the bonniest woman I've ever beheld. When ye smile —" Hamish shrugged. "I wished for ye to smile at me."

"Are ye always so forthright? Ye say things I dinna expect."

"I am with ye because I dinna want ye to wonder aboot ma intentions. I want ye to ken who I am and who ye'll marry if ye agree. But I am next to never this open. I dinna trust easily, Lia. Certainly nae here. But I trust ye. I dinna have aught to hide from ye. I've made ma mistakes, and I've done things I regret. I've erred like any mon, but I strive to learn from it. I danced with ye because I wanted to touch ye, have ye in ma arms. I talked to ye on the terrace because ye fascinate me. Ye are more interesting than any person here save Lady Gwendolyn." Hamish grinned at his great-aunt when she nodded without looking away from the animated conversation in which she was a lively participant. He knew the older woman listened to everything as a proper chaperone should.

"The mon who approached me as ye did is someone I've considered marrying. He hasnae officially asked to court me, but he has hinted he wishes to. He's kissed me, but nae the way ye did. Nay one has done that." Amelia watched Hamish as she confessed something she likely should have mentioned in the garden that morning. But too many other things swirled in her mind to recall Everett MacDonald.

"Do ye wish for him to court ye as well?"

"If I did, I wouldnae have kissed ye back. I forgot aboot him until now. He's in here somewhere, and I couldnae care less. He doesnae care aboot me any more than I care aboot him. He cares aboot ma dowry, and I cared aboot finding a mon I could tolerate siring ma children."

"Could ye tolerate me?" Hamish's stare held her in place. She shifted her legs beneath the table, so his right one was between hers.

"I dinna think it will ever be a question of tolerating."

"Would ye welcome me in our bed?"

"Our?"

"Aye, Lia. If we wed, there will be nay point in his and her chambers. Ye would never sleep in yers, and I prefer ma bed since it's longer than the one ma mother used. Ma feet would hang off the end. I warn ye now, if ye become ma wife, I dinna think I'll ever leave ye in peace. I shall chase ye until I catch ye each and every time." His wolfish grin made Amelia's core ache for something she could only guess. She wanted more kisses like the one they shared that morning. She wanted to explore the things she'd heard women discuss at court. Some were discreet and whispered, while others flaunted their knowledge to shock the virgin ladies-in-waiting. Either way, she knew enough to be curious, and there was only one man she wished to tutor her.

"Would yer half of the bed be cold some nights?"

Hamish's dark brows lowered, and his expression became a thundercloud. "Only the nights I'm on patrol or ye turn me away. I willna stray."

"Why would I turn ye away? Do ye think ye'll be that demanding that I shall need to hide just to get some sleep?"

"Aye. I will be that demanding. Though, I suspect I shall be the one hiding in ma solar to get a wee nap here and there. I think the woman I wish to call ma bride shall be as exuberant as me."

"Exuberant?" Amelia giggled. "Ye make it sound as though the entire keep would ken what we're aboot."

"If we're doing it properly." Hamish shrugged and winked. Amelia could only blink. This was the most improper conversation she'd ever had, and she loved every second. She'd never discussed marital relations with Everett, and the hint of doing so made her want to laugh. She could only imagine how distraught the man would become since she suspected he would have bedded her while they had all their clothes on and in the dark. Then he would have gone to his leman to enjoy himself. She didn't think he could manage the idea that a lady could be as randy as any man. Hamish certainly made her realize they could be. That she could be.

"Ye ken we talk aboot some of the more outlandish things, dinna ye, Hamish?"

"We're courting. Dinna ye think we should ken these things aboot one another?"

"Aye. But we've only spoken a few times, and it's always aboot things that would scandalize a court bent on debauchery." Stirling was hardly Sodom and Gomorrah, but it wasn't a place where everyone prioritized chastity.

"Do ye wish we didna? Have I offended ye, Lia?" Hamish's stomach knotted, and the quail he'd just swallowed felt sour in his belly.

"Nae at all. I just dinna think most people would approve. I couldnae care less that they wouldnae. It was an observation nae a judgment." Amelia chanced a peek at Gwendolyn, knowing the older lady listened to their entire conversation. But she felt safe discussing these things even if the dowager countess could hear. She didn't fear the widow's judgment or censure. She suspected the woman secretly encouraged them. At the very least, they entertained her.

The Sutherland men drew Hamish into the conversation until the music began. Hamish led Amelia into the crowd, and they lined up for the first dance. It was one that forced them to change partners. When Hamish found Henrietta standing in front of him, he forced his lip not to curl. She may have offered him what he suspected she believed was a seductive smile, but her eyes shot daggers. He could hear her warning, and he would be mindful not to taunt the woman again. Amelia would pay for his carelessness, and it would force her to accept the repercussions since he couldn't retaliate against a woman. He didn't want to place Amelia in her cousin's crosshairs again.

"Laird Sutherland, I beg your forgiveness," Henrietta said. "I was unconscionably rude. My cousin boasted aboot how she'd ensnared you and that she would lead you around by the bollocks. I grew angry that she would speak aboot you in such a way, so I pointed out where you'd been. You caught our conversation at the wrong moment, and I was too livid on your behalf to curb my tongue. I know how it appeared, but it was the very opposite."

Hamish looked down at the upturned face and girded himself against grimacing. Her anger was genuine, but so were her lies. He wanted no part of it, and he believed nothing she spewed. But he would be more circumspect. He also wouldn't lie like she had. "Ma lady, I ken what I heard. I'm certain ye felt vera justified in yer arguments. But I can defend maself with ma words as well as I can ma sword."

The music forced them apart before either of them could say more. It brought Hamish and Amelia back together. She looked questioningly at him, having observed his conversation with Henrietta but not being able to hear it.

"Lia, she claimed to defend me and that ye boasted aboot leading me by the bollocks. She didna defend me, and ye can lead ma bollocks wherever ye like." Hamish grinned and waggled his eyebrows. Amelia felt herself flush. That was the randiest comment they'd exchanged yet.

"I suppose I will since ye said ye will chase me."

"Aye, and I said I would catch ye. Is that what ye want, *leannan*? Do ye wish me to carry ye off like a beastly Highlander?"

"Resorting to bride stealing?"

"If I must. I've met the vera bonniest woman, and I intend to make her ma wife. If I must run off with her, then so be it. I wonder if she would go willingly."

Amelia slid her hand to his chest as she tilted her head back. "If I havenae run screaming from ma father's enemy yet, and I've jested aboot the bed I would share with him, I dinna think the mon would need to carry me anywhere but to our chamber."

"Jested?" Hamish wasn't sure what to make of that. Had she not meant any of it?

"*M'eudail*, dinna fash. We spoke with humor, but neither of us said aught we didna mean. I dinna ken what the days and sennights hold in store for us. I dinna ken if we will suit in ways other than this, but I think we will. I intend to find out."

"I—"

"Laird Sutherland! Where is Laird Sutherland?" A voice boomed over the heads of all who gathered in the Great Hall. Hamish recognized it. He took Amelia's hand and towed her through the crowd.

"Liam? I'm here." Hamish pushed people out of his way, ensuring no one would bump into Amelia. When they reached the doorway, he and Amelia stood in front of Liam and Kyla. "What's happened?"

CHAPTER 8

Amelia tightened her grip on Hamish's hand, worried about his relatives' arrival at court. More specifically, why Liam Sinclair bellowed Hamish's name. She'd met him before at court, and she knew him to be a warrior of unparalleled skill, but he was also a sage diplomat. He wasn't one to catastrophize, and it was a long ride to bring Kyla to visit Stirling, a place she'd only visited once or twice. She smiled at Kyla, whose gaze darted to where she held Hamish's hand. When their gazes met, Amelia saw kindness but speculation. She shifted her attention to Liam, not wanting Kyla to read too many of her thoughts.

"Hamish, we need to speak immediately. And nae here." Liam wrapped his arm around Kyla and turned. The man took no interest in the milling crowd or the whispers that swirled around them. He took one step forward before another voice boomed.

"Sinclair, why are you causing a stir in my Great Hall?" King John stood on the dais, his fists on the table, as he leaned forward. It could have appeared imposing, but with his rotund middle, baldpate, and pale skin, his bearing held little authority.

"I would speak to ma brother-by-marriage, Yer Majesty. We will take our conversation elsewhere, so ye may return to yer meal. Good evening." Liam dipped his head now that he faced the dais. But his attempt to leave was waylaid.

"Approach. I would know what brought you here." The king straightened and flapped his hand, beckoning Liam forward. There was no chance he would leave Kyla alone anywhere on the castle grounds, so she came along with him. Hamish followed, and since he hadn't let go of Amelia, she joined them. But when they were nearly to the high table, Amelia let go of Hamish's hand. He glanced down at her without moving his head. His expression warned her not to argue. He wanted her with him.

"We are aware of something that concerns the Sutherlands." Liam offered nothing more, and the silence drew out when Balliol expected further details, but none were forthcoming.

"Sinclair, do not keep me waiting."

"This is a matter for the Sutherlands. It's naught that need concern the crown." Liam's tone remained casual, which it had except for when he called out to Hamish. His arm hung loosely around Kyla's shoulders, but he'd positioned himself with his feet planted hip-width apart like a warrior taking a stand. He would not budge physically, nor would he budge on his commitment to keeping the topic private. The Clan Sinclair tánaiste raised his chin in defiance to the king. He had a healthy fear of any monarch who held the power to strip his clan of everything. But John Balliol had never impressed nor intimidated him. The Sinclairs were the king's only connection to Orkney and the Shetlands. They'd also brokered a peace with the Sutherlands and were no longer openly hostile to the Mackays. They rarely quarreled with the Keiths or the Oliphants, who also held land in the Earldom of Sinclair.

John Balliol needed Donnell and Liam Sinclair more than they needed him. They were as far from the border as anyone could reach short of diving into the North Sea. It was unlikely any battle would reach them. But they were loyal to Scotland and held a reputation for fierceness. When war inevitably came, King

John recognized the Sinclairs' importance— not only to fight, but to influence the other clans to stand behind him. There were other contenders for the throne, so his hold on his title was precarious on his best of days. When success— meaning not being forced to abdicate or not being killed —rested on the shoulders of clans like the Sinclairs, King John knew to proceed with care.

"Use my antechamber then." Balliol's tone turned solicitous, but none of the four standing before him thought it altruistic. He would have people listening to the conversation through peep-holes or insist his guards remain, who would then report to him. What he overlooked was none of his guards and none of the courtiers he would likely choose spoke Gaelic. The quartet standing before him did. Liam nodded before he and Kyla turned toward the Great Hall's doors. Hamish and Amelia made to follow them, but Roy blocked them.

"You are not taking my daughter with you."

"Aye, I am. If Lady Amelia is to be the next Lady Sutherland, then whatever this is concerns her. Even if she doesnae become Lady Sutherland, I trust her counsel and wish to ken what she thinks. Ma brother-by-marriage isnae a mon to overreact. What-ever he's here to tell me likely means I need Lady Amelia's sound advice."

"You would heed advice from a woman who knows naught aboot politics?"

"Ye are a daft sod if that's what ye think. There isnae a lady-in-waiting here who couldnae inform the king of every alliance or feud in this country. They hear it all. And ye are a bampot if ye canna remember the advice yer daughter's given ye twice in ma presence. Ye'd do well to heed it, and I will heed whatever she tells me. Move, Ross. Ye're keeping ma brother and sister waiting."

By the end of the moon Kyla and Liam had spent with Hamish after he'd accepted the lairdship, neither man considered themselves anything less than brothers in the truest sense. Liam's younger brother had finished fostering away from Dunbeath in the past moon, and Hamish no longer had brothers, and those he'd once had he'd never respected. He saw no need to use the qualifier most of the time.

"No. You are not married, and there is little likelihood you will. Whatever your problems are, Amelia isn't involved." Roy suspected Liam's reason for being there, and he didn't want his daughter involved. It only increased the chance she would side with Hamish.

"I gave the earl permission to court your daughter, Ross," King John interjected.

"I'm well aware, Your Majesty. But courting is no guarantee a marriage will take place. I do not want my daughter thrust into the middle of whatever this is and have her be in danger. I will keep my daughter safe."

Hamish nearly choked as he swallowed his snort. If Roy Ross meant to keep his daughter safe, he wouldn't have sent his daughter to court during a period of civil unrest. He wouldn't antagonize Hamish and cause a physical altercation that nearly trampled Amelia. Before he could speak on her behalf, Amelia stepped forward to whisper in her father's ear.

"Ye are bound and determined to see this fail, but in the meantime, there is much I could learn. Ye are making a scene once more, and ye dinna come across as a doting father. Ye come across as a mon grasping at aught in a sea that's sucking him into its depths." She would never violate Hamish's trust and share anything spoken in confidence to her. But she would manipulate her father as much as he manipulated her. He was a master at the technique, but she'd learned it from her mother. When she stepped back, her gaze locked with his.

"My daughter swears the Sinclairs will ensure her safety. I ken Liam's a mon of integrity, so he won't let aught befall her." Roy shifted his focus to Hamish, his lips wishing to curl into a smirk.

"So is Hamish. It's why I'm proud to call him brother." Liam didn't know the details of the latest intrigue between Hamish and Roy, and he grew tired of the standoff. He would make it clear to everyone that the alliance that ended the Sinclair and Sutherland feud was more than scratches on a parchment. He would remind Roy, too. He and Kyla stepped away, and Hamish ushered Amelia to go ahead of him. Hamish would have enjoyed nothing more than jamming his shoulder into Roy's as he walked past, but that would gain him nothing. The two couples left the Great Hall and went next door. A guard opened it to reveal a comfortable antechamber where kings often met with visitors or courtiers before meals. They gathered near the unlit fireplace.

Kyla stared at her brother until he looked at her, then she launched in Gaelic. "Are ye courting? Or are ye handfasted?"

Hamish grinned at his little sister who'd only dared be blunt to him. When she was, it was often painfully so. "The king granted me permission to court Lia, but Ross is set against it. He keeps insisting I'm doing it to get ma own back on him. I am nae."

"Of course, ye arenae. A marriage will last longer than he lives. Ye arenae committing yerself for a lifetime just to peeve him for a few more years." Kyla's pragmatism was one of her most endearing qualities to her husband. But as her gaze shifted to Amelia, she wondered whether the other woman saw its worth.

"Ye arenae wrong, Lady Kyla. Ma father will likely live at least another score, mayhap a score-and-a-half, but that is only a third of the time I will spend with Hamish." She looked up at Hamish. "Yer brother isnae cruel. He wouldnae use me like that."

Hamish released her hand and wrapped his arm around her shoulders just like Liam still did with Kyla. They were as alone as they would get, and he trusted his family even if he didn't trust the guards or the security of the chamber. He drew her to his side, and she leaned into him willingly. "What's happened?"

Liam glanced at Amelia before directing his attention to

Hamish. He had to trust Hamish knew what he was doing by having Amelia present. "We ken Ross sent his men to attack yer villages wearing Gunn plaids. Tomas Gunn insists ye are accusing them to start trouble where it doesnae exist. But he'll use a fight with ye to justify the war he wishes to wage against the Mackays."

Hamish rolled his eyes before responding. "Angus Mackay was a mercenary in France before he unexpectedly inherited that lairdship. He'd slip into Clyth Castle and kill Tomas in his bed before getting into a war with them. The only reason he hasnae done that to the Ross is because the mon's an earl. Tomas is naught but an eejit."

"Anyone with a sound mind kens that aboot Angus, but nay one's ever described Tomas as aught more than a fool," Liam responded. "In the meantime, he's using the excuse that ye and Roy are already blaming them for something the Rosses did. He thinks to shove that blame back on the Rosses and say it's them raiding the Keiths but wearing Gunn plaids again. Tomas kens ye get along with the Keiths, so he wishes to get revenge through them. He thinks people will believe Roy is attacking the Keiths because he canna do more to ye."

Liam paused since the matter was so complicated, even he had to think through the explanation as he spoke. When Hamish nodded, he continued.

"Tomas thinks claiming it's the Rosses dressed as Gunns, attacking the Keiths will only increase the hostilities between ye and the Rosses. To reach the Keiths or the Mackays, it means Tomas's ridden on parts of ma clan's land. Between Tomas and Roy, they're likely to tear the Highlands apart. After Berwick and Dunbar, we canna underestimate the likelihood Longshanks will attack. When he does, we'll have a war to keep our independence from the bluidy Sassenachs. We dinna need this right now."

Amelia didn't know where to look. She expected this to concern her father and clan, but now she felt listening betrayed her clan. She knew the next step would be Hamish and Liam planning their retaliation. She'd drawn her proverbial line in the sand by coming in here with Hamish and the Sinclairs. But she'd manipulated her father by saying she'd spy for him. She wouldn't betray Hamish. She wished she were anywhere but Stirling Castle.

Hamish could only imagine how conflicted Amelia must feel now that the facts were before them. This indirectly involved the Rosses, but it was Roy's tactics that were the catalyst. He knew Roy would demand Amelia share everything she heard in here. He knew she wouldn't betray him, and he also knew loyalty to her clan would trap her in the middle. She would have to say something. He slid his arm down to wrap around her waist and drew her to look at him.

"If ye wish to leave and nae hear more, I understand. Yer father will learn all of this soon enough. If ye feel ye must tell him, then ye should."

"If ma father is going to hear aboot this anyway, then it doesnae need to come from me. I dinna want to hear more, and I wish we could all leave. But ma concern for yer clan's wellbeing is stronger. I ken Tomas Gunn. His uncle was married to Father's sister. Father considered him as a potential husband several years ago. I wouldnae say he courted me in the sense ye wish to here. But he came to the keep several times, and we remained an extra sennight after they hosted the Highland Gathering. Father decided he didna need the alliance that badly because they arenae as strong as other clans, and while Tomas's uncle— and ma aunt's husband —is now dead, the Gunns and Rosses were already once bound by marriage. Father had been happy to maintain good relations by threatening the Mackays with the Rosses joining Tomas during any fight the Mackays had against the Gunns. He had nay intention of sending warriors. He believed he could intimidate Angus because he hadn't been laird vera long. This was aboot three-and-a-half years ago. Just before I came to court."

Hamish's arm instinctually tightened around Amelia's waist. He didn't enjoy hearing another man had considered— had the opportunity —to become Amelia's husband. It was years ago, so they hadn't known each other, much like the night he went to the Merry Widow. But jealousy flared as he wondered if she'd held his hand, let him kiss her, wished to marry him. His mind shouted *mine*. Amelia rested a hand on Hamish's chest, and she felt the steady beat that was surely faster than normal. The other was slightly lower on his abdomen. She'd felt the muscles jump when her palm touched his leine. Even after he relaxed, the peaks and valleys of his washboard stomach pressed back against her hand. Their gazes met, and passion sparked. If they were alone and it wasn't a time of crisis, they would have resumed their kiss from in the garden.

"Hamish, naught ever came from it. Mother insisted I come to court for at least a year before I wed. I accepted to escape Tomas. By the time the queen might have released me to marry, Father had already moved on. There was never a serious chance I would marry him." She patted Hamish's stomach. "But I ken how he thinks. I overheard him speak to Father more than once. The mon doesnae ken how to keep his voice down. He never wished to marry me. He would have for an alliance that would allow him to attack the Keiths successfully. He believes Laird Keith marrying Lady Marion, rather than her father accepting his suit, is a personal slight. It is. Laird Chisholm never would have let his daughter wed any Gunn. That it was Tomas only confirmed it. But rather than take it out on the Chisholms, he blames Ruairi Keith."

When Amelia turned to look at Liam and Kyla, Hamish didn't release her. Instead, his hands rested over her belly. She liked the feel, especially when his hands pressed her back against his chest. The Sinclair couple watched her intently, but she didn't feel either passed judgment while she stood in Hamish's embrace. Liam appeared disinterested in what lay between Hamish and her, and Kyla appeared amused but happy. She continued to share her thoughts now that she could see Liam and Kyla and felt Hamish wrapped around her.

"Tomas is ambitious to the point of recklessness. Ye ken he canna stand the sight of any Sinclair. He'd hand ye all to the devil if he could. He's relying on the Sinclairs and Mackays nae getting along, even if ye arenae fighting right now, and the Sutherlands and Gunns are at peace. He figures the Rosses are far enough away that they canna actually do more than steal some plaids. He obviously doesnae see us as allies now that we arenae related by marriage. This emboldens him to attack the Keiths. But the mon forgets all too easily that yer clans surround him on three sides. The sea is against his back. Now that ye're allies, I dinna ken how he thinks he can attack anyone without all of ye pouring onto his land. Ye may nae care for the Mackays, but yer father—" she looked at Liam "—and Angus both dislike Tomas more than they dislike each other. Tomas still needs to marry. He believes a victory against any and all of ye will prove him a powerful laird deserving of another powerful laird's auldest daughter."

Kyla nodded. "The Keiths are just the first step. Tomas believes if he can force the Oliphants to surrender to him, then he can force them to side with him against us. He wants more influence within the Earldom of Sinclair. He kens Da may have oversight of the lands, but the Sinclairs themselves arenae big enough to fight the Mackays, the Oliphants, and them."

Amelia listened to Kyla refer to her father-by-marriage as Da and that she believed herself a Sinclair. She sensed the fondness between Hamish and Kyla, but she could tell she no longer considered herself a Sutherland. It made her wonder if part of her would always associate who she was with being a Ross. She wondered if she would fully embrace being a Sutherland with no reservations. She wasn't sure. She pulled herself out of her ruminations to continue to listen to Kyla.

"Tomas must think the Sutherlands arenae ready for a battle, and he must doubt the strength of our alliance. He underestimates there's a reason the Sinclairs have an earldom, and they dinna. Same for why the Sutherlands have one. Neither clan is weak nay matter what challenges they face."

Liam picked up where Kyla left off. "We came to tell ye aboot the incursions and to plan with ye for how we move forward as one. We dinna trust messengers making it back and forth safely." He glanced at Amelia. "Do ye need help to resolve the matter with the Rosses? Ye're needed back in Sutherland."

"How fares our uncle, Kyla?" Hamish couldn't answer that without asking his own question first.

She grimaced, making Amelia wonder why Hamish's sister held such disgust for their family member. Kyla spoke unemotionally when she responded. "He's maintaining the keep, and he sent war bands out to seek any survivors or stragglers from Roy's attacks. He sent word to us aboot the staged raids. That made us question the Gunns' reaction since we were certain it wasna really the Rosses harrying the Keiths. That's when we learned the Gunns had ridden upon our land. Uncle Henry isnae ye, but now that Father isnae alive, he's more responsible than he ever was before."

Hamish mulled over his options as he gazed down at Amelia. If he left, it would end their courtship. He didn't know when he would return to Stirling, and he didn't doubt Roy would betroth her with haste the moment his horse's tail swished past the gate. Her assessment of the situation confirmed yet again why he knew she was the best woman to become his wife. She brought knowledge and connections, but she also could analyze situations and assess them without getting lost in emotion. She was steadfast in her counsel, and that's what Hamish needed. No one raised him to be laird. That was his older brother's role. But her mother raised Amelia to be a chatelaine, and she clearly understood politics. Having her by his side would help Hamish grow into the role thrust upon him.

"If I receive reports and send missives, do ye believe Uncle Henry could continue to lead for the next moon?"

Kyla and Liam looked at each other before Liam responded. "If that's the only option, then aye. He could."

"It isnae the sole option, but it is the only option if I wish to court Amelia. I'm certain ye ken now why I wish to marry Amelia." Hamish peered down at her upturned face as she turned back to face him. He would gladly get lost staring into her eyes for hours at a time. "Other than Kyla, I dinna ken another woman who could be laird. Hell, half the men I ken shouldnae be lairds compared to them."

Amelia beamed at him, and he wished they were alone. Liam glanced at Kyla, and they exchanged a knowing look. They'd been just like Hamish and Amelia only a few months earlier. Now they had no reason to hide their affection or desire since they were married.

"Hamish, what's yer plan then?" Liam asked, regretful that he would interrupt the couple's private moment, but he had his own reasons for needing Hamish's decision.

"I'll send a missive to Uncle Henry telling him ma expectations. Then I'd receive regular reports from now on. Mayhap I'll have a couple of ma men sail rather than ride for most of the journey. I continue to court Amelia. If she agrees to marry me, then we wed at Balnagown before going to Dunrobin."

"Ye'd want us to marry at Balnagown?" Amelia's brow furrowed. She couldn't imagine him living past his first step under the portcullis.

"I think ye would like yer family and people to see ye before ye move away and join a new clan."

"Willna yer people want to witness that since I'll be the new Lady Sutherland?"

"They'll have ye for the rest of yer life. Yer family willna see ye as often. If ye wish to marry there, then we will. If ye wish to marry here or Dunrobin, then ye need only tell me. Assuming ye decide we should wed."

"Ye make it sound like I'm the only one who needs to decide."

"Ye are, lass. I already ken."

Amelia smiled again, warmth suffusing all of her. Hamish observed Liam and Kyla step away and put their heads together as though they had something important to discuss. Liam's wink told him they were conspiring to give Amelia and him privacy. He pulled her tight against his chest, and she glanced over her shoulder at the Sinclairs then over Hamish's at the guards. Since she could barely see the men, she knew she was too short for any of them to see much of her. Hamish's expansive back shielded her from prying eyes. He cupped her left cheek as he lowered his head. Their lips met, and it was just as searing a kiss as the one they shared in the garden that morning.

She opened to him, growing accustomed to the arousing yet slightly strange sensation of Hamish's tongue being inside her mouth. She grew brave and pressed hers forward. His hand slid from her cheek into her hair as he cupped her head. She kept her hands on his chest since wrapping her arms around his neck would only make it irrefutable to the guards that they were kissing. Neither wanted it to end. They both had to remind themselves they weren't alone and to keep their hands from roaming. When they pulled back, they shared three pecks before their gazes locked. Amelia hadn't spoken with the same certainty as Hamish had about their future, but she felt it. She'd met plenty of Highlanders at gatherings, and she'd met men from all parts of Scotland and even foreign countries while at court. But none of them appealed to her. They definitely weren't a consideration now.

"Hamish," Liam interrupted. "If ye're staying here, then Kyla and I will rest for a couple days before returning to Dunbeath. Yer sister needs a break from traveling."

Hamish's brow furrowed. He didn't understand why Amelia stepped forward tentatively but offered Kyla an embrace.

"Felicitations?" Amelia wondered.

"Aye."

"What are ye celebrating?" Hamish looked at his sister then his brother-by-marriage. Then it dawned on him. "Am I to be an uncle?"

"Aye," Kyla chirped. Amelia stepped back, and Liam engulfed his petite bride in his arms. "Poor mon nearly drove me barmy while we traveled back to Dunbeath from Dunrobin. I was poorly and sleepy. He wouldnae give me any peace until I admitted ma suspicions. The midwife confirmed it."

Amelia knew they'd only been married a couple moons, but she suspected they couldn't keep their hands off one another. Just the way they looked at each other, never mind how Liam held his bride now, told Amelia that it likely wasn't difficult for Kyla to get with child so quickly. As she felt Hamish step close to her again, she shifted to make room for him to embrace his sister. As she watched them, she wondered what it would be like to know she carried a bairn she made with Hamish. She wondered what it would be like to spend their nights in each other's arms as they made love. As she observed him, she didn't get the sense he'd ever treat coupling with her as just rutting to get her with child. But mayhap she read too much into their kisses. She considered it might be more emotional for her than for him. But when he reached out his hand to her after grasping forearms in a warrior handshake with Liam, her concern fell away. His smile and the way he glanced at her belly told her he shared her sentiments.

"I ken ye should return to the other ladies, and I'm feeling ma fatigue. But mayhap ye would walk with me tomorrow while Liam and Hamish talk. Liam willna let me out of his sight here, so Hamish will have to join us." Kyla looked past Amelia and smirked at her older brother, but her smile was conspiratorial with Amelia.

"Thank ye." Amelia loved her brothers, but they would never be close like they were when they were very young. She hoped Kyla would become a close friend.

The Sinclairs led the way from the antechamber before continuing on to the passageway leading to the stairs that would take them to the Sinclairs' suite, rooms set aside for the earl's or his family's visits. Hamish looked forward to retiring to his, but he longed for the time when he wouldn't be alone. Hamish and Amelia watched them walk away before he brought Amelia's hand to his lips. Then he watched her slip back into the Great Hall. The ladies-in-waiting gathered, so he knew they would soon retire. It surprised him that the queen was leaving the Great Hall so early, but he didn't fear abandoning Amelia to her father for too long. As he wound his way through the keep to the same floor upon which Kyla and Liam had their suite, he knew someone followed him. He just couldn't tell who.

CHAPTER 9

The next sennight passed with a mixture of bliss and torture for Amelia and Hamish. They walked together for the first three days while Kyla and Liam remained at court. Just as Kyla suggested, Amelia kept her company while Hamish and Liam spoke because Liam refused to let Kyla out of his sight at Stirling. He was a doting husband who trusted no one with his wife's safety but himself. Between being a former Sutherland and now a Sinclair, along with her beauty, Liam feared the type of attention Kyla would receive if left to navigate court alone. She wasn't well versed yet in the duplicity of courtly society.

Once those first few days ended, it became harder for Hamish and Amelia to have time to talk. While the pair had walked with the Sinclair couple, they'd all spoken as equals. The men valued the women's opinions, and the women appreciated being listened to. After the Sinclairs left, the queen insisted upon Amelia always walking with the other ladies-in-waiting. So, the first two mornings, Queen Isabella excluded Hamish from the walk altogether. But for the last two mornings, he and Amelia "happened" to meet near the doors before the other women joined them after the morning meal. They led the way outside and into the gardens, which forced the queen to accept Hamish's company, even if she made it clear he was unwelcome. It was at the end of one of their walks when Hamish noticed the undercroft in the shade. He wondered if he might convince Amelia to steal a few moments alone with him.

"I must visit the fletcher before the upcoming hunt," Hamish stated, apropos of nothing during a rare lull in their conversation. "I wonder if he will be busy."

"If ye go soon, ye can catch him after the men finish at the targets but before the midday meal. But be brief. He isnae a mon keen to miss any meals."

"I've seen him. I ken what ye mean." Hamish wracked his mind for a reason for her to go with him or to meet him in the undercroft afterward. It wouldn't matter if he didn't go to the fletcher at all. "Would ye care to see the falconry? I ken it's near the fletcher."

Amelia looked in the direction in which the arrow maker and the hunting birds lay. She realized their route would take them past the undercroft with its cool and dim spaces no one would visit during late morning. She glanced up at Hamish. "Aye. I would."

"Can ye walk there with me? Or would ye have to meet me?" Hamish ensured his words wouldn't carry on the light breeze that lifted the hair from Amelia's shoulders in a tantalizing wave.

"I can meet ye there. I canna tarry for too long, but I will find an excuse," Amelia answered as they, and the rest of the queen's entourage, reached the end of the gardens. She whispered, "Give me five minutes."

Hamish turned to face her and offered her his hand, as had become their routine at the end of their walks. Amelia rested her palm in his before he brought the back to his lips. He brushed his against the smooth skin as his thumb stroked hers. But it only lasted a couple heartbeats before he let her go. He bowed as the queen passed them, and Amelia fell into line with her fellow ladies. He watched them go into the keep before he hurried to the fletcher. He would use the few minutes he had to check on the order of new arrows he's placed. He would attach his own feathers to the end, being very particular about them, but he knew the man's expert craftmanship for the wood projectiles. He paid and gathered his quiver before slipping into the undercroft. He stood beneath an archway, out of sight but where he could spy Amelia.

"Lia," Hamish stage whispered. She was looking for him when she appeared to stroll by. But he already knew her well enough to tell it was her purposeful walk that was meant to fool people into thinking she merely glided from one place to another. He'd strolled with her many times in the garden and along the river-bank when they went riding. He could tell the difference. She glanced around before joining him. They retreated into the shadows.

"This way," Amelia murmured. She took his hand without a second thought and led them into the area near the buttery. She scanned their surroundings until they reached a door to a store-room she believed was empty.

"Wait," Hamish breathed. He shifted and pressed her to his far side. He eased the door open and peeked inside. The outside light was so dim it did little to illuminate the storage area. But he was certain there was no one inside. When they stepped in, and he shut the door, it pitched them into darkness. A sole window near the ceiling did little to circulate the stifling air or allow light into the room with stacks of grain. But neither cared.

They came together in a needy kiss that held no finesse but all their unsatisfied longing for one another. Their hands roamed over the other's body, savoring each inch they discovered. Hamish dropped his quiver to the ground. He kept his sporran between them, worried his turgid length would frighten her. If only he'd known how much she longed to discover what lay behind it. But Amelia was too timid to suggest anything or move it herself. She feared what he would think of her brazenness, even if he seemed to enjoy her eagerness.

Soon mere kisses weren't enough. Hamish lifted her, and she wrapped her legs around him, grateful her full skirts allowed her the room to do that. He'd spied a table while the light was behind him. He could see its vague outline, so he moved toward it, careful not to bump into it when he got close. He placed Amelia on the flat surface as they continued to kiss. He moved without haste as he drew her skirts up to her ankles. When she didn't protest, he bared her calves and slipped his hands around the muscled flesh.

Amelia's legs wrapped around Hamish's as his hands ran up to her thighs. When he grasped them, she tried to pull herself closer. She clutched his leine and arched her back. She cupped his neck then his jaw. She ran her fingers through his hair and down his back. His palms inched up her thighs until her reached her hips. He pulled her to the edge of the table, but his sporran finally irritated them both too much. He pushed it around his waist, allowing his sword to press against her sheath. It was the first time she'd felt a man's arousal pressed to her mound. Amelia's moan was nearly his undoing.

"Do ye ken what it means?" Hamish was unaware of how much Amelia knew about how couples came together.

"I ken what it means," Amelia assured him.

As though speaking to one another silently, Amelia leaned back at the same time Hamish leaned forward until her shoulders brushed the tabletop. He lifted her hips, so he could notch his rod at her entrance. If they had no clothes between them, he would have thrust and entered her. Claimed her. Instead, they moved together just as they would one day when they could finally join as one. His fingers bit into her flesh until he worried he would leave marks. When he eased his hold, Amelia's hands flew to his through the clothing that separated them, pressing his fingertips deeper.

"I'll leave marks yer maid will recognize," Hamish whispered.

"She prepares ma bath, but she doesnae help me with it. It wouldnae cause suspicion if she only saw me in ma chemise for a few days. I would ken they're there though. I would see them." Amelia felt his breath beside her ear when he'd whispered. Now it tickled her neck as he kissed along it, tightening his grip as he did. She let go of her hesitation and gathered his plaid over his backside. She sat up as best she could while he continued to kiss her neck and shoulder. Her hands grasped his chiseled behind. She'd felt nothing like it. When she squeezed, she felt his rod jerk. She didn't know why he groaned then froze. She feared she'd done something wrong, but he was soon moving against her as he had before. It ignited need unlike anything she'd felt before. She ached but didn't know what to do to ease it. She didn't know what to ask for or what to tell Hamish to do.

In turn, Hamish appreciated the darkness since Amelia couldn't see how his cheeks heated. The moment she'd grabbed his backside and pressed him tighter against her mound, he'd lost control and spent himself. He feared she would know why his cock jerked between them. But she made no sign that she understood what had just happened. That he hadn't shocked her, and that she hadn't recoiled in horror or amusement, made him even hungrier for more of her. While he might have found his release, he was unconvinced he should take their interlude far enough for him to bring her to climax. He wanted to offer the relief and pleasure he'd found, but he didn't want to ruin the moment by doing something she didn't want or that might scare her.

They continued to move together, kissing and touching, until voices floated to them outside the storeroom. They froze, both looking toward the door. Whomever was outside passed close enough for them to hear footsteps. It was a bucket of frigid water. It reminded them of all they risked if they were found together. It would force them to marry but not with the respect they believed their partner deserved. Neither worried for their own reputation but that of the person they were growing to love.

Hamish stepped back, his ardor cooled from the interruption and his no longer aching bollocks. He helped Amelia arrange her skirts, then eased her to her feet. They wrapped their arms around one another, neither ready to leave their little hideaway. After the lust came a moment of loving affection. The last kiss they shared was little more than a peck before Hamish gathered his quiver, and they slipped out of the room to go in opposite directions.

WITH THE KING'S permission to court, neither the queen nor the Mistress of the Bedchamber, who oversaw the ladies-in-waiting, could deny Amelia time with Hamish in the afternoons. He went to the lists after his walks with Amelia, refreshed himself before the midday meal, and went riding with her after they'd eaten. They took a contingency of Ross and Sutherland guards, but Roy insisted Henrietta accompany them as a chaperone. She unsur-prisingly proved to be a constant irritation to both Hamish and Amelia. She inserted herself into every conversation and often forced herself between them when they rode or walked. When Amelia wasn't looking but guards were, she'd smile coyly at Hamish and even winked. He attempted to pay her no attention, which was a challenge since she liked to brush against him any chance she had.

Amelia noticed everything Henrietta did. It infuriated her more than hurt her. She expected her cousin to disregard her feelings in everything. She always had since they were children. But her flagrant attempts to seduce Hamish were beyond the pale. Amelia didn't fear Hamish's intentions straying. It was the inconvenience of Henrietta always being present that led Amelia to thoughts of violence. She appreciated Hamish's tact when he maneuvered around Henrietta, figuratively and literally, and always came to her side. Henrietta was a skilled rider, but she hadn't spent as many hours in the saddle as Hamish, nor did she have the natural balance and strength Amelia possessed. Once Hamish realized this, he urged Amelia to race with him. They'd charge ahead, leaving Henrietta behind with two Ross guards. It was those times when Amelia felt freest and that Hamish believed her the loveliest. Her laughter and twinkling eyes beguiled him.

"Will ye join the hunt this evening?" Hamish wondered as they stood together beside a stream midway through the third week of their courtship. They'd sneaked away to the storeroom almost every day since their first interlude, but they never carried things further than they had the first time. Both wanted far more, but neither felt comfortable admitting it. Hamish didn't want to frighten Amelia with the full force of his ardor, and consequently, Amelia feared being far too forceful if she asked for or did more. They were quietly driving each other mad with unspent lust. But it was more than that. Each day spent in each other's company, and each touch and kiss became a way to show how deep their feelings grew. They spent as many hours together as they could, but it never felt enough.

Their horses guzzled the chilly water as the couple held hands. They knew Henrietta wouldn't join them for at least ten minutes given her staid pace.

"I dinna ken if I can. I'd like to." Amelia's wistful expression made Hamish committed to ensuring she rode out with him and the other hunters. He drew her in for a kiss as his free hand rested low on her back. His ring finger and little finger brushed against her bottom. He turned them, so Amelia's back was to the stream. He risked her rejection and others spying them because they were in the open, but he slid his hand down to cup her behind. She leaned into him, pressing her breasts to his chest. Lust pushed the kiss to new heights each time they came together. He squeezed her backside as he released her other hand. He skimmed up her ribs until it slipped between them to cup her breast. When she grew bolder with her kiss, he groaned. The sound surprised him since he hadn't intended to make one. After their first rendezvous in the storeroom and hearing people walk past, they were always careful to remain quiet. But he longed for her, and he didn't mind letting her know the effect she had on him. She fisted his leine, holding him close lest he step back before she was ready to end the interlude. When they were breathless, their lips pulled away, but their bodies remained pressed together.

"Lia, I ken we're in public, so I willna do more. But, lass, the way ye tempt me." He grinned and shook his head. Each kiss they shared tucked away in the undercroft or along the stream when they stopped to water their horses grew more passionate by the day. But it wasn't solely lust. It was far deeper than that.

"And ye dinna think ye tempt me?" She'd never believed the notion women couldn't and shouldn't enjoy physical relations with men. She hadn't held out hope she would ever enjoy it. But Hamish's kisses promised more than she'd dreamed of when she'd considered marriage in the past.

"I hope I tempt ye, *leannan*. I hope I tempt ye to want me in all the ways I want ye." They hadn't spoken of their emotions toward one another, but Hamish could wait no longer to know if Amelia felt what he did. It worried him that she was inexperienced, so curiosity drove her. It worried him that she enjoyed his company but wasn't falling in love the way he was. In turn, Amelia secretly shared the same fears.

"Do ye nae ken I'm attracted to ye? Dinna ma kisses tell ye that?"

"They do, but— is it just —is that all?" Hamish stumbled, then blurted his thoughts. Her hesitation was soul crushing.

"Do ye feel more?"

Hamish realized she feared he wanted her to admit her feelings, then wouldn't reciprocate. She feared being made a fool. "A lot more, Lia. So much more."

"Nay one has ever made me feel important before. Ye ask how I'm doing and truly listen. It isnae done as a courtesy before speaking aboot yerself. Ye ask me aboot things we've spoken aboot before. Nae because ye werenae listening and canna remember. Just the opposite. Ye listen and make me feel like ye care aboot what I say. I dinna think most women at court ever have this."

"What ye say interests me," Hamish told her. "But even when we arenae talking, I enjoy yer company. It brings me peace to stand here at the stream with ye and just look toward the Highlands. I enjoy seeing the excitement in yer eyes when we race. Yer patience with the banshee impresses me when I would like to do naught more than throttle her." Hamish glanced over his shoulder, knowing Henrietta and the other guards would catch up soon.

"I am nae patient. I just ken I canna kill her and have nay one notice." Amelia only partly jested. Her cousin had been particularly hideous that morning during the meal and their walk. She'd spoken to the other ladies, hinting Hamish used Amelia as an excuse to spend time with her instead of the other way around. She alluded to him preferring her over Amelia. She didn't think anyone believed Henrietta, but she didn't appreciate anyone listening in case it gave credence to the rumors Henrietta attempted to spread.

"She willna come on the hunt, will she?"

Amelia laughed derisively. "Nay. It's one thing she kens she canna be the center of attention at. She kens the men willna take any notice of her when they can prove their manhood while taunting one another."

"Good."

They stepped apart as they heard the approaching hoofbeats. But Hamish refused to let Amelia be out of his reach anytime they stopped during their rides. He held her hand and turned so the two of them faced downstream. Henrietta had to be their chaperone, but she didn't have to be part of their conversation. He figured if they got a head start as she climbed down from her saddle, pride would keep her from chasing after them.

"Hamish?" Henrietta called out. He pretended not to hear her. "Hamish!" She veritably squawked his name.

With a sigh and a glance down at Amelia, they turned around. "Aye."

"Can ye check ma saddle? Something doesnae feel right."

Hamish shot a glance to one of his warriors. Guilt tugged at him, but he proceeded anyway. "Gareth was a stable lad before he started training in the lists. He kens far more than I do aboot tack and horses." It wasn't entirely true. The man was five years older than Hamish, so he'd started working before Hamish could. That extra time with horses was the only thing that justified the claim he knew more. Hamish had been tending to his steed since he was ten summers. There was little he didn't know about the animals.

"But—"

Hamish had already turned away, and Amelia followed. His stride was long, so his pace wasn't faster than usual. But it forced Amelia to take two steps to his every one. She knew she looked as though she sprinted to keep up. But they were soon in a copse of trees that hid them from the others. Their kiss was hungry as they devoured one another again. Admitting their feelings, then being interrupted left them even more unsatisfied than their brief daily trysts. Both of his hands cupped her backside after she pushed his sporran out of the way. She tilted her hips forward, wanting to rub herself against him. When he held her tight and rocked his hips, she thought she would lose her mind with need. She could think of nothing more than how she wanted more.

"Lia, it's just as well we arenae alone. Otherwise, I would ravish ye. Mayhap it's the fresh air or being able to see ye in the bright light, but I want ye more than I ever have. And I dinna ken how that's possible."

"Is it ravishing if I want it just as much?"

"Would ye ravish me then?"

"Och, aye, *m'eudail.*"

"I canna hear ye call me that enough, *mo ghaol.*" They both froze for a moment, gazes locked, before Hamish cupped her cheek. "I let that slip, but ye are ma love. I ken it hasnae been nearly long enough for most people to believe what I feel is more than infatuation, but I ken what I ken. This isnae fleeting."

Amelia lifted her chin and offered him a soft kiss before responding. "Ye are *mo chridhe* because ye have ma heart. I would call ye ma heart in Gaelic or Scots, French or English. Any language speaks the truth. This isnae fleeting for me either, Hamish. Ye and I both ken the moon is for everyone else to accept us. Even if we kenned each other years, there would still be things to discover aboot each other once we married. Either way, we will have to learn to live with each other. But how I feel willna change."

"Yer wisdom is likely what I love most aboot ye." He squeezed her backside with both hands. "But I'm fond of the rest of ye, too."

"Ma laird?"

Hamish and Amelia froze again, but not because they liked what they heard. He released her as a guard approached. "Aye, Martin?"

"Campbells are approaching. Ah— ah —if they stop, and Lady Henrietta is the only one there— I thought ye might wish to speak to them, too." Hamish's guard didn't let his gaze stray to Amelia, but it was clear he warned them Henrietta would gossip.

"Thank ye." Hamish wrapped Amelia's arm around his as they walked back with Martin, who fell in behind them just before they stepped out of the trees. It wouldn't look like he fetched them and was leading them back. He kept an appropriate distance that made it look like a guard following his laird. They'd just reached the rest of their party when the Campbells' laird came into clear sight. If they could see his face, then he could see theirs. None of the approaching riders slowed.

"Sutherland," the laird said with a dip of his chin.

"Campbell." Hamish returned the greeting in kind before the riders continued. He wished to sigh with relief, but he felt Henrietta watching him. He knew he'd had an extra shadow more than once, and he suspected it was Henrietta. The only reason he hadn't confronted whoever followed him was because he didn't wish for anyone, particularly his new nemesis, to claim he'd chosen to speak to her alone. It never took him long to lose his pursuer. He didn't know Stirling Castle better than anyone who lived there, but he was better at tracking than being tracked.

"You should have greeted him properly, Hamish. Then he would have known he was welcome to stop," Henrietta chided.

"Ma lady, use ma given name one more time, and ye will come to learn nae to anger an earl." Hamish led Amelia past her stunned cousin. He knew he shouldn't have reacted, but scowling at her for her informalities did nothing. Rude as he was, he wished others were around to hear him. Then it might squelch the rumors he knew she attempted to spread. Even without Amelia, he would never consider someone as conniving as Henrietta.

AMELIA STOOD with her father in the bailey as his diatribe about her not joining the hunt garnered more and more attention. When the trio had returned from their ride, Henrietta and Amelia joined the other attendants in the queen's solar while Hamish read a newly arrived missive from his uncle. Now a group gathered with their horses to ride out for the late afternoon hunt. The nearly autumn sun would provide light for several more hours.

Amelia cringed internally as Hamish approached. She realized he'd overheard her father lecturing her about how she couldn't attend the hunt because women weren't welcome, which wasn't entirely true, and that he wouldn't tolerate her flirtation with Hamish in front of everyone. Most people would have taken little notice of her presence if he hadn't been caterwauling. When Hamish came to stand beside Amelia, he kept his voice low.

"Ross, Lady Amelia is ma guest. She rides with me."

"She is not your guest. She is my daughter."

"She is to be ma wife. Ye can keep refusing, but Lady Amelia being here tells ye her choice. She rides with me." Hamish escorted Amelia to her mount.

"Ye ken ma feelings because I told ye earlier," Amelia said. "But the animosity between ye and Father still concerns me. I fear what he'll do next."

"Lass, whatever he does isnae yer fault. He's a mon who makes his own choices. If his pettiness is so great that he'd risk his clan's wellbeing, then that is his burden."

"But—"

"Wheest, *mo ghaol*. It will all come right. Dinna fash."

"I trust ye, but I dinna think ye're right. Mayhap me riding out isnae such a good idea. We dinna need to antagonize him."

"Lia, do ye enjoy hunting?"

"Aye. I've told ye I do."

"Then ye're coming." Hamish lifted her into the saddle before turning to his horse. He'd told the stablemaster to ensure their horses waited together since he'd expected Roy to cause a scene. He swung into the saddle not needing the stirrup, then adjusted his plaid as he watched Amelia ensure her skirts covered as much of her legs as she could. "Do ye ride astride?"

"I can."

Riding sidesaddle kept Amelia and Hamish from truly

pushing their horses when they raced. It made Hamish anxious about them going too fast. He looked around and noticed there were still plenty of mounts without their riders, and the king hadn't arrived. He got off his horse and signaled the stablemaster he trusted.

"Is there a proper saddle Lady Amelia can use?" Hamish whispered.

"Aye. I can find one, ma laird."

"Please do, but wait a moment." Hamish walked around to Amelia's horse. He acted as though he checked the girth, which he'd done while they talked a moment ago. When he reached up for her, she leaned forward. He spoke as he lifted her down. "Something seems off. Timothy will set it to rights."

He handed the reins to the man while Amelia looked up at him befuddled. She turned her head to watch her gelding follow the stablemaster. Her brow furrowed before looking back up at Hamish. "There's naught wrong with ma saddle. If I am nae ready when the king arrives, it willna matter what either of us wants. Everyone will leave me behind."

"First of all, I willna leave ye behind. I never will. Second of all, the king willna arrive until everyone is mounted and been waiting at least ten minutes. It wouldnae surprise me if the mon is watching us from a window to ensure he keeps *everyone* waiting."

"There's still naught wrong with ma saddle."

"I dinna like it." Hamish put his hands on his waist, his thumbs tucked into his belt.

"Mayhap standing like that makes others think twice aboot questioning ye, but it does naught to intimidate me. What is wrong with ma saddle, Hamish?"

"There isnae aught wrong. I just dinna like it."

"Dinna be obtuse. Ye ken what I'm asking. Are ye trying to pick our first quarrel?"

"Nay, but ye are stunning with the ire flashing in yer bonnie eyes." Hamish winked. He truly enjoyed seeing her like this, even if his conscience nagged at him not to start an argument. But he feared she would refuse a different saddle if he told her while there was time for her to stop the stablemaster. He didn't doubt she would prefer to ride astride, but for propriety's sake, she would never ask.

"And ye may still be the brawest mon I've ever seen, but that doesnae mean we arenae aboot to argue."

"Ye say the kindest things, lass." Hamish didn't hesitate when he leaned forward to kiss her cheek. Amelia's head whipped from side to side, terrified someone was watching them. Plenty were.

"Hamish," she hissed.

"Ye ken ma affection is genuine, but it doesnae hurt for others to see. We both ken what Henrietta's been trying to do."

"Aye, and people will say ye're laying it on thick to distract from yer affair with her."

"Say things like that, and I might kiss ye senseless so nay one doubts ma feelings for ye."

"Causing a scandal would force us to marry," Amelia admitted.

"That isnae how we will start our life together. I willna countenance any speculation aboot the Countess of Sutherland's virtue."

Amelia stared at Hamish. She knew marrying Hamish would make her a countess, but she'd never heard anyone use the title in relation to her. She nodded.

"Lia?"

"I just hadnae truly considered the title I would inherit when we marry." Nervousness that she wouldn't live up to the expectations of a countess flooded her.

"*Leannan,* there is little more to being a countess than being the lady of a clan. Ye will be a natural at both. One more reason why I ken ye're the right woman for me." He took her hand and brushed his thumb over the back of it before letting go. They waited five more minutes before a stableboy led Amelia's gelding to them.

"Timothy said this should work for ma lady." The boy didn't wait for any response before hurrying back to help with other steeds. Hamish checked the saddle before turning to Amelia. He put his hands around her waist, but she placed hers on top of his to halt him.

"Ye truly wish to cause a scandal, dinna ye?"

"I truly wish to keep ye safe. If ye can ride astride, ye should. The mounts will jostle one another, and the men will race. Ye ken that. This is a larger hunt than the ones ye're likely used to. I'd feel better with ye on this saddle."

She gazed up at him, her hands sliding up his arms until they rested just beneath his elbows. "Thank ye, *mo ghaol*. Thank ye for insisting I come when ye ken I wouldnae be allowed to without ye. Thank ye for worrying aboot me and wanting to take care of me."

"Always, Lia. Always." Hamish lifted her into the saddle. They hadn't actually said I love you yet. He wanted to, but he wouldn't say it for the first time in a crowded bailey. He'd intended to do it in the woods, but they were interrupted. He swung back into his saddle just as the horn blew to announce the king's arrival. It was obvious he expected more fanfare for his arrival. Only the most ambitious courtiers greeted the monarch. Everyone else merely wished to get on with the hunt.

"Stay near me, Lia."

"Keep up, Hamish."

CHAPTER 10

The riders trotted through the gates before cantering down the hillside that led to the woods outside Stirling Castle. They would pass through it before reaching a meadow for the hunt. Hamish ensured Amelia stayed beside him the entire time. It was immediately obvious the new saddle was a better choice than the sidesaddle. Riding astride made it easier for her to maneuver her horse among the crowd and to lie over the horse's withers as they passed below low-hanging branches. She was an expert on a woman's saddle, but she was a natural riding astride. Hamish hadn't realized it until he saw her, but it relieved him to think she would be safer when they journeyed to Dunrobin. That made him picture them in the laird's chamber and all the things they would do together with the door shut.

The kisses they shared only whet his appetite. He wanted more, and he was certain she did, too. He longed to introduce her to true ardor. He longed to discover it for himself. He'd bedded other women and enjoyed himself, but nothing compared to the near overpowering urges Amelia stirred within him. Every time he glanced at her, he needed to shift in his seat. His bollocks ached, and his rod had its own mind. He hadn't explained what happened during their first tryst, and he'd maintained better control of his lower half since then. But it took all his concentration and resolve since he slid his hands beneath her skirts each time. He never brought them close to her mons, and while she slipped her hands beneath his plaid, she never moved them near his shaft.

Her hair streamed out behind her as they entered the meadow, and the wind had already pinkened her cheeks. But it was her smile. She relished the excitement of their brisk ride and the ensuing pursuit. They'd discussed hunting, and he knew she didn't see it as a sport but as a means to support her clan or the people residing in the castle. Whatever was caught that day would go to the keep's kitchens to be served the next day or cured for the winter.

"There." Amelia nudged her chin to the left while most of the riders steered to the right. Hamish immediately spotted the animals hiding in the tall grass, observing the riders as they decided whether to scatter. The stable hands had tied her bow to both saddles, and she wore her quiver. As they'd trotted through the field, she'd unfastened the weapon. She let other riders pass her, and she knew Hamish would follow her rather than the pack. She nudged her horse forward but at a walk. "Can I take the shot?"

"Of course. Ye spied them." Hamish watched in amazement as she lifted her bow and nocked an arrow as her mount continued to walk forward. He reined in, not wanting two enormous beasts approaching the deer to startle them. He marveled at her strength to rise in the saddle, draw back the string, and launch the arrow with precision at a distance he doubted would allow the arrow to fly far enough. He underestimated her skill. The projectile whipped through the air and landed in a stag's neck. He knew it imbedded in the main artery, and the animal fell. Before it landed on the ground, Amelia released her next arrow. It flew just as true and impaled a doe in the heart.

"If those fawns were any younger, I wouldnae have shot their mother. They're auld enough to fend for themselves," Amelia justified as Hamish joined her.

"Ye dinna have to explain. I would have done the same." Hamish rode alongside her as they went to inspect her kills. Before they drew too far from the rest of the hunters, he released an earsplitting whistle that would signal they'd bagged an animal. The young deer were too stunned to flee when their parents died, but they bolted as Hamish and Amelia drew close. Amelia climbed out of the saddle at the same time as Hamish. "Ye should wait for me, Lia."

"Why? Do ye fear they'll come back to life, and the stag will gore me?"

"Nay. If ye get on and off yer horse by yerself, I willna have an excuse to touch ye." He shot her a wolfish grin as they walked toward the slain animals.

"Is that all ye think aboot now that I've let ye kiss me?" Amelia teased.

"That's all I thought aboot before *ye* kissed *me*." He nudged her shoulder with his.

"Wheest, ye daft mon."

"If I'm daft, it's yer fault. Ye drive all other thoughts from ma mind."

"How ye blather." Amelia shook her head before she kneeled beside the buck. Hamish inspected the hind. It surprised him just how deeply the arrow rested in the deer's heart. The projectile had flown with more force than Hamish expected.

"Amelia, how'd ye learn to shoot like this?"

"Believe it or nae, Father taught me. He doesnae mind me hunting. Truthfully, he complained aboot the propriety of me joining the group, but I ken he fears for me amongst so many horses and men. Ma horse is as large as any of the others, but ye ken how the men are. They dinna care aboot aught but the competition for the animal and the king's praise. He wouldnae admit it, but he worried I'd be knocked from or thrown from ma horse."

They had no time to say more as a group of riders approached. He recognized mostly Lowlanders since they wore leggings and doublets, but there were two MacLeods of Assynt, a MacDonald, and four Mackenzies in the group. It was obvious the Highlanders ignored the Lowlanders, and the sentiment was mutual. How they'd wound up together, Hamish was unsure.

"Well done, Sutherland." The MacDonald rider nodded to Hamish.

"These arenae ma kills. It was Lady Amelia who took down both."

The men laughed, and Hamish scowled while Amelia ignored them. She drew her dirk and was ready to pry the arrows loose. Her ease with her knife spoke to her experience and should have been proof enough.

"Come now, mon. We ken ye're courting the lass, but ye dinna need to pretend. We dinna believe yer flattery," a MacLeod stated.

"Samuel, shut yer gob." Hamish withdrew one of his arrows and ran his thumb over the fletching. "These dinna match what's in those deer. And before ye say I already pulled mine out, do ye see more than one wound on either animal? Do ye see any other bluidy arrows? Nay, ye dinna. *Lady Amelia* took down what I'm certain will be the largest stag today." While he knew women well into their nineties would be called lass, he didn't like the informality. And he also knew he didn't exaggerate about her accomplishment. The male deer was one of the largest he'd ever seen. He'd known it was big from a distance, but it was massive up close.

He strode back to his horse and pulled rope from his saddlebag. He returned to Amelia's side and tied the four sets of hooves into matching pairs. He wasn't entirely sure he'd be able to lift the doe alone. The stag would be impossible since he was certain it was close to four hundred and fifty pounds. He was certain the hind was well over two hundred and seventy when he lifted the hindquarters to gauge the weight. That was the same as some of his heaviest warriors he'd trained to carry. It would be a struggle, but he grew confident he could— if he could lift it to his shoulders.

"Rather than gawping with yer mouths open, get down and help me with the beasts. Two of ye must take the stag. MacDonald, take ma mount, please." Hamish gave directions to men he'd known for years. Each was a laird, tánaiste, or second-in-command. Only two moons ago, two out of the three groups outranked him. Now, not only did he bear an equal title to two of them, but he also outranked all of them as an earl. He didn't give the orders because of that, but he noted that drastic shift in his status. Blessedly, the Lowlanders remained quiet, though he witnessed their ongoing skepticism that Amelia killed the deer. It annoyed him.

"Ma laird, I willna be able to reach any of the branches sturdy enough to carry the stag," Amelia stated quietly. She wanted to hurry, so most of the men would return to the hunt. The attention made her uncomfortable, but she had to admit there was little more she could do. The stag needed binding to two solid branches, so a couple men could heft it and carry it back to the cart where they'd place all the kills.

Hamish stepped beside her and didn't speak as softly. "Which one of them are ye talking to because if it's me, ye ken I'm called Hamish." He would ensure all the men understood he supported Amelia, and he knew the men would gossip as much as the women. He wanted them to tell the world he only granted Amelia that privilege. Men who'd outranked him only recently now had to address him by at least his clan name unless he gave them leave to do otherwise in public. Thus far, he hadn't.

Amelia's stare told him she didn't appreciate his forthright manner as much as he'd hoped. But she knew people watched them, and she couldn't remain annoyed long when his expression changed to one of contrition. His back was to the others, so she knew they couldn't see either of their faces. He blocked her from their view just as he had the guardsmen when they spoke to Liam and Kyla in the king's antechamber. She offered him a smile that grew into a grin.

"Hamish, would ye find me a couple branches, please?"

"Aye, ma lady." He winked at her, and each time he did, she experienced a rush of giddiness. But she forced a neutral mien when he stepped away.

"One of ye come along. Ye ken none of us can reach high enough without sitting on someone else's shoulders. Sticks willna do the work." He looked pointedly at the Lowlanders who appeared ready to turn back. None were small men; each having fought along the border against the English for years. They just weren't as huge as the brawny Highlanders.

"We'll get them, Sutherland." The Elliot tánaiste offered, and the other men from his clan dismounted and followed. Amelia remained quiet while the rest made small talk, waiting for the men and branches to return. Hamish stood beside her and only commented when asked questions directly.

It didn't take the Elliots long to carry two branches strong enough to bear the buck's weight. The Mackenzie tánaiste and second offered to take care of it as they tied a branch between each set of hooves before hoisting the wood onto their shoulders to carry the deer to their mounts. They would tie the buck to their saddles and ride with it between them. In the meantime, Hamish lifted Amelia onto her horse.

"Lady Amelia, how did you keep them from spooking if you stood so close?" Dennis MacLeod asked. The assumption that she'd had to not only stand in one spot but practically be on top of the deer to hit them annoyed Hamish, but he concentrated on lifting the hind and accepting help to balance it across his shoulders.

"We walked our horses until we were, I'd say, nearly a hundred and fifty yards away."

"Closer to two hundred, ma lady," Hamish corrected softly. She'd shot from a distance that tested even the most experienced archers firing from a battlement.

"Not possible," the MacLeod of Assynt second-in-command scoffed.

Hamish turned toward the man as he bounced the animal to a more comfortable position. "Have ye ever kenned me to exaggerate, Dennis?" The man was one of the few at court who Hamish considered a friend and with whom he'd allow the informality of exchanging given names.

"Well, no. But the strength needed to fire from that distance. That's not what a la—woman can do."

Hamish suspected Dennis was about to call Amelia a lass before catching himself. "Ma lady, how long have ye been hunting?"

Amelia still wished they could just find the cart, dump the animals, and go back to hunting. "Since I was eight summers."

"Is that when ye learned to use a bow and arrow?" Hamish pressed. He already knew the answer.

"Nay. Ma father wouldnae let me hunt until I had experience with the weapon. He didna want me shooting someone in the arse by accident. I started with the bow when I was six summers." Amelia grinned to lighten her explanation, maybe even downplay pointing out that she'd been shooting for nearly two decades.

Hamish's expression clearly said, "see," without him uttering another word. He took his first step with the girthy hind and focused on not stumbling as he gritted his teeth. Since the female was so heavy, he knew the men who carried the male must have struggled, too. Amelia walked her horse at Hamish's speed and refused to ride off with the others when he suggested she rejoin the hunt. She didn't want to leave him behind, and he was glad she stayed nearby. He simply didn't want her to feel like she missed out because of his slow pace.

When they reached the cart that already had several felled deer, Hamish turned and leaned back to lower the one he carried. The two Mackenzies, Amelia, and Hamish stared at the rickety cart, then the stag. If they piled it on top, there would be no room for anything else. Its antlers alone would make it awkward to position it to fit. It was obvious the Mackenzies would have to carry it back to the keep, or it would have to be handed off to another pair of riders.

"Sutherland, must you show up everyone?" King John boomed as he approached. "We know how strong you are without you carrying your kill back like a conquering barbarian. Which of you two took down that beauty?" He peered at the stag.

"Your Majesty," Ulrich Mackenzie answered. "Neither of us shot this animal. Lady Amelia did."

King John's expression was so patronizing Hamish wanted to punch him. "Did you see the lady do it?"

"No, Your Majesty. But we saw the lady's fletching on the arrows in their chests."

"Their?" The king's brow furrowed.

"Aye. This stag and that hind on the top. She killed both of them."

Balliol looked at Hamish, then Amelia, then back to Hamish. "Laird Sutherland, you don't have to give the lass credit just because you wish to make a good impression."

Hamish stepped away from the cart, lifted Amelia from the horse, and slid his arm around her waist. His possessiveness and protectiveness radiated from him. "Lady Amelia, do I still need to make a good impression on ye?"

"Nay, ma laird. Ye already have."

"I'm proud of ma lady. She shot both animals, and she has the bluidy arrows with her fletching on them. None of ma arrows have bluid on them. And she didna give me any of hers to shoot with either. Ross, ye ken how well yer daughter can hunt since ye taught her. Did she do this?"

Roy nudged his horse forward, forcing other riders to move apart. He looked at both animals, then his daughter. "Absolutely."

Both men looked at the king, daring him to contradict two earls. The monarch nodded. "Well done, Lady Amelia. Naught else comes close so far, and the hunt is now over. We have no need for more."

Many grumbled. Having not bagged any animals themselves, several hunters wished to continue since there was more daylight. Anything not eaten in the next day or two, someone could cure and store, so they saw no reason not to continue. As the king's entourage rode back to the castle, Hamish and Amelia heard the whispers spreading about her success. Some voices carried louder than others. Until a booming comment from a man at the rear reached Hamish, he ignored them.

"That bitch didna kill a damn thing but the mood. He's sniffing up her skirts so high he's coming out the top. Likely after licking and sucking every bit in between. He'd do aught for that cunny. If ma wife had her tits, I might nae spend most nights in the tavern or plowing ma leman."

Hamish pulled his horse to such an abrupt stop it reared back, shaking its head. He ignored his mount's dismay and wheeled it around. He urged his horse forward against the flow, and people had no choice but to move aside lest he and his steed barrel through them.

"Get down," Hamish barked. He swung out of the saddle and strode over to the offensive man. He gave the man no opportunity to dismount on his own. Hamish grabbed the Highlander's leine and plaid, yanking him free of his horse and veritably tossing him to the ground. Hamish's boot landed in the man's belly. "Get up. Now, Chattan. I'll give ye a chance to die on yer feet."

Laird Malcolm Chattan knew his life was forfeit. He glanced

at his new son-by-marriage and blessed the saints he'd married his daughter off to the chieftain. He would leave his clan's future in the hands of a young man who would one day lead Clan Chattan and Clan Mackintosh. He stood and reached back for his sword. He wasn't as fast as Hamish.

Hamish slid his sword from its sheath. Its tip pressed against Malcolm's Adam's apple as Malcolm wrapped his hand around the hilt and withdrew his own weapon. Hamish poked him and pressed him back before taking his own step back, lowering his sword to waist-height. Amelia watched in horror. Humiliated by the comments everyone heard. Self-conscious about a physical feature that always embarrassed her. Terrified she would watch Hamish kill a man before her eyes.

"Ye deserve a thrashing for speaking aboot any lady the way ye just did. But to speak of the lady I love and am going to marry, ye had better pray I make this swift. I willna. But ye can pray." Hamish slashed his sword through the air, nearly severing the man's left arm mid-bicep. He thrust his sword into the wound and twisted, making Malcolm howl. "Ye didna think we could hear ye. Ye thought it would be all right to disparage the future Countess of Sutherland because ye thought I wouldnae ken. Ye thought ye were funny. Dead men dinna laugh."

He took an offensive stance but waited for Malcolm to raise his sword. He wouldn't execute the man, nor would he allow anyone to claim he murdered a man unprepared to defend himself. The wound gushed blood, and Malcolm would soon weaken, but he could still fight. Hamish knew his opponent had nearly lost a leg from a similar wound six years earlier. If he'd survived that to make it off the battlefield, he could survive a little longer.

"Ross, take Lady Amelia back to the keep." Hamish hadn't raised his voice to make his wish known. The steel in it told everyone what they already knew was inevitable.

Amelia stepped forward, but well away from either man's

reach. She looked at Hamish, then Malcolm, who she addressed. "Ye're vile. Yer wife is lucky she didna have to bear ye in her bed that often. And now she will be a widow. She's the true victor in this battle." She turned her head to Hamish. "I stay. Ye stood by me when nay one thought I killed those deer, and ye're standing by me now to defend ma honor. I'm going nay where. He willna be the first dead body I've seen. I'm a Highlander."

She stepped back to where her father had tried to keep her. She crossed her arms and nodded to Hamish. Their eyes locked when she turned her attention to him, and they remained that way until she dipped her chin. To him, it signaled the beginning of the true fight. He attacked but toyed with Malcolm. He nicked the man's other arm and both legs. He cut a deep wound from the man's right ribs to his left hip. His opponent put up the fight Hamish expected, which was better than most men could do.

"Do ye recant what ye said?" Hamish demanded.

"Aye. Ma apologies, ma lady."

"Have ye asked the Lord to forgive ye?"

"Aye, I have."

Hamish thrust his sword through the man's heart, yanking it back before severing Malcolm's neck from his shoulders. He walked over to the dead man and lifted his head by the hair, holding it up to the Mackintosh, new Laird Chattan. "I made sure it'll stand on yer high table. Let yer people ken who did this. Dinna slight the Earl of Sutherland, or ye willna come out the winner. I defend what's mine."

He let the head drop before wiping his sword across Malcolm's plaid, then sheathing it. He walked over to Amelia, entirely uncertain how she would react. She might have made her supportive pronouncement, but seeing him kill someone so violently might have changed her mind. Instead, she curtsied to him. When she stood, she clutched a handful of his leine, tugging hard as she went onto her toes. Then she did something no one expected. She kissed him.

Nothing prepared Hamish for Amelia's kiss, but he reacted immediately. He wrapped his arm around her waist, tunneling his free hand into her hair, and lifted her off her feet. He knew if they were alone she would have wrapped her legs around his waist. He was determined to experience it again before dawn. The kiss wasn't a polite peck. It left no one in doubt the couple would wed and probably have a bairn in nine moons to the day of the ceremony. Neither cared about the whispers, the king's comments, or Roy's insistence that they stop. Amelia's father tugged at Hamish's shoulder before stepping around him and trying to push him away. He only wound up with his fingers trapped between them when they both tightened their hold on each other.

"Sutherland, I shall lob off your tongue like you did Chattan's head if you don't get it out of my daughter's mouth," Roy murmured to his now inevitable son-by-marriage. But that could only happen if he lived to step before the altar. Roy's commitment to keeping them apart grew exponentially as his daughter and the man he now assumed was her lover continued to make a spectacle of themselves. When Hamish finally put Amelia back on her feet, their foreheads pressed together.

"I love ye more than aught, *mo chridhe*," Hamish whispered.

"Nae possible because ye canna love me more than I love ye, *mo ghràidh*. Thank ye for defending me."

"Always. I might have claimed ye in front of all these people in word and deed, but I am yers, Lia. Forever."

She cupped his cheek. "I ken."

As Hamish straightened, he winked at her. "Dinna think that's how I'm proposing."

Amelia's belly clenched and not from lust or excitement. She didn't want to meet her father's gaze or anyone else's. She wanted to exist in a bubble with just Hamish. But their actions would have repercussions. Neither thought otherwise. She just didn't know how severe they would be, even if she was certain they would be immediate.

"You were to wait a month, Sutherland. That is the time you asked for, and that is the time I gave you." Balliol's displeasure was clear in his voice and his expression as he came to stand beside the couple on the opposite side from Roy. "I didn't give you permission to wed, only to court."

"And I havenae proposed yet, so I ken we arenae betrothed. But naught changes the fact that I will marry Lady Amelia, so it doesnae matter who kens now since they'll all ken after." It was only after he finished speaking that he turned his focus from Amelia to the king. He trod dangerous ground, and he knew it. But word was spreading through the castle that the English would soon attack. The only questions were where and when. King John needed the Sutherlands too much to punish Hamish too severely. While his clan lost a number of warriors during the fight with the Rosses, they hadn't lost all of them from Dunrobin, and he had other men trained to fight who lived farther afield from his keep. His father and brothers might have mismanaged the clan, but their deaths hadn't ended the clan's strength. Just the opposite. The king knew that. It's why he hadn't passed a verdict in the matter with Roy.

Hamish slid his hand into Amelia's and led her to her horse. She enjoyed the feel of his hands around her waist as he lifted her. She enjoyed watching him swing into the saddle with no need for the stirrup. The thoughts that sight conjured when she observed his strength... They turned their steeds toward the keep and waited for the king's standard bearer to lead the way. The cart trailed behind, and many had almost forgotten why they were away from the castle.

"Henrietta, you're failing." Roy loomed over his niece, knowing he scared her and not caring. After the way Amelia and Hamish behaved only an hour earlier, he admitted his desperation to himself. If he didn't force Hamish away from Amelia, they would do something that would make Amelia's reputation unrecoverable. Then no man would take her.

"It's not my fault, Uncle. He's never alone long enough for me to get his attention. Without even a passing word or look, it's hard to get people to believe what I tell them."

"Then your skills aren't what you promised," Roy sneered.

"And I thought you were going to make sure one of his men walked in on us in his chamber. When are you arranging that?"

"Tonight. The story will be that he defended Amelia so strongly because he feared people were aboot to learn his true feelings for you. He wants her because she's an heiress, but he loves you." Roy knew that stretched the realm of plausibility, but it wouldn't matter the reason if someone found them naked in bed together.

"You'll have to drug him to get me into his chamber. He'll

never take me back there, and if he's a light sleeper like all warriors, he'll gut me the moment I walk through the door."

"I ken. I've paid a servant to slip a sleeping draught into his chalice. He'll retire early and will be sound asleep by the time you're able to join him. It should last a few hours, so I will time sending one of his men to the chamber for when he should no longer appear drugged." Roy paid the woman a small fortune to ensure she carried out his task without complaint. He finished their negotiations by warning the widow that if she failed, he would kill her. Then he'd take the coin back and let her children starve.

"Very well. I need to ready myself for the evening meal." Henrietta peered past the tapestry that hid the alcove Roy practically dragged her into. Her affinity for her uncle rapidly waned as he pressured her to do more than she knew she could. But she wanted Hamish in truth. The more time she spent chaperoning Hamish and Amelia, the more she wished he directed his feelings toward her. She longed for someone to be as devoted to her as Hamish clearly was to Amelia. And she knew it wasn't puppy love either. He wasn't mooning over Amelia. He respected her cousin and enjoyed her company. He saw Amelia as his equal and Henrietta as a fly to be swatted. She'd burned her bridge to ash by using his given name. Now it was too late to try something more subtle.

"Lady Henrietta, where did you come from?"

She'd had her head down once she stepped into the passageway and didn't see Andrew Fraser watching her. Now the clan tánaiste positioned himself in front of her. Her head jerked up as she nearly slammed into the massive Highlander. He was nearly as big as Hamish, only a couple inches shorter and likely less than a stone lighter. She knew his reputation, even if he spent more time at court than at home.

"Fraser, excuse me. I didn't see you."

"I know you didn't. Where did you come from? And what are

you doing in this passageway? There are only alcoves along here, then the kitchens." He knew the answers to his questions. He wished to see what lie she would tell.

"I came from Balnagown, and I was walking in this passageway. Excuse me." Henrietta shifted to step around him. She knew it trapped her uncle as long as she stood talking to Andrew. She also knew she would be late to join the other ladies. She prayed she could somehow make it seem plausible that she'd met with Hamish. As she looked at Andrew, she realized she could be vague and insinuate it was Hamish by saying she spoke with a dark-haired, brooding Highlander. She wouldn't be lying if she said that.

Andrew grinned and leaned to whisper in her ear. "I don't like your uncle, so I will keep you here as long as I can just to keep him stuck in that alcove. And unless you wish me to ask you again at a more inconvenient time, what are you doing here?"

"You seem to already know if you know my uncle is here, too."

"Och, lass. That does naught to reassure me. He is a mon at court without his wife. You are a bonnie young woman without a husband. You've just came out of a hidden alcove, distracted and in a hurry. And I've seen you watch your uncle."

"You've watched me?"

Andrew knew that would be what she focused on. That's why he'd saved that observation for last. "Of course, I have. You're an intelligent woman, my lady. Playing a flighty fool does you little good. You think to elbow your way into every situation and make yourself the center of attention to prove your importance. You'd do well to realize that silence will win you a husband."

"I'm to be seen and not heard like a naughty wean?" Henrietta scowled.

"No. You are to not be seen, so you can hear everything. You understand politics better than most, but you have no execution when it comes to ingratiating yourself into circles to learn more.

Clearly, your uncle expects you to report to him. But he's done naught to teach you how to gain the information he wants. Aught you share with him, you've put in at least twice the effort needed to gain it. You should be more like your cousin." Andrew grinned, knowing his barb would prick her temper. The only time Henrietta enjoyed being compared to Amelia was when someone preferred her to her saintly cousin. She stepped around him, and this time he let her. But only so he could snag her arm and wrap it around his.

"Let go before I scream."

"You won't do that. You might have evaded answering my questions outright, but you won't avoid answering to the queen, which you will if anyone finds you alone with me."

"Sod off."

"That's no way to speak to the mon you're going to marry."

Henrietta tripped over the hem of her gown; her attention stolen by his comment. "I am not marrying you." She looked up at him. "Has my uncle already betrothed me?"

"You needn't sound so frightened. He hasn't, but he will."

"No, he won't. You aren't who he wants me to marry." Henrietta lifted her skirts to ensure she didn't trip again as she tried to hurry away. She knew they were still close enough for Roy to watch, even if he could no longer hear them. Andrew knew the same thing, so the moment they rounded a corner, he pulled back a tapestry and tugged Henrietta with him. "What are you doing? Leave me alone."

Andrew heard the genuine fear in her voice this time, and he was prepared for it, even if he didn't like it. He pressed her into the corner of their own alcove, so she couldn't slip past him. But it put more distance between them. "Henrietta, whatever you're conspiring to do to Hamish will explode in your face. It will leave you with no reputation and no marriage. He will not marry you. Naught you can do will change that. Whatever scandal you think to cause will do naught to dissuade Lady Amelia from him. Nay one will believe he's chosen you over her after today. You will look like a whore, and nay one will have you."

"What happened today?" That her uncle hadn't explained the urgency only made her aware he'd run out of patience.

"Hamish killed Laird Chattan for insulting Lady Amelia. The mon disparaged her and spoke of her like she was naught more than a whore. We all heard him. Hamish challenged him, but before their fight began in truth, your cousin insisted upon staying. She said he wouldn't leave her side, so neither would she leave his. Once Hamish won— which was never in question — she kissed him. Not a peck on the cheek. Not even a peck on the lips. No one should have witnessed the kiss they shared. The only reason they aren't at the kirk right now is because Hamish is the Earl of Sutherland. The king can't force him. And the only reason Hamish isn't there by choice is because he said he would propose to Lady Amelia properly. Your uncle could do naught to stop it, nor did he insist they marry immediately. He's counting on you to interfere. I'm warning you against it."

"Because you intend to marry me?" She huffed indignantly.

"Aye. Your mother and aunt trained you to be a chatelaine, so you can become a laird's wife. But no one's trained you to be a courtier's wife. You're suited to it by instinct, but you don't have the skills. You can learn them, and I intend to train you."

"Like a dog or horse. No thank you."

"Like a warrior." Andrew crossed his arms, flexing his chest.

"I don't want you."

"Do you genuinely want Hamish? Do you genuinely want your uncle, or just the attention he might give you?"

Henrietta schooled her features, but it made her uncomfortable that anyone should know of her infatuation with her uncle. It humiliated it. "I owe you no answers to your questions. Move, Fraser."

He allowed her space to pass him, but he shot out his arm before she could. "We both know the answers to all my questions.

I already know the answer when I ask you to marry me. You know it too, but I'll give you time to accept it if you don't go through with whatever plot your uncle hatched. If you do, there will be no option but for me to claim you now. I will not allow you to destroy your good name for Roy Ross. He's not worth it. And I will not miss my opportunity to marry a woman who will be good for my clan and good for my career."

"I would be wonderful for you. You'd be useless to me."

"Because I'm a second son? Never to be an earl? Those are true, but you crave power and importance. Will you have those things locked away in the wilds of the Highlands? Hardly. You'll next to never come to court, so they'll all forget you. The title will do you no good among the Sutherlands. You'll use it once a year, assuming you attend the Gatherings. Live here at court, and you will lead the matrons."

"And watch your infidelities paraded in front of the entire court? That holds no interest to me."

"Don't confuse my brother for me, Henrietta. You ken we aren't the same mon. A marriage doesn't have to be a love match for the groom to mean his oaths." Neither Andrew nor Henrietta fully believed he'd be faithful, but then, neither fully believed Henrietta would be either.

"You are a courtier with your pretty little speeches that have now made me late. I am not interested." Henrietta pushed aside the tapestry after peeking around the edge. When she saw no one for ten seconds, she rushed away. The conversation disconcerted her. No man had ever stated such an unwavering interest in her, even if it were only for his political gain. She didn't want to wed any man who couldn't elevate her title from mere lady to lady of the clan. She'd initially believed she'd wind Hamish around her little finger, but it hadn't taken long to realize that would never happen. She sensed the same about Andrew, which made him wholly unattractive despite a handsome face and braw body. Taking Hamish from Amelia and becoming a countess were the only reasons Hamish remained attractive to her. In the recesses of her mind, she knew she could never have a romantic relationship with Roy, so she appreciated his strident personality. But the man she married would bend to her will, not the other way around. And if that meant trapping Hamish by being found naked in his bed that night, so be it.

AMELIA PAID no attention to Henrietta, but her cousin arrived late to the queen's solar as all the ladies gathered to walk to the Great Hall. She was winded and distracted, adjusting laces her maid clearly hurried to tie. She looked around the massive gathering space, and Amelia followed Henrietta's gaze first to Roy, then Andrew, then Hamish, where it remained. Amelia watched Andrew Fraser stare at Henrietta before Amelia shifted her attention to her father, who watched them both as they took places beside each other on a bench. When she finally gazed at Hamish, she already knew his attention was on her. Her left eyebrow flicked up for a moment in acknowledgement that she sensed something was amiss too, but she didn't know what. With the barest glance at Hamish as she entered, she knew his attention was solely on her. Mayhap he sensed something was off on his own, but she knew he was aware from watching her.

The meal progressed at a snail's pace for Amelia. She wanted the music to begin, so she had a reason to dance with Hamish. After their kiss that followed Hamish killing Malcolm, the queen refused to countenance Amelia sitting with Hamish alongside Lady Gwendolyn. The Mistress of the Bedchamber took her to task for being a wanton and warned the queen would send her away from court if another incident like that afternoon's transpired. That alone was motivation to kiss Hamish since she longed to leave. She had since she arrived at Stirling but doubly now that she wished to make Dunrobin her home.

As the meal dragged on, Hamish found himself feeling unwell. He rarely suffered from headaches, but one began behind his eyes. It sapped his energy with each course. But he was determined to dance with Amelia and arrange a rendezvous. He wouldn't fall asleep without kissing her again. He wanted to admit his feelings without an audience this time, and he wanted to show her by bringing her to release finally. He'd returned to his chamber and bathed, taking himself in hand as he pictured her as she hunted. His own Artemis, goddess of the hunt. He'd pictured how she looked when she spoke aloud her commitment to stand by him. His own Athena, goddess of war and practical reason. He remembered the feel of her body pressed to his and her taste. It had taken little time for him to reach his climax. Embarrassingly fast if he'd had a partner. As fast as it had the first time they sneaked into the storeroom.

By the time the servants pushed aside the tables and benches, his head felt leaden. His mind grew foggy, and he wished to find his bed and fall into a sound sleep. But his desire to talk to Amelia and hold her again was far stronger. He grew dizzy for a moment as he stood, making him wonder if he was falling sick. He surreptitiously touched his forehead, but he didn't feel feverish. He had no other symptoms, so he shook it off and approached Amelia.

"Hamish, what's wrong?"

"Naught, *leannan.*"

"Ye're pale, and yer eyes are glassy. Are ye ill?"

"A headache that will be gone by morn." He fought not to yawn. It had been a long day, but no worse than he was used to. It was far easier than days spent atop his steed, patrolling his clan's land.

"I dinna believe ye. Ye need to sit down before ye fall down."

"Wheest, ma love. What I need is to hold ye again." He slid his arms around her as the music began. It would keep them together, but it was a lively tune. He struggled not to miss a step to a dance he'd performed since he was an adolescent, learning it with his sister. His vision blurred, so he closed his eyes and danced by feel.

"Hamish, let me fetch ye some ale."

"Fetch? Ye arenae ma dog, but I wouldnae mind if ye scratched behind ma ear." He offered her a smile, but it appeared like a grimace. His head pounded, and he wanted nothing more than to climb into bed. Alone. He feared he would be ill now that he stood. He didn't want Amelia seeing him in such a state. He had to admit defeat. "Mayhap I am a wee poorly. I—"

Hamish stumbled, then crashed forward like a mighty pine tree. Amelia tried to push him upright, but he was too heavy. They landed on the floor with a thud, Hamish's massive frame crushing her.

"Hamish!" It was Henrietta who screamed his name. Amelia could do nothing but look around; the air knocked from her lungs. "What did you do to him?"

Amelia shook her head, trying to push Hamish off her. But his dead weight was too much. Three Sutherland warriors pushed forward and lifted Hamish off her, laying him beside her. She sucked in deep lungfuls that burned. She swept her gaze around the surrounding crowd.

"What did you do to him?" Henrietta hissed at Amelia. "Hamish, my love?" Henrietta tapped at his cheeks as she brushed hair from his forehead. Amelia still couldn't speak, forced to watch her cousin fawn over the man who loved her, not Henrietta.

"*Mo chridhe,*" Hamish mumbled. He reached toward Amelia, but Henrietta shifted, so it appeared he reached for her. His hand landed on her breast, but he jerked it back. Even in his stupor, he knew what he felt wasn't Amelia. He struggled to open his eyes, but they felt glued shut.

"I'm here," Henrietta whispered none too quietly. "I'm here." She stroked his cheek as Hamish's chest rose with a deep inhale then sighed. His body relaxed for a moment before he shuddered and swiped at Henrietta's hand. "Shh, my love. The healer will come." She wrapped her hand around his and brought it to her heart. "It doesnae have to be a secret any longer."

Amelia rolled to her side and sat up. She crawled to Hamish's side, but Henrietta blocked her. She wouldn't get into a shoving match with the other woman.

"Lia? Lia!" Hamish thrashed, knocking Henrietta off her knees. "Lia!"

"Wheest, Hamish. I'm right here." Now that Henrietta had fallen onto her bottom, Amelia could finally reach Hamish.

His eyes fluttered open before drifting shut. He groaned and shook his head. "Lia? *Mo chridhe?*"

"It's all right. I'm here. Hold ma hand." Amelia lifted both of his and squeezed.

"It's ye. Someone else— all wrong. Ye, ma Lia."

Amelia wanted to smirk at Henrietta and hoot with joy. He'd denounced her cousin, and in his stupor, he wanted her. Everyone heard. Instead, she focused on what needed to be done.

"Help me get Laird Sutherland to his chamber," she instructed his men. "He isnae ill. Someone drugged him."

That drew gasps from the crowd. King John stepped forward as the crowd parted for him. "What do you mean he's been drugged?"

"He was pale with glassy eyes. But he isnae running a fever. He was sluggish while we danced, then he collapsed. Asleep. I saw him twitch, and his sigh. His deep breathing. He roused himself long enough for us to see he isnae unconscious. Someone must have put a draught in his ale." Amelia kept her gaze on Hamish, but she wished to point her accusations at Henrietta. It was far too convenient that she was right by his side. It made no sense why she would claim him so publicly. That was still something to be addressed, but not before she tended to Hamish. She feared what might be wrong if she were incorrect. She still wanted the healer to check on him.

She stood and stepped out of the way, allowing the Sutherland men to gather Hamish to carry him to his chamber. She looked around for Henrietta, wanting to know what her cousin was up to. She didn't care for what Henrietta insinuated with the comment about no longer keeping something a secret. If Hamish hadn't cried out for Amelia, others might have believed Henrietta and Hamish were secret lovers. Nothing caused her to doubt Hamish's commitment to her. But she feared the gossip Henrietta struggled to spread would now blaze like an inferno. Hamish might have publicly denounced Henrietta, but she held no doubts her cousin would make it about herself.

Her eyes scanned the crowd, which watched the men heft Hamish into the air. Two men linked their arms around and beneath Hamish's shoulders while two more men carried his legs. One discreetly ensured Hamish's plaid kept all the necessary bits covered. She spied Andrew Fraser dragging Henrietta away, his hand obviously manacled around her upper arm. She couldn't hear what he said, but she could see he was livid. She watched as he practically shoved her through a doorway. Then she looked for her father, who stood among several other lairds. She didn't doubt he conspired to seize Hamish's land, preparing for him to die from his malady. She was certain he'd fallen asleep, but speculatory comments buzzed through the crowd. Hamish had no obvious heir, which made his clan and his lands vulnerable to her father.

If Hamish wasn't well by morning, Amelia had no choice but to send an urgent missive to Liam and Kyla. She needed the Sinclairs.

CHAPTER 12

*H*amish put a hand to his forehead and found a cool cloth laying there. He eased his heavy lids open to find himself in a dark chamber with a low fire burning across the room. His head felt worse than it had earlier. He had no recollection of coming to his chamber. He tried to make sense of what happened that led to him being in his bed with a compress on his head. A scent wafted to him. It was one he knew. The one he vaguely remembered calming him earlier.

"Lia?" Heather. It was her.

"Aye, Hamish." A shadow moved, then she appeared. The dim candle on the bedside table illuminated her face. He turned his head away and found the chamber door open. He could barely make out two shoulders in the doorway. The plaids were faint, but he was certain they were the Sutherland pattern. His thoughts still felt muddled, but he understood it was for propriety. Otherwise, Amelia couldn't be there. Though he wished they would shut the door and pretend like she wasn't.

"What happened?"

"I believe someone put a sleeping draught in yer ale or food. Ale most likely. Ye fell asleep while we danced."

"What?" He tried to sit up, but he groaned and felt nauseous. He sucked in air through his nose before sitting up again more slowly. He felt the sheet pool around his waist, and he realized he was naked. He looked at his lap before looking at Amelia.

"Yer men." She nudged her chin toward him.

"Such a shame, lass. Though I'd prefer to be awake when ye see me for the first time." He waggled his eyebrows, then winced. "If I fell asleep standing, did I fall? Ma shoulder aches."

"Aye. Ye fell forward."

Hamish twisted and lifted her from the seat upon which she sat and placed her gently on the mattress beside him. "Did I hurt ye, *mo ghaol*? I landed on ye, didna I?"

"Ye didna mean to."

"That doesnae answer ma first question. If ma shoulder is swore, then I can only imagine what I did to ye. Are ye bruised? Did I do aught more? I'm so sorry, Lia."

"Haud ye wheest. Ye knocked the wind from me, but naught worse. I'm a wee sore, but I'll live. Ye scared me more than aught. I thought for a moment that ye—" Amelia didn't want to give voice to her thought. It felt like it tempted fate after what just happened. Hamish opened his arms to her. She glanced at the door, but the suite's solar was just as dimly lit as the chamber. It would be hard for anyone to see them. She leaned forward and blew out the candle, which put them in near complete darkness. She flinched as she lay on her side, but she wouldn't let Hamish know it was the side with the bruise.

"Ye're bruised on that side. I felt ye tense." He dropped his voice to a whisper. "Roll over, ma love."

"Nay. Then I will nae be able to see ye at all." She skimmed her hand up his arm until she cupped his jaw. She kept her voice equally soft.

"I didna mean to frighten ye." Hamish also felt wretched that he'd hurt Amelia in any way. "Ye canna be done with me that easily. Ye owe me at least three score years of chasing ye around a chamber and loving ye before ye can say ye're done."

"I'm never going to say that. But who says I willna chase ye?"

"Ye'll never need to. I'll be waiting whenever ye're ready." Hamish hoped she understood he meant more than the obvious. His hand rested on her waist but with no pressure since he feared causing her more pain. She let go of his cheek and reached back to slide his hand lower until he cupped the swell of her backside.

"Neither of us need wait. I can close the door, and I ken neither of yer men would speak against ye."

"Nae tonight. I want to truly be alone with ye, nae with ma men posted outside our door. I want to hear ye moan ma name. I want to hear ye cry out as I bring ye to yer climax. I dinna want anyone kenning I'm pleasuring ye. And ye will be ma wife before we make love for the first time. I willna risk anyone taking ye from me." It was what implicitly kept them from taking things further when they rendezvoused in the undercroft.

"That's vera noble of ye, even if it is annoying."

Hamish heard the humor in her voice and chuckled. He squeezed her bottom before gathering the back of her skirts. His hand skimmed up her leg until he could cup her backside again. He let it rest there a moment before sliding it toward her thigh, his fingers dipping between them. He drew her leg over his as he pressed her backward, so his body leaned over hers.

"There's naught noble aboot what I want to do with ye. Can ye feel how much I want ye?

She guided his hand over the outside of her thigh and around to the front. It rested on her mound before his thumb found her pearl. He rubbed slow circles as she titled her hips toward him. She might finally get the relief to the burning ache he stirred in her.

"I willna take yer maidenhead until ye're ma wife. I wish to save that for our wedding night, but I also willna endanger yer future in case aught happens to me before we can wed."

Amelia understood what he meant. He was a warrior. He could have died that day fighting Malcolm, even though she'd been certain he would prevail. She knew he could be called to ride out at any moment, and he might not come back. She recognized he was trying to protect her in case they never married. She would need to be a virgin for whoever she wed. But she didn't like it. Her body was impatient for more. Her core ached far more than her side. Its emptiness a gaping cavern she needed Hamish to fill.

They dared much lying on the bed together, let alone having Amelia's skirts hiked up, her leg over his, and his hand at her entrance. She darted her glance toward the men and wondered if they knew what she and Hamish were about. They'd made no sound she thought would carry to the guards since she laid beside Hamish. As her need built with every circle he drew on her button, she pressed her lips to his, opening to him. She wanted to moan her enjoyment, but she didn't make a peep. The kiss drew on until she wrapped her fingers around the outside of his shoulder and gripped his arm. Her hips thrust forward, and she squeezed her eyes shut. Her nails bit into his skin as her body went rigid. Her release left her breathless and in awe.

"Shh, let me keep going, Lia," Hamish whispered as she made to lower her leg. He didn't remove his hand, instead pressing harder as he rubbed faster. His first two fingers ran along the outside of her nether lips before his middle slid through her dew. He dipped his fingers into her entrance, and Amelia's kiss grew wild. Her hand went to his hair as she fisted it. The bed creaked once as she tried to rock her hips. They froze, but no movement came from the doorway.

She flexed her hips forward and let Hamish work his magic. Surely that was what he did because she imagined nothing could feel so all-consuming and freeing at the same time. She sucked his tongue as she shattered again. All Hamish longed for was to thrust into her, but he would have settled for her hand wrapped around his cock. But neither was possible. He would satisfy himself when he was alone.

Amelia thought differently. She pulled the sheet loose and slid her hand between them. She took Hamish by surprise, but he grasped her wrist. She shook him loose. "I want to try, *m'eudail.* Teach me."

"Ye will be the death of me. I dinna ken that I can be quiet like ye."

"Ye'll find a way." She slipped her hand around his turgid length. Her thumb brushed against the head of his rod. When Hamish sucked in a breath, she rubbed the sensitive top. She understood how men and women coupled, so she assumed she was meant to stroke him. She moved slowly, unsure how fast or how hard she should hold him. "I dinna ken what else I'm supposed to do."

"Just that," Hamish responded in strangled whisper. He shut his eyes and reveled in the sensations. It never felt as erotic when he took himself in hand, and it had always been a prelude to something more with the women in his past. None had stroked him purely for his enjoyment. A wish to devour her washed over him as his need increased. He would find a way to strip her naked and taste her. He didn't know when or where, or even how he could make it happen. But he was determined. And it wouldn't be in the dark either. All his senses would feast.

Amelia could tell he enjoyed her ministrations from the way his kiss grew more and more fevered. His hand covered her breast and kneaded the ample mound. If her free hand weren't beneath her, she would have reached back and loosed the ties. But if she did that, anyone who walked in would know what they'd done. She might roll off the bed in time to hide their intimacies, but a gown half hanging off her would damn them.

He stroked his fingertips over the swell of her breast before dipping them into her cleavage. He twisted his hand and eased his fingers beneath the neckline until he could feel her nipple. He ran it between his middle finger and ring finger until it rose to a dart. He filled his hand as he lowered his head to brush a kiss against the flesh he pressed upward. Then their lips met again. He tried to pull her hand free when he knew he could no longer hold back.

"Ye felt ma release. Ye willna deny me the same pleasure." Amelia tightened her grip and worked him faster until he gritted his teeth to keep from bellowing. His seed shot forth, and he knew some coated her hand. But she didn't pull away, instead offering him a loving kiss. While Hamish feared the sensation might disgust her, she enjoyed knowing she'd brought him to release. Her. No one else. Certainly not Henrietta. He was hers, and she would be damned if anyone claimed otherwise. For now, she would enjoy a few more minutes with Hamish before returning to her seat. Tomorrow, she would deal with Cousin Henny.

WHILE AMELIA STRAINED to glimpse Hamish as the ladies followed the queen to the gardens, Henrietta wished to be invisible when she spied Andrew observing her. Amelia had returned to her chamber an hour after her interlude with Hamish. They'd agreed he was out of danger and merely needed to sleep off the rest of the draught. They hadn't agreed when he stated he would enter the lists that morning, but neither wanted to argue, especially since they didn't want the guards to hear them. One Sutherland escorted her back to her chamber. Her roommate was a kind Lowlander, who Amelia knew she could trust not to tell everyone how late it was when Amelia returned.

Henrietta hadn't spent such an enjoyable night with Andrew as Amelia had with Hamish. He'd dragged her out of the Great Hall and back to the passageway with the alcoves, where he shoved her into one. He'd railed at her for her behavior, telling her she was a fool to put on an act no one believed. She'd humiliated herself, and he wouldn't tolerate his future wife making a fool of herself and him since he would announce their betrothal in the near future. She'd refused to consider him as anything but a pest. While he'd backed her farther into a corner, she didn't fear him. Neither could she manipulate him. That was what bothered her most. He expected her to bend to his will and wouldn't allow it to be any other way.

Amelia steadfastly ignored her cousin, which Henrietta appreciated. The latter was in no mood to face her familial nemesis. Henrietta felt testy now that she'd spotted Andrew, who'd crossed his arms and frowned at her. He would ruin everything she hadn't already.

"Lady Amelia, how does Laird Sutherland fair this morning? We saw ye watching him," Elouise MacMillan mused.

"He appears well. Wouldnae ye agree? I havenae spoken to him since I arrived at the morning meal with Mary." Her roommate glanced over at the pair when she heard her name. She nodded before returning to her conversation with three other ladies. "As ye saw, I had nay chance to speak to ma laird."

"After last night's spectacle, we'd all say he's yers." Elouise watched Henrietta rather than Amelia as she lobbed the barb. Neither Amelia nor Henrietta responded. "Why does he call you Lia?"

"Because I gave him leave to." Amelia turned her attention away from Elouise, but the woman wasn't done.

"And when was that?" Elouise pressed.

"The other day. Elouise, we will keep the queen waiting if you dinna walk faster." Amelia lengthened her stride, skirting past Elouise and Henrietta to join Mary and the others. She spent the next hour avoiding more questions about the previous night and trying to glimpse Hamish in the lists. But the distance was far too great, and she wasn't certain she would recognize him among all the men. However, she knew it was him the moment he approached the opening in the fence. A rider passed between them, blocking her view. She recognized the new arrival as Dugan Sinclair, Liam's younger brother.

She'd considered sending for the Sinclairs, but she'd done nothing to summon them. Dugan's arrival was coincidence. She watched him dismount and toss his reins to a stable boy who ran to meet him. He set his course for the lists but stopped at the entrance to look around. Amelia wondered who he sought. Hamish, her father, and Tieran MacLeod answered her question when they approached Dugan. Why?

As the men left the lists, Hamish and Roy walked beside each other, and it was the first time they didn't look ready to pulverize each other. It made Amelia fear something far worse than their feud was afoot. Dugan had walked with purpose to the lists, but now the four men strolled toward the keep. It would have appeared uninteresting if not for Hamish and Roy being together and not brawling.

Amelia looked around and noticed a rose bush ahead. She angled herself to speak to Rebecca Maxwell and her roommate, Mary. She pretended to be so engrossed in listening, leaning past Mary to hear Rebecca that she didn't notice the rose bush they walked past. She twisted to make her skirts flair just enough to snag her dress. She tugged, hoping it looked absentminded, and it made it worse.

"By the saints," Amelia huffed as she tugged again. She heard the rending fabric and breathed easier.

"Oh, dear," Mary burbled as she hurried to help Amelia free herself. "You've torn your gown. You'll trip over this hem if you're not careful."

Which was exactly what Amelia would have done if someone hadn't made a fuss. Lady Helen Buchan, the Mistress of the Bedchamber and a member of one of the few clans who supported John Balliol's ascension to the throne, turned toward them. Her aggrieved expression made Amelia want to roll her eyes. The older woman flicked her fingers, shooing Amelia away. It meant she had permission to leave the walk early to return to her chamber to change. She lifted her skirts an appropriate height and hurried out of the gardens. She refrained from running, but just barely. She settled on a brisk walk that brought her to the keep doors just after the men passed through. Usually, she was soft-footed, but she made sure the heels of her slippers tapped along the stone floor.

"Lady Amelia?" It was Hamish who turned first and recognized her. That made Roy stop and turn, which forced the other two men to halt their progress, too. "Ye seem in a hurry."

"Och, I snagged ma gown on a rose bush and tore the hem." Amelia curtsied to Tieran as the laird of the MacLeods of Lewis. She dipped her chin to Dugan, who would become tánaiste when Liam inherited the Sinclair lairdship, assuming Liam didn't have a son old enough to assume the role.

"Lady Amelia," both men chimed.

She wasn't sure what to do next now that she'd caught up to the group. "Dugan, I didna ken ye were coming to court. Lady Kyla and Liam were here nae long ago."

Dugan nodded and hesitated, as though he sought an excuse rather than an explanation. "Aye. The taxes are due soon, so I came to see aboot the amounts."

Amelia locked gazes with him, clearly unbelieving. There wasn't a chance Laird and Lady Sinclair didn't know the exact penny they owed. Even if they somehow didn't, Amelia doubted Liam and Kyla didn't know. Dugan thought her a fool if he expected her to believe that since she was an earl's only daughter. Everyone expected her to marry at least a laird and become a keep's chatelaine. It would make her responsible for keeping ledgers that recorded expected tax payments. She didn't look away until Dugan did first. She shifted her attention to Hamish. He held out his hand to her, which she eagerly accepted.

"Nay," Roy hissed. "We aren't involving Amelia. It's not safe. Hamish, I draw the line on this. I absolutely forbid it. I will not risk her neck." He kept his voice a heated whisper as though the walls had ears in the passageway in which they stood.

"As far as anyone needs to ken, Dugan came to discuss our troubles with the Gunns. Tieran is Dugan's best friend. Lia can come with us."

"And when it gets out that we're not talking aboot that?" Roy continued to scan the passageway. "You might be fine risking my daughter, but I'm not."

"The only risk is remaining here clishmaclavering. Ye ken I'll tell Lia everything, anyway. She may as well hear it from all of us."

Roy stared at Hamish before relenting. "Very well. But we meet in my suite. It's the only way to justify Amelia's presence."

"That will give me an excuse to nae change ma gown immediately. If Father summoned me, there is little Lady Helen can do."

Tieran had remained quiet, but now he shifted his gaze from Amelia to Hamish. "Why would ye tell Lady Amelia aught?"

"Because she will be Lady Sutherland when John Balliol abdicates the throne."

CHAPTER 13

*A*melia's gaze darted from Hamish to Roy to Tieran to Dugan before coming back to rest on Hamish. Knowing they couldn't get away with walking hand in hand through the keep, she accepted his arm when he offered it, letting him wrap hers around his, and they followed Roy. Tieran walked to Amelia's right, and Dugan brought up the rear. She thought it odd that no one walked beside her father, but she realized the men surrounded her. She wondered if it was a habit for the men to guard the woman or if they thought they had an immediate need to protect her. Hamish patted the hand that rested on his arm. None spoke until Roy let them into the Ross suites. Amelia remembered staying there when she was a child and the first few days after she arrived at court to become a lady-in-waiting.

"What—" Amelia started.

"Shh," Hamish whispered. She watched as the men moved around the room to various spots along walls. She stared in stunned silence as they each picked up scraps of linen and poked them into peepholes. She had no idea anyone spied on her family. It made her wonder if anyone spied her with Hamish the night before since his chamber was in a suite much like the one in which they all stood now. When her gaze met Hamish's, he offered her a reassuring smile. She didn't know if that meant there were no holes in his walls or if he'd already plugged them. It shocked her that all four men knew exactly what to do without a word.

They were one chair short, so Hamish stood behind Amelia's. His hands rested on the back of the x-shaped seat. His thumb brushed her back three times before he rested it on the crossbar. She waited for someone to explain Hamish's comment, but when they remained in silence, she twisted to look up at him.

"Lia, we represent four of the most powerful clans in the Highlands and Hebrides." Hamish looked at Tieran, who led a branch of the MacLeods that was distantly related to the ones on Skye. Both dominated their respective islands. "We might be far from the border when war comes— and it is —but Balliol will insist all of us send warriors."

In private, few referred to King John by his title. Since none respected him, none wished to think of him as their sovereign. He'd allowed the wolf in the henhouse by encouraging King Edward to influence Scotland's politics and royal heredity. Hamish hadn't agreed when the royal advisors sought Longshanks' help after King Alexander died, leaving only the Princess Margaret of Norway as his heir. The young girl died not long after the former king. It left Scotland bereft of clear succession. Accepting Edward's advice indebted them, and the English king reminded them at every turn.

Amelia watched Hamish as he spoke, but when he finished, she turned toward her father. "Ye dinna trust the Auld Alliance, do ye?" The treaty between the Scottish and French didn't promise the country would send soldiers to fight alongside their Celtic allies. It promised to keep the English busy with ongoing conflicts on the Continent. For such a small country, England had a unique ability to fight wars on many fronts without failure. It drained English coffers, but since Edward stole anything his men could touch, it kept him from utterly bankrupting the country.

"We dinna." Roy abandoned his courtly accent among his northern peers. It told Amelia he was at least somewhat at ease despite being shut into a tight space with Hamish. Their anxiety must be severe for them to put aside their hostilities, especially with Amelia present, to discuss the current politics. "The French are failing to engage the English. They appear ready to retreat and regroup. Before sending more fighters to France, we believe Longshanks will send more men across the border. He did it easily enough when he took Berwick then attacked Dunbar. The Earl of March wasna prepared for the battle, and it was over embarrassingly quickly for the Lowlanders. We canna afford for that to happen again."

"None of ye would discuss this with the threat of being convicted of treason if ye didna have an alternate to Balliol already in mind. The Bruce?" Amelia observed her father, but she reached back to cover Hamish's hand when it rested on her shoulder. None spoke their answer aloud in case someone could hear them, but they each nodded. The linen-plugged holes ensured no one could see in, so they were safe to answer that way.

"With the peace in Gascony, the French have little reason to hold up their end of the agreement," Tieran explained. "We canna trust Balliol to lead us if we must combat the full might of the English army." Tieran put the situation diplomatically. If the English and French ceased their war, the French were useless to the Scots.

"Ye ken ye'll have a fight among the clans to get the Bruce on the throne while fighting the English to keep their armies off our land. How will ye do it? Balliol might be useless, but he isnae without support. Longshanks will fight us if for nay other reason than just to keep Balliol on the throne."

"Aye," Dugan agreed. "And it doesnae help that the Bruces are

Lowlanders. He'll depend on us Highlanders and Islanders, but nae everyone trusts him. He'll need our clans to rally behind him to bring the others."

"But he doesnae even have all the border clans," Roy pointed out. "I canna blame them at all for siding with the English if it will keep their people safe. But it willna. When war comes, the English will trample them if they dinna put up a fight. And that's a fight they can only win if we come down from the Highlands to fight beside Robert."

"The Bruce is the Earl of Carrick, and that came with minor properties in England. His tenants sent word the English are encroaching," Dugan warned. "Da had a missive from the Mackay who had word from the Kennedys. The Mackay messenger was lucky he didna lose his head the way he rode toward our keep, waving his sword. He said it was to catch the light and get our attention. Daft lad. Ye ken the Mackay and the Kennedy were mercenaries until just a year ago. They battled the English on behalf of the French. They ken how the English fight. The message warns Longshanks is coming here. To Stirling," Dugan announced.

Hamish looked down. "Ye leave tonight. I dinna care if the mon isnae coming for a moon or a year. Ye leave tonight, Lia." His decision was immediate and without needing contemplation.

"We arenae wed yet. I canna go to Dunrobin without ye. Ye said I leave tonight. Ye didna say we." Amelia rose and faced Hamish.

"Ye must go to Balnagown until I can come for ye," Hamish insisted. Amelia's lips firmed. She wouldn't argue with Hamish in front of the others, but the heat flashing in her eyes warned Hamish the conversation wasn't over. He looked past her shoulder at Dugan. "How soon?"

Dugan's expression tightened. "A sennight at best. It may nae be safe to send anyone away from the keep. We canna be sure he hasnae sent men ahead to scout."

Amelia had looked over her shoulder at Dugan, but now she stared at Hamish.

"Nay, Lia. Neither yer father nor I can linger. We must leave and get back to our clans. We canna lead men if we arenae with them. Ye are nae staying here. I'll travel with ye until we get to Balnagown. Then I must go on to Dunrobin and rally ma warriors. That's why Dugan came. It wasna just to tell us the English are coming. It was to set a meeting place for us and our allies."

"Edward will come here. Stirling is the key to all of Scotland. It's the gateway to the Highlands and where Balliol resides. He's convinced he'll have an easy victory after Dunbar. The mon might be a brilliant strategist, but his hubris prevents him from believing the Scots can defy and defeat him. He might believe we'll await him here, but I suspect he doesnae fathom the defense ye'll muster. I understand why ye wish to bring the Highlanders and Islanders down here. If too many of the Lowlanders travel north, it will alert him. Besides, it's nearly autumn and could snow. The Lowlanders havenae enough meat on their bones for the Highlands." Amelia grinned at the end, feeling like she might have overstepped. While their southern neighbors might think the Highlanders were heathens and barbarians, the disdain flowed both ways. The Lowlanders couldn't weather the northern climes and carried shorter and skinnier swords. The latter was a constant source of mirth to the brawny and wild Highlanders and Hebrideans who preferred the claymore, or double-handed broadsword.

"Ross, this is why I'm marrying yer daughter. When I ride out to fight, I want to ken someone's leading ma clan I can trust. Someone who will understand the war and the other clans. Someone strong enough and bright enough to defend our people. She's intelligent, and I love her for it." Hamish gazed into Amelia's eyes and brushed the backs of his fingers against her cheek the entire time he spoke. He dropped his hand when he was done, not wanting to antagonize Roy while they were getting along.

"Ye're marrying?" Dugan asked.

"Aye."

"Nay."

Amelia and Hamish answered together, almost drowning out Roy's disagreement. Hamish and Roy were back to scowling at one another, but Amelia sensed the hostility from Hamish wasn't as strong as it was the morning after they met. She couldn't be sure about her father, but he seemed to rein in his temper.

"Did ye nay speak to Liam and Kyla before ye came here?" Hamish wondered.

"I did. They said ye were keen on one another, but they didna ken ye'd agreed to aught. We need the Mackenzies and Campbells on board for this to work." Dugan brought the conversation back to what they needed to discuss, sensing it would be a poor idea to press the issue further in front of Roy. "Wallace and the Bruce are headed here, but ye ken Balliol canna ken the Bruce is nearby."

"And John Comyn?" Tieran interjected, having sat quietly until then. He'd witnessed Hamish and Roy's brawl in the bailey and how Hamish defended Amelia's honor the day before. However, he hadn't realized Hamish intended to wed before the imminent attack, despite the kiss he witnessed. He respected the man more than he did most mainlanders.

"A burr in Robert's arse," Roy responded. "But he's committed to getting Balliol off the throne. At the very least, so his arse has a chance to warm it."

John Comyn was another contender for the throne and Robert the Bruce's most significant opponent. They would work together to free Scotland of the English, but it would surprise no one in that chamber if a fight to the death didn't erupt between the Comyn and the Bruce.

"Longshanks will order his men to find Wallace during the

battle. He willna rest until he punishes Wallace for leading the revolt," Dugan pointed out.

"Wallace has done his sworn duty as the Guardian of Scotland, but he willna be long for this world if Edward captures him," Roy stated ruefully. He'd fought alongside William Wallace, and he admired the warrior. He was a Scottish patriot, but he was King Edward's most reviled enemy. Roy knew if the English ever captured Wallace, they would draw and quarter him before beheading him. Edward would likely send a limb to each corner of Scotland to ensure the Scots understood he held dominion over them. It's what spurred Roy to help lead the attack on Carlisle alongside six other earls. He wanted Edward to know he had no such power over Scotland. He would rather the Guardians and even Balliol lead them than allow Edward to have another say in anything to do with Roy's homeland. Unfortunately, many along the border weren't prepared for the English retaliation once the Highlanders returned north.

"Dugan, are ye going to approach Neil since he's here?" Hamish asked his brother-by-marriage's younger brother. His resemblance to Liam was uncanny. They were mirrors of their father. Dugan spent the previous five years fostering with the Campbells, and Neil was like a second older brother to him. He and Neil shared similar coloring, though the latter's was even darker than Dugan's chestnut. Neil's dark hair and eyes, along with his reputation on the battlefield, had already earned him the moniker of the "Black Campbell." If they had the Campbells fighting alongside them, they would be in an excellent position for victory.

"Aye. Neil's here to seek the king's permission to marry the MacDonnell laird's daughter." Dugan sounded less enthusiastic about that than going to war. He'd kept his opinion to himself last he saw Neil, but he knew the woman was too independent for his foster brother. Neil would break her spirit before he ever admitted he would benefit from her counsel once he became laird. Dugan liked the young woman and knew she could do better, but he could never say as much. He prayed she gave birth to two sons soon after their marriage, so Neil would leave her alone.

Hamish frowned, and Amelia grimaced. Tieran looked away. Only Roy looked uncertain, but he could guess. He suspected the young woman was like his daughter, but unlike Hamish, Neil would berate her for having her own thoughts. She'd do well to keep them to herself. As he considered that, he assessed Hamish. The young man hadn't been wrong either time he pointed out Roy would have approved of him if not for his Sutherland name. It forced Roy to accept he was fighting a losing battle trying to keep Hamish and Amelia apart. But he wouldn't allow his daughter to become a widow. He wouldn't agree to the ceremony until after this impending battle. He prayed by the end, a wedding between the two would be moot.

"Dugan, how long are ye staying here?" Amelia looked at the youngest man in the group. He was only in his early twenties, but his bearing spoke of a man already experienced in the art of war.

"Long enough to speak to Neil and a couple others I trust. I dinna want this getting back to Balliol."

"Are ye going straight back to Dunbeath?"

"Aye." Dugan's brow furrowed at Amelia's questions.

"Wonderful. Tell Kyla and Liam they should meet us at Balnagown in three sennights. Assuming there isnae a war before then, they're coming to our wedding." Amelia shot her father a challenging glare before turning to Hamish. She whispered to him, "I ken ye wished to ask me. And I didna ask ye at all. But ye're nae leaving to fight in a war without making me yer wife first. Ye're coming home to me, and the family we shall make together. In the meantime, I will shoulder the burdens ye leave behind. Ye are nae alone in this, *mo ghràidh.*"

"*Tha gaol agam ort.*" I love you. "Ye couldnae be more perfect."

He dropped a peck on the tip of her nose, very aware of the other men in the chamber.

"Amelia—" Roy's tone brought them both back to reality.

"Nay, Father. Ye ken ma feelings for Hamish are genuine, and his are the same for me. But if we are on the cusp of a war with England, and ye're here to rally the clans together, then ye must make peace. Who will believe our clans can fight as a unified army if the Earl of Ross and Earl of Sutherland canna get along? If it becomes the Earl of Ross against the Earls of Sutherland and of Sinclair? Do ye think the Bruce and Wallace want ye showing up to fight the English while ye're trying to run each other through instead? If any of ye want their trust, then ye canna squabble." Amelia rested her hand on Hamish's chest. "The same goes for ye. I need to trust ye willna antagonize ma father. I dinna want to attend either of yer funerals because ye murdered each other instead of the bluidy English."

"Aye, lass. Ye have the right of it." Hamish smiled down at her, and she remembered what they'd done the night before that sent the same rush of heat through her as his gaze did now. It made her glad she had her back to the other men because they'd surely see the way she blushed. She wiggled her toes in her slippers.

"How will ye explain leaving court when it was Balliol who sent for ye?" Tieran questioned Hamish and Roy.

"I'm going to tell the king the truth. The Gunns are causing more trouble and saying it's Rosses dressed up like them. Ye have reason to return home for that," Dugan interjected with an explanation.

"Vera well. That gives me as much reason to leave too." Roy stood and stared at Hamish. His daughter's arguments were sound, even if he wished Hamish would have the courtesy to die in battle rather than take Amelia to Dunrobin. But he knew when to retreat. If they could broker a truce, then it would benefit both clans more than the feud ever would. When he decided to make peace, he raised his arm. But Hamish already extended his. He scowled, not liking that the younger man beat him to the pact. They shook forearms, and Amelia beamed at them. Amelia stepped around the chair, prepared to hurry back to her chamber to change gowns. But Roy's voice carried to her.

"Dinna confuse for now with forever."

$\mathcal{A}$melia's brothers waylaid her as she left her chamber for the noon meal. She stifled her groan, but she wasn't excited to see either of them. She knew they would bombard her with questions about why she attended the meeting of lairds and Dugan, and they would want to hear from her what the men discussed. They would disdain her presence all the while benefiting from her astute understanding of politics and her keen memory for conversations.

"One of the Johnstones said he saw you chasing after Hamish this morning." The younger of the two brothers didn't bother greeting her.

"I chased after nay one, Lio." Amelia pulled her chamber door shut, taking a step forward that pushed between her brothers.

"The mon said you had your skirts up your calves and were practically running," Lionel pressed.

"I tore the hem of ma skirts. That's why I'm leaving ma chamber. I had to change. I lifted them, so I wouldnae trip. I entered the keep after Father, Dugan, Hamish, and Tieran." She hoped burying his name in the list might downplay his presence. She knew it was a dream.

"Father said you joined them in our family suite," Tormud inserted.

"I did. Hamish wished for me to hear the conversation."

"Why?" Both brothers demanded.

"Because I will be Lady Sutherland soon. When ma husband rides out, I need to ken why he's leaving, and I need to have some idea of where he's going. I'll have duties to lead our clan and protect our people. I canna do that if I dinna ken the threats we may face."

"'Our clan.' 'Our people,'" Tormud parroted. "You are not a Sutherland, and you never will be."

"Aye, I will. And ye can run straight back to Father and tell him this, too. If he stands in the way of ma marrying Hamish, we'll elope or handfast. I've reached ma majority. I can decide for maself. Hell, I could argue we're already married by consent since I've told him at least three times that I wish for us to wed. I'm nae arguing with either of ye. Ye are keeping me from joining the queen."

"You weren't so concerned aboot that when you were locked in a meeting with Father and your lover." Lionel raised his chin and looked down at her.

"Ye can wipe that sneer off yer face before I do it for ye. I'm as impressed with ye now as I was when we were weans, and ye thought ye caught the biggest fish. Ye preened around like a bonnie wee prince until ye realized I'd caught three fish twice the size of yer measly one. Hamish hasnae done aught to compromise me. Ye willna besmirch his honor or mine with that accusation. There is naught to be gained from saying such if ye dinna want to tarnish yer own reputation since ye're ma brother."

"You latched onto Hamish, and that's the only reason they allowed you in that meeting. Father didn't want you there," Tormud insisted.

"Ye're an arse." Amelia set a course for the stairs and didn't wait to see if her brothers joined her. She hoped they wouldn't, but she knew they would.

"You know what I mean. Don't be so touchy."

Amelia spun around, her skirts flaring around her like petals on an opening flower. "Ye tell me Father doesnae want me. Ye tell me the only reason they accepted me was because of Hamish. I'm nae being touchy. Ye're being an arse. I didna see either of ye there, but I ken ye were in the lists with him. Father didna invite ye, but neither did he send me away. Now tell me who he doesnae want." She crossed her arms, tapped her toes, and raised her chin to look down at them. She was far better at the imperious gaze than her brothers. They merely appeared supercilious when they tried.

"You have a waspish tongue, Amy," Lionel snapped.

"She has a tongue as sharp as her mind, and that's why I'm marrying her." Hamish's voice rose from within the stairwell. Amelia looked over the rope railing to see Hamish two floors below them. Wonderful. Their voices carried. Who knew who else might have heard them? Hamish changed course and continued up the stairs from the floor upon which his chamber lay. "If ye canna say aught kind to yer sister, then ye willna say aught to her at all. She doesnae have to listen to ye insult her just because ye share parents. If yer sister wishes to spend time with ye, *she* will find ye. Nae the other way around."

He came to stand beside Amelia with his thumbs tucked into his belt, feet hip-width apart. He looked at the younger men who were both nearly a match for him in size. But at nearly ten years his junior, they didn't have the same experience or bulk Hamish had. His body was far denser with muscle than their late adolescent ones, and he'd had two brothers he'd wrestled with as often as he'd wielded a practice sword against them. He exuded the confidence that came from victory on and off the battlefield. Neither Tormud nor Lionel felt up to testing him. They nodded to Hamish before looking apologetically at Amelia.

"I'm sorry," Tormud admitted.

"Me, too," Lionel seconded.

Amelia looked at her brothers and knew they meant their contrition, but it didn't lessen the sting that they'd said what they had. And they likely wouldn't have retracted it if Hamish hadn't interrupted. He wrapped his arm around her waist before continuing.

"I didna hear how yer conversation began, but I can guess. I dinna care how yer sister came to join us. I'd already asked yer father, and he'd refused. I didna want to make a scene in the lists or the bailey, but I kenned Lia spotted us. I kenned she followed us. I kenned she was behind us before I turned around. I wanted yer sister at that meeting, and I dinna care who didna agree. As far as I'm concerned, she's as good as Lady Sutherland already. I respect her opinions, want her advice, and support her decisions. If ye canna do the same, then ye can stay out of our bluidy way." Hamish turned Amelia so the couple could head down the stairs.

He knew Tormud and Lionel gawked at them from above. He knew he couldn't make an enemy of Tormud, or their clans would never have peace. But he also knew they were both young and wished to impress their father. In time, they would mature and realize Amelia's worth. He'd witnessed Roy's acceptance of Amelia's wisdom, so Tormud and Lionel would come around eventually. However, that didn't mean he needed to allow them to abuse Amelia with their cruel words. He heard them follow Amelia and him as they wound their way to the second floor, where the queen's solar lay. When the chamber's door came into view, he felt Amelia tense, then relax, but not with ease. With resignation.

"Lass, nay matter what happens with the war, I will whisk ye away from here soon. I promise."

"I ken. Thank ye. It isnae so bad, but Henrietta's caused nay end of trouble. I dinna want to deal with more. She likely kens by now that I found ye and Father. She'll likely neglect to mention he was there when she tells the world I was locked away with ye, Dugan, and Laird MacLeod. She'll conveniently omit that we met in the vera suite our uncle also occupies when he comes to court. Ye may have called out to me last eve while ye were asleep, but that isnae stopping some people from spreading the rumor that our relationship is merely a disguise for the one ye have with Henrietta. That ye will marry me because I'm the heiress, but ye long for her. I ought to start ma own rumor that she canna be aught more than a mon's mistress because ye'd never take her to wife. But I willna because ye would never keep a mistress, and I willna plant the notion that ye would."

"Even if I wasna going to marry ye, I wouldnae have one. I dinna believe in them. I wouldnae dishonor ma vows before God, ma wife, and ma people. Besides, lemans are also far more fuss than they're worth. An unloved mistress will expect things only a wife may claim, and she can be a horror to live with when she never gets what she wants. And that's recognition that they might force the laird to marry one woman, but he'll always want to bed another. A beloved mistress only lives a life of pain, kenning the mon can never devote himself to her in truth. She spends a life watching another woman have all the things she longs for with the mon she loves and who loves her. And the wife. Well, regardless of whether she's kind and fair or simply horrid, she lives with being played a fool every day for the rest of her life, pitied or ignored. Nay. I willna do that to any woman or ma clan. And I have nay need to consider it when I have ye."

Amelia strained to whisper in Hamish's ear as he leaned to his side, bringing his ear closer to her lips. "Will ye love me like a wife but bed me like a mistress?" She pulled back and offered him the most innocent mien she could muster. But it didn't last. She waggled her brows and winked, just like he so often did to her.

Hamish knew no one else was in the passageway but Amelia, her brothers, and him. He stopped so abruptly Amelia took a step past him. He tugged her back to him, wrapped his arms around her, and practically inhaled her as he kissed her soundly. He wanted to let his hands roam over her body, but he had enough sense not to do it in front of her brothers. The guards might not allow them to wear their swords in the castle, but every man had at least one knife. Highlanders had plenty. He straightened and chucked her chin with his forefinger. "Dinna doubt it for a second, lass."

Amelia stood, staring and breathless, before she smiled again. She reached around and patted his backside before sliding out of his arms and dashing the last few feet to the queen's solar. She stopped, composed herself, then looked in his direction and blew him a kiss. Hamish's grin warmed the scant few inches that his kiss didn't overheat.

Hamish turned back to Tormud and Lionel, who both stood with their hands on their dirks. "I hope ye both find women ye can love like I love yer sister. Ye'd do well to look for women like her. Especially ye, Tormud. A woman like Lia is what truly makes a clan strong. It isnae the brute force a laird brings with his sword. It isnae the booming voice that carries over a battlefield. It's the lady who cares for every member of her clan. The lady who can take on the mantel of laird when her husband rides out, kenning he might nae come back. The lady who raises a lad into a mon worthy of being a laird. Dinna think for a moment it's a father or fostering that does that. It's the mother from the day they conceive the bairn until the day she goes to our Lord. Ye dinna appreciate her now, but mayhap ye will when ye're signing yer name to a betrothal contract, praying yer wife is as fine as yer sister."

He walked past the brothers as they stared at the door through which Amelia disappeared. Hamish was gone by the time they turned to look at one another.

AMELIA WATCHED her cousin skirt the crowd in the Great Hall, trying to get back to the safety of the pack of ladies-in-waiting. She knew Henrietta slipped out to the garderobe, but she watched as Andrew Fraser trailed her into the crowd. Henrietta clearly wished to avoid him. But his longer strides and broader build made it easier for him to move people out of his way, as opposed to Henrietta, who had to squeeze between people and pull in her skirts to keep from anyone's foot pinning her in place. She'd almost made it to the other young women when Andrew stepped around an elderly couple and positioned himself in her path. Amelia coughed to hide her chuckle as Henrietta's eyes narrowed. Even from a few yards away, she could see Henrietta's cheeks flush with anger. If only she were closer and could hear their conversation.

"What do you think that is aboot?" Elouise asked.

"I dinna ken, but I certainly would like to," Amelia admitted.

"If we can't know that, then the rest of us want to know why you suddenly sound so unnatural. Ever since Laird Sutherland arrived and started paying you court, you speak like an uncouth heathen."

Uncouth heathen? Redundant. But the only one who's uncouth is ye, ye bluidy bitch.

"This is how I've spoken all ma life. It's only coming here and having to tolerate ye intolerant Lowlanders that made me change. I dinna need to impress anyone anymore. I can be who I've always been. *A Ghaidheil.*" Amelia locked gazes with Elouise, knowing the woman was one of the least likely to back down. But the lanky blonde only nodded. For the first two years Amelia was at court, she'd wished she were willowy like Elouise. Her counterpart was more proportionate than Amelia, who was bustier than the others. Even her broader hips did little to balance her upper endowments. She'd felt like a Highland coo amongst the mythical unicorns who were the elegant ladies-in-waiting. But she'd grown more comfortable and accepting of herself in the past year, and she sensed it was that confidence that drew Hamish from the start. It was certainly a characteristic he praised. He put on no pretenses, and Amelia found it freeing.

"A ga-what?" Elouise couldn't be bothered to even try to pronounce the Gaelic word.

"A Highlander."

"*Gur math a thèid leat.*" Good for ye. Rose MacLeod whispered behind Amelia. She was a MacLeod of Assynt, a lesser branch of the MacLeods of Lewis that lived on the mainland. Their shared progenitor distantly related her to Tieran, but they got along like siblings. She knew the woman was one of Kyla's few childhood friends. She'd seen them talking while Kyla visited court.

"What was that?" Elouise squawked. Amelia looked over her shoulder at Rose, and they both laughed.

"*Bu chòir dhuinn uile Gàidhlig a bhruidhinn dìreach airson dragh a chur orra.*" We should all speak Gaelic just to bother them. Amelia looked for the handful of other Highland women who the Lowlanders easily outnumbered nearly two-to-one. All of them looked toward Amelia since she spoke her suggestion loud enough for the others to hear.

"You will not!" Henrietta snapped as she returned to the group, catching what Amelia suggested. "There's a reason we aren't in the wilderness anymore. Just like the Holy Spirit led Jesus out of the desert, we've been led out of the Highlands."

"*Cò leis? Iadsan? Gun fhuil buailteach.*" By whom? Them? Nae bluidy likely. Rose's lilting voice belied the cynicism in her response. She'd faced the same intense scrutiny all Highland ladies-in-waiting received upon their arrival. Just as Amelia had, she'd adopted the courtly Scots language. She'd only spoken Gaelic a handful of times in her year at court, and that was when she was certain no one could overhear her.

Amelia spied Hamish at the same time Henrietta did. Unfortunately, Henrietta was closer. She batted her lashes at him when he looked in Amelia's direction. Since Henrietta was in front of

Amelia, it appeared like he looked at the former when he smiled at the latter. Henrietta set off to join Hamish before Amelia could do anything. She knew Hamish wouldn't make a scene, so it would likely force him to dance with her cousin. She watched, and just as she predicted, Henrietta positioned herself between Hamish and a large man with his back to them. It forced her close to him, and she took the opportunity to press her body to his as she whispered to him. Amelia could only imagine the trouble Henrietta concocted.

In turn, Henrietta watched Amelia from the corner of her eye. She knew it pained Amelia to watch them, and she enjoyed it. She knew Hamish didn't want her, but she couldn't understand why. She couldn't fathom, besides Amelia's dowry, how he could want someone so plump and dowdy as her cousin. Despite all Hamish had so publicly stated, she believed there was still a slim chance to convince him to choose her. She cared not what Andrew Fraser insisted.

"I'm so happy to see you fully recovered, my laird. You gave me quite a scare." Henrietta turned a doe-eyed mien to Hamish, who didn't spare her a glance as he watched Amelia. The woman he wanted shrugged. There was nothing either of them could do to divert Henrietta's attention without bringing everyone else's to them. "You've been so light on your feet when you dance. I've enjoyed watching you, waiting for my turn to partner with you."

Hamish knew she purposely spoke loud enough to make it impossible for him not to take her hint. "Would ye care to dance now?" *I care that I dinna want to.*

"Yes, my laird. It's wonderful being back in your arms." This time, Henrietta used a stage whisper that carried nearly as well as her normal volume.

Hamish realized his mistake the moment he leaned forward to whisper in Henrietta's ear, but there was nothing he could do to change the appearance, so he spoke to her, anyway. "Cease, lass. Ye ken just like everyone else. I'm nae interested."

"Och, I ken. It was an excuse to dance with you. Amelia asked me to give you a message. After last night when she spent most of it in your chamber, she's trying to be more discreet. She wants to meet you an hour after everyone retires. Since she knows she can slip in and out of your chamber, she said she would go to you."

Hamish believed not a word of what Henrietta spewed. He already suspected either Roy or Henrietta arranged for someone to drug him. He also suspected they'd wanted him deeply asleep so they could do something to him. Now that Henrietta spoke of a woman, albeit Amelia, coming to his chamber in the middle of the night, it made him certain Henrietta's intentions were nefarious. It wouldn't surprise him if she showed up, then had her maid conveniently find them together. They knew he'd have to be drugged to let her into his chamber, so she had some other plan to compromise him that evening.

"Thank ye, ma lady. I will be ready." Hamish walked away as soon as the musicians played the last note. He caught Andrew's attention and gestured for him to follow Hamish to the far end of the Great Hall.

"What do you want, Sutherland?"

"It's nae what I want. It's what ye want. Lady Henrietta."

"I never said I wanted the lass," Andrew hedged.

"I never said ye did. That doesnae change ye wanting her. Are ye prepared to marry her?"

"Aye." His answer was swift.

"Ye dinna fear she'll stab ye in yer sleep?"

"Nay. She'd stab me while I'm awake. But she'll make a good courtier's wife." Andrew watched Hamish, uncertain where the conversation headed.

"She thinks to convince me Lady Amelia wants a late-night rendezvous with me. She told me Lady Amelia will come to ma chamber an hour after everyone retires. Ye are going to find yer accommodations for tonight are far better than what ye have. Ye are going to wait for her to climb into ma bed with ye. I'm certain she'll come to ye naked as a bairn. When she does, some friends and I will arrive, supposedly to meet ye there. We will make sure ye're betrothed before the sun rises."

"Why would I be in your bed?"

"Ye were sotted and thought to rest until I arrived."

Andrew considered the suggestion, and he recognized the merits. "So, the lass compromises me in my already compromised state. That's a first."

"Mayhap, but do ye really wish to wed her?" Hamish tried not to curl his nose in disgust. He didn't want to know whether Andrew held any genuine affection for her. If the man didn't, Hamish feared he might feel guilty about his duplicity. Then he reminded himself that he wasn't conspiring to do anything different from what she planned to do to him.

"I do. She won't be an amiable woman to live with. And I doubt she'll be faithful once she bears me a few sons. But I can accept that because she's smart enough to pick powerful men and attractive enough to get them into her bed. She's intelligent enough to know information is power, and that's what she craves."

Hamish stared at Andrew. He couldn't hold a more opposite view of marriage if there were one. But he knew his ideas were the rarity. He recognized Henrietta's disdain for most men, seeing them as weak targets for her to dominate. The only reason she considered Hamish was for the title of countess. Otherwise, he was exactly the type of man she avoided. Andrew would be too if he weren't willing to give her exactly what she wanted with as many men as she wanted. She would never coerce Andrew, but she wouldn't need to since their marriage would inherently be based on her manipulating everyone else. As far as Hamish was concerned, they could have each other.

Hamish's gaze scanned the crowd as he twisted to put his right hand out of view while he fished inside his sporran. He withdrew the key to his chamber. He kept nothing in there of true importance. He burned the missives he received after reading each three times to commit them to memory. He locked the little money he brought with him in a chest he hid between the wall and bedframe. He didn't worry about allowing Andrew into his chamber unattended.

"How will you ken when to arrive?"

"Dennis and Tieran MacLeod will come with me along with Dugan. They'll wait with me down the passageway in Dugan's chamber. When we ken Henrietta's gone inside, we'll wait ten minutes, then enter. Ye must leave the door open for her, and ye must be sure she doesnae lock it behind her. I dinna think she will since she'll have someone coming to catch ye— me — anyhow. But she willna be able to pretend it didna happen if Dennis, Tieran, Dugan, and I see it. I'll send Dennis to summon Roy, and I'll make sure he lets a few other people ken along the way."

"Nay. He tells Roy, and I can tell the king in the morning. But nay one else hears aboot it. I need her convinced to marry me, and we can weather a minor scandal. But this can't be bandied aboot like a bunch of fishwives clishmaclavering. She must have some semblance of a reputation when she meets me at the altar. The point to marrying her is to further our positions not to ruin them before they've begun."

"Vera well. I willna encourage him to say aught to anyone else, but if other people see or hear aboot it, I canna stop that."

"That's fair. I just don't need any of them being the town crier." Andrew needed to coerce Henrietta because he was in no mood to keep watching her make a fool of herself. But he didn't need everyone to know he had to work so hard to convince her.

"Fraser, what will ye do when people call her fickle or a light skirt because she'll go straight from chasing me to marrying ye?"

"Blame Roy." Andrew grinned. They both turned to look in Roy's direction. As though sensing them, the older man shifted his focus from a MacMillan delegate to Hamish and Andrew. He looked decidedly uncomfortable with them together.

"He's desperate to ken what we're talking aboot. He's sure we're plotting something, but he doesnae ken which of a dozen ways we could torment him." Hamish tried not to feel too smug, but he couldn't help it. And he didn't really try that hard.

"Do you need to speak to the others?"

"Aye. I came straight to ye after speaking to the little harridan. We've talked long enough and ken each other well enough for it to make sense ye would go to ma chamber for us to continue talking or even play a few rounds of knuckle bones." Hamish stared at Andrew for a long moment before they both nodded. They weren't friends, so they would have to trust each other. They'd never had trouble doing that on the battlefield the few times they'd been on the same side. But they weren't long-standing allies anywhere. Hamish slipped away to tell Dugan, Tieran, and Dennis. The latter was a member of the lesser branch from Assynt like Rose. They were cousins, and Dennis was one of the few men among the hunting party who'd only been a second-in-command. Since that was all Hamish believed he'd ever be, they'd shared that in common since Hamish was a second son, and Dennis was a laird's nephew.

Once he'd made his rounds to the other men, he sought Amelia. He would tell her the plan since he didn't want her to misconstrue why Henrietta would go anywhere near his chamber. He signaled for her to step onto the terrace like they had the night they met. He guided her to a shadowy corner and kept his voice low.

"Henrietta told me ye wished to see me tonight after everyone retires. She said ye told her to tell me ye would come to ma chamber an hour after the Great Hall empties. I ken that is as great a lie as the devil told Jesus in the desert." When Amelia snorted, he paused.

"It's naught really. It's just that Henrietta said we'd been led out of the heathen Highlands like the Holy Spirit led Jesus from the desert. That's why Gaelic has nay place at court. If she had her way, it would have nay place anywhere. It's funny that I should hear two such comparisons."

"Aye, well, only one of us is right. She wishes someone to find her with me, assuming I sleep naked. I willna be in ma chamber when she arrives, but neither will it be empty."

"Andrew?"

"Aye."

"I dinna think he realizes just how horrid she can be. She will never forgive him for trapping her, even if that's exactly what she planned to do to ye. And she will never forgive ye for yer complicity in this. It's one thing to ignore her, but to spurn her by forcing her to marry another mon— it willna go well, Hamish. She's held grudges against ma brothers and me since we were weans. She has a long memory." Amelia had an uneasy feeling about the plan, even if she would concede it was the most likely to rid Hamish of Henrietta and to force her to cease plotting to divide Hamish and Amelia. She knew her cousin would get her own back on Amelia somehow. It was only a question of when and how.

CHAPTER 15

*H*enrietta glanced down the passageway as she took the last step to bring her onto the floor with the family suites. There weren't nearly as many doors on this floor as there were on the bachelor and bachelorette floors. She passed her family's rooms before going past the Earl of Moray's apartments. She glanced down the passageway to the Sinclairs' door before putting her hand on the doorknob to the Sutherland chambers. She pressed softly, waiting for a noise. When none came, she inched it open, glad that it didn't creak like hers did. She swept her gaze around the dimly lit room with a table and four chairs. The fire was low, and she only had a single candle, so she watched each step after shutting the door. Part of her wished to lock Hamish in with her, but it would defeat the point if her maid couldn't reach her.

When she came to the first bedchamber door, it was open. No one was in bed. She moved onto the second and found what appeared to be a massive mountain slumbering in the bed. The lightly snoring form was on the far side of the bed, facing away from the door. It was too dark to see anything more than that. Once she was just inside the door, she slipped off the light kirtle she'd changed into. It was easy for her to unlace since the ribbons were in the front. Much like she'd crept through the solar, she tiptoed to the bed. She waited before drawing back the covers. She spied a bare back, and she took a moment to marvel at the visible muscle even when the body was at rest. She didn't know everything that could pass between a man and woman, but she knew enough to happily anticipate Hamish bedding her.

She whipped her chemise off her head and tossed it on the floor between where she stood and where her kirtle landed. She put one knee on the bed, testing it like she had the door. When there was no sound, she climbed on, kneeling once both feet were off the floor. Still nothing. No sound from the bed, and the body didn't stir. That made her suspicious. It would have been one thing the night before for Hamish to not rouse at her arrival since he'd had the draught. But for a warrior to not wake the moment someone entered their chamber frazzled her nerves. But she set the candle on the bedside table, then shifted onto her side, facing away from him as she drew the covers over her. Her heart pounded with fear, knowing all the ways this could do wrong. She forced herself not to count the seconds, but it felt like forever before she heard a noise outside the bedchamber. She pushed up on her elbow enough to blow out the candle. She inched closer to the body, and when it didn't stir, she slipped her arm over the man's waist on top of the covers.

The colossus groaned as he rolled over, nearly squashing Henrietta. She rolled back as the man shifted onto his other side. He nuzzled her neck as his hand slid along her naked body. She held her breath, terrified. But the feel of a massive hand massaging her breast made her core ache. The way his fingers played with her nipple, tweaking it enough to make her back arch. Then his hand slid to between her legs. Instinct told her to widen them. She prayed her maid would walk in, so she would catch them with his fingers dipping into her quim. She also prayed the woman took her time, so she could enjoy what was happening.

She did nothing to stop him when he pushed the sheet down between them, since it still covered her body. But she knew when her maid walked close enough with a candle, she'd be able to guess where his hand was. However, it was so dark now that she couldn't see the details of his face, so she knew, with the low light of one candle, her maid wouldn't actually see him touching Henrietta. She had some modesty, even if her maid saw her naked daily.

His hand found her pearl and rubbed. She squeezed her eyes shut as sensations she didn't know or understand made her ache for more of what she knew would happen when they coupled. She needed her maid to arrive before it got to that stage. She still wanted to be a maiden on her wedding night. But she would enjoy the ministrations for now. Fingers gliding along her entrance and a thumb rubbing her sensitive bud made her shift restlessly, and she couldn't stifle her moan. Mayhap that would spur her maid to enter. She turned her head, but she could make out no features since he still nuzzled her neck. Pleasure burst through her as she grabbed his arm. She moaned again, far louder than the last.

"Henrietta, ye came," a raspy voice whispered beside her ear. She understood the double entendre, especially now that she understood the feeling she just experienced. The hulking form pressed up on his elbow and kissed her, continuing to pleasure her at the same time. She burrowed her fingers into hair that suddenly felt too short to be Hamish's. Just as she pulled back, she heard the heavy tread of several men's boots, then a set of four candles illuminated the chamber.

Henrietta screamed as she yanked at the covers while trying to push Andrew away. "No!"

"Ma lady?" A woman's voice came from behind the group of men.

"Emily, find my clothes," Henrietta sobbed. She looked at Andrew, unbelieving, before she shifted her focus to Hamish. "Why aren't you the one in bed?"

Hamish shrugged. "I wasna tired yet. Fraser, I told ye to wait for me, nae to wrinkle ma sheets."

Henrietta turned tear-filled eyes toward Andrew and whispered, "How could you do this to me?"

"You made no effort to discover who you climbed into bed with. You assumed you knew. It's your fault for not."

"If I had known, I would have stopped you."

"You could have known. If you had, and you'd said stop, I would have. You climbing into bed, then wrapping yourself around me told me you agreed to sharing this bed with me. You're naked. That told me all I needed to ken. You wanted the mon in this bed. You didn't care who it was."

"I did care. I care very much. You deceived me."

"Like you were going to deceive an entire court? You were going to claim Hamish seduced you and compromised you."

"One foul deed doesn't justify another."

"But it does beget another." Andrew looked over at the men and Emily. "Leave and shut the door. I wish to speak to my bride in private."

"No! Don't leave me in here with him." There was genuine fear in her voice.

Andrew cupped her jaw gently and pressed her to look at him before he nodded. Hamish was the first through the door, so he collected the candles and put them on the mantle before they all left. Henrietta pushed Andrew's hand away, and he let it drop.

"Etta, neither of us just lied. I warned you against this course of action. I warned you I would marry you even if you followed through with your plan. We both know I'm not who you *think* you want, but I am the mon you're best suited to. I can live with your duplicity. Hamish never could. You'd be miserable for a title no one ever uses. You'd do your uncle's bidding to be a spy, but

Hamish already knows that. He would trust you with naught. You'd run his keep and maintain the ledgers, but you'd never know aught of importance. Your usefulness to your uncle would end far faster than you imagine. Then he would abandon you to the Sutherlands. Hamish would be kind to you, but he would never love you. You would feel more alone than you ever have, even once you bore him children. Is that what you want?"

"You think you know so much. You know naught." Henrietta's denial was weak, and she heard it. When Andrew cupped her cheek again, she didn't resist him nudging her to look at him.

"Etta, we may never love each other. I don't know. But I will always treat you gently. I will always respect you in public and in private. I understand you in a way you are yet to realize, but that also means I trust you. I know who you are and how you think. We're far more alike than you realize." Andrew pressed a kiss to her temple. The pet name and the affection wreaked havoc on her.

"How can you be so sure?"

"Because I've watched you for years. I knew of your infatuation for your uncle. You don't love him as aught more than an uncle. And you don't truly long to be his wife. What you want is to be recognized for what you can offer. You want a mon who won't bend to your will, but neither will he stop you from making every other mon do just that."

"Are you truly that ambitious?"

"Aye, and so are you."

"You won't be faithful, will you?"

"I won't promise I will remain that way. But that is how I will start. What aboot you?"

"Get me with child a few times soon, and I will be until then. For the same reasons you stray from me, I will stray from you. If it's good for me or both of us, then I will bed who I have to. You may return to my bed after you sire our children if you continue to please me like you did tonight." Henrietta peered down her nose at a man twice her size. She didn't stop Andrew when the hand that rested on her jaw slid down her neck to cup her breast. He bent his head and licked her nipple before sucking it into his mouth. Her fingers tangled in his hair again, pressing his head to her. But he pulled away.

"You will be a maiden when we wed in three sennights. But if you wish for more before then, then you need only tell me."

"I want more. I want everything short of losing my virginity." Henrietta snapped her mouth shut. She wouldn't have consented to that with Hamish. She didn't know why she did with Andrew. But as she gazed into his eyes, she knew she was honest with him and he with her in a way neither of them was with anyone else. "If we were to love each other, would you still go to other women's beds?"

"I don't know. Would you go to other men?"

"If it served you and our clan, then yes. If you make me feel the way you did tonight, then it wouldn't be for me."

"That is how I feel, but I wasn't sure if I should say it. If tonight is a hint to how things will be, I'll never feel like I *want* to seek pleasure elsewhere."

They watched each other for a long time, seconds slipping into minutes before they came together for a kiss that threatened to make them forget they were in someone else's bed with people waiting for them.

"Henrietta!" A roar from the solar yanked them apart. Henrietta's eyes filled with fear even stronger than when Andrew said he wished to speak to her alone.

"You are mine now, Etta. He can do naught you don't want. You are auld enough to agree to a marriage, and he never could have forced you to say your vows. Nay priest in Scotland would wed an unwilling bride."

"He could withhold my dowry."

"Let him. The Frasers may not be as wealthy as the Rosses, but we are not impoverished. We don't need your dowry now, and all you will do to serve our clan will be worth far more than some coin and plates."

Henrietta's mind warred with itself. Andrew offered her everything she wanted. It was as though he lived within her mind to know her so well. But she still didn't want to accept not becoming a countess, or not marrying a man as powerful as Hamish. And she would always resent Amelia for taking Hamish before she had the chance to woo him. She would always resent that Hamish chose a plump, plain, and pious woman over her. She was certain Amelia would never stray from her vows no matter who she married or how it would serve her clan. She squinted her eyes at the closed door. Her anger simmered until her uncle bellowed her name again. Terror soon replaced it.

"He's irate. I've never heard him like that before."

"Dress and wait in here until I come for you. Lock the door if you're truly fearful."

"You're really going to protect me, aren't you?"

"Henrietta, I would protect you out of duty no matter what. But I'm protecting you because you deserve it. You do his bidding with no appreciation or recognition. Naught would change once you married Hamish. I will not stop you from telling him things *we* agree are appropriate. I won't ignore you when I don't need something from you. And I already appreciate that being a courtier isn't easy, so I will always appreciate you." Andrew watched the woman who'd attracted him for years. He'd told himself to be patient, waiting quietly for Henrietta to get over her puppy love for Roy. But the moment he realized how seriously Roy wanted Henrietta to wed Hamish, he knew he had to act. He dressed and looked back at Henrietta, who remained in bed with the sheets up to her neck. He nodded before stepping out.

"What the bluidy hell do you think you're doing with my niece, Fraser?"

"You wanted her to slip into bed with a mon to force him to marry her. You succeeded." Andrew returned Roy's glower with a smirk. If Roy stated Andrew wasn't the one he wanted Henrietta in bed with, he'd have to admit aloud his machinations to trap Hamish, who stood off the side listening. Roy knew Andrew had maneuvered him into a corner with five men standing in front of him. He'd already sent Emily away on pains of death if she whispered a word about this.

"You took advantage of my niece." Roy crossed his arms as Andrew stalked forward.

"Dinna shovel that shite at me," Andrew hissed, allowing his burr back into his voice since it made it so much more intimidating than his courtly Scots. "Ye've taken advantage of her and yer daughter since ye dropped them off and rode back to Balnagown. Ye've manipulated a young woman who sees naught but the sun, moon, and stars when she looks at ye. Her mother couldnae give a damn aboot her, but ye took interest in her because ye saw the same things I do. Ye made her think she was important to ye beyond just the news she fed ye. Ye made her think ye valued her when we both ken ye will replace her with some other spy. Ye'll probably make Lionel stay here until he must fight the next battle."

"I'm still her laird. I willna sign the contracts, and ye willna get a penny." Roy dropped all his pretense as well.

"I already told ma bride I dinna need or want it. What I want is her. She kens I believe she's far more valuable over the course of our lives as ma courtier wife than some coins and plates. Before ye interrupted, we'd negotiated our own marriage contract. Push me too hard, Ross, and she and I will handfast. I already ken she wouldnae repudiate it, and I sure as hell willna."

"Och, ye would. The only way ye'd keep her for more than a year is if the church commands it." Roy raised his voice, knowing Henrietta would hear him through the closed door.

Andrew lunged forward and wrapped his hand around Roy's throat, pushing him into the wall. He kept his voice dangerously low. "She may never love me, and I can accept that. But I love her." He stepped back.

Hamish, Tieran, Dennis, and Dugan heard him. They glanced at each other, realizing Andrew spoke the truth. In whatever perverted sense it was, Andrew loved her. None of them would judge the soon-to-be newlyweds, but neither would any of them want the relationship Andrew and Henrietta embarked upon. Yet everyone in the chamber knew it would suit the couple perfectly.

"Sign a contract, Ross. Henrietta and I will go with ye now to draft and sign. If ye refuse, then we'll be married by dawn," Andrew threatened.

"Nae if I lock her in her chamber," Roy countered.

"Ye still have to get her out of this chamber," Andrew threw back. "There is much ma bride can learn outside the Privy Council chamber, but she will never hear for herself what happens within. I will. Ye need me as much as ye do her." Andrew looked at the other men. "We all ken what's coming. We all ken where our allegiance belongs and where it will go. Dinna act like having me alongside the current king willna help everyone in this chamber when the future takes a different path. Ye may nae have included me in yer last meeting, but ye should have. I'm the only here who spends one boring day after another in the Council chamber. I work for each piece of information I remember. Let me wed Henrietta without contesting it, and I will make sure ye learn all I can share."

"Can or will share?" Roy snarled.

"Like I said, ma bride and I already negotiated our betrothal contract. Ye will ken what I can let her tell ye." Andrew turned on his heel and stalked back across the chamber. He knocked once before easing the door open. Henrietta rose from the end of the bed, her hands still clasped. He offered her his, and she hurried to him. With his back to everyone else, he murmured, "We may have to handfast. If we do, do nae for a moment imagine I will let ye go after a year and a day."

"Do not think your Highlander tones can scare me. I know you now, Andrew. And I know I will gut you before Mass the day you *think* to walk away from me." Henrietta stepped forward until their bodies nearly touched. Andrew dipped his head and pressed a kiss to her lips that she received, leaving no one to wonder if they at least lusted for one another. Andrew straightened and took Henrietta's hand. Hamish, Dugan, Tieran, and Dennis watched in silence as Roy led the couple from the chamber. Hamish shook his head.

Match made in hell if ever there were one. Now, where's mo leannan?

CHAPTER 16

Amelia stood in the shadows as the door to the Sinclair suite opened. She watched Dugan, then Hamish enter. She waited for Tieran or Dennis, but neither joined them. Once Hamish shut the door, she stepped forward. He crossed the room and engulfed her in his embrace.

"It's done," he swore. She rested her head against his chest. She prayed he was right. "What are ye doing in here, lass?"

"I heard something ye need to ken." Amelia looked past Hamish to Dugan. "Ye should ken, too. As I was leaving the Great Hall, the king and James Hannay were speaking when the king came to bid the queen goodnight. They suspect people are plotting to force Balliol to abdicate."

"Mayhap one day. But we arenae in a position to replace him yet. We call it suspicioushood. The Greeks called it paranoia. Either way, he has it," Hamish responded.

"But he isnae wrong to worry," Dugan pointed out as he came to stand near the couple. The Sinclairs, Sutherlands, and Rosses supported Balliol abdicating. "Did either say aught aboot what they were going to do?"

"Nay. Balliol asked Hannay for his counsel. He wants the

border clans on his side, but he wants to be sure the other Galloway clans remember their shared lineage. If it werenae for his mother, he would have little claim to aught. Lady Dervorguilla was his link to the auld Celtic lairds, and he needs to maintain those alliances now that she's dead."

"The Hannays are as likely to support Edward and allow him to cross their land as they are to keep supporting Balliol," Hamish mused.

"I ken. That's why I came to tell ye. Balliol didna sound confident that he'll grow auld as king. He's frightened of Edward coming. He said he expects the attack within the next sennight. His informants told him it would be here at Stirling." Amelia watched Hamish as she imparted the last piece of information. His hold around her waist had loosened when she stepped back to talk to both men, but he pulled her close now.

"That means Longshanks has warriors near here. Ye canna travel home. The roads out of Stirling willna be safe for a lady." Hamish loathed the idea that Amelia could be anywhere near a battle, but he accepted it was their way of life. He wouldn't rail against the unfairness of the situation. He would ensure she was safe and knew how to exit the keep if the English overran it. "We canna stay here all night, *leannan*. Let's go, so Dugan can get some sleep."

"Sutherland, I ride out before dawn. I need to get back to Dunbeath, tell Da and Liam what's happening, and return with warriors." Dugan glanced toward his bedchamber.

"Ye need to return to Dunrobin for the same reason. Balnagown is on the way for both of ye. Can we go together?" Amelia wanted to be nowhere near a battle against the English. The ones she'd heard of between clans were bad enough. She didn't want to look out a window embrasure and see the men clashing or hear the noise or inhale the inevitable stench. But more than that, she knew Hamish would ride out with a full contingent of warriors and that would likely keep his uncle in his current position, leading the clan in Hamish's absence. She knew from their walks that it didn't thrill Hamish to have the man overseeing the clan. She knew there was no one adequately fulfilling the chatelaine's duties.

"Yer father willna agree," Hamish pointed out.

"He has Henrietta to deal with. And he'll need to get our— the Ross —warriors the same as ye and Dugan. I'll be safest with guards from three clans. I can travel in trews and keep ma head covered. I'll look like a lad. What do the English call them? Squires?"

"Dugan, ma men and I will be ready to ride half an hour before sunrise. We'll meet ye in the bailey."

"Sounds good." Dugan nodded to Amelia, then turned toward his chamber. Hamish led Amelia to the door. He counted to one hundred once he opened it. When all was quiet, he led Amelia to his chambers. He'd kept the key to the bedchamber. If anything went amiss, and Andrew broke his trust, he could still lock the door that led into the solar from inside the bedchamber. The moment they were alone behind a locked portal, they couldn't keep their hands off one another.

"Ye should plan with yer captain," Amelia panted.

"Ye should be in yer chamber sleeping," Hamish acknowledged.

"We should discuss what's going to happen."

Neither was interested in any of those three things. Their lips met, and Hamish's tongue swept every nook and cranny of her velvety mouth. Her hands roamed over his chest and back, reveling in the parts she hadn't been able to reach or see the night before. She felt the cool air climb her legs as he gathered her skirts from the back. She pushed his sporran from between them. His massive, calloused palm feathered over her backside until he cupped both halves. She rocked her hip against his until he pinned her to the door and ground his length along her mound.

"Hamish," Amelia moaned. Her body ached for relief she

knew only he could give. Her clothes felt as though they trapped her, and she wanted to be free of them. As though he read her mind, he tugged at her laces, loosening them down her back. She tilted her head away as he kissed along her neck. He bared one shoulder, nipping at the pale skin before uncovering the other. He lifted her, guiding her legs around his waist as he carried her toward his bedchamber. But he stopped halfway. He didn't want to take her to the bed where Andrew and Henrietta laid naked not that long ago. He turned toward the other bedchamber. It was the lesser of the two, and the one he'd used as a child with his brothers.

He considered closing the door, but he decided against it. He didn't want anyone to slip in without him hearing. Shutting the door might protect Amelia from anyone easily seeing them, but that meant they could get closer without Hamish knowing. He wouldn't accept that risk. He walked to the foot of the bed and sat with Amelia on his lap.

He kissed along her neck until he found the erotic spot behind her ear. She moaned and ground her mound against him. His hands ran up and down her bare thighs before guiding her to ride his cock, only his plaid keeping him from entering her. He pulled her gown down her arms until he exposed her chemise covered breasts. She leaned back as he kissed the tip of each nipple.

"Lia, we canna couple, but I can pleasure ye again."

"I want to pleasure ye, *mo ghaol*. I want to touch ye like ye touch me." She tried to inch back on his thighs to reach beneath his *breacan feile*, but he caught her wrists.

"I want to feel yer hands all over me, *leannan*. But if ma sword gets anywhere near yer bare sheath, the temptation will make me a weak mon."

Amelia grinned as she ran her hands over his abdomen, up his chest, and around to his back. "There is naught weak aboot ye."

"Ma willpower to deny ye is vera fragile, lass." Hamish

gripped her backside and pulled her close to him. "I ken ye should return to yer chamber, and I shouldnae touch ye more than I already have."

"Hamish, we're marrying. Whether it's vows said on a kirk's steps or a handfast, we will wed. I ken ye fear leaving me without a maidenhead if aught happens to ye before we can say those vows. I dinna have such a fear. I ken ye will do all ye can to always come home to me, especially once we have a family. I ken ye love me. How could I nae? Ye show it in all ye do and all ye say. I'm the luckiest woman alive for how ye love me. I dinna care aboot anyone else. As far as I'm concerned, I'm already yer wife. If we were in the Highlands, and it were the middle of winter with nay priest nearby, we could marry by consent. There's nay one in Scotland, nae even in the Lowlands, who could contest the validity of a marriage by consent. It's as binding as a church wedding. Even more binding than a handfast. Aye, there are priests here in Stirling who could perform our marriage. But ma consent isnae based on them. It's based on me loving ye. I've told ye and others more than three times that I wish to marry ye. By the rules of consent, we are wed."

"Ma heart and ma mind have believed ye're ma future since the moment I met ye. I ken ye've read aboot the ancient Romans and Greeks. Did ye ever read the tales aboot Zeus separating mon from woman to make two forms?"

"Nay."

"I remember reading aboot it in one of ma father's books. It was probably the dustiest tome in his solar. He certainly couldnae have cared less aboot the ancients. But I found it fascinating. I remember reading the tale with Kyla. I dinna ken if she recalls it. I should ask since I think she'd appreciate it now that she has Liam. In one story, it explains how mon and woman came to be. In the beginning, mon and woman shared a body and a mind. Four arms, four legs, and two faces. They were one, back-to-back. But Zeus grew frightened of the power they had. He worried they would rise against him because they were so equally matched. He split them, creating two separate beings. Ever since then, men and women have searched for their perfect match. The one who completes them and puts them back together as they'd once been. I dinna believe in Zeus or any power he had. I dinna believe that's how mon and woman came to be since we all ken God took one of Adam's ribs to create Eve. However, I believe in the idea that two bodies once shared the same spirit. I didna before I met ye, but I do now."

"I may be much smaller than ye, but I will always protect yer back. Ye are the other half of me. I felt whole the moment we touched. I didna realize that's what it was that night, but I've accepted it as the truth since then. But I think God created mon and woman to be joined chest-to-chest." Amelia waggled her eyebrows as she pressed her hips forward and cupped her breasts for Hamish. "Even if it isnae tonight, one day, our bodies will be one. Ye are the one who makes ma soul complete. Ye are the one God meant to be my mate."

"I love ye, Lia." Hamish slid his right hand from her bottom over her hip and down to her mons. His thumb found her pearl and rubbed. Their gazes locked, but soon pleasure forced Amelia's eyes shut. She rode his thumb and the fingers he pressed along her seam. Her head fell back, the cords in her neck straining as her breasts bounced. Hamish suckled her left one through her sheer, thin chemise as she clutched his leine on his shoulders. His free hand gripped her hip, moving her at a pace that was agonizing delight.

She mewled with dismay when he stood and turned them around. She thought he would end things when he let go of her nipple. But he laid her on the bed and pushed up her skirts. She flattened them, so she could watch as his head descended between her thighs. Then she felt his tongue on her slit. He licked with the tip before laving her with it flat, covering all of her netherlips. His tongue dipped within before his lips sucked on her bud. She fisted the bedding as she observed everything he did. Two fingers pressed into her sheath, and her hips came off the mattress.

"*Mo chridhe!*" Amelia cried out as the ache in her core tightened before bursting into waves of pleasure. Her hips undulated as Hamish continued to draw on her pearl. He kissed the inside of her left thigh as his thumb replaced his lips and tongue. He rubbed circles, alternating between soft and rough, slow and fast, light and hard. It drew out another two climaxes before he knew she would grow sensitive. He kissed her exposed belly and rested a hand on it. She covered it with both of hers as she propped herself up on her elbows. "One day."

"Aye. If we have a dozen or if we have naught, if we have all lasses and nae a single lad, I will love ye nay matter what. Any child we have is a blessing we made together. If we never have a bairn, I ken we still share more gifts from our Lord than most. I'm nae marrying ye for yer womb. Ye ken that, dinna ye?"

"Of course. I never imagined for a moment that ye only wanted to breed me. Naught ye've ever done makes me think ye want me for aught less than all of me."

"I desire ye in a way I never have aught before. I crave touching ye and being touched by ye. I want to make love to ye in every way a couple can. I want to fall asleep inside ye, Lia. I want us to be one in heart, body, and soul."

"We are two out of those three. Only ye want to wait for the third. I willna pressure ye to do aught ye dinna want to." Amelia grinned and waggled her eyebrows again. "But I want all the same things."

"I long for those physical things. I canna hide that." He eased onto the bed and lowered himself to her, careful not to trap her beneath his greater mass. But he flexed his hips, so she could feel his unspent yearning. "But there is so much more to ye than a body made to make me sin. Ye are brilliant. I ken I've only seen a hint of how intelligent ye are. I look forward to a lifetime of yer counsel. I didna imagine I would be laird. I never wanted it or to be the tánaiste. Ma younger brother did. I was content as the captain of the guard, training ma clansmen and leading them into battle. Ye were raised to be a chatelaine. It's nae that I'm ignorant of how to run a clan, but I still dinna ken all a laird must do. I wasna privy to it. I ken I can rely on ye to teach me what Liam and Kyla didna have time to."

"Ye are a fine mon to admit what ye dinna ken and to ask for help. It warms me to ma toes that ye want that help from me." Amelia brushed hair from his forehead before tucking it behind his ear.

"I do. I want us to leave in the morning, but I'm nae convinced it's safe to have ye on the roads. But neither do I like the idea of ye being here if a battle rages outside the gates. Ye've said ye could travel as a lad. Is that really what ye want?"

"It may be ma only choice if I'm to leave here. I didna want to be here during a battle. Nae when ye need to gather yer men. I ken how ye feel aboot yer uncle. The sooner we wed, the sooner I can take ma place as yer chatelaine. I ken ye canna leave me entirely in charge of the keep and yer garrison, but I could help."

"I'd have ye be the captain of ma guard before ma uncle." Hamish shook his head ruefully. "He's a skilled warrior, and I trust him in battle. But he isnae a leader. If he had been, mayhap he could have kept ma father in check, but he couldnae. He'd rather drink. I'd like to have ye at Dunrobin when I ride out with ma men."

"Then that's what we shall do. Father, Tormud, and Lionel can come to Dunrobin. We can wed there."

"What aboot yer mother and the rest of yer clan?"

"I'd like them to be at ma wedding, but there isnae time."

"Nay. I willna have ye miss the wedding ye deserve. We ken the English approach, but we dinna ken when they will arrive. We dinna ken how they will strike. We can go to Balnagown, and Liam and Kyla can join us like ye planned. I'll take ye to

Dunrobin, and we will wait for orders from Wallace or Moray." Hamish pulled back to kneel. Amelia followed him up and reached for his brooch. He captured her wrists, but she shook his hands loose. She unpinned it, tucking it into his sporran that sat near his lower back. She drew the length of plaid down from his shoulder. "What do ye want, *leannan?*"

"To spend the night with ye. We will be on the road for days, and ma father and brothers will be with us. We'll have nay time alone together. I'd spend this night with ye." Amelia lowered her hands and waited for Hamish's response. She squeaked when he pounced. He pushed her back onto the bed and rolled them, so she was on top, sitting astride his hips. He cupped her breasts, kneading them through her undergarment. She plucked at the ribbons on her shoulders, and the thin linen pooled around her waist. He drew his hands out from beneath the material and finally touched her bare skin. He squeezed and gently pulled, guiding her to lean forward, so he could suckle her uncovered nipples. He nipped, licked, and sucked as she moaned. She yanked at his leine until it came untucked. She demanded, "Off."

With a chuckle, Hamish sat up enough to whip the offending shirt over his head. He loved the hunger that entered Amelia's eyes as she looked at him. He returned his mouth to her right breast as his hands ran up and down her back. She rocked and rose over and over, wishing there wasn't so much fabric between them. When he wrapped his hands around her waist, she didn't expect him to lift her off or for them to wind up standing. But she soon understood as he unfastened his belt as he toed off his boots. She laughed as he hopped on one foot, almost losing his balance as he tried to lick her nipple, take off his belt, and slip out of his boot at the same time. She kicked off her slippers, let her gown slip to the floor, and reached beneath her chemise for her stockings. When she put her hands to her waist to push down the undergarment, Hamish stopped her.

"We canna both be bare, or ye ken what will happen."

Amelia failed to smother her giggle at his forlorn expression. "Dinna fear. I will protect yer honor and yer innocence, ma laird. I willna ravish ye." She left the chemise in place. But she forgot her jests as Hamish allowed his plaid to unravel after taking off his stockings. He caught it in one hand, shielding his rod, but little else. She exhaled, "Hamish."

"Aye, lass?"

"Ye're— ye're —exquisite." She tentatively ran her hands over his chest, down to his ribs, and around his hips before traveling up his back. She stepped around him, trailing her fingertips to pass over faded scars and hewn muscle. She kissed his back before sliding her arms around his waist. She leaned against him, her breasts to his back, her cheek to his shoulder blade. He drew her around to stand before him. She marveled at every inch before he let go of his plaid. She gazed down between them, unprepared for what he revealed. She'd seen her brothers and other men pishing in the distance when she traveled. She'd seen her brothers when they were all younger and swam together. But she'd never seen a man endowed like Hamish, nor had she ever been able to brush her fingers against a man. It was entirely different now that she could see all of him, as opposed to guessing what it looked like beneath the sheet that had covered him the night before. His rod twitched, and she yanked her hand back before she could touch him. "Did it— did it do that on its own? Or did ye—"

"A bit of both, *mo ghaol.*" He grinned at her, and it set her more at ease. She'd felt it move before, but beneath his plaid it seemed different. She skimmed her nails down his belly until she reached his rod. Her gaze met his, and she waited. When he nodded, she drew in a fortifying breath and wrapped her hand around his length. She wasn't sure what made her nervous. She supposed it was a fear of disappointing him, despite what they shared in the room across the solar the night before. Being able to see him heightened everything for her. While he'd never detailed his past with women, neither had he pretended not to have one. "Touch me how ye want, Lia. All of it feels amazing."

It was a new angle, both of them standing. She moved tentatively as she tested stroking him. When he did nothing to correct her, she slid her hand faster, one tantalizing stroke at a time. It was her turn to watch the cords in his neck strain as he let his head loll back. She watched his chest rise and fall faster as she increased the speed of her hand.

"Lia," Hamish groaned.

"Aye. Tell me what ye want."

"This. Just keep touching me. Lord, how I've dreamed of this every bluidy night. How I've ached for it to be yer hand instead of mine. Dinna stop, *mo ghràidh*."

"I willna." Amelia considered how Hamish had just pleasured her. She considered the girth that rested in her hand. Then she considered whether she was brave enough to carry out what she wanted. He squeezed his eyes shut as his hips rocked slightly. She sank to her knees and licked the tip.

"Lia!" Hamish's head whipped forward as the tip of her tongue swept over the head of his cock. She shifted her gaze up to meet his, and he'd seen nothing so erotic in his life. He fought not to spill his seed right then and there. She returned her attention to her ministrations. Running her tongue from stem to stern before swirling it around the width of the bulbous top. She remembered how he'd sucked on the pearl that was the key to her pleasure. She wrapped her lips around the head and sucked. He hissed, "Fuck."

When she jerked back, her eyes wide with concern, Hamish regretted his oath. He knew she didn't understand. He cupped her cheek, brushing his thumber along the petal-soft skin. He nodded his encouragement with a soft smile. She opened to him again, this time sliding him farther into her mouth. She inched down his length, uncertain if she could keep going. She didn't realize the torture she inflicted upon Hamish, who wanted to thrust into her over and over until he found his release. But he would do no such thing. He feared terrifying her. He didn't want this to be the only time she offered such delight. More importantly, he didn't want to ruin the moment with her. He wanted to treasure every second of their first time truly being intimate.

As she grew more confident, she took more into her mouth each time her head bobbed until she had most of his length within her silky recesses. What she couldn't manage, she stroked. She was determined to master this skill, so she could one day take all of him. But she recognized her limitations this first time. She hummed as she felt him grow against her tongue. He pulsed before trying to pull away.

"Lia, I shall spill ma seed soon. Stop."

She batted away his hand when he tried to press her shoulder back. He did it again, trying to ease his hips back. "Hamish, ye didna run from me when ye brought me to release. Ye seemed to enjoy it. Let me at least try."

"But I dinna want to scare ye. Ye may nae like it."

She stroked him as she licked beneath his rod, swiping her tongue over his bollocks. "I understand what will happen, so it willna scare me. We willna ken if I do or dinna like it until I try." She slid her mouth down again, redoubling her efforts. His hand slid into her hair, loving the silky strands. He gathered it into both hands, watching as she brought on his climax. Her eyes were closed as she concentrated, and he had never felt so loved as he did in that moment. The physical satisfaction paled compared to seeing how much Amelia wished to please him. How she was willing to try something new to reciprocate what he'd given her. How she focused solely on him, as though the rest of the world mattered not at all. To them, it didn't. At least, not that night.

"*Lia!*" Hamish bellowed as his hips jutted forward. She gripped his backside and held him to her as she swallowed over and over. He groaned as his release subsided, his chest burning and his stomach muscles aching from flexing. He eased Amelia off her knees and lifted her into his arms. He carried her to the bed and pulled back the covers. He was exceedingly gentle as he laid her on the mattress and slipped into bed beside her. "I love ye."

"I love ye, *mo chridhe*. I wasna sure ye would enjoy that as much as I enjoyed yer mouth on me."

"If I enjoyed it any more, ma heart would have leapt out of ma chest." Hamish drew her palm to rest over his pounding heart. He pressed a kiss to her lips and drew her closer into his embrace. "Ye belong in ma arms in the bed we will share until the end of our days. I wish I never had to sleep without ye again."

"Only on the nights ye are away from the keep."

Hamish pushed up on his elbow to gaze down at her. "I told ye I have never kept a leman, and I never will. But ye ken I willna seek any other women, dinna ye? Nae at a tavern. Nae at another keep. Nae here if I must travel without ye."

"Whether ye loved me or nae, ye wouldnae do that. I ken yer views on marriage. Even if we hadnae talked aboot it, I've seen what ye think aboot Henrietta's ideas. I've seen how ye look at philandering men and women. I ken ye dinna believe in straying from yer vows. I think ye could loathe yer wife and still remain faithful."

"Aye. But I dinna loathe ma bonnie bride. Just the opposite. I adore her."

"I adore ye, too, Hamish." She settled with her eyes closed. She sighed, completely content.

"Rest, wee one. I will wake ye in time for ye to return to yer chamber."

"Ye need to sleep too. The days will be just as long for ye as they are for me."

"But I'm far more used to going without rest. I wish to see every moment I have with ye. I dinna want to miss any of it. When war calls me away, I want to have these memories to cherish. I—"

"Hamish! Hamish!" Pounding on the suite's door carried into the bedchamber. It was muffled, but they both heard it.

"Wait here. It's Tieran." Hamish scrambled from the bed, grabbing his plaid, and wrapping it around his waist. He hurried from the chamber, shutting the door behind him. Amelia threw back the covers and searched for her gown and chemise. She crept to the door as she pulled the under gown over her head. She opened it a sliver and put her ear to it.

"Wallace and Moray have Abbey Craig under their control and are amassing their armies there. De Warenne is across the river. The battle is nigh."

melia's mind whirled at the news of how imminent the battle was. Questions bombarded her mind from every direction. Would she be able to leave Stirling? When would Hamish, and her father and brothers ride out? What would they do without their full armies to fight alongside them? What if the unthinkable happened to Hamish?

That threatened to steal her breath as she rushed to don her gown, but she knew she couldn't leave the chamber while Tieran was there. It was far too damning. She wasn't fully presentable, and Hamish went out with only his plaid wrapped around his waist. She longed to open the door a crack rather than a sliver to hear better, but she didn't know where they stood. Could Tieran see the bedchamber door? Would he notice it open? She put her ear back to it instead. That only slightly improved the sound, but it was still so muffled she figured the men stood closer to the door leading to the passageway than where she hid. She eased the portal open enough that it could no longer be considered shut. But she could see nothing besides the width of the door's thickness. She continued to strain to hear, but it was marginally better.

"When did the English arrive?" Hamish asked. He was certain John de Warenne, 6th Earl of Surrey, led the charge.

"Just before dusk. Wallace and Moray have the upper hand at Abbey Craig. The English must ken the disadvantage they're at. I dinna ken if they realize how soft the ground will be if they take a stand between their camp and the bridge. But they must ken where Wallace and Moray are." Tieran no longer sounded like a courtier. He was a Hebridean again, and a laird prepared for battle. Amelia could hear the succinct practicality in his voice.

"Ma guess is they think to send an envoy tomorrow or the day after. Negotiate something that will be to their favor and grossly insulting to ours. This came far sooner than we expected. I canna summon ma warriors, and neither can anyone else. The Lowlanders will only be a help if they followed de Warenne here." Hamish doubted many of the Lowland clans would know about the Earl of Surrey's advance. The English crossed someone's territory, but it would take time for the clans to inform one another. They fought each other nearly as much as the Highlanders did. It wouldn't be easy to pass the information nor rally enemies to trek north. But if any of the Lowland clans had managed to do so, there might be a chance they could surround the English. "Is there news of who came with de Warenne?"

"I didna hear. Moray came south from the revolt near Urquhart. The English retreated, and those men may have regrouped here with de Warenne." Tieran shrugged. Without more information from Balliol's scouts, they would know nothing for certain.

"Was there any word whether the Bruce is with Moray and Wallace? If I had to guess, I'd say the English will send James Stewart to negotiate. Bluidy traitorous bastard." Despite being William Wallace's fellow Guardian of Scotland, Stewart had capitulated to Longshanks' pressure and sided with the English rather than his Scottish brethren. "I'd also guess de Warenne will send a Dominican monk or two along to make it look like they come in peace."

As Amelia listened, she was certain the English weren't alone. They'd have Welsh bowmen and soldiers. They'd likely have some Scots as well from the Lowland clans that sided with Edward. That made her stomach churn with disgust. She had no respect for anyone who accepted Scotland being anything but independent. If the Lowlands wanted to belong to England, then she figured they could draw the border at Glencoe, and the Highlands could be Scotland. But she didn't like to consider her country losing so much land to the English. The border was already fluid, land in Northumbria changing hands by generation, if not more frequently. The English had encroached far enough.

"What do ye think Balliol will do?" Tieran asked.

"I think the same thing ye do. Put up a weak fight. Obviously, Longshanks and de Warenne believe we canna defend the keep if they marched this far north. It wouldnae surprise me if Lundie is among them. He turned traitor after the Capitulation of Irvine. Sir Richard Lundie, Lowlander and Longshanks' arse licker." An informant and tactical advisor to the English as well, Hamish was certain. He held as little respect for the knight as he did for James Stewart. They'd chosen their side, and it wasn't the one Hamish believed anyone with a drop of Scottish blood should choose.

"Lundie's the one we should worry aboot the most. He kens how we fight, and he kens Stirling. He's likely to suggest outflanking us," Tieran pointed out.

"Aye. But I wonder if the rest of de Warenne's contingent has as much faith in Lundie as the Earl of Surrey and King of England do. Ye'd think with those endorsements the Sassenachs would have more faith in him."

"Nae when he already switched allegiances once." Tieran shook his head. "He might have helped the English since changing sides, but they'll never completely trust him."

Amelia tried not to tap her toes. She had thoughts she wished to share, but she was stuck behind the door, hiding. She'd have to wait until Tieran left to share her ideas with Hamish. As though he heard her thoughts, she listened to him end the conversation with Tieran.

"Let me dress, and I will join ye and the others. Where will ye be?"

"Ross's suite." Tieran rolled his eyes. "He was ready to put a dirk to Fraser's neck when I arrived to tell him what I learned. Henrietta surprised me. She's accepted this marriage and defended Fraser. They were arguing when Lionel let me into the suite. She told her uncle something along the lines of accept the marriage in private and sign the contract, or she'd make yer and Lady Amelia's kiss look chaste. Something or other aboot stripping naked and entering the Great Hall to find Fraser, then— I dinna even ken how the lass kens aboot what she suggested. I pray for her sake the stones under her knees arenae too cold."

Amelia covered her mouth, fearful the men would hear her snort. She could envision the argument between her cousin and father. And after what she did with Hamish, she could picture Henrietta doing something similar. She wouldn't do it naked in the Great Hall, but she would make sure they caught her. After all, Henrietta had planned to do the same to Hamish. At least, the getting caught part.

"Thank the Lord and all the angels Fraser got her away from me. I dinna ken if he's waiting for sainthood or hell. But he's far more likely to spend eternity sweating." Hamish glanced toward the chamber in which he'd left Amelia. "I'll dress and join ye in a few minutes."

Tieran hesitated, then leaned forward to whisper to Hamish. "I ken Lady Amelia is in there. I willna say aught. Take yer time and say ye went to fetch her."

Hamish's jaw set, and his eyes narrowed. "Why do ye think that?"

"Because Dennis whispered that he waited in the passageway for Dugan to come out. They were going to speak to our men to ready themselves to ride out tomorrow. That's obviously nae happening. Dennis told me he saw ye and Lady Amelia come in here, but she hasnae left. Ye ken he's discreet. He only told me because he kenned I was coming to talk to ye. He warned me I shouldnae barge in."

"Whatever ye think happened in here didna." He put his hands on his hip. "I ken how it looks, but ma bride is in the same condition as the day before we met."

"I believe ye, Hamish. I've kenned ye since we were weans. I ken the mon ye are. Ye dinna go aboot defiling virgins. But ye'd better hurry before Ross sends Henrietta to her. He looked ready to throttle the lass, and he kens Amelia is aboot the only person who'd protect her besides Fraser. If Henrietta goes to Amelia's room, and Amelia isnae there, she'll go right back to causing trouble."

"Vera well. Give me ten minutes." Hamish turned away once Tieran shut the door behind him. Amelia flung open the one to the bedchamber.

"Tie ma laces, please." Amelia turned around, her skirts pulled high as she adjusted her stocking. She had one stocking and one shoe on. As Hamish pulled the ribbons tighter, she slipped on the second shoe.

"There," Hamish said with a kiss on the crook of her neck. She returned to the bedchamber with him as he donned his leine, then pleated his plaid. She spoke as he dressed.

"It's nae just Lundie ye need to worry aboot. I'd bet ma last penny Hugh de Cressingham is with them."

"Edward's treasurer?"

"Aye. He's been to court before. A more pompous mon ye will never meet. He thinks himself a great military commander. He's stubborn. He's likely to insist upon a direct attack if what I've seen of his personality is any hint. I dinna ken how he'd get an army across the bridge when it's so narrow, but if anyone can find a way, it's him. He likely has Sir Marmaduke Thweng and Sir Richard Waldegrave too."

"Who? Thweng? What sort of name is that?" Hamish wondered if it might be Welsh. They had more letters in their words than they needed. He'd seen it written once and couldn't make heads nor tails of it.

"I dinna ken. But the mon's from Yorkshire. I heard an Elliot and an Armstrong talking aboot him a while ago. I guess he's a knight, but the Elliot delegate said the mon wants to become at least a baron. Eager to prove himself."

"And the other? Waldegrave?"

"I ken naught of him besides the name linked to Cressingham and Thweng." Amelia shrugged as she handed Hamish his belt to slide beneath his pleated *breacan feile*. She watched him lie down to wrap it and the belt around him. When he stood, he retrieved his brooch from his sporran and pinned the extra yards over his shoulder. He rushed to get his stockings and boots on. They both took a longing glance at the bed before leaving the chamber then the suite. No one was in the passageway, so they walked hand-in-hand the few feet to the Ross apartments. Hamish knocked, and Tormud answered.

"Nay." The Ross tánaiste crossed his arms as he peered down at his sister. She looked around his shoulder at the men already in the solar before looking at Tormud.

"Haud yer wheest and let us in, Tor. I'm here, and I went to the last meeting Father held." Amelia's gaze bored into him as only hers could. He always relented because his older sister was far more obstinate than he ever could be. He stepped aside and admitted Amelia and Hamish. They walked to the table where Roy, Lionel, Dugan, Dennis, Tieran, Andrew, and three other men stood. Amelia spied the map unfurled on the table. She recognized the area surrounding the keep. She could guess what the chess pieces meant. She gazed up at Hamish, who raised his eyebrows to her. She glanced at the map, then back at him and shook her head once.

Hamish tapped Dugan on the shoulder, and the younger man stepped to his left to make room for Amelia and Hamish, who stood behind her. Hamish cupped her shoulders and gave them a reassuring squeeze. "Lia, what's amiss?"

Amelia tensed. She should have whispered her thoughts to Hamish and had him communicate them to the group. The three recent additions to the group were men she disliked and didn't trust to believe her. She'd encountered all of them, and each believed women were useless beyond procreating.

"What's the lass doing here?" Donald MacDonald demanded. He glowered at Roy, who in turn stared at Hamish. Unperturbed, Hamish stared back at Roy. The MacDonald representative directed the question to Amelia's father, not Hamish.

"Ma daughter is here at Sutherland's behest. She's attended other meetings and has sound reasoning. Ye'd be wise, MacDonald, to hear her out."

"I'm nae lis—"

"That map is wrong," Amelia interjected. "It's nae to scale. Ye ken the Forth widens to the east far more than this shows. This looks like it's passable, but ye ken it isnae. The real problem is Flanders Moss is closer than this shows. That marshland to the west and the Forth will force them to cross at the bridge. They canna ford the marshlands because it rained too much earlier this summer. It's bogland now. The English may nae recognize that, but if Lundie is with them, he will."

It had shocked her when her father came to her defense. He'd appreciated the information she shared, but he'd never publicly encouraged her to speak, and he hadn't taken her side on anything since she met Hamish.

Harrold Oliphant grimaced but nodded. "We had word a scout spotted Lundie upstream about three-quarters of a league. If he fords there, he could bring sixty horsemen over at a time."

Amelia waited, but no one mentioned Cressingham as they considered whether they should send word to Moray and Wallace, suggesting they send troops in that direction. "What aboot Hugh de Cressingham? Is he there with de Warenne?"

Harrold glowered at her, not pleased she knew so much. Hamish slid his arm around her waist and shot the aging Highlander a warning glare. He sounded far more civil than he appeared when he responded to Amelia. "Aye. They're together south of the river. Ma guess is ye're going to tell us what Cressingham will try."

Amelia swept her gaze across the men surrounding the table. She fixed her focus on her father for a moment before looking at each man as she spoke. "Many of ye visit Stirling and stay for sennights, even a few moons at a time. But there is only one of us in this chamber who lives here. That means there is only one of us here who kens what happens every day. If ye dinna want to believe I ken what happens when ye arenae here, then dinna. But ye're a fool nae to believe the ladies ken far more than ye realize. Unless she's deaf, a lady-in-waiting hears things because so many men assume we're too dimwitted to understand. Yet our families send us here to do more than surround a queen like she's a brood hen, and we're all her chicks."

Amelia locked gazes with Harrold, whose face was the shade of a radish. She wondered if he might have an apoplexy, but he nodded. However, that was only after he shifted his eyes to look at Hamish. Amelia could only imagine Hamish's expression. As though sensing her thoughts, he gave her ribs a squeeze.

"Amy, what say ye then aboot Cressingham?" Roy asked.

"The mon is Longshanks' treasurer. He didna become such because he's free with his coin. He will argue Lundie remaining upstream to outflank Wallace and Moray's army is too costly. He's impatient, so he willna want to wait for them to ford the river and ride down to fight. He also wishes to be the hero of the battle. He will take command and likely have Thweng in charge of the cavalry. Think of the glory he would claim if he led an entire army to victory over a bridge that only fits two horses abreast. That such a slow-moving army could beat the inept Scots." Amelia shrugged.

"Ye say ye've heard these things, but how have ye heard them?" Donald demanded.

"I've lived here for three years. People come and go, and I have an excellent memory. Lowlanders speak aboot the English they encounter. Courtiers discuss occasions where Balliol and Longshanks communicated. I canna fly, nor can I just appear in a place by whim. I hear things when I walk through the keep. It's noisy in the Great Hall at the evening meal. People talk over one another, and some voices carry. Laird Chattan proved that." She felt Hamish tense behind her. Her hands hung by her sides. She patted his left thigh twice in reassurance. It wasn't a judgment against him for killing the man. She held no regret for that. The man brought it upon himself.

"Is there aught else ye ken?" David MacKinnon asked. He was the third man Amelia knew and didn't care for. He was the one she trusted the least since he'd tried to convince her to slip away from the evening meal with him more than once.

"De Warenne will hang back. He willna lead any charge. The mon wishes to see another day, so he can lead yet another attack. Considering I've never once heard anyone speak of someone injuring de Warenne, I doubt he fights in many battles. If he does, he leads from the rear. Ma guess is he stays back there, so he can run when the tide turns. He blames the men he assigns to lead different divisions when they fail and hails himself a hero when they win. If ye wish to get de Warenne, ye will have to attack from the rear. A fight is a fight. It's nay one's fault but his own if he doesnae think to protect his back. A sword through his heart will kill him nay matter which direction it enters." Her lips turned down in a quick frown, and her eyebrows twitched as if to say, "oh, well."

"Ross, why is Tormud yer tánaiste? Yer lass should be yer next laird. It isnae impossible," Donald teased.

"She canna lead Clan Ross when she's leading Clan Sutherland beside me. That's why," Hamish responded. He leaned around her and grinned. "Mayhap ye can be Lady Sutherland, Clan Sutherland's tánaiste and Countess of Sutherland. I fight one battle ye strategize, and nay one will ever come knocking at our gates again."

It was impossible to miss the pride and sincerity in Hamish's voice. His uncle was his tánaiste for now, but Hamish would gladly replace the aging warrior with a propensity for drunkenness with the savvy woman standing before him. When the other men laughed, his grin fell.

"I'm nae jesting." Hamish raised his chin. "Which of ye wishes to face a battle ma bride plans?"

The laughter ended, most of the men glancing at the map before assessing Amelia. It was Dugan who spoke up first.

"The only person I'd fear as much is ma sister-by-marriage. Now that the Sutherlands and Sinclairs are allies, and with Lady Amelia soon at Dunrobin, people would be wise to stay away."

Hamish shifted his focus to Roy, wondering if the man would finally accept his impending marriage to Amelia. He refused to consider any other future, and it seemed others in the room were already assuming it was a foregone conclusion.

"Sinclair, ye assume I wish to share ma daughter's intelligence. Mayhap I shall take her back to Balnagown as ma own counselor alongside Tormud and Lionel." Roy crossed his arms, glowering at Hamish.

"I'll be sure to visit regularly, Father," Amelia interjected. "Do any of ye think Wallace and Moray will attack preemptively? They could send men upstream to outflank the English."

"Nay," Hamish said from behind her. "They're likely to allow a few waves of English knights over the bridge before launching their defense. They'll strike them down, then cut off the rest of the English from crossing. They dinna need to kill the entire army. Just enough to leave de Warenne limping back to the border."

"How soon do ye think de Warenne will give the order?" Dennis wondered.

"He'll wait at least a day or two," Hamish responded. "He believes having a battle against the English looming will intimidate us. He'll send Stewart and some monks over to negotiate. A sign of goodwill. He'll even wait to see if we concede before a sword is drawn."

"If anyone needs a sleeping draught, it's him," Amelia mused. "Let him oversleep."

Everyone chuckled, but she saw some speculative looks exchanged. Perhaps someone would poison the officious man. It would still leave far too many Englishmen seeking to subdue the Scots, but it would at least be one less. The conversation continued with discussion of which clans fought alongside Moray and Wallace. The latter brought border clans that had already traveled north: the Hays, Elliots, Cunninghams, Dalziels, Hamiltons, MacDuffs, and MacDonalds. Highland clans also followed Wallace, so everyone in the Ross suite expected to see Grahams and MacLeods. There would also be clans Moray and Wallace led together such as the Mackays, Munros, Frasers, Erskines, Napiers, Lennoxes, Malcolms, and Macphersons, along with several others. Andrew Moray brought the northern clans of MacRuaries, Campbells, MacDougalls, Mackenzies, Comyns, and Cheynes. While the English forces would likely number over nine thousand, Moray and Wallace led an army of at least six thousand. Six thousand who knew the terrain and shared the common goal of defeating the English and driving them out of Scotland for good.

"Ma father is likely camped at Abbey Craig since he was with Wallace and Moray at Dundee," Andrew Fraser pointed out. "I will ride out in an hour to join him. Ross, dinna pray me dead. I still intend to marry yer niece. I must prepare ma men to join me, so I bid ye goodnight."

Everyone looked around, and Andrew's announcement signaled the end of the conversation. There was little else they could discuss that night. It was implicit each man standing at the table would join Moray and Wallace, even though none spoke it aloud as Andrew had. Amelia sighed as her father rolled up the map. She turned in Hamish's embrace and gazed up at him.

"When will ye go?"

"Tomorrow eve. We canna all ride out at the same time. It would raise too much suspicion. The MacDonalds will likely leave with the Frasers. Ma men and I will leave with Dugan. I would remain here as long as I can in case something happens to the keep." Hamish watched as everyone but Roy and his sons left the suite. Amelia wondered what he didn't want the others to hear. "Ross, do ye ken Lia's way out?"

"Aye," Roy responded to Hamish's purposely vague question, but Lionel and Tormud appeared lost.

Hamish took Amelia's hand and led her into the bedchamber Roy occupied. Amelia's brothers followed while Roy put away the map and chess pieces. Hamish guided them to the wall on the right of the headboard. He pushed aside a tapestry and ran his fingers over the surface until he felt the small notch. He pressed, and a door unlatched.

"Lia, there are tunnels that lead out toward the town and the woods. There's also one that leads to the bailey. I will guide ye through them. We will be in there for a couple hours because I want to be sure ye can find yer way even in the dark. I need to ken ye can escape if the English reach the keep. The battle willna come to the town, and nay one will fight near the trees. But ye must be prepared that the English might flee to the woods. If they do, ye must get into a tree. I ken ye can climb them, so get as high into the leaves as ye can. When the battle starts, I want ye to change into trews and a leine. Dinna wear yer plaid. I will get ye a set of clothes from one of the stable boys. They'll be small enough for ye and nae in the best condition. Braid yer hair and tuck it beneath the collar. I ken ye already have sturdy boots. Smear dirt on yer face and under yer nails. Ye canna look like a lass. It'd be better if ye appear poor and of little consequence if anyone catches sight of ye."

All of Hamish's instructions made sense, but they terrified her. She didn't want to flee the keep, but she would if she had to. She didn't want to make her way into town or the woods on her own, but she would if she had to. The only thing she wanted without question was for Hamish and her to live long enough to start their life together. A battle in a day or two left them with no guarantees.

CHAPTER 18

For the next three hours, Hamish led Amelia through tunnels leaving from her father's chamber. He was working from memory since he hadn't explored them since he was a child. He'd imagined glorious adventures when he was a boy left to his own devices in the suite. He'd run his hands over the walls in the room he shared with his brothers and found the latch. With a torch and no one to check on them, he and his brothers spent hours roaming through the hidden passageways. It had been a score of years since then, but it came back to him as he pictured the routes they'd discovered. He led her to his suite, where he wanted her to remain once the battle began, so they began their exploration from there.

After the first hour-and-a-half, he sent Amelia ahead of him just beyond the torch light. He wanted her to know the path by touch and by memory in case she had no opportunity to take a torch. He wanted her well-equipped to escape at a moment's notice. He'd already made her swear she would go to his suite as the first bell chimed. It was nearly dawn by the time they finished. They both had cobwebs in their hair and dirt under their nails from trailing their hands along the walls in the dark.

They emerged from the secret network of tunnels to pick the sticky white strings from each other's hair. They scrubbed their faces, necks, and hands at the ewer and basin in Hamish's chamber.

"What will yer roommate say aboot ye being gone all night?" Hamish wondered as he patted his face dry.

"I told her I would likely spend the night in ma family's suite. She kenned I went to look for ma father. I said naught aboot finding ye. She already kenned it without me saying."

"When must ye join the queen?"

"Nae for several hours. She isnae an early riser. Ye ken it's midmorning by the time we have the first meal. It's nae like home where we rise with the sun for morning prayers and to start a full day of work. The late mornings are a blessing after how late the evening meal lasts."

Amelia ran her fingers through her hair again. As she finished, Hamish gathered it and drew it over her shoulder. "Can ye guess how many times I've pictured yer hair strewn across our pillows? The feel of it when I stroke yer hair just before we fall asleep? The way I wish to wake with it draped over ma chest?"

"Probably as many times as I've pictured ye resting against those pillows as I undress for ye. As many times as I imagine stroking yer chest just before we fall asleep. Just as many as I wish to wake in yer arms."

"Ye truly see our future together, dinna ye?" Hamish couldn't completely quell the inner voice that continued to warn him Roy might succeed in keeping them apart.

"I dinna see any future without ye. Do ye doubt ma love or ma intentions?"

"Nay. I wonder if ye fear fate might interfere."

"Nae fate. Ma father or a war. And I fear they will try. But I refuse to let either of them. Hamish, ma life will be with ye for as long as ye'll have me."

"Till ma last breath." Hamish's response was swift and definite. He drew Amelia into his embrace. "I ken couples who ken each other for decades and never fall in love. They might grow fond of each other but never in love. But I also ken Kyla and Liam. They both say they started falling in love the day they met. It only took a few weeks for them to be certain of their feelings. They took their time to share them for fear of rejection. I dinna think we're all that different from them. And a better matched couple I have never seen."

Amelia smiled softly. "I have. Us." She tightened her arms around his waist and rested her head against his chest. "I love ye, *mo ghaol.*"

"Just as I love ye, *mo chridhe.* Lia, I've shared ma fear I will leave ye before I can wed ye. That fear grows stronger every moment we get closer to me riding out. I want to ken I'm coming back to ma wife. I want to ken ye have the protection of ma name and yer father's. I want to ken even though ye have never lived among the Sutherlands, ma clan will be in excellent hands if aught happens to me, and ye choose to go to Dunrobin. Even if it's only temporary. I want to ken naught will keep our futures apart nay matter how long or how short that may be."

"As yer wife?" Amelia hoped she understood what Hamish proposed.

"Aye. We canna justify saying we married by consent when there are priests here and in town. But we can handfast."

"Unpin yer plaid and dinna dilly dally." Amelia reached for the brooch herself, but Hamish's height made it difficult to reach. He chuckled and removed the laird's pin that had been in his family for generations. He dropped it into his sporran before they wrapped the plaid around their clasped hands.

"I pledge a life with ye filled with love, devotion, faithfulness, and respect," Hamish began. "I promise to lay ma head in a bed I share with only ye. I promise ye the first and last bite of any meal. I promise to listen to yer counsel and share the decisions as ma partner as we lead our clan together. I will never keep ma feelings a secret from ye or anyone else. Ye are the only one I have, do, and will love until the end of ma days. I plight thee ma troth."

"I pledge a life with ye filled with love, devotion, faithfulness, and respect," Amelia repeated. "I promise to offer ye a home ye return to each day filled with comfort and relief. I promise to listen to ye and offer all the support I can as we lead our clan as partners. I promise to always welcome ye into our bed with open arms and a willing heart. I will always honor ye as ma laird and keep our quarrels private. Ye are the only one I have, do, and will love until the end of ma days. I plight thee ma troth."

"I love ye, Lia. This isnae for a year and a day. It's until we can stand in front of a priest. It's until we breathe our last."

"I willna repudiate ye now or ever. I love ye, Hamish."

With their hands still bound, their kiss began with tenderness so filled with love that it made both hearts ache. But repressed longing and urgency from knowing they had so little time with one another brought a maelstrom of need. As their free hands roamed over each other, they shook the plaid loose. They only pulled apart long enough for Hamish to yank his leine over his head. They fumbled with Amelia's laces, nearly knotting them.

"If ye had yer clothes here, I'd slice the damn laces and buy ye new ones," Hamish muttered as they finally pulled them loose. Their kiss was no less heated as the rest of their clothes piled on top of their shoes. Hamish lifted Amelia, her sheath rubbing against his rod with each step as he carried her to the bed. She marveled at his strength as she clung to him when he climbed onto the bed, one arm wrapped around her and the other bracing him as he leaned forward. She reached back and drew her hair out from beneath her, letting it fan out across the pillows. Hamish groaned as he rocked his hips, realizing she fulfilled one of his many fantasies.

He reached between them as he rested his weight on his left forearm. This time it was a growl when he discovered the dew already coating her netherlips and sheath. He pressed his thumb against her button, igniting an aching burn within Amelia's core. She thrust her hips, begging for him to bring her relief.

"Hamish, please."

"Soon, *mo ghaol*. Soon." He continued to press his thumb against her. Now drawing slow circles that drove her to the brink of madness. Her fingertips and nails pressed into his back as she arched beneath him. He inched down the bed until his head rested between her thighs, his arms sliding beneath them. They pinned her hips in place as his fingers peeled her netherlips open. He laved her entrance before flicking her pearl. Her sigh followed a gasp, the sensation still so new. He dipped his tongue within, reveling in how ready her body was and how eager her responses were to his ministrations. He reveled in knowing he was the only man who'd been intimate with Amelia. He had a moment's regret that she wouldn't be able to say the same about him. But he was working on instinct at he continued to lick and suck, having never performed such a personal act on a tavern wench. He'd limited his other experiences to means that would protect him from disease and siring children. His first time had been the last time he shared this with Amelia. There was much for them to still discover together.

He once more firmed his lips around her nub, sucking and flicking until Amelia's fingers snagged his hair, fisted it, and pressed his face closer. Her body tensed, her knees squeezing against his ears. He watched the waves of climax ripple along her belly until she sighed again. Her eyes were shut as she rode a wave of ecstasy. It wasn't until she opened them that she realized what she'd done to Hamish's head. Her legs fell open, and she released his hair.

"Sorry." She winced.

"That was the loveliest sight I've ever beheld. Dinna apologize. I wasna sure if I'd— if ye'd…"

"Hamish, what is it? Ye're blushing."

He pushed up and shifted to hover above her. "We've never

spoken of ma past. This is hardly the time to do it, but I should tell ye. This was only the second time I've done that. I couldnae bring maself to want to do something so intimate with a woman who wasna mine alone. I never wanted to be aught like ma brothers who whored any day of the week. They risked much by going to different women any time the mood struck. Do ye ken there is a way for a couple to join without risking the woman getting with child?"

"Aye. I saw horses breeding when I was aboot eleven summers. I asked our unfortunate stable hand if that's how all animals got each other with child. I didna ken how the backend of a mare was made. It's nay as obvious as a stud, so I thought there was only one place for them to join. Suffice it to say, he told me people dinna have bairns the same way because he didna ken what else to tell the laird's wean. Since he didna say people dinna couple that way, only that they dinna have bairns that way, I reasoned people must come together somehow, so that only left one other choice for how to breed a woman as opposed to how I assumed it happened to a horse."

"Ye ken I dinna see us having bairns together as breeding ye, dinna ye?"

"I ken ye see me as more than a brood mare, but at eleven, I didna have any other way to explain it to maself."

"Ma ever-practical lass." Hamish kissed her, and their conversation ended as need for a physical connection supplanted the need to discuss the mechanics. Amelia reached between them, wrapping her hands around Hamish's rod. Their brief distraction did nothing to lessen his readiness to join their bodies. He prayed he didn't finish as embarrassingly quickly as he had their first time in the storeroom or when he was in the bath alone. Amelia's hand felt divine. He could only imagine how it would feel to finally be inside her.

"Hamish, I dinna want to rush ye, but can we— are ye ready to—?"

"Aye," Hamish blurted. He felt his cheeks heat again. He hadn't been nervous around Amelia before, feeling his experience was enough to guide and satisfy her. Now he had a rush of nerves. As she stroked him, he returned to rubbing her pearl. When they both drew close to release, Hamish guided his sword to her sheath. Their eyes locked before he thrust into her. Her eyes squeezed shut, and her mouth opened on a silent scream. "Lia, I'm sorry. I'll stop."

"Dinna ye dare! I am yer wife now, and I intend to enjoy ye performing yer husbandly duties. Give me a wee moment." Amelia inhaled deep breaths, calming the shock from the abrupt intrusion and the sensation of being stretched to the brink. As she told her body it was hale and to relax, the pain eased away. When she opened her eyes, the concern in Hamish's melted her heart. No one had ever looked at her with such love and worry. She cupped his jaw and lifted her head to kiss him. It was languid and conveyed as much as the way they would soon move together. "I'm all right, and I want to ken."

"I want to ken, too." Hamish drew back his hips and eased forward again when all his rod told him to do was thrust as fast and as hard as he could. But they both wished to know what it meant to make love. The emotions. The physical sensations. He forced restraint he thought might kill him. But he felt Amelia's body adjust and welcome him more easily with each stroke. He kissed her cheeks, her neck, her lips, her jaw. Everywhere his lips could reach. Her hands began on his back, but soon slid lower. She'd discovered the grooves on the sides of his hips that fit her hands to perfection. She left them there until she grew restless. She now understood the longing her body experienced. She knew what she needed.

"Hamish, I'm close, but I need more. I willna break." Amelia pulled his hips, encouraging him to piston his length into her core. Their kisses grew ravenous and without finesse. They wished to devour one another, and the world outside that bed ceased to exist. Amelia pressed her feet into the mattress to leverage her body to meet each thrust. "Aye. Like that... More... Harder. I swear I willna break... Aye."

"Ye shall make a beast of me. I dinna want to hurt ye."

"The ache I have to find ma release is what hurts. I need ye." Amelia slid her hands to grip his buttocks and pressed, encouraging him to lose his vaunted control. Their bodies created a symphony as they moved together, a periodic mewling sound from Amelia and a growl from Hamish.

"Hamish! Och, Hamish!" Amelia cried out as a wave of pleasure spread from deep within her sheath to her belly and out to her limbs. Her heart beat wildly, and she struggled to catch her breath. Only a moment after she cried out, Hamish followed her.

"Lia!" Somewhere between a bellow and a groan, Hamish's voice filled the chamber. His rod pulsed over and over, and more seed than he thought he had spurted forth. While perhaps the new way of coupling increased his enjoyment, he was certain it was because he made love to Amelia. He'd shared nothing like it before. He brushed hair from her damp temple before dropping soft pecks on her lips. He eased his right arm around her waist and brought her with him when he rolled onto his back. She rested her head on his chest and felt as much as heard his heart pounding. She told herself theirs beat to the same rhythm. She drew her legs up and cuddled with him. She loved how one of his massive palms rested on her bottom while the other hand's fingertips ran along her spine.

"I think ye excel at yer husbandly duties. I think I shall be a vera demanding wife."

Hamish chuckled. "Ye willna need to demand aught because once we reach Dunrobin and our chamber, I dinna think we'll ever stop." He tightened his arms around her and kissed her forehead. "I never imagined I could love someone as much as I do ye. I never imagined I could share something— something— so— so awe-inspiring. I ken I could never have aught like this with someone else."

Amelia pushed up to rest her left forearm on Hamish's chest, then rested her chin on her arm. "Ye really hadnae done it that way before?"

"Nay. It wasna that I thought to save maself for a wife. But I'm immensely glad I did. I— um— I hadnae— nae until the last time we were in here."

Amelia's brow furrowed until her mouth opened into a perfect O.

"Och, lass. That expression makes me think of something else we did in here." Hamish's shaft twitched within Amelia just as it was softening. It made him wonder if he could manage another round. But he chided himself for forgetting Amelia was likely sore or would be. However, she felt him and shifted. They watched each other as Amelia sat up. Hamish grasped her hips and rocked her, guiding her until they both found a rhythm that satisfied them together. "I dinna ken how I can go again, but St. Columba's bones."

Amelia tested rising and falling along with the rocking. This new pace set them both ablaze. Hamish pistoned his hips as she rode his length. Unbeknownst to each other, both appreciated how much horseback riding Amelia had done over the years. She leaned her hands on his chest as she sailed toward the wave's crest before going over the top and slipping into what she was certain was paradise. Her inner muscles contracted, and Hamish pinned her hips to his as he ground her mons against his pelvic bone, once more spilling within her.

"Ye shall be the death of me, *mo ghaol*," Hamish panted.

"I'd better nae be. I like this too much to be done with it," Amelia giggled.

"Demand away, ma bonnie bride." Hamish accepted her kiss before they gazed at each other until Hamish's body finally relented and could no longer remain buried deep within her. It was a dose of reality neither wanted. "I wish I could summon a bath for ye. As much as I enjoyed that, I fear ye willna feel the same in the morning."

Amelia climbed off of him and sat facing him. "If I am sore, it'll be a reminder of what we shared. I wouldnae have it any other way, and I willna just have to picture it. I will soak in a hot bath before I begin the day. Until then, I shall enjoy the few more hours we have together. Rest, husband. I canna have ye falling asleep in battle."

She shifted and laid on her side facing Hamish. He drew her top leg over his, sliding one between her thighs. She draped her arm over his waist and nestled close, her head resting on the pillow just above his shoulder.

"Do ye wish to let anyone ken, Lia?" Hamish knew they would have to face the world soon enough.

"Only if we must. I like the notion that we have something to share just between us. But I also dinna want ye arguing with ma father on the eve of ye both riding into battle. I dinna want to say goodbye to ma father, possibly for forever, and be at odds with him. If it's a matter of our safety, then aye. But otherwise, let's be circumspect."

"Vera well. But I will draft an agreement between us before ye leave. We'll sign it and seal it with our rings. If we're nay telling anyone, then ye canna wear ma ring on yer finger. It would be too big, anyway. But I want ye to hold it while I am gone. I'll make sure the priests have the agreement before I ride out tonight. They're the only ones I trust nae to open it. If aught happens to me, it will attest to ye being ma wife. Ye are the Countess of Sutherland. Ye willna be gainsaid aboot aught."

"Aye, ma laird. The ever-wise Earl of Sutherland."

"Wise enough to fall in love with ye." They shared another kiss before both dozed off. They had little time to sleep before someone pounded on the door once more.

CHAPTER 19

Hamish and Amelia looked at each other before turning their heads toward the open bedchamber door. Both were grateful Hamish's habit was to always lock the suite door, so no one could enter without his knowledge. But the doors weren't indestructible, and it sounded like someone intended to burst through with their loud knocking.

"Can we nay have a few moments alone?" Hamish grumbled. "Dinna dress. I like how ye look now." He climbed out of bed, and just like the last time someone interrupted, he wrapped his plaid around his waist without pleating it. And just like last time, Amelia crept to the door with her chemise in her hands. She eased the door open a hair's breadth, but it was enough to hear Hamish open the door. She donned her chemise and turned her head to examine the bed. She thought to hurry and make it, but her gaze landed on the proof of her innocence. That was more important than whomever was in the solar. Hamish would tell her everything. She dashed to the bed and yanked the bottom sheet from the two corners on her side before racing around to the far side and pulling those corners free. She felt clumsy as she hurried to fold it, then shove it between the footboard and

Hamish's trunk. She pulled the remaining sheet and blanket up, tucking and turning it down just as a maid would.

She snatched her stockings from the remaining pile of clothing as she assessed her housekeeping skills. Naught looked different from how they found it. She donned her stockings as she once more listened at the door. Her eyes widened when she heard the new arrival's voice. She was certain she recognized it.

"Wallace and I will lead the initial surge from Abbey Craig. Moray will wait and bring men around to the side, cutting the English off from the bridge. Our forces will have to split into two lines, half fighting those trying to retreat, but are caught between our forces, and those who will try to push across the bridge," Robert the Bruce explained.

"Where would ye have me?" Hamish asked.

"Anywhere that'll keep the Black Campbell from killing the MacDonald and the MacDougall amid the chaos." To Amelia's ear, Robert didn't sound like he jested.

"Duncan willna do aught in the midst of battle but kill as many Englishmen as he can. It's afterwards that ye should worry aboot. Inevitably, the bluidy MacDougall will have something to say aboot how we all fought, and that'll include the Campbells. Duncan takes forever to calm after battle. He'll lop Charles MacDougall's head from his shoulders and kick it back to Glenorchy."

"Aye. Then the MacDonald won't wish to be outdone, and he'll pick a fight with Samuel Fraser, which means Andrew will take on Magnus MacDonald and his bluidy eejit son. The mon is more likely to get lost and wind up supping with the fish. How Magnus sired such a dolt as Mitchell is anyone's guess."

"I'll ride beside Duncan. Ye should ken the Frasers and Rosses are aboot to enter an alliance."

"How the bluidy hell did that happen?"

"Lady Henrietta decided she and I should wed. Roy likely gave her the idea, and if nae, he at least watered it until it took root. I didna consider her because I can barely stand the lass. It's her cousin, Roy's daughter, who I love. I'm marrying Amelia as soon as this bluidy battle is done."

"Amelia? She's always been so demure compared to Henrietta. God bless Andrew for taking that shrew home. Besides, between your uncle Henry and Henrietta, that's too much of a bad thing to have at your keep. The names must be a sign."

"Aye. That thought passed ma mind more than once. Amelia isnae demure so much as astute and diplomatic. She's the smartest person I ken. She puts ye and Wallace to shame. If she were a mon, Wallace and Moray would have naught to do but ride their horses. I ken I've only seen a hint of how strategic she is. There isnae a better woman to lead our clan alongside me. And she's the bonniest lass I've ever seen."

"She's pretty, but don't exag—"

"Finish that thought, Bruce, and there will be one less contender for the crown. There isnae anyone more beautiful to me."

"Settle, mon. I didn't mean aught by it."

"Aye, ye did, or ye wouldnae have started to say it. We've kenned each other for years, and I will support ye and yer cause. But speak a word against ma bride, and I will leave ye without yer teeth. I have nay tolerance for it."

"You're besotted," Robert mused. His Lowlander accent was more pronounced with those two words than before. Hamish didn't care for the judgmental tone.

"Aye, and I will be from now until eternity. Do ye want Dugan and his men to ride alongside me and mine?" Hamish changed the subject before he lost his temper. He was certain Amelia listened at the bedchamber door. He didn't want her to hear anyone disparage her, and he had no patience for such noise buzzing in his ears.

"You, the Sinclairs, the Campbells, the Rosses, and the MacLeods will be among the first wave down the hill. You all have the best horseflesh and the best horsemen. But we'll need you on foot to form the schiltron instead. Moray will keep his men, the Frasers, the MacDonalds, and the Grants with him to come around the side and intercept the second wave of Englishmen. Watch yourself with those Welsh bowmen. If your lass's temper is aught like her father's, I don't need to wake to a blade against my throat. I don't think she'd forgive me if aught happened to your bonnie face."

"She wouldnae. And she wouldnae sneak up on ye. She'd let ye ken she's coming. Dugan and I dinna have many men between us. How many did the Black bring? I ken Tieran came from Dundee, so he has five score waiting for him." They would need a sizable force to create a schiltron, an impenetrable wall of targes and pikes.

"Duncan brought triple that. He summoned men from every branch and sept."

"That's four hundred between them, and Dugan and I each bring a score. That isnae nearly enough, Robert. We need at least triple that to fight enough English to devastate de Warenne's army. Ye ken we must eliminate at least two or three thousand of their men before blocking the bridge for the last four or five thousand. That bridge is narrow. It'll take hours for that many to cross. We'll have too many men to push through to meet Moray's. Even with additional waves following us, and the slow crossing for the English, we need more. By the time we come down from Abbey Craig and fan out, several hundred English will likely be upon us. Who can ye put out front with us?"

"If you'll fight alongside Lowlanders, then—"

"Of course, I'll fight alongside them. They may nae fight like us, but they ken the English better than we do." Hamish referred to his fellow Highlanders and the Hebrideans. They didn't conform to the polite rules of battle the English imposed. Battle was a melee to them, not a choreographed dance. It meant they often overwhelmed their English opponents. But Hamish respected the Lowlanders. None of them had survived long enough to fight alongside him without learning to win.

"Very well. The Elliots, Cunninghams, and Hays will join you."

"Wallace and Moray will agree?" Hamish didn't want to expect more allies if they wouldn't come.

"Aye. There's sense in what you say, and I doubt you'll be the only one saying it. The Wallaces and Bruces will be with you, too. That should increase the numbers to over one thousand." Robert the Bruce put his hands on his hips as he looked toward the window embrasure. "This battle is likely to decide the path this war shall take. A group of earls attacking a town will look like naught but a rowdy gathering when history looks back upon this war. Berwick and Dunbar were merely a hint of what's coming. Stirling Bridge will be the first true battle where we show Long-shanks we won't bend the knee to him ever again."

"What of Balliol?" That was the one genuine concern Hamish had. He watched Robert's gaze slowly shift to him. He couldn't read the man's mind, but he sensed what was coming. "He willna be a concern by the time the first mon draws his sword, will he?"

"He won't. He knows what's coming. He will abdicate tomor-row. If he refuses, we'll lock him in his dungeon until we've won the battle."

"Ye dinna want him to fight alongside ye? At least give him a noble death?"

"Bah," Robert scoffed. "If he survives, it'll make him look like he's still a credible monarch. He isn't. You know that. I know that. All of Scotland knows that. But neither can we guarantee he'll die on the field unless one of us executes him. Wallace, Moray, Comyn, nor I will tolerate that. Whoever takes the throne next can't come to it by foul deed alone."

"If he's here, de Warenne will send men. The castle's garrison canna withstand an attack with so many men."

"We know. We've been circulating a rumor the king and queen are away. The rest of the royal court is with them."

"But anyone here could tell the English the truth," Hamish pointed out.

"They would have to reach the English first. Our scouts would cut them off first and kill them. No one has seen him outside the castle wall since before the hunt."

"Aye, and that means nay one saw him leave."

"They left with a long day of travel to begin with, so they departed before dawn," Robert reasoned. Hamish remained unconvinced, but there was nothing arguing would gain him. He wanted Robert gone so he could discuss the news with Amelia. He also knew he needed sleep. While Amelia exaggerated he might fall asleep on the battlefield, he didn't need to be exhausted before the fight began. He wouldn't risk defeat when he now had so much to live for.

"Ma men and I will ride out through the postern gate tomorrow night. I would let them have tonight undisturbed. I'm sure they ken the order is coming. We will prepare, then join ye at Abbey Craig. Ye should be away soon. Dawn is upon us. Someone might recognize ye."

The Bruce's gaze darted to the bedchamber door, but it was the one Andrew and Henrietta used. The one Hamish should have been using that night.

"Aye. I wish to return to ma bed. I was asleep when ye pounded on ma door, and I wish to be asleep again before the bells ring for morning prayers."

"Sleeping? Two nights before a battle? I know what I was doing a few hours ago, and what I will do tomorrow night. It wasn't sleeping. At least, not alone." Robert grinned.

Hamish took a menacing step toward his friend. "Ye are a widower. I am a bridegroom. I'm nae interested in tupping a whore. And if ye think to imply something improper aboot ma Lia, then I will end our friendship right now. I told ye. I will support ye and yer cause, but ye've almost insulted her once. I'm nae so forgiving a second time."

"Your honor has always been of the utmost importance to you. But you aren't married yet. And even if you were, the lass must know what men are like."

"Bruce, let me clear aboot this, so ye can tell any and everyone else. Amelia Ross will be the Countess of Sutherland. This isnae an arrangement to bring peace between our clans. It's a love match. I willna have anyone else. Nae in ma bed. Nae against a tavern wall. Nae in a tent. Nae rolling around in the dirt. She is as good as ma wife, and I have nay interest in betraying her."

"Speak like that, and people will say she leads you around by the bollocks."

"She can lead ma bollocks wherever she wants." Hamish put his hands on his hips. "I am nae bedding anyone but ma wife. I love her, and I'm nae attracted to anyone else. And dinna tell me to close ma eyes and picture her. I'm auld enough that I dinna judge ma manhood by ramming it into any quim I can find. I'm auld enough to ken I can wait until I'm with ma wife and willna expire on the spot if I dinna get off. Ye can do as ye please, and I will do as I please. Go and speak to Ross. I'll pass the information to Dugan."

"Very well. Goodnight then." Robert gave him one last look, unsure what to make of the resolute man he knew avoided marriage like the plague only weeks ago.

"Goodnight." Hamish couldn't wait for Robert to get out of the suite. He hated Amelia hearing the insulting things the Bruce said. But more importantly, he needed to discuss the news. More than ever, he wanted to be sure she could escape if she needed to. He walked to the bedchamber door and pressed it open.

"Lia?"

"Aye." Amelia's voice came from behind the door. She stepped around it. "I heard the Bruce leave, but since I couldnae see aught, I couldnae be certain ye were alone now. Mayhap someone listened without speaking. I wanted to be out of sight."

"Did ye hear everything?"

"Aye. I appreciate ye defending me, but ye canna pick a fight just because someone says something unkind aboot me. I understand why they do." Amelia leaned away as she finished, and Hamish's face was a mask of anger.

"I will never tolerate anyone saying or doing aught unkind to ye. I willna turn a blind eye to it. It's completely unacceptable for anyone to treat ye in such a way. And what kind of husband would I be to allow it? Mayhap nae every mon believes ye to be the most beautiful woman. Mayhap the mon thinks his own wife or lover is. But that doesnae mean I dinna think it. I dinna exaggerate, and I willna let anyone claim I am. And as for tupping camp followers, I never have. I dinna want to ken just how many other men the woman beds before coming to me. At least I couldnae keep count with a tavern whore. Turns ma stomach over to think aboot it."

"I believe ye. Ye dinna need to explain. Do ye wear armor when ye go into battle?"

"Aye." Hamish walked to the trunk at the foot of the bed and squatted. When he pulled it forward, he noticed something white fall behind it. He recognized it as a sheet, but he didn't understand why it was there.

"Ye must pack it with yer belongings. I canna walk through the keep with it without someone wondering what it is and why I have it. It's the proof we're wed." Amelia didn't know if Hamish's clan would expect them to fly the bedsheet from the laird's chamber window, but she would be prepared in case anyone questioned her. Hamish unlocked the chest and opened the lid. He dropped the sheet on top before rising. He stepped to Amelia and encircled her in his embrace.

"Are ye in pain?" Hamish whispered.

"Nay. A little sore, but naught that will bother me. I promise. I can couple with ye again. I want to before ye leave."

"I want the same. We'll find a way to be alone tomorrow before I ride out. But if it's too much, then we wait. What matters to me is holding ye just before I leave. I want that as ma last memory before riding off."

"A hot bath will set me to rights. Yer armor?" Amelia looked around him at the chest. She'd glimpsed something before he placed the sheet over it. Hamish spent the next ten minutes showing her the gambeson, or padded doublet, with the long, tight sleeves. He rarely wore it since it restricted his movement. His cotun was sleeveless and made from leather, which was harder to slice. It required less padding. He would wear that to ride away from the keep in case any English lurked for an ambush. But he admitted it was unlikely he would wear either into battle. Most Highlanders avoided them since they made it challenging to wield their massive claymores. The tight garments restricted their arms' range of movement, making it difficult to raise the double-handed broadsword above their head.

Before he repacked his armor and laid the sheet on top, he removed a quill, ink, wax, and a sheet of parchment. Together, they drafted the letter than detailed their handfast and pledges. It also stated Hamish's wishes for his clan's future and Amelia's if anything should happen to him. He made it clear it was Amelia's decision whether she returned to court, returned to Balnagown, or went somewhere else if she didn't wish to remain at Dunrobin. It acknowledged any son she might already carry would be the next Laird Sutherland, Earl of Sutherland, regardless of where she resided or gave birth. Both satisfied with the contents, they each signed before Hamish heated two dollops of wax he and Amelia pressed their signet rings into. While they waited for the wax to harden, Hamish slipped his ring from his forefinger and took Amelia's hand. It was far too large for anything but her thumb. Even then it easily spun, but it wouldn't fall off.

"I enjoy seeing ma ring on yer finger. I will give ye a proper one once I can bring it."

"I'm nae worried. I ken we're married. I'm more disappointed

I canna wear a kertch than nae having a ring. A ring is harder to spot from a distance. A kertch tells the world I'm married. I think they look horrible, but I'll be proud to wear mine."

"I ken why ye must, especially as lady of the clan. But keep that hideous thing off yer head when we're at home. I'll burn them if I must. Don it before leaving the walls, but ye dinna need it at the keep. Everyone will ken who ye are. I want to see yer hair spread across yer back and imagine weaving ma fingers through it."

"Ye willna be doing that. It'll be braided or pinned up. I canna wear it down like a maiden. And it willna be practical with ma duties to have ma hair down. I used to braid it all the time at Balnagown."

"Must ye make me cry?" Hamish adopted a mien of someone pretending to sob. "Dinna take away what I'm looking forward to most aboot having us share a home. I want to gaze upon ye whenever I can find ye."

"Daft mon. Ye say the barmiest things."

"Ye heard the Bruce. I'm besotted. I canna help it." Hamish sounded utterly unapologetic, and that warmed Amelia's heart. She felt nothing less than extraordinary when she was with Hamish. She knew he didn't believe she was perfect, but he thought she was perfect for him. She shared that sentiment in reverse. He was perfect for her.

"Help me with ma kirtle. We must give this to the priests before anyone questions where we are. It's later than we realized."

"So much for sleep," Hamish mused. He sighed as he looked at the bed.

"Mayhap we can sneak back here for a couple more hours." Amelia winked at him. They crept from the suite, through the solitary passageways, until they reached the kirk within the keep. The priests were about to begin one of the daily prayers services as they slipped inside. With no one in attendance, a beleaguered priest agreed to accept the parchment. They were as quiet as church mice before returning to the Sutherland suite. They stole three hours of sleep before they knew they could no longer hide. Amelia nearly jumped out of her skin when she heard Henrietta's voice as she closed her chamber door.

"You fucked the mon I was supposed to marry."

CHAPTER 20

"That's ridiculous," Amelia responded. *There was never a chance Hamish would have married ye, ye bluidy banshee.*

"If you hadn't thrown yourself at him, he would have chosen me. But you made yourself so easily available. You trapped him. Lured him like a kelpie."

"Hamish Sutherland canna be lured into aught he doesnae want. The mon is nae easily swayed."

"You convinced him to sniff around you and now tup you. He has but one thing on his mind when he sees you."

"Mayhap tupping me is all he wants." *It's nae.* "But at least he wants me. The only thing he sees when he looks at ye is a woman he so desperately does *nae* want to marry that he let another mon lie in his bed to trap ye into wedding that mon instead. What does that say aboot how desirable he finds ye?"

"I hate ye, ye piece of shite!" Henrietta flew at Amelia, claws raised and ready to attack, her brogue flavoring her words. Before she could sink her nails into Amelia's arms, the latter slapped her cousin. The sound rang in the room, and stunned Mary, who watched from where she sat on her bed. Henrietta gave Mary no hint she would pounce the moment Amelia walked in. She'd been wary to admit Henrietta to the chamber, but she'd thought the woman was harmless.

"I have nay an ounce of love for ye when Hamish wants it all for himself." Amelia shoved Henrietta away. "Cease. All ye want is attention. Ye dinna care what kind it is as long as ye're the center of it. Ye're desperate and grasping. I have never wanted aught since I got here but to leave. Ye love court. Hamish isnae a mon who will come here often. He prefers the Highlands. Ye wish to carry the title Countess of Sutherland, but nay one would call ye aught but Lady Sutherland or ma lady. Ye want a braw mon to want ye. Ye have Andrew Fraser. I didna realize it, but now I can see it. Andrew loves ye, Henny."

"Dinna call me that!" Henrietta screeched. Amelia had done it on purpose. She was ready when her cousin flew at her again. She stepped aside, letting Henrietta take a step past her, then grabbed a handful of her hair. She fisted it and steered Henrietta to her bed. She forced the flailing and irate woman facedown onto the mattress.

"Cease!" Amelia commanded. She turned her head and looked at Mary. She mouthed, "Find Fraser."

Amelia didn't know if he'd truly ridden out already, but she wanted her roommate gone. When Henrietta tried to push up and onto her fists, Amelia sat on her back. She pushed her backside harder against Henrietta.

"Get up, ye— ye —elephant. Aye. Like the ones Hannibal brought across the Alps."

"Ye didna listen to all of that lesson, did ye? Hannibal defeated the Romans."

"But he never took Rome. Ye willna take Hamish. I listened."

"Henny, I didna need to take aught. Hamish came to me."

"Stop calling me that!"

"Henny, Henny, Henny." Amelia knew she sounded like a child, but years of turning the other cheek to Henrietta's unkindness— even cruelty at times —finally came to an end. "Ye have a mon who wants ye. Dare I say even loves ye. If he were an earl, ye'd be wed to him by now. But he isnae, so that single thing makes him nae good enough for ye. But what do ye offer a mon like Hamish? Ye canna tell the truth to save yer life. Ye canna be happy for anyone who isnae ye. Ye canna do aught that doesnae benefit just ye. Ye canna be the lady of a clan until ye mature. If ye marry Andrew, one day ye might be ready. We canna guess what the future holds for a warrior. But the Sutherlands need someone who thinks aboot more than herself."

"And that's ye? Ye're only thinking aboot yerself by pursuing him. Ye could think of me and what I want for once. But nay. It's all aboot St. Amelia and what the earl's daughter wants, she gets." Henrietta's voice rose with each word until she screamed at the end. Amelia was certain anyone passing the chamber could hear every word. The door bursting open and slamming against the wall supported Amelia's suspicions when she recognized Andrew stalking toward Henrietta. He said nothing but scooped her over his shoulder after Amelia scrambled to get out of the way.

"Put me down!"

"Nae until we're in private, and ye can unleash yer venom on me alone. Ye willna speak to yer cousin that way. I heard it all, Etta. From when Lady Amelia walked in here to just now. I was coming to escort ye to the morning meal. Ye and I are marrying, and I willna have the ghost of another mon in our bed. I will exorcise him from yer head. At least I ken I dinna need to worry aboot yer heart. It's too frozen to let anyone in."

Amelia watched in stunned silence as Andrew carried Henrietta from the chamber. It amazed her to witness Henrietta putting up no fight after her initial rejected command. Mary entered the chamber, wide-eyed and speechless.

"He was already in the passageway?" Amelia asked.

"Aye. He is far calmer than he was a moment ago. I feared he might kill her. I don't jest. The mon has more patience with her than anyone should. I heard he told your uncle he loves her. He must. Why else would he put up with that? His clan doesn't need an alliance with yours, and they don't need her dowry. He must really want *her*."

"He seems to. She will never forgive me for this slight as she sees it. But if Andrew can keep her away from me, then I willna complain." Amelia wanted a bath and to find Hamish again. He was going to find her clothes from a stable boy.

THE DAY PASSED in a frenzy as the keep buzzed about the imminent battle outside the walls. Amelia didn't see hide nor hair of her cousin, but she ran into Andrew. He merely promised Henrietta would no longer be a problem. Fear must have crossed Amelia's face, for Andrew assured her he didn't need to beat Henrietta to make her come around. She fought not to grimace as her father and brothers approached her.

"Amy, we're riding out in an hour," Roy explained. "I want you in your chamber with the door barred. Make Mary go in there too. Only let your maid in with food."

Amelia noticed her father was back to his Lowlander speech. She looked at her brothers, and she sensed they were eager to leave. They likely still felt a sense of adventure riding into battle. But she knew neither took it lightly. She opened her arms, and the three siblings embraced.

"Be careful. I'll pray for yer safe return. Stay together. I love ye." Amelia kissed them each on the cheek before stepping back. Despite how angry she'd been with her father lately, she feared for him riding out to battle. She accepted his embrace just as she had when she was a child before he rode away. She whispered, "Come back to us, Da."

"Dinna fash, ma wee lassie. Ye arenae done with me yet," Roy whispered in her ear.

Amelia leaned back enough for their gazes to meet. "I dinna want ye to leave without us resolving things aboot Hamish. I'm marrying him. I need ye to accept that. It's nae just what I want. It's what's best for our clans. We're already powerful in our own right, but allying with the Sutherlands will only make the Rosses prosper rather than losing our livestock, people, and lands to them. Ye ken if he wasna his father's son, ye would welcome him. But he's his own mon. Please, Da."

Roy observed his daughter and knew time was running out. Henrietta had failed at her mission. But his conscience screamed it was just as well. He may have wanted to make Hamish miserable, but he didn't want to make Amelia miserable. With a deep inhale, he conceded with a nod.

"Then ye accept our marriage?"

"Aye. I will speak to him. But ye wed at Balnagown."

"Vera well."

"And we post the banns once we get there."

"We dinna ken when that might be. Ye ken just like I do the banns are a tradition. They arenae church cannon or the law of the land. If it takes longer than three sennights from this coming Sunday, then we arenae waiting." Amelia didn't wish to wait a day, but it also registered in her mind that if she was already with child, they would have to reveal the handfast regardless of whether Hamish survived. If that happened, her father might finally kill Hamish. She watched him narrow his eyes at her. The suspicion radiating from him. "He canna be away from Dunrobin forever."

"He can go home for those sennights and come for the wedding just the way every other noble couple does it." Roy's penetrating stare had never intimidated Amelia the way it did her brothers or other people. She tilted her head to the right and merely returned his stare. It became a battle to see who would blink first. As had been the case since she was three-and-ten, Roy blinked first. Even back then, he blamed it on his aging eyes. "Very well."

Amelia wished to sigh since her father once again sounded like a courtier. Instead, she strained to kiss him on the cheek and accepted another hug. "Is this the last time I will see ye before ye leave?"

"Aye. It's why we sought you. I want you to go straight back to your chamber."

"I will, but I must see Hamish first. He promised to get me a set of clothes from one of the stable lads. If I have to leave, he doesnae want me looking like noblewoman. He wants me to look as little like a woman as I can."

"You know your way around the tunnels? Well enough you won't get lost forever?"

"I do. We spent three hours going through them. I had to prove to him I could do each in the dark several times. I'm confident I can."

"If it comes to it, you must find Henrietta. I don't know if Andrew made any plans for her."

Amelia's lips drew in, and she glanced toward the stairs that led to the bachelor chambers. "Andrew planned to escort her to the morning meal before he left. I dinna ken what delayed his departure. Mayhap he didna want to leave without saying goodbye. Henrietta was in ma chamber and began ranting at me so loudly Andrew heard her in the passageway. He carried her off. I dinna ken where they went, but it wasna to her chamber. I checked."

"Bluidy hell. I don't have time for this. Lionel, go to the stables and look for the Frasers there. Tormud, go to the mon's chamber and see if he or Henrietta is there. If she is, take her to our apartments. Amy, I want you there with your cousin instead of your chamber. At least you can put two doors between you. I know you aren't getting along, but you must survive each other to survive this battle. Take Mary with you if you must. I'd feel better with you there than in a chamber on the ladies' floor. That's the first place they'll go."

"All right, Father." The time for sentimentality was over. With a kiss on the forehead and a last goodbye to the three men, they went their separate directions while Amelia went in search of Hamish.

"THIS IS WHAT I COULD FIND." Hamish handed over a stack of clothes to Amelia. He'd struggled to find a stable boy whose clothes would fit. Any who were Amelia's height had already filled out. She would swim in their clothes. Any slim enough were too short. He thought he'd found the best combination. He would have paid dearly for it if the stablemaster hadn't walked past and realized for whom he gathered the clothes. Hamish learned Amelia always offered the boys treats on Beltane and Hogmanay. She never issued the men or boys orders, and she usually cared for her horse herself to save them the work. She treated each of them with respect and kindness. After the stablemaster gave the two boys warning glares when Hamish asked how much, he slipped them several coins when the older man walked away. He handed them over with a wink. It would take them ages to earn enough for a new leine and a new pair of trews. Winter would come fast, and they would need the extra clothes.

"These will work. Who did ye get them from?"

"The blond with freckles, and the gangly one with carrot hair."

"Dinna call it carrots. Ma father and brothers have that hair. Our weans could too."

"And it will look a far sight better on them than it does anyone else. But ye ken which lad I mean."

"I do. The blond is Rabbie, and the gangly one is Kenny. I will make sure to slip them a little candy the next time I see them."

"*Mo ghràidh*, I paid them well even though the stablemaster made them hand the clothes over once they kenned they're for ye. I'm sure they'll appreciate the treats, but they didna walk away empty-handed," Hamish assured her.

"I didna think they would. I kenned ye'd be fair. It's just ma way of saying thank ye." Amelia looked down at the clothes. She knew she would have to retire to her family's suite soon and Hamish would ride out an hour after dusk. It had taken her longer than she intended to find him. The queen required all her ladies join her on a walk, then adjourn to the music room where Amelia played the harp until her fingers had deep grooves. It gave them normalcy. "When the battle ends, what should I expect?"

"I will come to ye as soon as I can. I will have to ensure we account for all ma men and that a healer tends ma wounded. I will have to meet with the other lairds to discuss what happened. It'll be hours before I can come here, but I willna dally."

"Father wants me to wait in our apartments with Henrietta and Mary. He fears ma chamber will be too obvious a place for the English to look if they breach the keep."

"It is. I saw Andrew before he rode out this afternoon. I believe Henrietta will be far more amiable after his conversation with her."

Amelia tensed as her eye widened. "Did he beat her?"

"Nay. I dinna think he even threatened her. I got the sense he found a different way to encourage her to be pleasant." Hamish arched a brow and shot Amelia a knowing grin. He laughed when her cheeks pinkened.

"Mayhap that's what she's needed all along. Will ye come to the Great Hall for the evening meal?"

"Aye. We'll dine together whether Lady Gwendolyn can chaperone or nae. I'll walk ye to yer family's chambers and say goodbye to ye there. I've already spoken to Danny and Martin.

They're to guard ye, so they will post outside the door. When ye and Henrietta are ready to retire, one of them will stand watch in the solar. Ye ken the way out through the tunnels. I dinna ken if anyone's aware of the way in. If anyone should enter either bedchamber, neither of ma men would likely hear ye scream if they're both in the passageway. Ye might only have the chance to scream once or knock one thing over to make a noise. They ken they're to have their swords and targes at the ready until I dismiss them."

"They canna have their swords in the keep!" Amelia pictured the royal guards discovering men standing in a passageway with their swords drawn. Hamish was one of the few exceptions to the rule and could wear his sword within the keep. Her father could too, but her brothers couldn't. The privilege of being earls, or maybe it was the danger of being earls. Amelia was certain it was the privilege because of the danger. But regular warriors could never carry them within the castle.

"Lia, the king willna say boo to a goose when he realizes those men are guarding ye. Between ye being ma betrothed and the Ross's only daughter, he willna risk our ire. Nae when they're there to protect ye because we're beyond the walls fighting to protect our country."

"Do ye expect the battle to begin at dawn?"

"Aye."

Amelia wiggled her toes in her slippers. "Would the king send for ye this evening?"

"I canna think why he would. Half the men are gone. I dinna think he kens who's coming and going. Nay one's asking or even telling him. Will the queen ask for ye?"

"Mayhap. But I dinna care."

"Let's retire now and send for a tray. Where do ye wish to go?"

"I dinna ken where Henrietta is, so I dinna want to go to ma family's chambers. I'd rather go to yers."

"Ours, Lia. We're married now. They're ours." Hamish was

unprepared for Amelia to do the same thing she'd done at the end of the hunt. She fisted his leine, went up on her toes, and kissed him. It left them breathless before he swept her into his arms. She rested her head against his shoulder, luxuriating in the way he spoiled her and made her feel precious. She closed her eyes and relaxed in his arms until they entered the suite. He put her down before going in search for a servant to bring them a tray with their meal.

"I ken more than the basics aboot medicinals. I used to spend time with the healer since she's ma mother's closest friend. I learned a lot when I was younger. When the battle is over, will there be aught I can do to help yer men or ma father's?"

"Only if they come back to the keep. I dinna want ye anywhere near the bridge. I dinna want ye to see it, smell it, or hear it. And I dinna trust yer safety from the English and the Scots alike. Men arenae in their right mind after a battle. The bloodlust is just that. Lust. Some men want naught more than to find a woman, willing or nae, to satisfy what energy they didna spend fighting. They will lock the gates before it begins. Ye stay within the walls unless ye must leave to stay alive. If ye can hide in the tunnels and nae leave the keep, that would be best. But ye ken what to do in case ye must."

Hamish carried two chairs to the fireplace as he spoke before poking the peat back into a blaze. They sat together until a knock signaled the food's arrival. Amelia shared what her father said about their wedding, and it eased her worries when Hamish agreed so easily. When they finished, Amelia gazed at the window embrasure. She couldn't see out because the hide hanging above it blocked her view. But there was little light peeking around the edges.

"Ye must go soon." Amelia struggled with fortitude as she prepared herself to say goodbye to Hamish for the first time.

"I have a couple more hours. We willna leave until it's fully dark. They may see men on horses, but they willna ken who we are. We'll ride away from Abbey Craig, and once we're out of sight, double back. Wait a moment, wee one." Hamish disappeared into his bedchamber and returned with two Sutherland plaids and the bed's pillows. She watched him as he spread one plaid on the floor before the hearth, pushing the rushes out of the way. He arranged the pillows before shaking out the second plaid. He laid that across the chair in which he'd sat. "Come here, ma love."

CHAPTER 21

Amelia kicked off her slippers, then rose to join him beside the plaid stretched out before them. Unlike their previous times together, neither rushed as they undressed each other. They both wished to savor every moment, knowing they might never have this time again. Their kisses were poignant, laced with hints of prayers and goodbye.

"There's naught I willna do to come back to ye, Lia. Ye are home. It doesnae matter where we lay our heads. Home is yer embrace, yer heather scent. Ye are who I'm returning to. Whether it's this battle or any other. Ye and the family we might have one day."

"I wish for naught more than to be yer respite and haven. Ma arms will be open when ye return. I will take care of ye as ye would take care of me. Ma home is in yer arms. The sound of yer heartbeat beneath ma ear, the feel of it beneath ma cheek."

They eased down to the blanket and rolled to face one another. There was no urgency to their caresses. Just the opposite. They relished each one. They explored their partner's body in a way they hadn't taken the time to do in the past. Hamish cupped her cheek as he kissed her, and she rolled onto her back.

He followed and hovered above her. He bent to lick her nipple before suckling. The feel of her body beneath his, the soft mewling each time he drew on the puckered dart shot pulses of arousal to his rod. But he wouldn't suddenly rush when they were reveling in the calm before the storm. He balanced on his right hip and forearm as his left hand trailed over her collar bone to between her breasts, stopping at her navel before sliding back up to cup her right mound, which he lavished attention upon just as he had the other. He alternated sides as his hand continued its quest until his fingers reached her mons. He cupped it, her heat warming his palm. His middle and ring fingers dipped within.

"Are ye sore, wee one?"

"Nay. But I ache for ye."

"I feel the same." He groaned when she wrapped her hand around his shaft and stroked. He eased his fingers into her, fearful he would ruin the moment if he pressed too hard against a tender place. Amelia's free hand disabused him of such worries. She pressed them into her farther. He took the hint and swept his fingers within her until he grazed a spot that made her contract around his questing digits.

"There. Right there," Amelia whispered.

He rubbed as her hips lifted off the floor. She cupped her right breast, unsure what to do with the aching flesh that felt neglected now that he focused on her sheath. But the sensation where he rubbed was so arousing and unusual she rested her fingers above where she could feel his. She pressed against it and moaned as her hips undulated. Hamish's thumb drew circles around her pearl before pressing and rubbing it in a rhythm that matched what his fingers did within her.

So focused on the new sensations was she that she absent-mindedly stroked his length, her thumb passing over the tip before sliding around the rim of the bulbous head. She tried to focus on the pace and her grip, but Hamish's attention to her pleasure distracted her. She felt the sensation she craved creeping to the surface. Sensing what she needed, he increased the speed and pressure until she called out to him.

"*Mo chridhe!*"

"There is naught as lovely as watching ye come apart in ma arms."

"There is naught that feels as lovely as coming apart in yer arms." Amelia laughed, making Hamish chuckle along with her. He was unprepared for her to push against his chest. He followed her silent command to switch positions. She nipped at his earlobe, drawing it between her teeth before kissing beneath and behind it. She trailed her kisses along his neck as she straddled him. He was prepared for her to position him at her entrance. Instead, she leaned forward, pressing her breasts against his chest. Then she inched backwards, her nipples skimming over his chest and belly until she kneeled between his legs. She watched him as she leaned forward once more. This time, licking the flared head, then the ridge that ran the length of his sword.

Hamish gathered her hair and held it in his right hand. As sensual as it was watching it fall around her shoulders, and as tantalizing as it felt brushing his thighs, he didn't want to miss a moment of the erotic picture she painted as her lips slid up and down. When the temptation grew too great, he closed his eyes and inhaled several times. But even denying one of his senses wasn't enough to slow his body's need to climax.

"Lia, I'm too close. I canna promise ma body will be so quick to recover as it was last night. I didna ken it would. I dinna want to finish like this. I want to make love to ye."'

"We are making love," Amelia responded with a last lick.

"Do ye want what we did before? Or do ye want to try something different?"

"I liked ye above me, so I could watch how yer body moves. It's a work of art. But I enjoyed how deep ye felt within me when I was on top. I dinna ken what else I might enjoy. I assume everything."

Hamish sat up and wrapped his hands around her waist, lifting her to straddle his hips before reclining once more. She guided him to her entrance and eased down his length. "Hamish, that's nearly as good as ma release. That feeling of ye entering me."

"I ken." He cupped her backside but did nothing else. He let her find what felt best before he thrust. They moved together like a couple who'd perfected their movements over years of coupling. It came with ease to them. When they both felt themselves creeping toward their climax too soon, they slowed, savoring their kisses while their bodies calmed. Hamish wrapped his arm around her waist and rolled them, bringing him on top. He pistoned his hips, his pelvic bone rubbing against her button, triggering her release.

"Aye!" Amelia called out. "I'm there."

Hamish watched her lovely expression again; proud he was the one who brought her such ecstasy. She pressed on his back, wanting their bodies to touch from chest to hips. He settled more, but not all, of his weight onto her. She kissed his shoulder, traveling from the outside to the crook of his neck, where she nipped and licked. It elicited a feral growl. His hips thrust in a rhythm that pinned her to the blanket. Try as she might, heels digging into the floor, she couldn't rock her hips. But she didn't mind. She knew he was a man known for his control. She'd seen it when he dealt with her father and Henrietta. Even when he'd fought the Chattan. But as he pushed up onto his hands, she watched the perspiration form on his forehead. Each time he surged into her was a little rougher. His right hand grasped her hip and lifted. She'd never imagined anyone could desire her so much as to have no restraint.

"Lia, tell me if it's too much. I dinna want to hurt ye. I willna forgive maself if ma pleasure harms ye."

"More. Harder." Amelia gripped his forearms as she undulated her hips, allowing him to sink deeper with each thrust. "Dinna stop. I'm so close again."

Hamish never wanted to stop. But he held onto the scraps of his self-control, waiting for her to climax again before he sought his own. When he felt her core spasm around him and once again watched the muscles in her belly flutter, he no longer had any reservations about finding his release. His head fell back with a groan as his seed flowed forth, emptying into her core. He gazed down at the woman he loved beyond measure. Once again, she pressed his body down to hers. He settled some of his weight onto her as she wrapped her legs around his and cradled his hips between her knees.

"That— that was different from how we started. I liked it. I liked it all, but it— I liked the roughness. Isnae that how men—with wenches —should I —" Amelia stumbled over her words, uncertain how to express her questions.

"That wasna how a mon tups a wench. That is a transaction, Lia. It's release in exchange for coin. I didna merely seek a climax. Ma feelings run far too deep for it to be something so simple. It wasna gentle like how we started, and mayhap to someone watching it might look like I tupped ye. But I'm nay walking away without looking back. I'm nae fishing for coins from ma sporran. I hope ye kenned how much I wished to show ye I love and desire ye."

"Ye did. I just dinna ken all the ways just like ye pointed out earlier. I didna think aught was wrong with it. Even if ye had said ye tupped me like a wench, it wouldnae have disappointed me. It'll only disappoint me, mayhap even hurt a wee, if we dinna do it like that again. I've loved everything we're shared."

Hamish breathed easier. He'd been uncertain what motivated her question.

"I ken putting ma mouth on ye isnae what many say a lady should do. That doing it really is for whore and wenches. But it doesnae seem that way to me. I enjoy the way it feels when ye do that magic with yer tongue. Why wouldnae I want to offer ye the same delight?"

"Magic and delight? Ye shall make ma head swell."

"Bah. Ye ken exactly what ye do to me. And ye ken it delights me."

"Ye delight me in all ways." Hamish's body softened, no longer cooperating with his wishes. He shifted onto his side, and Amelia rolled to look at him. "I enjoy these moments afterward as much as I do everything between now and when we started. I enjoy simply watching ye."

"Must ye always speak ma thoughts before I have a chance to?" Amelia drew her forefinger from between his eyebrows to the tip of his nose before tapping it. He grasped her bottom and pulled her close. His kiss nearly smothered her as he tickled her ribs. When she laughed so hard her cheeks ached, and she was breathless, she panted, "Kings."

Hamish stopped after one last tickle. He brushed hair back from her shoulder and rested his arm over her waist. She launched her own attack the moment she realized he thought they truly finished. She sat up and used both hands to tickle both sets of his ribs. It was hard with his left ones pressed against the pillow beneath him. Unprepared, he twitched and wriggled, unable to escape the onslaught. She'd noticed him suck in a breath or tense when she's discovered ticklish spots in the past. He'd made no other sign he would squirm, but he did now. He clasped her wrists together and lifted her arms over her head as he rolled them yet again, so he was back on top.

"Cheeky, lass. I will get ma own back on ye."

"Ye canna. I was getting back at ye. Ye started it." Amelia giggled as she raised her head to give him a quick peck. They settled, this time both of them turned toward the fireplace. Hamish adjusted the pillows to better protect Amelia from the harsh stone floor. He pulled the spare plaid from the chair where he'd left it, covering them both. Amelia helped adjust it until they were content. "Can we do this— lie together like this —in our chamber at home?"

"Aye. Ye can decorate the keep as ye wish. I ken we have an extra trunk in the lady's chamber. I could bring that into ours, then ye could fill it with pillows and cushions to spread before the fire."

"If I'm sleeping in our chamber, what will happen to the lady's?"

"Whatever ye want. If ye'd like to keep a bed there in case—"

"I dinna want to." Amelia interrupted with a decisiveness that made Hamish smile. He kissed her check before continuing.

"Then ye could make it into yer solar, I suppose."

"Is there a door that joins them?"

"Aye."

Amelia looked over her shoulder. "Then it will be the nursery until the wean is auld enough to have a chamber of their own. How many chambers are there?"

"Do ye plan to fill each one?"

"I might." Amelia waggled her eyebrows.

"There are eight on the family floor and eight on the guest floor. Our chamber is on the third. Ma grandfather moved it up there after a particularly violent raid by the Mackays. They made it into the keep. He wanted ma grandmother as far away from the doors as he could. He figured a Sutherland warrior would cut the intruder down before they could get to the laird's family if they had to climb an extra set of stairs."

"Two flights?" Amelia pictured herself lumbering up them when her belly swelled.

"If it's too much for ye when ye're with child, we can move to the second floor. Or we can permanently move down there."

"Did ye climb all those stairs when ye were a wean? How auld were ye when ye could take them on yer own?"

"Ma mother insisted we all have chambers on the second floor until we were six, and she trusted we could manage that many stairs on our own. We each slept in her chamber until we were three. Sometimes there was more than one of us in there because we overlapped."

"That was wise. But I dinna like such young weans being on a different floor from us. What if they become poorly in the middle of the night? I dinna want them crying for us, and we canna hear. Or worse, they try to find us in the dark and fall. I ken we may never need to consider this again, but just in case."

"Lia, if we never have bairns, then I'll just have more of yer time to spend pestering ye."

"Ye need an heir."

"It wouldnae be unheard of if a lad Kyla and Liam had were to become laird if I dinna have a son. It could be another member of ma extended family. I'm nae setting ye aside, and I'm nae siring a bastard to have one. I wouldnae give a child such a stigma, and I absolutely refuse to consider coupling with another woman. I willna even let such a suggestion reach ma ears." Hamish's insistence made Amelia relax. It was a fear any woman could hold. But another thought came to mind.

"Ye ken if I dinna get with child or we only have lasses, I would never seek another mon to sire a child."

"I never imagined ye would. I ken it could be as much ma fault as yers— rather it could be ma body's fault as much as it could be yer body's —that keeps us from having children. I dinna believe it's just the woman to blame. It's ma seed that must enter ye. Mayhap some dinna have potent enough seed or enough of it. Ye canna blame a woman for something made inside a mon."

Amelia rolled toward him. "Ye are the most exceptional mon. If others heard ye say that, they'd think ye weak or a bampot. When ye say such things, ye make me feel like a true partner. Ye make me feel respected. It's the same as when ye insist men listen to me."

"Ye are ma partner, and I do respect ye. I wish there werenae a need for me to get in the middle. They should listen to ye, regardless."

"Mayhap one day." Amelia felt wistful as she looked toward the window embrasure, but she wished she hadn't. "Hamish, it's dark out. It must be time for ye and yer men to go."

"I ken. I noticed. I'm just in nay rush, but I ken I need to get ma men settled, so they can sleep as much as possible." Hamish rose and helped Amelia to her feet. As they each folded a plaid, Hamish told her, "Keep one of these. If ye must leave the castle, then dinna take one with ye unless ye can find a satchel. Dinna wear it. I wish I were giving it to ye under better circumstances, but I want to ken ye have one of ma plaids to wear."

Amelia had noticed both had a faint hint of Hamish's scent. She shook out the one she held and folded it into a massive triangle since it was clear Hamish's *breacan feile* required more than the usual length of material. She wrapped it around her as a shawl. She rubbed her right cheek where it covered her shoulder. She set it aside to dress. While Hamish pleated his plaid, she returned the spare to the bedchamber and the chest in which he stored it. She spied the bedsheet and smiled. She had flashes of memories from the times they'd made love. Happiness suffused her, but she knew she couldn't linger.

Once they dressed, and Amelia had the plaid wrapped around her with her stack of lad's clothes in her arms, they walked down the passageway to the Ross suite. Neither wished to let go as they kissed goodbye. It was a series of kisses until Amelia feared she would burst into tears in front of Hamish. It was the last thing she wanted to do. She swallowed the lump in her throat the best she could.

"I will see ye when I see ye. I dinna have a lot of thread in ma sewing kit right now, so dinna need too much mending." Amelia offered a brave smile when all she wanted was to curl into his arms again.

"I shall tell the English they arenae to touch me, or they'll face ma vera angry wife." Hamish kissed her forehead, not eager to let go. But he reached past Amelia and pressed the door handle. "I love ye, *mo ghaol.*"

"I love ye, too, *mo ghaol.*" Amelia prayed it wasn't the last time she said that or heard it, but her mind screamed it might be.

CHAPTER 22

$\mathcal{U}$nlike the flurry of activity that took place the day Hamish and his men rode out of Stirling Castle, there'd been next to nothing to do for the past two days. Wallace and Moray prepared their army for battle the morning after Hamish and his men slipped out of the keep alongside Dugan and his warriors. But de Warenne overslept, and his troops approaching the bridge had to be recalled. It was an endless source of amusement. The Highlanders' booming laughter was surely heard all the way to the English encampment. At least, that was their goal. Hamish recalled Amelia making a comment aboot de Warenne being the one who should have had a sleeping draught slipped to him. Hamish wondered if her wish came true.

The previous day, de Warenne sent James Stewart and two Dominican priests to negotiate. They didn't bother approaching the castle gates. They went to Abbey Craig instead. They shouldn't have bothered. Robert the Bruce and John "the Red" Comyn went to the keep and veritably yanked King John from his throne. More than a hundred warriors followed the men, and the royal guards did nothing to block them as they swarmed the bailey. Hamish had watched as the man arrived at Abbey Craig as

King John. By the end of the meeting with the English envoy, Scotland was without a king. John Balliol had abdicated.

Hamish had stood three men to the right of William Wallace as he imparted his ultimate message to James Stewart. "Tell your commander that we are not here to make peace, but to do battle to defend ourselves and liberate our kingdom. Let them come, and we shall prove this in their very beards."

The Highlanders, close enough to hear, lifted their swords and targes, pounding their sword handles against their shields. The cacophony of noise traveled through the Scottish camp, and warriors from all the clans joined in. Hamish wondered how many of the English pished themselves hearing the various clans' battle cries among the rhythmic drumming. He wondered about their thoughts as they surely feared what the Scots might be doing to Stewart and the two priests. It was rare he considered himself a Scot. He was a Highlander. But while they waited as a unified force to fight their common enemy, he was the same as any man from the Lowlands. A Scot defending the land that had belonged to his family since the Picts dominated the land.

It wasn't until Hamish's third day at Abbey Craig that the time came. He, along with all the men, rose at dawn. They checked their weapons and donned their armor, if they wore any. It was just over three-quarters of a league from the abbey to the bridge. They descended the hill on horseback but dismounted an easy running distance before they reached the inevitable battlefield. The clans gathered in groups around their leaders, who led them in prayer and reminded them of what was at stake. Hamish looked around the score of warriors he'd brought with him to Stirling. They were men he'd fought alongside since he'd walked into the list for the first time at four-and-ten. They were men he'd trained since they were lads. He hadn't brought his best warriors since he needed them at Dunrobin to defend their home. But he held no doubts the warriors who stood with him were among the best in the land.

"But there for the grace of God go we *sans peur*," Hamish finished the Biblical proverb with the clan's motto of without fear. He and his men chanted, "*Ceann na Drochaide Bige*." The Sutherland war cry of "The head of the little bridge."

Like the other clans, they awaited the order to advance. But it didn't come. Hamish watched as a rider approached. He recognized the man as an Elliot delegate who'd followed that day's English emissary at a safe distance. Hamish, Roy, and several other men once more surrounded Wallace and Moray, this time joined by Robert the Bruce.

"That bluidy bastard de Warenne believed you sent me to negotiate. That we will concede defeat to avoid the battle. They sent a messenger across the bridge to tell me. I don't know what those priests or Stewart said, but I could practically see Stewart sweating and shaking his head as the mon approached me. I turned my horse and spurred it before the maggot finished speaking."

"They're on the move," Tormud stated as he pointed toward the Stirling Bridge. Hamish and the others hurried back to their clans once more. This time Hamish picked up a spear one-and-a-half times his height. He leaned forward to see Roy, who had Tormud to his right and Lionel to his left. Sensing him, Roy looked toward Hamish. They exchanged a nod.

"Ready and hold!" Moray bellowed, and the command echoed through the six thousand warriors gathered. "Hold!... Hold!... *Cha togar m' fhearg gun dìoladh.*" No one can harm me unpunished. He shouted the Scottish motto as the blend of Highlanders, Lowlanders, and Islanders poured forth.

Hamish took off with his targe fastened to his left forearm. His sword remained strapped to his back while his right hand carried the spear. As the hoard of Scots reached the oncoming Englishmen, they came together to form a schiltron. The formation, with its spears pointing outward in a wedge, appeared like a massive hedgehog advancing on the English. They made headway with a nearly impenetrable force until a score of English cavalrymen attacked the left flank, cutting down the men.

When it became clear the spear would no longer be his better weapon, Hamish drew his sword and swept it through one opponent after another. He'd fought the English enough times now to know where to look and aim for weak spots in their armor. His sword poked through several openings in the underarm, or the crook of the neck, or through the helm's eye slits. He parried until he could make his last thrust. He withdrew his weapon from one dead man's body and moved onto the next. Sweat poured from his forehead, but he didn't dare lose focus long enough to wipe it away, lest an opponent fell him. He shook his head, hoping to release some of it from his hair. His gaze swept the area, scanning for his men. He saw most. The Sutherlands and other clans who were part of the first wave continued to push forward, but they were becoming outnumbered.

"*Ceann na Drochaide Bige!*" The head of the little bridge!

"*Giringoe! Giringoe!*"

Hamish spun to look behind him as he heard his clan's war cry booming whence he came. The Sinclair battle cry that harkened back to their Norse heritage and the name of one of the clan's earliest castles nearly drowned it out. He spied his uncle leading his clan with Liam and his father, Donnell, riding alongside them. He was certain he saw Rosses to the right of the Sinclairs, who approached in the middle of the new wave of warriors.

"*Sans peur!*" Without fear. Hamish roared with his sword raised, pumping his arm in the air. Energized by the reinforcement's arrival, he turned once more. As he looked around again, he realized he'd only spun in a circle without stopping. He'd noticed the Sutherland, Sinclair, and Ross men as he rotated in place before pressing on. It became slow progress as he estimated at least a thousand men were in the English Vanguard made up of mounted knights and foot soldiers. He spotted two men who clearly led, but he didn't know which one was Thweng and which one was Cressingham. He spied the Welsh bowmen who spread out along the riverbank and began launching their arrows into the swarm of fighters. He wondered how many of the arrows lodged themselves in friend instead foe. With the way the melee churned and surged, a target could shift in a second.

"Wee brother! Ye canna have all the fun!"

"Dinna tease the lad."

Hamish looked to his right as mirror images in appearance— physical features and movement —pushed through to reach Dugan, who'd remained near Hamish throughout. The original contingents of Sutherland and Sinclairs fought together, unified as allies.

"Haud ye wheest and be useful," Dugan called back to Liam. The older sibling handed reins to Dugan, and Hamish recognized the man's horse.

"Hamish! Here!" Uncle Henry tossed a set to Hamish much like Liam did to Dugan. Hamish mounted his trusty steed and felt whole.

As Hamish leaned far to his left to strike an approaching horseman, sweeping him from the saddle, he noticed the Sinclair cyclops became a three-headed hydra. He and his brothers and father had never moved with such synchronicity. And their appearances were never so similar as to look like there were three versions of the same man. Donnell Sinclair could have passed for either of his sons. A man in his fifth decade, it was impossible to tell him apart from his sons, who were in their twenties.

"How much longer do ye think?" Lionel said as he came alongside Hamish. "There must be nearly— two thousand who have —already crossed. This field— canna hold much— more before —we're overrun." Lionel panted every few words, some punctuated with extra force as he beat back a foot soldier with his targe.

"I dinna ken." Hamish struggled for the three words, his throat so dry. He sucked in deep lungfuls of air whenever he could. He heard a roar of pain and looked over to see his uncle's thigh bleeding.

"Ye bluidy Sassenach son of a whore!" Henry rammed his targe into the English foot soldier's head before running him through.

"Are ye all right, Uncle?"

"Aye. If the Rosses canna kill me, then neither will the bluidy English. I see ye, Roy Ross. I will come for ye next."

Hamish would have much to explain, and he prayed his uncle would accept Amelia. It was a complication he'd pushed from his mind several times. He did the same now, focusing once more on the battle. The way the River Forth wound, it created an unfinished loop that now trapped the English on three sides with the Scots approaching from the front. But more enemy warriors kept pouring across the bridge.

"It canna hold all that weight forever," Hamish said to anyone who could hear.

"Aye. It will fall," Liam agreed. "But we must kill the bluidy bastards who've already made it across."

Hamish had no concept of how much time had lapsed since he helped lead the charge. It was as though time didn't exist during battle. He never had a sense of whether five minutes or five hours passed. He simply fought to stay alive, and now that he had Amelia, he fought doubly hard. During a moment of peace, he finally swiped his sleeve across his forehead and eyes, which had burned for ages. He noticed the sun had passed overheard, and they'd entered the afternoon.

"Watch or weep this night!" Andrew Moray rode toward the crush of warriors and the end of the bridge where English warriors continued to cross. A wave of fresh Scottish fighters surged forward, blocking the forward flow of combatants trying to cross the bridge. The new arrivals also prevented any retreat, successfully dividing the English army. With no way to move forward and no way to move back, the weight of so many horses and men caused the wooden bridge to creak and sway.

An almighty crack rent the air before a melody and harmony of ongoing splashes signaled the bridge's collapse. Many paused their fighting to stare as man and beast plummeted into the river. The current already carrying away some and sucking others below the surface. But the distraction didn't last long. Hamish and his brethren continued to cut through the English. Only about two thousand of the nine thousand strong English army crossed the bridge before its demise. These two thousand now faced the full Scottish force of nearly six thousand. With no reinforcements, the tide turned against the English. They'd already struggled to defend themselves; the offensive advantage ended the moment they clashed swords with the Scots. Their defeat came within minutes of Moray's forces joining the main body of the Scottish army.

Cheers went up from the Scots. Those cheers included taunts shouted across the river to the English. From atop his mount, Hamish could see down the river to where more English gathered. But they had no means to cross. He considered what Amelia said about Lundie taking forces upstream to flank and attack. Had he done that, the battle would have been entirely different. He looked down at the bodies strewn around him, searching for Sutherland plaids. His brow furrowed as he dismounted. He approached a body with a helm laying next to it. Someone had clearly knocked it off. Sightless eyes stared toward the heavens.

"Isnae this Cressingham?" Hamish asked as he swept his gaze among the clan leaders also looking for their fellow clansmen.

"Who said Cressingham?" William Wallace asked as he approached on foot.

Hamish pointed. "Him. His horse hasnae left him. The animal's armor has Cressingham's crest."

"That's him," Wallace confirmed. He laid his sword on the churned mud beside the knight and unfastened the man's armor. He rolled the dead body until he could raise the hauberk to expose the back. Hamish watched in stunned silence, like everyone else surrounding Wallace and the dead Cressingham, as the Scottish hero flayed a chunk of skin from the corpse. "I shall send a piece of this to each end of our glorious land, so our people know we are mighty and proud. We will defeat those who think to steal our lives and our homes." He held up the flap of skin. "I might even have a baldrick made to hold my sword."

Some cheered while others merely stared. But the examination of bodies continued beyond the dead English leader. Clansmen searched among the fallen, and piles of felled warriors formed as clans found spots to gather. Hamish didn't know anyone specific to look for beyond the men who'd ridden out with him.

"Uncle Henry, what are ye doing here?" Hamish asked the older man as Henry guzzled what Hamish knew was whisky from a wineskin.

"The Sinclairs passed us as they headed south. I kenned ye'd be out here with nae nearly enough Sutherlands to protect ye when ye have the bluidy bastards over there—" He jerked his chin. "—trying to cut ye down. I kenned ye would want our men to fight alongside everyone else to keep the Highlands for the Highlanders. We canna allow the Sassenachs any farther north, or they will come to God's vera country."

Hamish listened to his uncle who'd clearly ridden into battle soused. He'd still been an adolescent when Hamish realized his uncle fought far better intoxicated than sober. He didn't question it, accepting it for what it was. "If ye're here, who's leading our clan at home?"

A sinking sensation took root in Hamish's belly. The Rosses

weren't their only foe, and not all the Highland clans sent warriors to aid the cause.

"Ma Kyla," Liam called over. "Mama is running Dunbeath as she always does. Kyla stayed at Dunrobin after we rode out with Henry and yer men." Liam winked at his father as he teased the older man, and elbowed Dugan in return as they laughed at Liam's jest.

Hamish knew he and his clan had come a long way if Liam agreed to Kyla remaining at Dunrobin without him. He'd barely left her side the first sennight they were there after Hamish inherited the lairdship. Fear of his father kept the clan from ever protecting Kyla from the man's savage temper. She'd left Dunrobin and hoped to never look back. Now she believed it was no longer her home, but she could accept always being a Sutherland, even though now she was a Sinclair, too.

The next three hours passed in as much a blur as had the battle. Hamish helped identify his men and move them to where they lit a pyre. The massive fires dotted the field as the other clans did the same. There were too many bodies to carry home, and some clans had so many casualties it would likely be sennights before they could travel. Hamish counted himself lucky that out of the one hundred and seventy men wearing the Sutherland plaid, only sixty-four perished. After he'd helped his clansmen, the leaders of each clan's delegation met to discuss what happened.

"Where's Moray?" Roy asked of the group.

"Didna ye hear?" Tieran spoke up. "He was injured. Pulled from his horse. Nay one kens if he'll make it."

Silence fell over the gathered men as their gazes followed Tieran's finger to where a woman leaned over a body. Seeing the feminine form reminded Hamish of Amelia's offer to help. The moment the discussion was done, he jogged to the riverbank. The English had already retreated farther than arrows could reach. He knew the battle was done, and the Scots trounced the

English. He didn't fear another wave of fighting, so he set his sword beside him and scrubbed his hands with the chunk of soap he kept in his sporran for this purpose. He washed away most of the blood and grime from his hands before working on his face and neck. There was nothing he could do about his clothing, but he prayed he wouldn't be quite so frightening to Amelia.

"Did ye hear Moray's battle cry?" Dennis asked as he accepted the soap Hamish offered.

"Aye. Isnae that from the Compline prayer? 'Keep watch, dear Lord, with those who work, or watch, or weep this night, and give yer angels charge over those who sleep.'"

First Hamish with his Biblical proverb, then Moray with his phrase from the evening prayer. Hamish wondered if the Lord had anointed their side, leading them to victory.

"What's to become of Balliol?" A Sinclair warrior asked from nearby. "What aboot the country? We dinna have a king?"

Hamish had no answer to that, and neither did anyone around him. Many muttered, "we shall see," while no one wanted to admit the lack of an apparent heir was the very thing that brought the English into Scottish affairs. Hamish exchanged speaking looks with the men who'd gathered in Roy's solar before the battle along with the newly arrived Henry, Liam, and Donnell. They knew who they would support, but voicing it now was neither the right time nor the right place.

When there was nothing left to do, Hamish took his horse from the Sutherland warrior tending all the mounts. He opted to walk beside his steed, giving the animal a chance to continue resting. He looked at his uncle, their horses separating them. It was likely a good thing considering what Hamish was about to announce.

"Uncle Henry, I'm marrying Lady Amelia Ross as soon as we can get to Balnagown."

"Nay, ye are nae." Henry's face turned as red as Roy's hair. His anger radiated from him, and Hamish couldn't help but wonder if it was something about the name. Henry and Henrietta. Both were self-centered, yet willing to sacrifice for their clan. Both craved attention when they least deserved it. And both were a pain in Hamish's arse.

"Ye willna convince me otherwise, Uncle. I've already heard and dealt with the Ross's opposition. I love the lass. Our marriage will bring peace, hopefully. But even if it doesnae, nay one will keep me from ma bride. We will wed at Balnagown since it's on the way to Dunrobin."

"Ye are letting Roy Ross make an eejit out of ye. He's sending a spy into our home."

"If Roy had his way, he would have gelded me and sent me to the Shetlands by now. He still doesnae fully accept this, but it will happen. Ye will keep a civil tongue in yer head when ye're around Amelia. Ye will welcome her into our home, which is now hers. Ye will respect everything she says and does. If ye canna do that, then ye will find yerself in a croft in the village."

"Ye would choose her over me?"

"Aye."

"Ye ungrateful wretch," Henry squawked.

"Ye have spent yer life whoring and drinking when ye werenae picking fights. Yer skills didna come from the lists so much as trying to keep yer head attached when angry husbands chased ye down for fucking their wives. Ye did naught to help lead our clan until recently. I still havenae forgiven or forgotten how ye abandoned Kyla when she arrived at Dunbeath. Ye didna even greet Donnell. It's yer choice, but ye will be more than just passably decent. Ye will be on yer best behavior."

"Or ye kick me out on ma arse."

"Nay, I have men to help move ye into yer own croft."

"And where will I eat? I dinna have a woman to cook for me," Henry whined.

"In the keep. But if ye insult ma wife once, ye will sit below the salt. If ye do it a second time, I will find ye a home at one of the lesser keeps. Ye will live there until ye cock up yer toes. Am I clear?" Hamish's voice brooked no argument. With some men, he might have feared retaliation for the ultimatum. But he knew his uncle was a weak man. He could lead the clan when Hamish had to be away because he had enough sense not to touch the ledgers, and he could mediate an argument long enough for Hamish to return. If there'd been an attack, he could organize the warriors to defend their home with success. But beyond that, he had no aspirations to leadership, and he served little purpose outside the lists.

"Och, dinna get in a dither. I'll be nice to yer lass."

"She may be younger than ye, but she will be the Countess of Sutherland. Ye willna address her as lass or call her that in other people's presence. Ye will address her as ma lady and call her Lady Sutherland. Ye will lead by this example, Uncle. I'm unbending."

"I ken. Mayhap bedding her will take out that stick up yer arse. Ye might be a wee more flexible."

Hamish dropped the reins and was around the two horses' heads in a flash. He stood before his uncle, blocking the path. "That is precisely the type of comment I willna tolerate."

"I'm an auld mon. It will take me time to learn," Henry hedged.

"Ye have the time it takes to get to the keep." Hamish turned away and went back to gather the reins which Dennis had picked up. His friend gave him an approving smile. He just had to get through introducing Henry to Amelia, organizing his small army's trek home, a visit to Balnagown, and getting Amelia familiar with their home. His head swam at the prospect. But when the keep's doors came into sight, and he knew he was only a few minutes from having her in his arms, everything felt manageable again. "I'm going to find ma bride."

CHAPTER 23

"Hamish!" Amelia flew across the suite and launched herself into Hamish's arms. She cared not about the blood, mud, or stench. She cared only that he arrived on his feet, and his arms held the same strength to pin her against him as they always did. Their kiss was a desperate cry of reassurance that they both survived. From the suite's windows, Amelia witnessed the entire battle. She nearly drove herself mad envisioning what Hamish endured. Her nose curled over and over as she imagined the stench. It was muted, but the battle sounds traveled to the keep on the wind. She was certain she heard the cries of fallen men and their steeds.

She'd spied a man she was certain was Hamish as the first wave barreled toward the English. It was impossible for her to know for sure since the battlefield lay half a league away, but her heart insisted it was. She'd observed the additional Sutherlands, Rosses, and Sinclairs arrive as the battle became critical. She'd breathed easier knowing reinforcements would strengthen the Scottish army. Then she'd waited with bated breath as Moray and his forces intercepted the English, cutting their army into two. She'd cheered silently as the bridge crumbled.

Now Hamish had returned, and she felt the tension seep from her body. She stepped back, assessing him. She could see nicks and cuts that would need tending, but there was nothing alarming. She looked past him as her father and brothers entered. She squeezed Hamish's arms before darting to her family. Just like with Hamish, she ignored the smells and appearances. She embraced them as they each engulfed her in their arms. She was filthy by the time her family members had a chance to hug her. She rejoined Hamish, slipping her hand into his. She didn't want to be away from his side again now that she knew her family's fate.

She recognized a man who could only be Hamish's uncle since they bore a resemblance to each other that couldn't deny their relationship. She grew wary as the man eyed her like a horse at auction. She wondered if he would attempt to pry her mouth open and look at her gums. His speculative stare earned him a haughty one in return.

"Uncle Henry, this is Lady Amelia. Lia, this is ma uncle." *Unfortunately.*

Amelia's training screamed she should curtsy to the older man, but intuition said she shouldn't submit to him. If she did, it would set a poor precedence if she wished for him to respect her. She extended her hand to him, expecting him to bow. He gawked at it for a moment before offering a half-hearted air kiss above it. She would accept it with grace, reminding herself that the men fought a battle, then tended to their dead. Perhaps Henry was not at his best.

"Where's my Andrew?" Henrietta cried when no one else entered the suite. Amelia's head turned as Henrietta's possessiveness registered. Her cousin rushed forward, pushing between Roy and Lionel. Tormud snagged her around the waist, lifting her off her feet as she flailed.

"Settle, lass. He wished to refresh himself before he sought you."

"I dinna care aboot that," Henrietta insisted. She hadn't noticed her burr as distraught as she was.

"Did ye miss me, ye wee hellion?" As though summoned by her demands, Andrew strolled through the door. While he was hardly clean, he'd donned a fresh leine beneath his filthy plaid. What Tormud hadn't mentioned was he sported several sets of stitches, and blood had soaked his leine. Everyone watched in disbelief as Henrietta eased her arms around his neck, careful not to press against any wounds she couldn't see. Then she burst into tears. No one could hear what she whispered to Andrew, but he stroked her back as she calmed. "Wheest. Dinna fash. I warned ye. I'm nae finished with ye. Ye canna be free of me."

He whispered something to Henrietta as she stepped back. She merely nodded before turning to look at everyone's mystified expressions. "We handfasted earlier. I'm going with my husband." Her affected speech was back in place as she wrapped her arm around Andrew's. "Uncle, tell my maid to send my belongings to Andrew's chamber. We leave in the morning. I never wish to see you or Balnagown again."

Over her head when she turned toward the door, Andrew stated, "The price of peace." Then they were gone. Amelia turned a bewildered expression to Hamish. No one bothered asking where they headed.

"Could it really be so simple? Is she really gone from our lives?"

"So it seems. At least until we encounter her here or at a Highland Gathering."

Amelia looked at her father, who offered her a dismissive shrug before issuing a command. "Lio, get servants to bring us tubs before all of them are in use. Remind them who it's for." Roy looked at Hamish. "Clean yerself, mon. None of us are fit for Amy. She will see ye at the evening meal. Ye may sit with us."

Hamish smirked at the disdainful invitation. He wouldn't argue. "I shall deign to sit with ye, so I can enjoy Lia's company."

He smirked at Roy before growing serious. "I need to speak to ma uncle and Lia first. Ye've spoken to Tormud and Lionel, but I must have the same conversation with ma family. We must plan."

Roy stared as his lips pursed. Then he nodded. Amelia would have followed Hamish regardless of Roy's consent. But it made things mildly easier. The trio walked in silence to the Sutherland suite. They spent the next hour together as Hamish and Henry discussed the logistics of traveling home with fewer warriors and the ramifications of another loss of men to defend their clan. Lia remained quiet as they spoke, taking the time to learn more about how Hamish led. He asked her opinion throughout, but she preferred to listen.

"All that's left is the wedding. Uncle, if ye dinna think ye can remain civil at Balnagown, then travel home ahead of us. Ye willna do aught to cause trouble. I havenae forgotten what we lost at Roy's hands. But I ken what we've taken from him."

Henry grinned. "Aye. His only daughter."

"Damn it!" Hamish slammed his fist on the table. "Ye go straight to Dunrobin. I willna hear aught aboot it. Find a maid and request a bath, but leave before I say something I canna take back."

Amelia wrapped her arm around Hamish's and led him to the chamber they'd chosen. Hamish had moved his chest to the other bedroom while Amelia had spent hours in the music room on their last day together before the battle. He'd given her the key to the suite before he'd handed her the lad's clothing. "Hamish, I kenned we would get here when we could, but I came here as soon as I saw men heading back to the keep."

She opened the bedchamber door, and Hamish nearly wept with joy. A tub sat before a roaring fire with buckets of water nearly boiling on the hearth. Amelia stayed out of his way, filling the bath as he stripped, kicking his boots and clothes into a far corner before easing into the steaming taste of heaven. It eased his aching body. It was nearly too hot, but he cared not. He rested his head back with his eyes closed.

"Thank ye, ma love. Ye are the finest wife in the land."

"Ye're nae upset that I left the suite before ye returned?"

"The English never came near the keep. Ye werenae in imminent danger. I kenned ye'd use common sense if ye were. I appreciate yer thoughtfulness. I noticed ye hadnae ordered baths for yer family."

Amelia shook her head. "I did, but they hadnae arrived. I'm sure they did by now. But I couldnae say aught. If I told them, then Father would have taunted ye. If I admitted I'd included ye, he would have had an apoplexy before letting me come with ye. I'm certain he hopes I will be away from here before this bath could arrive."

"Ye are such a kind woman, Lia. And ye're dutiful. Ye put others ahead of ye, even when it isnae easy. If I werenae worse than a pigsty, I would invite ye to join me."

Amelia laughed before curling her nose as she looked at the murky water. She grabbed an empty bucket and scooped out water. She did this with four other buckets before pouring in clean water. She grabbed the lump of soap the maid set on the table with the drying linens. "Sit forward. I'll scrub yer back. I need to see if any of yer wounds are serious enough for stitches. They all need thorough cleaning."

Hamish gritted his teeth, knowing she was right. She was as gentle as she could be while still aggressively attending to minor wounds that could still turn putrid. As he bathed, he recounted what he could, omitting some parts he censored and some parts he couldn't remember. "Now that Balliol has abdicated, Isabella is nay longer queen. Ye are nay longer in service to her. We can leave when we want."

Amelia perched on the end of the bed as Hamish stood and dried himself. "Yer men need at least a couple days' rest before we're on the road. Ma father will feel the same aboot his men.

But the moment ye both believe we can leave, we do. With nay king, I pray we dinna have to return here for a long time. But I ken that also means we willna have a leader. I also ken that means there are more battles ye will fight. What happens now?"

"Wallace and the Bruce will track de Warenne and likely fight the next battle somewhere near Falkirk. Moray was grievously wounded. I saw him. It wouldnae surprise me if infection takes him within the sennight. If it doesnae heal, he willna live more than a couple months if he lasts that long."

"We are at war, arenae we?"

"Aye. One that will either tear our country apart or prove to the English there's a reason the Romans couldnae conquer us, so neither will they. But only time will tell."

It took nearly a fortnight before enough Ross, Sinclair, and Sutherland warriors were well enough to guard the injured and the lairds' families. They traveled to Balnagown at a snail's pace. Liam and Dugan rode ahead to Dunrobin with a small entourage to escort Kyla to the Ross keep. Roy sent a messenger ahead to inform Amelia's mother that she should welcome as honored guests those who would arrive before him. He also told her to prepare for Amelia's wedding. He'd been in two minds whether to tell her who the groom was and whether he should swear the Sinclairs to secrecy. It was Amelia who warned her father that he faced a temper far worse than his when it came to her mother. She didn't lash out. She would simply make him miserable by being uncooperative, barring him from their chamber, and putting everyone on edge. Her anger rarely lasted more than a couple days, but Amelia insisted it could be sennights before Margaret Ross forgave her husband for such a shock.

Everyone was weary as the combined Ross, Sutherland, and

Sinclair party rode under the portcullis at Balnagown. Amelia spotted her mother as she reined in. The woman guarded her feelings unless she wished to make it known someone displeased her. While Hamish helped Amelia down from her mount and waited until she was steady on her feet, she observed her mother's version of a warm welcome for Tormud and Lionel. She embraced both, then patted them on the back three times before pulling away. She accepted Roy's proffered kiss on her cheek. Then she turned to Amelia, whose heart was in her throat. Margaret offered her a rare smile that reminded Roy of when they'd met.

It shocked everyone how warmly she received Hamish, though she turned a cold shoulder to Henry, ignoring him completely. She clarified that her hospitableness was purely for Amelia's sake. The Sutherlands and Sinclairs joined the Rosses in the lists during the four days leading to the wedding. It took those four full days before the Rosses and Sutherlands quit antagonizing one another and no fights broke out in the training grounds or Great Hall. Irrespective of each other, each laird addressed his men, warning them that they wouldn't survive the day if they ruined the wedding for Amelia. Both men wanted it to be perfect, having seen the constant anxiety she suffered when the two clans came together.

When the day of their wedding finally arrived, Amelia spent it with Kyla and her mother. She grew close to her future sister-by-marriage with ease. They were like the sisters neither ever had. They were inseparable except for when Amelia was with Hamish and Kyla was with Liam. Both couples slipped away for covert moments alone. However, unlike Kyla and Liam, Amelia and Hamish could not retire together at the end of the night. At least not publicly. Hamish crept to Amelia's chamber in the middle of each night, guiding her to his chamber the next floor up from hers. It was above an unused chamber on the family floor. The newlywed Sinclair couple's, Dugan's, and Donnell and Arabella's chambers were at the other end of the hall from Hamish's. Amelia suspected her mother knew they'd already handfasted since the woman was nobody's fool. Liam and Dugan's mother, Lady Arabella Sinclair, Countess of Sinclair, seemed as aware as Margaret. Dugan had continued past Dunrobin to Dunbeath to escort his mother to Balnagown.

Liam and Hamish had been standing on the kirk's steps for ten minutes waiting as the time for the wedding drew near, but only because Hamish insisted they be early. "Stand still," Liam whispered for the fourth time as Hamish failed not to fidget. He ignored Liam's warning until the crowd suddenly parted. The magnificent sight that approached him struck him dumb. He'd seen nothing so lovely as Amelia walking toward him. He knew she'd spent the time from the day of the battle until that morning working on a wedding kirtle when he wasn't around. She'd poked him with a needle once when he tried to peek. When she reached him, he offered her both hands. She squeaked when he pulled her in for a kiss that should have waited not only until the end of the ceremony but until they were alone.

"Naught has ever been or ever will be as bonnie as ye," Hamish whispered as the priest wrapped a swath of Sutherland plaid around their wrists much like they had when they hand-fasted weeks earlier. They'd only confessed to Kyla and Liam, who admitted they'd handfasted after Liam survived a single combat, defending Kyla.

"Dearly beloved," Father Mark began. "We are gathered together here in the sight of God, and in the face of this clan, to join together this mon and this woman in holy matrimony; which is an honorable estate, instituted of God in the time of mon's innocence, signifying unto us the mystical union that is betwixt Christ and his Church; which holy estate Christ adorned and beutified with his presence, and first miracle that he wrought, in Cana of Galilee; and is commended of Saint Paul to be honorable among all men: and therefore is nae by any to be enterprised, nor taken in hand, unadvisedly, lightly, or wantonly, to satisfy men's carnal lusts and appetites, like brute beasts that have nay understanding; but reverently, discreetly, advisedly, soberly, and in the fear of God; duly considering the causes for which matrimony was ordained."

As often happened when they were together, Hamish and Amelia entered a bubble that insulated them from the rest of the world. This time the priest joined them. To both of them, only three people existed.

"First, it was ordained for the procreation of children," Father Mark continued. "To be brought up in the fear and nurture of the Lord, and to the praise of His holy name. Secondly, it was ordained for a remedy against sin, and to avoid fornication; that such persons as have nae the gift of contingency might marry, and keep themselves undefiled members of Christ's body. Thirdly, it was ordained for the mutual society, help, and comfort, that the one ought to have of the other, both in prosperity and adversity. Into which holy estate these two persons present come now to be joined. Therefore, if any mon can show any just cause, why they may nae lawfully be joined together, let him now speak, or else hereafter forever hold his peace."

Both tensed as they feared someone might actually speak out against their marriage. Neither turned their heads, but their gazes jumped to Henry, then Roy. The men were barely civil to each other, but they tried. When everyone remained silent, Amelia and Hamish shared a private smile.

"I require and charge ye both, as ye will answer at the dreadful day of judgment when the secrets of all hearts shall be disclosed, that if either of ye ken any impediment, why ye may nae be lawfully joined together in matrimony, ye do now confess it. For be ye well assured, that so many as are coupled together otherwise than God's Word doth allow are nae joined together by God; neither is their matrimony lawful. Wilt thee have this woman to thy wedded wife, to live together after God's ordinance in the holy estate of matrimony? Wilt thee love her, comfort her, honor, and keep her in sickness and in health; and, forsaking all other, keep thee only unto her, so long as ye both shall live?"

"I will," Hamish answered without reservation.

"Wilt thee have this mon to thy wedded husband to live together after God's ordinance in the holy estate of matrimony? Wilt thee obey him, and serve him, love, honor, and keep him in sickness and in health; and, forsaking all other, keep thee only unto him, so long as ye both shall live?" Father Mark turned to Amelia, a woman he'd once christened.

"I will." Amelia beamed as her gaze remained fastened on Hamish, just as his was on her.

"Who giveth this woman to be married to this mon?" Father Mark looked at Roy.

With ease that surprised everyone, Roy's answer was immediate and resolute. "I do."

"I, Hamish Alexander Angus Sutherland, take thee, Amelia Elizabeth Louise Ross, to ma wedded wife, to have and to hold from this day forward, for better for worse, for richer or for poorer, in sickness and in health, to love and to cherish, till death us do part, according to God's holy ordinance; and thereto I plight thee ma troth." Hamish sighed as he finished. He'd sworn fealty to his father as his laird and to Balliol as his king. He'd pledged to always protect his clan. And he'd begged Kyla's forgiveness for failure to protect her when they were growing up. But never had he meant words more than he did the ones he just spoke.

"I, Amelia Elizabeth Louise Ross, take thee, Hamish Alexander Angus Sutherland, to ma wedded husband, to have and to hold from this day forward, for better for worse, for richer or for poorer, in sickness and in health, to love, cherish, and to obey, till death us do part, according to God's holy ordinance; and thereto I give thee ma troth." Amelia knew they were already married. Their handfast vows weren't any less signifi-cant to her. But listening to Hamish, then reciting her own sacred vow, resonated with Amelia in a way she never fathomed.

Hamish reached into his sporran and produced a ring with an amber stone that reminded him of Amelia's hair. One of the features he loved best about her. He'd quietly asked Liam to help Kyla find it among their dead mother's belongings. "With this ring I thee wed. With ma body I thee worship, and with all ma worldly goods I thee endow: In the Name of the Father, and of the Son, and of the Holy Spirit. Amen." He slid the ring onto Amelia's finger, running his thumb over it. She curled her fingers around his as Father Mark gave the final benediction of their wedding ceremony.

"Those whom God hath joined together let no mon put asun-der. Forasmuch as Hamish and Amelia have consented together in holy wedlock, and have witnessed the same before God and this clan, and thereto have given and pledged their troth either to other, and have declared the same by giving and receiving of a ring, and by joining of hands; I pronounce that they be mon and wife together, In the Name of the Father, and of the Son, and of the Holy Spirit. Amen."

The gathered clans cheered as the couple shared another kiss that left no one in doubt their marriage wasn't arranged. It hadn't come about to secure peace. It was one between two people devoted to one another. They led the onlookers to the Great Hall for the feast. They tolerated three courses before they both wished to slip away. Hamish leaned over to Amelia.

"We dinna say aught to anyone. We simply rise and go to the stairs. I will carry ye. We canna risk ye tripping in our haste to leave faster than anyone can realize what we're doing."

"I ken. Are ye ready now?"

"Lass, I've been ready since I woke this morning." Hamish nudged Amelia's leg beneath the table when her hand slid beneath his plaid and up his thigh. He nearly choked over his hissed warning. "Lass."

Amelia giggled as she withdrew her hand. She glanced at Liam and Kyla, who both nodded. Without ceremony, Hamish and Amelia rose and stepped around their chairs. Some diners noticed them, but most did not. Hamish entwined his fingers with Amelia's as they made their way to the end of the dais, but before Hamish could take the first step, Roy's voice reached them.

"Ye willna retire yet. Everyone else hasnae finished their meal. Ye will wait for the bedding ceremony until our clan and our guests are done."

Hamish turned slowly and raised his chin. "There will be nay bedding ceremony. Nay one sees ma wife but me." This was the precise reason they wished to slip away.

Roy rose from his seat and walked over to the couple. "I have accepted yer marriage, but nae all of ma clan has. It will be the same for yers. Ye must indulge them. If ye want the peace ye claim, the peace I'm willing to accept, then they must see the priest bless ye and the bed. They must see ye are truly married. That there can be nay annulment. That there is a chance ye sire the generation that will bind our clans by blood."

"Ye can have the sheet in the morning. Nay one sees ma wife. If yer clan wishes to question ma honor, then let them. Ma clan kens ma word is solid. They willna question Amelia's. What ma wife and I do behind closed doors is nae for anyone to watch." Hamish could feel the tremors passing through Amelia's body. He knew she feared people watching her, and he knew she feared people discovering they'd already coupled. They were to spend the night in his chamber, and he had the bedsheet with the evidence in the locked chest.

"Ye are in ma keep. It's nae yer choice," Roy insisted, taking a menacing step toward Hamish, who tucked Amelia behind him.

"I warned ye once aboot threatening me when yer daughter is

near. Back up, Ross. This may be yer keep, but Amelia is ma wife. Ye have nay say in aught."

"I do until ye bed her. Until then, ye arenae truly married."

"Father, we already—" Amelia didn't finish when Roy turned such a disgusted look at her, then a venomous one to Hamish that she snapped her mouth shut.

"I kenned ye defiled her."

"Ross, ye have until the count of one to step away from Amelia. Ye and I can go to the lists right now. Single combat if we must, but if ye come any closer, I will take it as a threat to ma wife as much as it is to me. I dinna give a shite whose father ye are." Hamish put his hands on his hips, deceptively passive, even if it would intimidate most. He gave Roy a moment, but the older man did nothing. "One."

Instead of stepping back, Roy shifted his weight to the balls of his feet. Hamish knew Roy prepared to strike. It was the only signal Hamish needed. He drew back his right fist and swung. Because he was about to attack, Roy was prepared. He blocked the shot. But he didn't realize Hamish predicted the movement and already had his left fist flying toward Roy's face. It made contact, whipping Roy's head to the side. Chairs and benches scraped along the floor as men rose to defend their respective lairds. Roy stumbled backward, but when Hamish made no move to do more, he raised his hand in the air.

Hamish glowered at Roy. "Nay one." He turned back to Amelia and swooped her into his arms. She buried her face against his chest, and he felt the tears seep through his leine. "I'm sorry, *mo chridhe*. I will apologize right now. I'm sorry."

Amelia lifted her head, bewildered. "Hamish, ye didna upset me. The idea of a bedding ceremony is terrifying, whether I'm a virgin or nae. I dinna want so many people staring at me. I've heard enough comments aboot ma appearance. I dinna need anyone but ye seeing me without a stitch of clothing on. I'm upset because ma father didna heed yer warning. We've been through this before. Ye've already proven how ye react to aught ye think poses a threat to me. That was unnecessary, but I saw him shift his weight too. Ye merely moved faster than him. This isnae what I wanted on our wedding day. I refuse to take it as an omen, but it lowers a pall over our joy."

"Dinna let it, wee one." Hamish put her on her feet once they stepped into the chamber. He reached behind and turned the key in the lock. Then they couldn't strip fast enough. It was much like the first time they came together. Patience wasn't a virtue either was interested in having. Hamish's hand roamed over her bare shoulders and back as she cupped his buttocks. "I love ye, Lia."

"Ye are everything to me. Ma valiant protector. Ma champion. The one person I ken I'm always safe with because ye willna let aught happen to me. I love ye."

Hamish lifted her, and her legs came around his waist as they continued to kiss. But the door burst open, and voices filled their chamber. Amelia screamed as Hamish grabbed the spare Sutherland plaid at the foot of the bed. He wrapped Amelia in it as he lowered her to the floor. He spun with a roar, uncaring that he was naked. He stooped and pulled a dirk from his discarded belt. "Out!"

"We're here now," a drunk Ross warrior slurred.

"Bed her!" Cried out a woman. At the sound of the female voice, Amelia saw red. She snatched Hamish's leine from the floor and flung it at him as she stepped forward.

"Nay one sees ma husband unless ye'd like me to gouge yer eyes out with ma fingers. Leave. Now."

Many chuckled, but no one moved until Kyla and Arabella pushed through the crowd, Liam and Donnell on their heels. The chamber was enormous enough that more than a dozen people spread out to witness the scene before them. Amelia turned to Hamish, fury and fear mixed. When four Ross women stepped forward, reaching for the plaid that hid Amelia's naked body, Kyla and Arabella both drew dirks.

"Step closer to ma sister, and I'll gut ye," Kyla warned. "I dinna give a bluidy damn whose keep this is or who ye might claim to be. Ma brother and sister said nay. Get out."

Amelia recognized one woman as someone who worked in the kitchens. She was close to Amelia's age, and she'd been one of the unkindest when Amelia developed sooner than the others. Amelia knew she wanted nothing more than to witness Amelia's humiliation. When the servant's attention shifted to Hamish, and her expression was far too appreciative, Amelia lunged. The woman only remained unscathed because Hamish caught Amelia around the waist. He'd donned his leine, which came nearly to his knees, and kept her close to him. She opened her arms and encircled his waist, creating a Sutherland plaid cocoon for them.

"Drop the plaid. Get on with it." The same drunkard spoke again. He raised a mug of whisky and grinned. When he licked his lips and reached toward his groin, Hamish once more pressed Amelia aside. He wrapped his massive palms around the man's neck, lifting him onto his toes, and shaking him. The warrior wasn't little by any stretch, but Hamish's anger and need to protect Amelia gave him near superhuman strength and resolve. The man's eyes bulged as his face turned crimson. Ross guards tugged at Hamish's arms and pushed at his chest, but he didn't release the offensive onlooker.

While Hamish continued to the throttle the man as blood vessels burst in the man's right eye, three older Ross women hurried forward, skirting the six men trying to restrain Hamish. Hagatha, the midwife who'd delivered Amelia, nudged her aside.

"Come, lass. This willna end until ye're in that bed with yer husband. Turn toward me, and let me see." Hagatha angled herself away from the spectators. Kyla, Arabella, and the two other women formed a circle around Amelia. Margaret joined them when she could push her way through the crowd. No one moved when she announced herself, and they'd done just as little to allow Tormud and Lionel into the chamber. Roy was one of the first men through the door, having nearly yanked the chatelaine's keyring from his wife's belt. He stood to the side; his gaze fixed only on Hamish. He knew his daughter and son-by-marriage would likely never forgive him for this. And he loathed subjecting his daughter to the indignity. But he'd lived twice the life they had. He'd led the Ross clan since he was the same age Hamish was when he entered the lists. He'd been Laird Ross, Earl of Ross for nearly forty-five years. He knew his clan better than anyone. He knew people wouldn't truly consider their families united if the Rosses didn't witness the true wedding. It wasn't the vows exchanged. It was the possibility— the hope —a child would result from the wedding night coupling.

"It's done, lad," Hagatha said from behind Hamish. "She's under the covers."

Hamish glanced over his shoulders at Amelia, who had the sheet up to her chin. Hamish turned back to the man he would kill if he pressed ever so slightly harder on the man's windpipe. As it was, Hamish doubted the man would speak for at least a sennight. He released the intoxicated warrior with a shove and a knee to the groin. He swept his gaze around the people who invaded his and Amelia's privacy. He noticed many of his men stood with their backs to the bed.

"Bed her! Bed her!"

When the chant began, these Sutherland warriors materialized, forming a barrier between the Rosses and their laird and new lady. None even darted their gaze in Amelia's direction. Kyla stalked forward to stand in front of her brother. Arabella stopped beside her, and Liam hovered beside his wife, just as Donnell did the same to his.

"There is naught ye need to watch," Kyla warned. "If ye are so dissatisfied with yer own lives that the only excitement ye have is to watch others couple, then find yerselves a whore. Men or women. I promise ye, ma brother, ma husband, and ma father-by-marriage are nay the ones ye should fear. I'm nae so forgiving as ma brother. If any of ye women thought to ogle ma husband the way ye are ma brother, I promise ye wouldnae see the morn. Ye men are lucky Hamish didna kill any of ye. He has more restraint than me." Kyla lifted her dirk as she locked gazes with the woman she knew tormented her new sister. She spun the dirk in her hand, clearly comfortable with the weapon. She pointed it at Amelia's nemesis and smiled, taunting her. "The only reason I'm nae gutting ye is Lady Ross has been vera kind, and I dinna want to sully her rushes." She pointed to the doorway with her blade before stepping closer to the three women who'd first approached Amelia. Kyla lifted her knife high enough to be eye level with the one directly in front of her.

"Dinna think she willna do it," Liam warned. "Ma wife is with child, and a more fiercely protective woman ye will nae meet in her condition."

The women looked around as Margaret stepped forward. "I have tolerated this for long enough. I understand why our laird accepted this. It is so ye can see we are truly at peace with the Sutherlands. If ye dinna see how protective the Sutherlands and Sinclairs are of Amelia, then ye dinna see the strength of this alliance. Get out."

At the Countess of Ross's order, people gave one last look around before they filed out of the chamber. Amelia watched as her mother asserted herself as only she could. She'd prayed one of her parents, even one of her brothers, would step forward. She appreciated her family-by-marriage's dedication to her when her family disappointed her. But she considered what her mother said as she saw the distress in her father's eyes when he finally looked in her direction.

"Da, wait." Amelia sat up, the sheet tucked beneath her arms. Roy flinched. She shot Hamish a quelling glance. She looked at Kyla and nodded. She took Liam's hand and turned to the door. Donnell and Arabella followed them out of the chamber silently.

Lionel and Tormud were issuing orders down the passageway. "Hamish?"

Her husband turned toward her, and she could feel the anger still radiated from him. It practically reverberated in the chamber. She held out her hand, which forced him to walk past Roy unless he wanted to climb onto the bed beside her. When she gripped it, she kissed the back of it.

"Da, this is why ye opposed the marriage. Ye didna want this to happen. Ye wished to spare me. Why couldnae ye have just said so?"

"Because ye wouldnae have believed me, lass. Ye would have insisted Hamish could keep it from happening. Or people wouldnae be that interested. I've been laird twice the time ye've been alive. I've seen this exact situation at more weddings than I can remember. It's the benefit and curse of age. I ken things aboot life and aboot people that ye are simply both too young to believe. I ken their nature. I couldnae guarantee they'd even accept a marriage, let alone a wedding without a bedding ceremony. I feared the clan turning on ye. I feared for yer safety. But I canna ignore how much Hamish loves ye. And this would never have been yer home once ye married." Roy looked at Hamish. "I dinna think I will ever forgive yer father and brothers. I ken ye arenae them, but only time will tell how different ye are. We have a truce. If ye are the laird and the husband ye claim ye will be, we'll have an alliance."

This time, they extended their arms at the same time. They grasped forearms in a genuine act of respect. There was no posturing, neither testing who was stronger, who would back down first.

"Thank ye," Hamish stated. He could accept Roy's explanation and his willingness for a truce. It would be a while before he forgave him for the wrongs done to his clan or trusted the Rosses after the spectacle they just endured. But he'd wanted a truce since the moment he discovered Amelia was a Ross. Was. He glanced over at her with the Sutherland plaid around her shoulders. She was and ever would be a Sutherland. "I'd like to be with ma wife."

Roy and Margaret left Amelia and Hamish alone. They watched the door shut before he went to the portal, locked and barred it. He chided himself for his foolishness. They could have avoided the entire situation if he'd barred the door. As he dropped it into place, he looked back at Amelia. "I'm sorry I didna do this when we came in here."

"Ye shouldnae have needed to. Ye locked the door, and that should have been enough."

"I see the sense in what yer father and mother said. I dinna agree with them aboot how it happened, but it's over now." Hamish took off his leine and climbed into bed beside Amelia. She pushed the plaid to the foot of the bed. "They could have selected people they trust to be here. That isnae unheard of."

"I dinna ken that it would have satisfied the clan. I saw how yer men stood ready to protect us. I never needed to test their dedication to ye, and by extension me. But it willna be a bad thing to encourage yer— our —clan to accept me. When they speak of how they wouldnae allow anyone near me, it will help our clan see I'm already a Sutherland."

"Ye are such a practical woman. I'm still sorry it happened. I wouldnae have killed that mon, even if ye hadnae gotten into bed. But I wanted to. I havenae felt rage like that before. It wasna bloodlust like I've had before."

"It must run in yer family. Kyla didna look like she would back down. Ye must have taught her how to use that dirk."

"She wouldnae have. But that skill with a dirk to twirl it that way came from Liam. I made sure she kenned how to protect herself, but I didna teach her any tricks."

"Nay. From the moment of disbelief that flickered in his eyes, I assumed ye taught her. It wasna Liam."

Hamish chuckled. "It wouldnae surprise me then if she didna teach herself in a moment of boredom."

"I'm glad Dunbeath and Dunrobin arenae so far apart. I hope we can raise our children alongside theirs." Amelia reclined, opening her arms to Hamish, who hovered above her.

"There arenae enough days left in ma life to count all the blessings ye bring me. It willna always be an easy life together, but it's one I only wish to build with ye. When I went to court, I hardly expected love to come calling. But ye are as wild and as strong as the Highlands itself. Ye have been ma future since the day I was born."

"The sweet things ye say, ye daft mon. I love ye." Amelia lifted her chin to accept Hamish's kiss. As always happened when they were together, the only thing that mattered was the other. Their bodies moved together as though they'd always been one. Night passed into day, which passed into another night and another day for a sennight. When they emerged, still blissful, they embarked on the journey to Dunrobin on the path filled with Highland love.

"Blair, leave yer brother alone, young lady." Amelia scolded her five-year-old daughter as she watched a sticky hand swipe her eight-year-old son's last four dried apricots before shoving them all in her mouth and sticking out her tongue at Lachlan.

"Mama!" Lachlan bellowed with indignation.

"Bahaha!" Laughter from Kyla and Liam's two oldest sons, Callum and Alexander, came from behind Lachlan. Her son, who looked so much like Hamish, turned toward his cousins and raised his wooden sword.

"Ye let a wee lassie take yer sweeties," Tavish, the third son, taunted. But he was soon crying foul when his sister, the same age as Blair, pushed him over, stepped on him, and pulled the fig he was about to eat from his hand. Unlike Blair, however, Mairghread dropped it in the dirt and stomped on it.

"Dinna tease Blair," Mairghread commanded. Beside her stood Amelia and Hamish's middle child, Maude.

"Lachlan, stop whingeing. Ye canna carry a sword if ye sound like a wean," Maude explained. Amelia's six-and-a-half-year-old daughter had inherited her mother's practical nature while Mairghread had inherited Kyla's spunk.

Amelia and Kyla sat beside each other on the beach at Dunbeath. Four plaids, two Sutherland and two Sinclair, were spread out on the sand for their picnic. The mothers watched their children building stick and sand fortresses near the water's edge, but all of them knew better than to get close enough to get wet. They all knew if they got too close without their mother or aunt, then they all had to go home.

"Auntie Amy?"

"Aye, Magnus." Amelia looked at Kyla and Liam's fourth and last son who was barely nine moons older than Mairghread.

"Did ye ken Mama's a selkie?"

"Nay, I didna. How do ye ken?"

Magnus turned to Kyla. "Mama, show Auntie Amy. Go on. Go."

"Magnus," Kyla warned.

"Sorry, Mama. Please, Mama, will ye show Auntie Amy how much the seals love ye?"

"When Papa and Uncle Hamish join us after they finish in the lists. Then I'll go in, but I willna leave Auntie Amy alone with all ye heathens." Neither Kyla nor Amelia were unable to manage all eight children on their own. Neither clan was at peace with the Gunns, and in recent months, there had been more raids than ever before. Neither mother would leave the other to defend all seven.

"Can ye tell me why ye think yer mama's a selkie?" Amelia asked Magnus.

"Och, that's simple," Mairghread interjected as she handed the dirty fig back to Tavish and a clean one to Maude.

"Aye," Callum called out. "Ye should see how she swims with them."

Alexander, the most solemn of the five Sinclair siblings, walked over and sat on Amelia's other side. "Mama can swim out with them, and they never fear her. They will come close, but they dinna threaten her. Even when they have their pups. It's nae natural. Nay one else can do that."

"Mama shed her selkie skin when she fell in love with Da," Tavish explained, joining the family storytelling. "She became a woman, so she could live with Da and have all of us."

Amelia smiled at the young children now surrounding her. The four Sinclair sons were the mirror images of Liam, and while Mairghread looked a great deal like Liam, it took only one look at Kyla to realize they were mother and daughter.

"Mama?" Lachlan asked, now more interested in the story than his stolen apricots. "If Auntie Kyla is a selkie, and she's Da's sister, does that mean he's a selkie too?"

"Nay," a booming voice belonging to Liam answered from the path leading to the beach. "Yer da's a bodach."

"I'm nae an auld, grumpy mon," Hamish responded with a voice just as deep and loud. "Ye are. Ye're the one who landed on his arse twice more than me."

"I only did because our bluidy men got in the way. I didna want to run yers or mine through. And it only counted as once. I went down, but ye didna let me up before ye rammed me again with yer targe."

Amelia and Kyla giggled as they watched their enormous husbands jostle each other as they came to join the family picnic.

"Da!" Eight youthful voices squealed together as they launched a coordinated attack on the two seasoned warriors. As the men sat, the children clambered over their fathers and uncles. Amelia and Kyla sat back, enjoying their husbands tossing the children in the air and rolling around with them. Completely distracted by the men, the children didn't notice as their mothers stripped down to their chemises and waded into the North Sea.

"It's so bluidy cold, Kyla. How does it never bother ye?" Amelia asked as a wave sprayed water up to her shoulders.

"I feel the cold. I just tell maself it could be colder. We could be Norse." Kyla chuckled before diving under a wave. Amelia followed her, just as strong a swimmer having been raised along the North Sea coast too.

When they both surfaced, they splashed water back and forth until four seals barked. The lumbering animals slid off the rocks upon which they sunned themselves and swam toward the women. Neither Amelia nor Kyla feared them. Each species kept a healthy distance, but to the children cheering on the shore, it appeared as though the seals spoke to the women. When the animals lost interest in Kyla and Amelia, they swam back. Hamish and Liam stood at the shore with the toes of their boots in the surf, and spread their warm plaids open waiting for their wives. They bundled their women into them and kissed their respective wives soundly.

"Mama's one, too!" Lachlan hooted as he jabbed his wooden sword into the air. He was only four months younger than Callum, who nodded.

Early afternoon slipped into evening before the two families repacked their picnic. The adults trailed behind a passel of sleepy children. The couples smiled knowingly. Their offspring would fall into their beds exhausted and unlikely to disturb their parents. Hamish nipped at Amelia's ear as they approached Dunbeath's postern gate.

"I love ye, *mo ghaol*, but I'm too tired to chase this eve."

"I will take mercy on yer aging body." Amelia tickled the ribs covered in only muscles and skin. "And I will only make ye find me in that enormous bed."

They stopped to a share a kiss much like the first one they had in the Stirling Castle gardens nearly a decade earlier. A new king sat upon the throne, but the only peace they knew was what they made in a home filled with Highland love.

You can enjoy practical Maude's story in *A Wallflower at the Highland Court*. Cheeky little Blair finds love in *A Saint at the Highland Court*. And the patient oldest son, Lachlan, finds his match in *A Beauty at the Highland Court*.

House of Clan Sutherland is a spinoff from the other series I've built in this world. It follows the lives and loves of Lachlan's, Maude's, and Blair's children.

Would you like to read Liam and Kyla's story? Discover how *The Clan Sinclair* began with *Their Highland Beginning*. Fall in love with Callum, Alex, Tavish, Magnus, and Mairghread. Their children find love in *The Clan Sinclair Legacy*.

You can read the books in all my series as standalones, but it's always nice to feel like part of the family when you get to know each member.

And if you're curious about Henrietta and Andrew, you can learn more about them in Magnus's story, *His Highland Pledge*, and the first book, *A Spinster at the Highland Court*, in my *The Highland Ladies* series.

Celeste Barclay, a nom de plume, lives near the Southern California coast with her husband and sons. Growing up in the Midwest, Celeste enjoyed spending as much time in and on the water as she could. Now she lives near the beach. She's an avid swimmer, a hopeful future surfer, and a former rower. When she's not writing, she's enjoying the California sunshine with her family.

Visit Celeste's website, www.celestebarclay.com, for regular updates on works in progress, new releases, and her blog where she features posts about her experiences as an author and recommendations of her favorite reads.

Have you read *Their Highland Beginning, The Clan Sinclair Prequel?* Learn how the saga begins! This FREE novella is available to all new subscribers to Celeste's monthly newsletter. Subscribe on her website.

www.celestebarclay.com

Join the fun and get exclusive insider giveaways, sneak peeks, and new release announcements in

Celeste Barclay's Facebook Ladies of Yore Group

Have you chatted with Celeste's hunky heroes? Is this your first book by Celeste Barclay? To learn more about her other books and series or to get exclusive insider treats and deals, subscribe for free to chat with the men of Celeste's *The Highland Ladies* series.

Chat Now

THE CLAN SINCLAIR

His Highland Lass **BOOK 1 SNEAK PEEK**

She entered the great hall like a strong spring storm in the northern most Highlands. Tristan Mackay felt like he had been blown hither and yon. As the storm settled, she left him with the sweet scents of heather and lavender wafting towards him as she approached. She was not a classic beauty, tall and willowy like the women at court. Her face and form were not what legends were made of. But she held a unique appeal unlike any he had seen before. He could not take his eyes off of her long chestnut hair that had strands of fire and burnt copper running through them. Unlike the waves or curls he was used to, her hair was unusually straight and fine. It looked like a waterfall cascading down her back. While she was not tall, neither was she short. She had a figure that was meant for a man to grasp and hold onto, whether from the front or from behind. She had an aura of confidence and charm, but not arrogance or conceit like many good looking women he had met. She did not seem to know her own appeal. He could tell that she was many things, but one thing she was not was his.

His Bonnie Highland Temptation

His Highland Prize

His Highland Pledge

His Highland Surprise

Their Highland Beginning

THE CLAN SINCLAIR LEGACY

Highland Lion **BOOK 1 SNEAK PEEK**

Liam Mackay gazed at the bustling Orcadian village of Skaill, on the isle of Rousay. He thought of how it reminded him of his clan's village, outside the walls of Castle Varrich in the Scottish Highlands. As he crossed the dock, he noticed the massive longboats that Norse traders sailed to conduct trade on the island. With his father's jet-black hair and emerald eyes, few would believe Liam had Nordic heritage, but it had connected his family to Orkney for ten generations. He swept his eyes over the crofts nearest the marina of sorts. He watched as a tall blonde woman stormed out of a house and slammed the door shut. The fury on the woman's face made him think of his mother when she was angry with Liam and his younger brothers and sister. But the woman before him, statuesque and voluptuous, couldn't resemble his petite brunette mother any less. Her tall stature belied her curves until she leaned forward to fill a bucket at the well.

"Elene, come back here. We are not through speaking," an older woman called from the doorway to the croft Elene Isbister left. The younger woman continued to fill the bucket as though no one spoke to her, but Liam watched her face grow red, and it wasn't from exertion. His path carried him toward the well, but he could have continued past to reach his destination. Instead, intrigued by the stunning blonde and the scene playing out before him, he stopped at the well as the woman finished raising the bucket. She poured the contents in her own pail before letting it drop back into the cavernous pit. Unaware of Liam, she jumped when he stepped forward and grasped the crank.

Liam's emerald eyes met deep sapphire, the shade of the Highland sky in autumn. Liam observed the surprise, then wariness, in her gaze as she stepped away. He drew the full bucket to the ledge and dipped the community ladle into the cool water. As he sipped, Elene took two steps back before turning away, disconcerted by the handsome stranger. However, her feet grew roots as the older woman stormed toward her.

Liam kept his head down as he lowered the bucket, chiding himself for his nosiness but unwilling to move away. The older woman glanced at him dismissively before settling her attention on Elene.

In Norn, the language of Orkney, the woman continued her chastisement. "I didn't tell you that you could leave. We were in the middle of talking."

"No, Mother. You were in the middle of talking, and I was in the middle of not wanting to hear any more. I cannot believe you're considering marrying him."

"Not considering. I've already decided. When Gunter returns in a sennight, we will wed. Then we will all move home with him."

"Home?" Elene scoffed. "Norway hasn't been our people's home in ten generations. And you are a fool if you believe he will allow me to remain."

"You're old enough to marry."

"Getting married is a far sight different from being sold!" Elene made to step around her mother, but the older woman was just as quick.

"You exaggerate."

"And you believe a slave trader over your own daughter."

"Gunter is not a slave trader. You would smear his name because you aren't getting what you want, you selfish child."

Clearly not a child, Elene stood to her full height as she gazed at her mother, who was at least two inches shorter than her daughter. "Selfish," she repeated her mother. "I hadn't realized Katryne and Johan raised themselves."

"I am their mother."

"But I raised my brother and sister. I lost my chance to marry while you lost yourself in barrels of mead." Elene swung her glare at Liam, who'd remained near the arguing women while he spoke to his two ship captains. Despite speaking Gaelic, Liam sensed Elene knew he understood her conversation with her mother. It explained her accusatory glare.

"That was my grief."

Elene released a dismissive puff of air. "That was your habit. You haven't missed Father in years. You welcomed Petyre into our home almost every night, and Father hadn't been dead two moons."

"We need a man to provide for us," the older woman sniffed defensively.

Elene gawked at her mother before she laughed. "We do not need a man to provide for us. You might need one because you can't stand to be alone for more than a day. But I work our fields and hunt out supper. Petyre, and now Gunter, come into our home and eat the food I provide. I should have accepted Duncan's offer before he grew fed up with waiting."

"You didn't love him."

"You mean like you love Gunter?"

"I do love him," Elene's mother insisted.

"More fool are you," Elene muttered.

"Come inside. You're causing a scene."

"I'm not the one yelling. And I can't. I must bring Bess this water, feed the chickens, muck out the stalls, then milk Bess. I haven't time to argue when I know you refuse to believe me."

"He is not going to sell you!"

"He will. Or he'll force me to bed him. He will not feed and clothe another adult without getting something in return. He told me."

Highland Bear

Highland Jewel

Highland Rose

Highland Strength

Highland Devil

THE HIGHLAND LADIES

A Spinster at the Highland Court

BOOK 1 SNEAK PEEK

Elizabeth Fraser looked around the royal chapel within Stirling Castle. The ornate candlestick holders on the altar glistened and reflected the light from the ones in the wall sconces as the priest intoned the holy prayers of the Advent season. Elizabeth kept her head bowed as though in prayer, but her green eyes swept the congregation. She watched the other ladies-in-waiting, many of whom were doing the same thing. She caught the eye of Allyson Elliott. Elizabeth raised one eyebrow as Allyson's lips twitched. Both women had been there enough times to accept they'd be kneeling for at least the next hour as the Latin service carried on. Elizabeth understood the Mass thanks to her cousin Deirdre Fraser, or rather now Deirdre Sinclair. Elizabeth's mind flashed to the recent struggle her cousin faced as she reunited with her husband Magnus after a seven-year separation. Her aunt and uncle's choice to keep Deirdre hidden from her husband simply because they didn't think the Sinclairs were an advantageous enough match, and the resulting scandal, still humiliated the other Fraser clan members at court. She admired Deirdre's husband Magnus's pledge to remain faithful despite not knowing if he'd ever see Deirdre again.

Elizabeth suddenly snapped her attention; while everyone else intoned the twelfth—or was it thirteenth—amen of the Mass, the hairs on the back of her neck stood up. She had the strongest feeling that someone was watching her. Her eyes scanned to her right, where her parents sat further down the pew. Her mother and father had their heads bowed and eyes closed. While she was convinced her mother was in devout prayer, she wondered if her father had fallen asleep during the Mass. Again. With nothing seeming out of the ordinary and no one visibly paying attention to her, her eyes swung to the left. She took in the king and queen as they kneeled together at their prie-dieu. The queen's lips moved as she recited the liturgy in silence. The king was as still as a statue. Years of leading warriors showed, both in his stature and his ability to control his body into absolute stillness. Elizabeth peered past the royal couple and found herself looking into the astute hazel eyes of Edward Bruce, Lord of Badenoch and Lochaber. His gaze gave her the sense that he peered into her thoughts, as though he were assessing her. She tried to keep her face neutral as heat surged up her neck. She prayed her face didn't redden as much as her neck must have, but at a twenty-one, she still hadn't mastered how to control her blushing. Her nape burned like it was on fire. She canted her head slightly before looking up at the crucifix hanging over the altar. She closed her eyes and tried to invoke the image of the Lord that usually centered her when her mind wandered during Mass.

Elizabeth sensed Edward's gaze remained on her. She didn't understand how she was so sure that he was looking at her. She didn't have any special gifts of perception or sight, but her intuition screamed that he was still looking.

A Spy at the Highland Court

A Wallflower at the Highland Court

A Rogue at the Highland Court

A Rake at the Highland Court

An Enemy at the Highland Court

A Saint at the Highland Court

A Beauty at the Highland Court

THE HIGHLAND LADIES ALWAYS

A Sinner at the Highland Court

BOOK 1 SNEAK PEEK

I hate him. I hate him. I hate him. How can he do this to me? How could he pick her over me? That fat sow. Kieran will regret this till the day he dies. He and she both. This is her fault. All her fault. I hate her too.

Madeline MacLeod felt the four walls of her tiny convent cell closing in upon her. Her brother, Kieran, had dragged her from Robert the Bruce's royal court at Stirling Castle and dumped her at Inchcailleoch Priory earlier that week. She refused to accept that any of her words or actions had caused her fall from grace. She'd only spoken the truth each time she told Maude Sutherland how unconventionally curvaceous she was. Why her brother wanted to marry a woman who looked more like a tavern wench than a lady was beyond Madeline.

He just wants a good rut. He'll realize what a dreadful mistake he's made when he takes her home to Stornoway. He will realize that tupping her won't be worth the humiliation of having such a plain-faced, round as a barrel, heifer for a wife. He could have had Laurel Ross!

As Madeline listened to the bells toll for yet another Mass, she grimaced. All she seemed to do was pray these days, but God certainly wasn't listening because she remained at the priory despite her fervent appeals. She kneeled among the other novices, postulants, and nuns eight times throughout the day and night as they followed the Liturgy of Hours. The bells in the background signaled Prime, so she knew it was still very early. She'd already attended Matins in the middle of the night and Lauds at sunrise.

Madeline glanced out the narrow window set high in the wall, thinking that the masons must have designed it so the women couldn't escape. The sunlight, weak and dismal, matched Madeline's mood. When she lived at court, six o'clock in the morning was an hour she'd never seen.

Now that she lived at the convent, she'd already been awake for an hour and a half.

Madeline dragged herself from her cot and her introspection. She could feel her anger simmering below the surface, and if she wanted to avoid another outburst—which would result in two days of wearing a hair shirt for penance — she would do well to calm herself. She splashed freezing water from the washbasin onto her face. It was refreshing, but it only reminded her of the austerity she now faced daily. Already dressed in her postulant's dark gray gown, she'd tucked her roughly shorn hair beneath her wimple, and a large wooden cross hung around her neck. The undyed wool of the dress made her skin itch, and it chafed the open cuts upon her back. But it was far better than the hair shirt they forced her to wear the third day she arrived. She'd lashed out at another postulant who bumped into her as they entered their pew. The postulant was formerly a lesser noble, and Madeline reminded her that she, Madeline, was the sister of a laird and a former lady-in-waiting to Queen Elizabeth de Burgh. Madeline's voice carried, but the other woman was more discreet in her own set-down, as she pointed out that Madeline's brother was the one to banish her from court.

A Hellion at the Highland Court

An Angel at the Highland Court

A Harlot at the Highland Court

A Friend at the Highland Court

An Outsider at the Highland Court

A Devil at the Highland Court

PIRATES OF THE ISLES

The Blond Devil of the Sea **BOOK 1 SNEAK PEEK**

Caragh lifted her torch into the air as she made her way down the precarious Cornish cliffside. She made out the hulking shape of a ship, but the dead of night made it impossible to see who was there. She and the fishermen of Bedruthan Steps weren't expecting any shipments that night. But her younger brother Eddie, who stood watch at the entrance to their hiding place, had spotted the ship and signaled up to the village watchman, who alerted Caragh.

As her boot slid along the dirt and sand, she cursed having to carry the torch and wished she could have sunlight to guide her. She knew these cliffs well, and it was for that reason it was better that she moved slowly than stop moving once and for all. Caragh feared the light from her torch would carry out to the boat. Despite her efforts to keep the flame small, the solitary light would be a beacon.

When Caragh came to the final twist in the path before the sand, she snuffed out her torch and started to run to the cave where the main source of the village's income lay in hiding. She heard movement along the trail above her head and knew the local fishermen would soon join her on the beach. These men, both young and old, were strong from days spent pulling in the full trawling nets and hoisting the larger catches onto their boats. However, these men weren't well-trained swordsmen, and the fear of pirate raids was ever-present. Caragh feared that was who the villagers would face that night.

The Dark Heart of the Sea

The Red Drifter of the Sea

The Scarlet Blade of the Sea

VIKING GLORY

Leif **BOOK 1 SNEAK PEEK**

Leif looked around his chambers within his father's longhouse and breathed a sigh of relief. He noticed the large fur rugs spread throughout the chamber. His two favorites placed strategically before the fire and the bedside he preferred. He looked at his shield that hung on the wall near the door in a symbolic position but waiting at the ready. The chests that held his clothes and some of his finer acquisitions from voyages near and far sat beside his bed and along the far wall. And in the center was his most favorite possession. His oversized bed was one of the few that could accommodate his long and broad frame. He shook his head at his longing to climb under the pile of furs and on the stuffed mattress that beckoned him. He took in the chair placed before the fire where he longed to sit now with a cup of warm mead. It had been two months since he slept in his own bed, and he looked forward to nothing more than pulling the furs over his head and sleeping until he could no longer ignore his hunger. Alas, he would not be crawling into his bed again for several more hours. A feast awaited him to celebrate his and his crew's return from their latest expedition to explore the isle of Britannia. He bathed and wore fresh clothes, so he had no excuse for lingering other than a bone weariness that set in during the last storm at sea. He was eager to spend time at home no matter how much he loved sailing. Their last expedition had been profitable with several raids of monasteries that yielded jewels and both silver and gold, but he was ready for respite.

Leif left his chambers and knocked on the door next to his. He heard movement on the other side, but it was only moments before his sister, Freya, opened her door. She, too, looked tired but clean. A few pieces of jewelry she confiscated from the holy houses that allegedly swore to a life of poverty and deprivation adorned her trim frame.

"That armband suits you well. It compliments your muscles," Leif smirked and dodged a strike from one of those muscular arms.

Only a year younger than he, his sister was a well-known and feared shield maiden. Her lithe form was strong and agile making her a ferocious and competent opponent to any man. Freya's beauty was stunning, but Leif had taken every opportunity since they were children to tease her about her unusual strength even among the female warriors.

"At least one of us inherited our father's prowess. Such a shame it wasn't you."

Freya

Tyra & Bjorn

Strian

Lena & Ivar

www.ingramcontent.com/pod-product-compliance
Lightning Source LLC
Chambersburg PA
CBHW050007120726
47903CB00006B/1675